Stonewall Jackson's Elbow

Stonewall Jackson's Elbow

An Owen Allison Mystery

John Billheimer

Five Star • Waterville, Maine

First Edition
First Printing: September 2006

Published in 2006 in conjunction with Tekno Books
and Ed Gorman.

Set in 11 pt. Plantin by Christina S. Huff.

Printed in the United States on permanent paper.

Library of Congress Cataloging-in-Publication Data

Billheimer, John W.
  Stonewall Jackson's elbow : an Owen Allison mystery / John Billheimer.—1st ed.
     p. cm.
    ISBN 1-59414-462-1 (hc : alk. paper)
    1. Allison, Owen (Fictitious character)—Fiction.
2. Government investigators—Fiction. 3. Bank fraud—Fiction.
4. West Virginia—Fiction. I. Title.
    PS3552.I452S76 2006
    813'.54—dc22   2006000063

For Bob Owen

From quiet homes and first beginning,
Out to the undiscovered ends,
There's nothing worth the wear of winning,
But laughter and the love of friends.
—Hillaire Belloc

Acknowledgements

This is a work of fiction. Names, characters, places, and incidents either are the product of the author's imagination or are used fictitiously. Any resemblance to actual persons (living or dead), events, or locales is entirely coincidental.

Every work of fiction reflects some matters of fact. As always, I am indebted to a number of people who helped me get a few facts straight. These include Brian Bouthillier and Steve Gimonetti, for insights into the trading of baseball memorabilia; Lisa, Denis, and Gail Boyer Hayes of the firm Hayes, Hayes, and Hayes, for legal advice; Bob and Dale Lewis for pharmaceutical details; David Meade for information on drug effects, enforcement, and rehabilitation; Brad Porteus, for particulars on eBay procedures; and Dr. Ann Younker, for insights into Alzheimer's testing. Any blame for misstatements in these matters belongs to the author.

In the interests of spreading the blame, I wish to acknowledge the contributions of the Wednesday Night Wine Tasting and Literary Society, whose members help to keep me upbeat, upstanding, and up-to-date. Membership in this quasi-elite group includes:

Sheila Scobba Banning
Bob Brownstein
Ann Cheilek
Mark Coggins
Ann Hillesland
The "displays" in the Museum of Fakes and Frauds were

culled from a variety of sources. The two references which proved most helpful were *Hoaxes and Scams* by Carl Sifakis (Michael O'Mara Books, London, 1994) and *The Museum of Hoaxes* by Alex Boese (Dutton, New York, 2002).

It's a Barnum and Bailey world;
Just as phony as it can be.
—Harold Arlen, "It's Only a Paper Moon"

After all, what is reality anyway?
Nothin' but a collective hunch
—Jane Wagner,
The Search for Signs of Intelligent Life in the Universe

Prologue:

The Missing Millions

Nobody knew for sure where the money went. Seven hundred and fifty million dollars. Three quarters of a billion. A hick bank in a hick town, and it stacked up to be one of the biggest failures in the history of the Federal Deposit Insurance Corporation.

Nobody was even sure whether the late J. Burton Caldwell had a hand in looting his own bank. Sure, he'd run off a few inspectors by brandishing a shotgun, but that was all part of his image. After the loss became public, one of the inspectors was quoted as saying, "Old Burt didn't seem bright enough to do that much damage."

But old Burt had been bright enough to build the assets of the First National Bank of Contrary from ten million dollars to nearly one billion dollars in a little less than thirty years. Burt Caldwell had come to Contrary, West Virginia, early in 1970. Just where he'd come from was never certain. At various times, he claimed to have run banks in rural Tennessee, Alabama, and the Philippine Islands. He also claimed to possess a degree from Harvard, but that university reported having no record of his attendance.

Caldwell was promoted to bank president shortly after arriving in Contrary. He immediately started to extend the bank's reach by driving to Huntington, Charleston, Lexington, and Pittsburgh to offer discounted mortgages to doctors, lawyers, and other professionals.

"I plumb near wore out two cars a year in them early days," Caldwell told *FORBES* magazine in the mid-nineties. By then, his Contrary Bank had grown to nationwide prominence by buying up, repackaging, and reselling federally insured mortgage loans. While his discounted mortgages had taken the bank's assets from ten million to ninety million, his repackaged loans, coupled with nationally advertised interest rates two points above the market level, sent the bank's assets soaring toward a billion dollars. *U.S. BANKER* named the First National Bank of Contrary the most profitable small-town bank in the country for four years running.

Burt Caldwell relished being in the national spotlight and cultivated his country-boy image. He drove a Ford pickup, wore bolo ties with his two rumpled blue serge suits, and breakfasted six mornings of the week at Tatum's diner, just across the street from his bank. A *Wall Street Journal* profile quoted the proprietor, Patty Tatum, as saying, "Man's common as cow flop, but he'd wrassle a live chain saw for his people."

In addition to his Contrary neighbors, Caldwell's "people" were his bank employees, called "Burt's skirts" by the townsfolk. A lifelong bachelor, he followed a female-only hiring policy for years until a disgruntled male job applicant sued. Caldwell railed publicly against the court ruling, hired the litigant, and subsequently boasted privately that even when his banking operations topped a billion dollars, he only took on enough males to justify his investment in the urinal.

Burt Caldwell worked long hours, rarely took a vacation, and lived frugally in a modest brick house within walking distance of downtown Contrary. Of course, as the *Wall Street Journal* profile noted, ninety percent of Contrary was within walking distance of the downtown.

He branched out in the early eighties by purchasing a small farm in a hollow near the county line, where he stabled a series of undistinguished racehorses. The local saying had it that "If Burt wanted one of his nags to finish in the money in the fourth race, all he had to do was enter it in the third race. They needed the head start."

Aside from his work and his stables, Caldwell's only known passion was the Museum of Fakes and Frauds he started in Contrary just after he became bank president. He opened the museum in a tiny side room of his bank with a few fraudulent Civil War artifacts, a display of counterfeit money, and placards celebrating the scams of spiritualists and phony psychics.

In the mid-eighties, Caldwell moved the room's exhibits to the largest house in Contrary, a red-brick Victorian that he purchased from the retiring president of Consolidated Coal, and expanded the museum to include a Hall of Hoaxes, Basement of Bunkum, Corridor of Cons, and several Swindle Suites. Within five years, the museum had become a statewide tourist attraction, and Caldwell had filled two warehouses with counterfeit paintings, forged documents, phony manuscripts, fabricated memorabilia, and artifacts from several notorious scams.

Burt Caldwell was killed in 1998, when his pickup ran off a winding West Virginia road on a foggy morning and plunged fifty feet into a dry creekbed. Federal investigators who'd been cowed by Caldwell's sharp tongue and waving shotgun waited out a short period of mourning before sending a team of eight auditors to examine the books of the First National Bank of Contrary. Acting on a tip, two of the auditors drove straight to Caldwell's farm, where they surprised four bank employees in the act of burying five hundred boxes of records in a forty-by-forty-foot excavation cut into the dirt floor of an abandoned barn.

Alerted by the attempt to entomb five truckloads of

records, the federal comptroller's office sent in ten more auditors. The auditing team closed the bank after a four-month investigation revealed that six hundred million dollars in loans had been sold but remained on the bank's books as assets. In addition to these missing millions, the auditors identified another one hundred and fifty million in unexplained administrative expenses.

Although the auditors could pinpoint the amount of missing funds as "seven hundred and fifty million, plus or minus ten million dollars, one way or the other," no one had a clue where the missing money had gone. A federal judge sentenced senior bank vice president Mary Kay Jessup, one of Burt's first skirts, to thirty years in prison for mail fraud, conspiracy, and attempting to obstruct a federal bank examination.

Where J. Burton Caldwell had lived quietly and frugally, Mary Kay Jessup lived noisily and expensively. She drove a bright red Cadillac convertible and at the time of her arrest was finishing a four-million-dollar home in a county where over half of the residents were below the poverty line.

Throughout her trial, Jessup claimed she was innocent and was being hounded by federal regulators who needed a scapegoat and were jealous of her success and her generous salary and bonus arrangements. At her sentencing, she professed no knowledge of the whereabouts of the missing millions. Unmoved by this claim, the federal judge ordered her to pay $750,218,644.22, plus interest, in restitution, attached her car and house, and further stipulated that she pay fifty dollars a month toward the total bill while in prison.

On the theory that the burial of records might have been preceded by the burial of loot, four out-of-work coal miners began digging up grave-sized plots on Caldwell's ranch, using metal detectors to help them decide where to sink their spades. The federal government got wind of this activity when the miners uncovered a long-buried septic tank. Officials forced the miners to fill in the holes on the five acres they'd despoiled, confiscated their metal detectors, and posted round-the-clock security guards on the property. Rumors began circulating that the guards themselves were using the confiscated metal detectors to continue the search during their off hours.

While most local residents maintained accounts in the bank, few had balances in excess of the hundred thousand dollars insured by the FDIC. Fewer still could muster anything bad to say about J. Burton Caldwell. "Old Burt always had a kind word for everybody in my diner," said Patty Tatum. "He couldn't have known what was going on."

Most of the larger account balances in the bank were maintained by high-rolling out-of-state investors attracted by the bank's widely advertised high interest rates. These investors, who stood to lose everything in excess of the hundred-thousand-dollar insurance limit, were much less understanding than the locals and insisted on a far-ranging investigation.

When the investigation failed to turn up any sign of the missing millions, FDIC officials froze the assets of the First National Bank of Contrary and took over its operations. They also assumed ownership of three lackadaisical racehorses, a museum dedicated to displaying bunkum, and two warehouses packed with forgeries, fakes, and fabrications. None of these assets seemed likely to make up any significant part of the seven-hundred-and-fifty-million-dollar difference between the bank's looted assets and the claims of angry depositors. And the missing millions remained missing.

Chapter One:

Bogus Bibles and Counterfeit Cards

Owen Allison stood in front of the museum exhibit and was struck once again by the way history was blown off course by the winds of chance. A shying horse, a nervous picket, a random shot in a shadowy wood, and the fortunes of war could shift enough to alter the fate of nations.

The last time he'd seen the exhibit, it was in a small side room of the First National Bank of Contrary and he'd been a college sophomore. Now it was nearly thirty years later, and the exhibit had been moved from the bank to the rambling brick residence that housed the Museum of Fakes and Frauds.

Two crossed muskets formed an X at the rear of the exhibit, and a patina of dust covered the two gray Confederate kepis that flanked a pedestal made from four black leather Bibles. Displayed like a rare gem on a gray silk scarf draped over the Bibles, the knobby bone fragment was smaller and more yellow than Owen had remembered, but it still held the same fascination.

A placard leaning against the bottom Bible identified the bone fragment as STONEWALL JACKSON'S ELBOW, and a neatly lettered plaque beside the exhibit explained how the general came to be separated from his left arm.

The evening after he'd outflanked and overrun the Union forces at Chancellorsville, Jackson had ridden out a little ahead of his troops to reconnoiter. When random shots echoed nearby, he rode back toward his own lines, only to be fired on by nervous Confederate sentries from the 18th North Carolina regiment, who mistook his party for Union cavalry in the shadowy woods.

Two of Jackson's aides were killed on the spot and Jackson himself was struck by two bullets that shattered the bones of his left arm. A third bullet pierced his right palm. Jackson's left arm was amputated the next morning and buried near the battlefield as the general was removed to a field station far from the fighting. He died of pneumonia a week later, issuing battle orders to absent subordinates in a fevered haze before closing his eyes and murmuring, "Let us cross over the river and rest under the shade of the trees."

Thirty years ago, the sketchy account of Stonewall Jackson's death on the hand-lettered plaque had inspired Owen to dig into the annals of the Civil War. Up until that time, he'd had less than a nodding acquaintance with U.S. history. The nuns who had taught him in high school preferred to focus on the struggles of various priests to convert certain Indian tribes, and history was not a required course for engineering students at Marquette University.

Intrigued by the story of Jackson's death, Owen read several biographies of the general, the collected works of Bruce Catton, Douglas Southall Freeman's *Lee's Lieutenants*, the memoirs of Grant and Sherman, and a variety of other Civil War literature. He visited the battlefields, including Chancellorsville, and saw for himself the monument commemorating the spot where Stonewall Jackson fell, the marker designating the burial site of his severed arm, and the field station where the general died.

Several of the historians Owen consulted singled out Jackson's death as the turning point of the Civil War, arguing that if Jackson had been Robert E. Lee's second-in-command at Gettysburg two months later, the road to surrender might have led to the north instead of south to Appomattox. Lee himself, on first hearing of Jackson's wounds, said, "The General has lost his left arm, but I have lost my right arm," giving support to the argument that Jackson's survival might have led to the survival of the Confederacy.

Owen was willing to credit the series of what-ifs that could have let Jackson survive Chancellorsville. If random firing hadn't spooked the general's horse and the North Carolina sentries; if Jackson hadn't ridden out ahead of his lines, or if he'd done so a little earlier or a little later; if the dark woods hadn't masked his identity, he might have lived. Reverse any one of those conditions and he might have lived.

Owen was much less willing to credit the argument that the Confederacy might have prevailed if only Jackson had been on hand to flank Meade's Union forces at Gettysburg. The idea that the outcome of a cataclysm as complex as the Civil War might have been altered by the reversal of a single turning point had always seemed overly simplistic to Owen.

To him, life was an infinite series of turning points, of roads taken or not taken, strung together like the knots in an ocean-wide fisherman's net. Change the outcome of a single event and you were faced with a whole series of paths and choices that could be quite different from the paths and choices you'd actually faced.

Shying horses and random gunfire hadn't figured in the chain of choices that had brought Owen back to his native West Virginia to contemplate Stonewall Jackson's elbow. A rigged bid, a painful divorce, and a few cases of fraud worthy of exhibits in this museum could be found at key junctions along the network of paths that had led him back home.

Seven years ago, he'd been living in Palo Alto, California, with a wife and a small business consulting in risk analysis. When he lost a rigged bid on a state job he'd counted on too heavily, his business went belly up and he'd taken a stopgap job with the Department of Transportation in Washington, DC. His wife refused to leave her Palo Alto law practice to join him in Washington, and his marriage couldn't survive the separation.

Owen's job in the federal government hadn't survived his own impatience with bureaucracy and a scandal that originated right here in Contrary, when he discovered that the city fathers were collecting a subsidy from the Transportation Department for operating a twenty-bus system, running only two buses, and pocketing five hundred thousand dollars a year.

Since leaving the federal government, he'd tried with sporadic success to restart his consulting business and had spent the last year back home in West Virginia helping to nurse his widowed mother through the onslaught of ovarian cancer. Now, pushing fifty and looking back over a string of failures, Owen realized that he probably would have spent much of the last year here with his mother whether or not his business and marriage had failed, and that his marriage might have failed even if his business hadn't. And Lee might have lost at Gettysburg even with Stonewall Jackson.

"My dad was named for that guy," a voice behind Owen said.

Owen turned to see Jeb Stuart Hobbs, a tall, broad-shouldered teenager who had recently moved in with Owen and Owen's mother following the deaths of his own parents.

"Probably has a lot of namesakes around here," Owen said. "He's one of West Virginia's most famous natives."

"Oh, yeah? Was he born hereabouts?"

"Up in Clarksburg."

Jeb Stuart pointed at the center of the display. "Is that really his elbow?"

Owen shrugged. "It's somebody's elbow. One of the North Carolina soldiers who fired on Jackson's party claimed he recovered it after the general's arm was amputated. Carried it around for good luck."

"Gross. Was it good luck?"

"Not for Jackson."

Jeb Stuart gave Owen a "duh" look.

"Could have been good luck for the North Carolinian, though," Owen said. "He survived the war. One of those muskets in the display was his."

"So that could be the musket that really killed the general?"

"Could be. Nobody knows for sure. There were a lot of shots fired and it was pretty dark. There's a better chance that's the musket that wounded him than that he was carrying one of those Bibles when he was shot. The Bibles are fake for sure."

"Why would anybody fake a signature in a Bible?"

"Money. Jackson was as famous in his time as any of today's rock stars or baseball players."

Jeb Stuart took Owen's arm. "Oh, hey. Baseball players." He gave the arm a perfunctory tug. "Come on. I want to show you something."

"Do we have time before the auction starts?"

"This won't take long." Jeb Stuart led the way up the broad maple staircase of the ornate house and down a corridor labeled THE HALL OF HOAXES. He stopped halfway down the hall and pointed at a large glass case built into the wall. "There."

In the back of the display case were two New York Yankee jerseys whose shirttails bore the forged signatures of Babe Ruth and Lou Gehrig. Hanging on pegs above the jerseys were a Red Sox batting helmet that probably never belonged to Ted Williams and a right-handed first baseman's mitt that definitely never belonged to the left-handed Stan Musial, even though someone had thoughtfully applied his autograph to it with a magic marker.

Jeb Stuart's finger was pointing at the front of the display, where a posterboard backing showcased a pyramid of baseball cards. At the apex of the pyramid was a counterfeit copy of the rare 1910 Honus Wagner card that had been auctioned at Sotheby's for four hundred fifty-one thousand dollars.

Just below the Honus Wagner counterfeit were two more recent cards depicting Atlanta Braves players with the negatives reversed, so that the right-handed Henry Aaron was batting left-handed and the script on the front of Dale Murphy's jersey spelled sevarB, or Braves backwards. The display estimated the value of the photo-reversed Aaron card at one hundred dollars, and the Murphy at thirty dollars.

Jeb Stuart tapped the glass of the display case in front of the Aaron card. "There. See that? It's just like the one you

21

gave me. Guess you'll be wanting it back now that you see what it's worth."

"Nope. It's yours. I'm a Braves giver, not an Indian giver."

Owen had given Jeb Stuart a shoebox filled with the baseball cards he'd collected in the early 1960s, keeping only a few of the cards depicting the Cincinnati Reds players that he'd idolized growing up. It turned out that the value of the cards in the shoebox had caused a gap between them that they papered over with mutual kidding.

When he made the gift, Owen had known vaguely that baseball cards had become a red-hot collector's item, but he couldn't believe that cards he'd bought for a penny in bubble-gum wrappers when he was in grade school could be worth much more than one or two dollars today. The gap began to open when Jeb Stuart started checking the value of the shoebox cards in a catalog and reported that one of the cards, from Pete Rose's rookie year, had a catalog value of eight hundred dollars.

Owen thought he'd taken the news with a poker face, but judging by Jeb Stuart's reaction, he must have lit up like a cartoon Scrooge McDuck with dollar signs for eyeballs. The boy suddenly became quiet, as if he'd just reported that he'd lost eight hundred dollars instead of finding a hidden treasure. After a long silence, Jeb Stuart said, "Uh, maybe you'd like to keep some of these cards and sell them instead of giving them all to me."

Owen blinked back the dancing dollar signs and tried to sound like a mature adult instead of a greedy cartoon character. "No. They were a gift. If it hadn't been for you, they'd still be at the bottom of one of those old chests in the garage."

"But you didn't know what they were worth when you gave them to me."

Actually, figuring out what the cards were worth was far from straightforward. Catalog values were heavily dependent on the condition of the cards, rated from poor to mint, with six levels in between. The Pete Rose rookie card was valued at eight hundred dollars in mint condition, but Owen's cards had endured a lot of handling. Like Rose himself, the images had become smudged and frayed around the edges.

Owen didn't like the idea of trying to assess the condition of his cards and assign a dollar value to them. To him, their primary value was in the memories they evoked of his childhood baseball fantasies. He noticed, though, that he still thought of them as "his" cards and he couldn't quite shake the image of himself as a shoebox Scrooge, locking his treasures away in a vault, fondling them periodically, and auctioning them one at a time to the highest bidder.

Under ordinary circumstances, he told himself, he would have laughed it off and been happy for the boy's windfall. But Owen's personal finances had been shaky ever since he'd moved back to West Virginia to look after his mother. It hadn't been easy to establish himself as a consultant locally, and state contracts sometimes came with kickback requirements that he refused to pay.

For the six months since Jeb Stuart had moved in with Owen and his mother, Owen had enjoyed acting as a surrogate father to the boy. Now it seemed that what had started as a charitable impulse with his baseball cards was taxing their relationship. It didn't help Owen's equanimity to realize that the sixteen-year-old was handling the situation more maturely than he was, insisting that it was all right with him if Owen wanted to take the cards back and sell them.

The auction that they were scheduled to attend today had helped them take a step toward resolving the issue. Owen's collection of cards covered the 1960s, and Jeb Stuart had done a good job of contributing cards from the 1990s, but the years between were spotty. They'd come in response to ads saying that the FDIC was auctioning a portion of J. Burton Caldwell's collection of artifacts, including some of his baseball cards. The possibility of obtaining bargains at a government-sponsored auction seemed like a good way to fill in the blanks in their combined collections.

"That's our Pete Rose rookie card," Jeb Stuart said, pointing to the bottom row of the pyramid of cards in the museum display case. Owen couldn't be sure, but he thought he heard the boy emphasize the possessive "our." The card in the case was a counterfeit, flanked by other counterfeit cards from the rookie years of famous players. Catalog values of the genuine items were listed under the phony cards and ranged from one hundred fifty dollars for a Mark McGwire to twenty thousand dollars for the Mickey Mantle from the 1952 Topps collection.

Owen and Jeb Stuart bent to look at the counterfeits in the bottom row of the pyramid. Each card was brightly colored and perfectly centered, with smooth edges and sharp corners, prime examples of mint catalog condition.

"Sure look real," Jeb Stuart said.

"All it takes is a printing press and a little larceny. You could pay for the press just by selling a few of those Mantle cards."

"You'd have to be careful, though. Experts must be able to spot the fakes."

"And a buyer would have to be crazy to shell out that kind of money without consulting an expert." Owen straightened and looked at his watch. "Maybe we better start for the auction. The warehouse is down by the creek."

"The flyer says they'll auction off the phony art and other stuff first, before the baseball cards."

"I'd like to get there early and look around. Caldwell's warehouses are supposed to be a bigger show than this museum."

"The cards will be real, though?" Jeb Stuart nodded toward the display case. "Not fakes like these?"

"A little of both." Owen shrugged his shoulders. "I sure wouldn't know how to tell the difference, though."

Chapter Two:

Half the Magic

The warehouse where the FDIC was auctioning a portion of J. Burton Caldwell's collection sat squeezed between Blackwater Creek and a pair of abandoned railroad tracks at the foot of Contrary's Main Street. Two sunglass-wearing security guards with white plastic cords leading from their right ears to their collars were stationed outside the main doors of the concrete block structure. A matched pair of guards without sunglasses stood just inside the doors, watching over twenty rows of folding chairs that faced a podium standing on wooden pallets. Secretaries sitting at two long tables flanking the podium assigned numbers and auction paddles to prospective bidders.

Owen signed up with one of the secretaries and was given a catalog of the items to be auctioned and a paddle with the number 42 printed on either side in bold black numerals. They seemed to be assigning paddles in numerical order, but forty-two bidders didn't seem like a lot of competition for the amount of goods listed in the catalog and highlighted in the newspaper ads. Relatively few of the folding chairs were occupied, and the high ceilings and wide expanse of the concrete interior made the head count seem lower than it actually was.

Rather than sitting, most of the attendees were wandering through the eight rows of storage racks that stretched the length of the block-long building. Owen joined Jeb Stuart and followed the signs leading to the items to be auctioned that day, which were on display in the first row.

Jeb Stuart headed straight for the storage racks containing baseball memorabilia. A row of racked bats formed an open fence in front of two long tables holding an array of batting helmets, balls, jerseys, and baseball cards. Most of the balls and bats were autographed, although a sign warned that few of the signatures had been authenticated.

Jeb Stuart picked a bat from the rack, gripped it by the handle, examined the trademark, and assumed his batting stance. "It says Ken Griffey Junior." He strode toward an imaginary pitcher and took a slow half swing, stopping his stroke where the bat would meet the pitched ball. "What do you think? Think it was really his bat?"

He handed the bat to Owen, who went through the ingrained male ritual of turning the trademark up and taking a half swing. "That's the problem with most of this stuff," Owen said. "If they could prove it was real, they could sell it for big bucks. Or if they could prove it was phony, there'd be a place for it in the museum."

Owen replaced the bat and nodded toward the end of the display tables. "That looks like what we came for."

Two shoeboxes sat at the far end of the memorabilia table. Both had been taped shut. A few current baseball cards had been scattered in front of the display, and a placard explained that the boxes were filled with cards collected by J. Burton Caldwell in his search for counterfeits. No claims were made for the cards in the shoeboxes, although most were believed to be authentic.

"Most are believed to be authentic," Owen read. "Not exactly a ringing endorsement."

"We don't get to look at the cards before we bid?" Jeb Stuart asked.

"No. Let the buyer beware."

"We'll still bid, won't we?"

"Oh, yes. That's the fun of it. My father used to say only half the magic is in the suspense of the bid. The other half is in the surprise of the opening."

Owen's father had died just after Owen's tenth birthday, but he remembered attending estate auctions with his dad in the rural areas of West Virginia. The estate sales were a form of recreation for Wayne Allison, who was on a first-name basis with most of the auctioneers in the state and who loved nothing more than bidding blindly on locked chests, taking a chance on their contents.

He always waited until they returned home before opening the treasure chests, heightening the suspense and drawing Owen's mother into the ritual. Part of the ritual was Ruth Allison's exasperation when each new footlocker, campaign trunk, or hope chest appeared on their front porch. Most of the closed chests yielded up nothing more than old, moth-eaten blankets or clothes so far out of style and size that they went directly to the parish hall for the next rummage sale. There were times, though, when real treasures would emerge from the auctioned chests. Owen remembered retrieving two boxes of toy soldiers from the folds of an old army blanket, and one cedar chest contained a full set of silverware that his mother still used on special occasions. Nearly forty years later, many of the chests still lined one wall of his mother's garage, now filled with her own family's cast-off treasures.

Owen left Jeb Stuart hefting the bats racked in the baseball section and wandered off to look at the rest of the items to be auctioned. A dozen black Maltese Falcons hovered over a display of movie memorabilia like overweight vultures too lazy to pounce. The display included four pairs of ruby slippers of different sizes, "similar to those" worn by Judy Garland in *The Wizard of Oz*, a telephoto lens purported to be the one used by Jimmy Stewart in *Rear Window*, and several movie posters stacked in a display bin. According to the auction catalog the posters, all forgeries, would have commanded anywhere from one thousand to twenty thousand dollars had they been originals.

The first poster in the display bin was a two-sheet reproduction of the *Citizen Kane* advertisement showing a young Orson Welles standing, legs apart, hands outthrust, smiling as if he were about to burst into song. The image conveyed none of the movie's content or power, but it seemed appropriate to Owen that the poster would find its way into J. Burton Caldwell's warehouse, since Caldwell's collection reminded him of the vast store of antiquities amassed by Charles Foster Kane in Welles' movie. Owen thought of Caldwell as a minor-league version of Kane, and, by implication, of William Randolph Hearst, the model for the Kane character.

Owen moved from the movie memorabilia to displays and bins of counterfeit artwork that took up nearly half of the warehouse space devoted to auction items. A group of prints depicting various stages of a foxhunt had been framed ornately and were to be auctioned off as a unit. Other groupings depicted sad, round-eyed children in the style of Charles Keane and splashy, colorful sporting scenes that looked as if they could have been done by LeRoy Neiman but weren't.

Owen passed slowly in front of the paintings, keeping pace with a few other viewers, like patrons in a sparsely attended museum. He paid little attention to the other viewers until the flow ahead of him bunched and split to pass a woman who wasn't moving at all, but rather stood in front of a single painting, writing on the back of the auction guide. The woman's coal-black hair was cut in a close-cropped shag, and she wore gray slacks and a white blouse whose short sleeves exposed a muscular upper arm and the tattoo of a dagger that undulated as her right hand moved the pen over the catalog pages.

Owen stopped one painting short of the woman and pretended to examine the work in front of him, an oil painting depicting Christ and an adulteress done in the style of Vermeer. The adulteress was tattoo-free. From somewhere in his past, he recalled reading the admonition, "Never sleep with a woman who's wearing a dagger tattoo," but the source of the quote hovered just beyond the reach of his memory.

The woman in question was examining a painting of a bright orange arrow on a field of tiny rectangles of varying brown hues. The painting triggered a reaction in Owen and he said, "Amazing," aloud, startling both himself and the woman. She looked at him as if he'd just mouthed an obscenity, folded her catalog under her arm, and moved off down the row of art work. Owen mentally amended the barely remembered advice to include, "Never converse with a woman who's wearing a dagger tattoo."

"It is pretty amazing, isn't it?"

The voice came from behind Owen, and he turned to see a tall, attractive woman with clear blue eyes and gray-streaked brown hair tied back in a severe bun.

"I mean," Owen said, "it looks exactly like a Paul Klee. I guess, though, because it's here, it must not be."

The woman smiled. "No. It was painted by an Englishman named John Myatt who copied Klee's style. The really amazing thing about the forgery, though, is that Myatt's accomplice, a man named John Drewe, managed to plant a bogus history of the work in the archives of the Tate Museum."

"So they passed it off as authentic?"

"For a little while. Myatt and Drewe foisted off at least two hundred paintings as the work of different artists before they were caught." She nodded toward the imitation Klee. "That painting sold for thousands of dollars and was featured in two traveling museum shows before it was exposed as a fake. Now no museum will touch it." She shrugged. "But it's still the same work of art."

A man wearing blue jeans, a plaid work shirt, and a baseball hat with a United Mineworkers logo passed between Owen and the painting. The rail-thin woman on his arm paused and said, "My land, they want five thousand dollars just to open the bidding on that."

The man tugged at the woman's arm and started to walk away. "For that kind of money, that there orange arrow ought to be pointing to a buried treasure."

The thin woman hung back for a moment, then followed the man's lead. "I don't know. I kind of like it."

"I kind of like it too," Owen said to the woman with gray-streaked hair after the couple had moved on. "It's really quite remarkable."

"Did you come here to bid on it?" the woman asked.

Owen didn't want to admit he'd come to bid on baseball cards, but there was no way he could afford the five-thousand-dollar minimum bid for the fake Klee. He shook his head. "It's a little too rich for my blood."

"Mine too, unfortunately."

Owen nodded toward the painting of Christ and the adulteress. "Did the same team produce that fake Vermeer?"

"No. That was done by a Dutchman named Hans van Meegeren, around the time of the Second World War. He managed to fool a lot of people with his Vermeers. Even sold one to the Nazi high command."

"Well, he would have fooled me too. But that's not hard to do. I'm afraid I don't even recognize most of the artists whose works are being copied." Owen pointed to the painting on the other side of the fake Klee. It was a particularly ugly abstract of what appeared to be the head of a rabid pit bull done in shades of black with a lolling red tongue surrounded by vivid white frothing. "Take that painting, for instance. Is that a self-portrait of the artist?"

The woman raised her eyebrows. "Careful now. You could be hurting my feelings."

Owen backtracked, trying not to blush. "You're not the artist?"

"No, but I am the museum curator." She held out her hand. "Victoria Gallagher."

"Owen Allison. Outspoken but ill-informed art critic."

"You're right about that painting. It is hideous. But I'm not responsible for it. Burt Caldwell purchased most of the paintings in this building before he died."

"And now you're getting rid of them."

"I wanted to keep the Klee, but it wasn't on display in the museum and the feds thought it would bring a good price. They're trying to get as much as they can to cover the bank's losses."

"Miss Gallagher. There you are. We're trying to get this auction started." A short man with a neatly trimmed black moustache, an officious air, and a badge identifying him as Mitchell Ramsey, FDIC Project Manager, stood with his arms folded, waiting to be obeyed.

Victoria smiled and took her time extending her hand to Owen. "Well, it was nice meeting you. Good luck with your bidding."

Owen liked the solid feel of her hand and the way she moved at her own pace, refusing to be hurried by the bureaucrat. He wished he had enough money to buy the fake Klee and let her keep it in her museum.

Owen rejoined Jeb Stuart and the two of them found seats in the far corner of the last row of folding chairs.

Mitchell Ramsey strode to the podium and announced, "All right people, we're trying to get this event started. Will you bidders please take your seats so the auction can begin?" His voice echoed off the cavernous walls.

A few people emerged from the rows of warehouse racks and began to fill in the empty seats, but many stayed behind, examining the items to be auctioned and other museum artifacts.

Ramsey glared down from the podium as if he could fill the empty seats through sheer willpower.

The woman with the dagger tattoo took a seat in the first row. Watching her, Owen recalled where he'd read the warning against women with similar markings. Someone had made the warning a part of an updated version of Nelson

Algren's three-part advice to young men. Owen remembered Algren's original version clearly, and decided to share it with the young man sitting beside him while they waited for the auction to start.

"There was a writer in my father's generation," he said, "who laid down three rules for young men starting out in life: 'Never eat at a place called Mom's. Never play cards with a man named Doc. And never lay down with a woman who's got more troubles than you.' "

"I can't remember ever wanting to do any of those things," Jeb Stuart said. "What brought that on?"

"They've updated the rules for your generation."

Jeb Stuart smiled and leaned forward, expecting that a joke would follow Owen's buildup.

Owen held up one finger. "The first updated warning is, Never eat in a restaurant that revolves."

Jeb Stuart frowned. "I didn't know there were any." Owen reflected that Jeb Stuart had been outside Appalachia only once, to visit him when he lived in California. "Maybe that rule only works in big cities." He held up two fingers. "Second, never play poker with a man named for a city."

Jeb Stuart's frown deepened. "You mean, like, say, Saint Joseph?"

"Not exactly who I had in mind. But you probably wouldn't want to play poker with him, so he fits the rule. My guess is, the rule makers were thinking of the Cincinnati Kid."

"Would that be, like, Ken Griffey Junior?"

It dawned on Owen that he'd have to construct a few bridges across the generation gap if he wanted to be an effective guide for his new charge. "No, the Cincinnati Kid is a fictitious character. A card sharp. Steve McQueen played him in the movie."

"Steve McQueen? Sounds like they updated the rules for your generation, not mine. What's behind all this advice, anyhow?"

"Actually, it was the third updated rule that made me think of any of them."

"And that is?"

"Never sleep with a woman who's got a dagger tattoo."

Jeb Stuart looked at Owen as if he'd just chanted a psalm in Swahili. "It never would have occurred to me."

"That's because you didn't run into the woman in the front row over there." Owen pointed out the woman with the shag haircut. In the sitting position, her short-sleeve blouse covered the hilt of the dagger, so that only the blade tip and blood droplet were visible.

Jeb Stuart shook his head. "That's gotta be your generation we're talking about. Half the girls in my high school have tattoos. It's no big deal."

It'll be a big deal when they turn fifty and sagging skin starts to distort the tattoo artist's draftmanship, Owen thought. But he kept the thought to himself, knowing that the teenage Jeb Stuart could never imagine turning fifty.

Less than one-third of the folding chairs were occupied with bidders and some people were still wandering through the racks, viewing J. Burton Caldwell's acquisitions.

Mitchell Ramsey announced once more that the auction was about to begin. He introduced Victoria Gallagher and the auctioneer, Red McCann, a tall skinny man wearing red suspenders whose thin, hawk-like nose looked as if it could open cans. Then Ramsey cupped his hand over the microphone, still hoping to attract more bidders, while the auctioneer stood beside the podium, fiddling with his red bow tie.

No one else came to fill the empty chairs. After a long silence, the man in the United Mineworkers cap shouted, "Hey Red, wake me when you get to the livestock."

The audience laughed.

Ramsey grimaced and retreated, joining Victoria at the side table and leaving the podium to the auctioneer.

The first catalog item to be auctioned was a group of twenty oil paintings attributed to several different modern artists, but authored by none. The paintings went for two thousand dollars, attracting just two bids above the stipulated minimum.

When the second group of twenty paintings failed to attract more than two bids, Mitchell Ramsey shouldered aside the auctioneer to plead with the crowd. "Ladies and gentlemen, the proceeds from this auction go toward retiring the debt of the First National Bank of Contrary, a debt primarily owed to its depositors, your friends and neighbors. Keep that in mind when you're deciding whether to bid."

Actually, Owen thought, most of the money was probably owed to out-of-state fat cats attracted to the bank by Burt Caldwell's widely advertised high rates of interest. He doubted that many Contrary residents had deposited more than the hundred thousand covered by FDIC insurance, even though his mother had one hundred twenty thousand dollars in her savings account and had given up hope of recovering the uninsured twenty thousand.

The next item to be auctioned was the imitation Paul Klee painting Owen had admired with the museum curator. The bidding started at five thousand dollars and attracted several spirited bidders, with three and four paddles shooting up in unison.

As the paddles went up in response to the rapid-fire chants of the auctioneer, Owen recalled the excitement he felt when he was ten years old attending backwoods estate auctions with his father. His skin tingled and he shoved his own paddle under his seat so he wouldn't be tempted to make a bid he couldn't afford.

By the time the bidding on the fake Klee reached eighteen thousand dollars, the only two bidders remaining were the woman with the dagger tattoo and a bearded, overweight man with one arm sitting two rows in front of Owen and Jeb Stuart. While the one-armed man seemed to agonize over each bid as if it were a physical effort to raise his paddle, the woman with the dagger tattoo invariably raised her paddle immediately following his offerings, advancing the bid by one thousand dollars each time. The two competitors took the level up to twenty-five thousand dollars with repeated increases of five hundred dollars from the one-armed man and one thousand from the dagger lady.

"Twenty-five thousand dollars," the auctioneer announced, staring at the one-armed man. "Do I hear twenty-six?"

His paddle shaking, the one armed man jumped the bid to thirty thousand.

The oohs and ahs of the crowd were silenced by the dagger lady's quick response of thirty-one thousand.

Owen made a mental note to update Nelson Algren's rules still further, to "Never converse, sleep with, or bid against a woman with a dagger tattoo."

"Thirty-five thousand," the one-armed man said, raising his voice on the final syllable so it sounded more like a plea than a bid.

"Thirty-six." The dagger lady didn't even bother to raise her paddle.

The bidding proceeded in increments of one thousand dollars, with each bid from the one-armed man coming more and more slowly. When the dagger lady bid forty-two thousand he shrugged heavily, causing his empty sleeve to bounce, and shook his head, declining to bid further. The auctioneer banged his gavel and awarded the painting to the woman with the dagger tattoo.

The crowd applauded. Seated at the front table, Mitchell Ramsey beamed and Victoria Gallagher met Owen's eyes with what he interpreted as a sympathetic look.

None of the other paintings commanded anywhere near the amount bid for the imitation Klee. The painting coming the closest was the fake Vermeer painted by the Dutch forger Van Meegeren, which the one-armed man claimed with a bid of fifteen thousand dollars. Most of the individual paintings sold for between one and two thousand dollars. Owen hoped that the level required for a winning bid would be lower when the auctioneer got to the baseball items.

The level of the winning bids started to drop when the movie memorabilia came onto the auction block. The covey of plaster-of-paris Maltese Falcons went for two dollars a bird, while the dagger lady won the Citizen Kane poster with a bid of two hundred and fifty dollars. The ruby slippers brought an average of five hundred dollars a pair, even though each of the four pairs was a different size and there was no evidence that any of them had been anywhere near the feet of Judy Garland.

The first batch of baseball memorabilia to be auctioned off included a duffel bag filled with a dozen assorted autographed bats which a man with a Cincinnati Reds cap won for six hundred dollars. Jeb Stuart urged Owen to bid on the Ken Griffey Junior bat they'd both hefted and Owen started the bidding at forty dollars. He intended to bid no higher than fifty, but got caught up in the competition and heard himself bidding seventy-five before the Cincinnati Reds fan took the bat with a bid of eighty dollars.

Owen could feel his heart racing and his adrenalin pumping with the excitement of the bidding. He barely had time to register Jeb Stuart's disappointment over the lost bat before Red McCann held up the first of the sealed boxes of baseball cards that had brought them to the auction.

Owen's opening bid of one hundred dollars for the box was immediately doubled by the one-armed man two rows ahead of them. Owen responded with a bid of two hundred and fifty dollars, only to hear the woman with the dagger tattoo bid four hundred.

The one-armed man bid five hundred dollars, which Owen had set as his personal limit. The dagger lady took the level well beyond that limit by bidding seven hundred and fifty dollars. While Owen hesitated, wondering whether he could afford to bid higher than he'd intended, the one-armed man rendered the issue moot by raising the bid to a thousand dollars.

Jeb Stuart looked at Owen expectantly. Owen shook his head and whispered, "Too much." The boy's head and shoulders dropped, increasing Owen's frustration.

The one-armed man and the dagger lady staged another bidding war, with the man again growing more hesitant each time he lifted his paddle to bid and the lady immediately raising the bid by one hundred dollars almost before his paddle had returned to his lap. Finally, after seeing his bid of thirty-five hundred dollars topped by her response of thirty-six hundred, he shrugged and withdrew from the bidding.

"The box can't possibly be worth that much," Owen whispered to Jeb Stuart. "Someone must have culled it for anything really valuable, even if they were only looking for forgeries the museum could exhibit."

Jeb Stuart's lips were drawn into a thin disappointed line. He didn't answer Owen, but nodded toward the podium, where the auctioneer was holding up the second of the two shoeboxes full of baseball cards.

Without much hope, Owen started the bidding again at one hundred dollars. When the one-armed man bid two hundred, Owen raised the bid to two hundred and fifty. The one-armed man turned in his seat to see who was bidding against him. No other bids were heard.

The auctioneer frowned and said, "Let's hear some bidding, ladies and gentlemen. If the last box was worth thirty-six hundred, this box must be worth at least three."

The one-armed man shrugged and nodded to Owen, then turned in his seat without entering another bid.

The auctioneer announced, "Going once." His eyes scanned the crowd for another bid. "Going twice." It seemed to Owen he was deliberately slowing his countdown. "Sold." The gavel banged down and Owen and Jeb Stuart exchanged low fives beneath the seat backs.

After the final item had been auctioned off, Owen and Jeb Stuart were standing in line waiting to pay for their successful bid and claim their shoebox when Victoria Gallagher approached him.

"Congratulations," she said. "You must be pleased. It looks as if you got a real bargain on that box of baseball cards."

"Either that," Owen said, "or the woman who won the other box paid a lot more than it was worth."

"Oh, we got a bargain, all right," Jeb Stuart said.

"You must be pleased yourself," Owen said. "That imitation Klee brought in forty-two thousand dollars."

Victoria pursed her lips and shook her head once. "I hated to see it go. I was getting quite fond of it."

"It's funny what people will bid on," Owen said. "Judy Garland's ruby slippers are on display in the Smithsonian, yet you got five hundred dollars a pair for slippers that never touched her feet."

"We don't know for sure that the slippers never touched her feet." She smiled. "We have papers saying that two of the pairs came from the MGM prop department."

"You had papers saying that the Klee painting was an original." Owen didn't know how to interpret her smile. "You don't really believe that Judy Garland actually wore any of those slippers in *The Wizard of Oz*?"

"There's a chance she did." Victoria paused and gave him the same enigmatic smile. "Maybe she did. I think those people bid on the magic of that 'maybe.' "

Owen could imagine Nat King Cole singing about the Mona Lisa strangeness of that smile. "But there were four different sizes of slippers."

"All the more likely that one of the sizes fit Judy Garland. There's still the magic of that 'maybe.' I'm sure the winning bidders are happy with that."

Owen shook his head. "If Prince Charming had four different sizes of glass slipper, he would have wound up marrying an ugly stepsister."

Victoria laughed. There was nothing enigmatic about her laugh. "Maybe. You just never know."

The line moved up and only two bidders stood between Owen and the long table staffed by three cashiers and overseen by two security guards and Mitchell Ramsey. A cell phone rang behind the table.

Ramsey ripped his cell phone from his belt clip, glared at it, and stepped behind a temporary partition. His voice carried over the temporary barrier. "It's a pissant town. Most of the paintings barely brought in enough to cover the cost of their frames."

Victoria blushed and looked down at her shoes. One of the security guards went behind the partition.

Ramsey lowered his voice, but certain words could still be heard on the other side of the barrier. "Pissant" seemed to be a favorite, and the figure "two hundred grand" also rang out over the cashiers' heads.

Before Owen reached the front of the line, Ramsey charged out from behind the partition and the cashiers' table, fastening his cell phone to his belt. Seeing Victoria, he stopped and said, "Next time, we take the goods to DC and auction them there. I need you to help me with the inventory for that." When Victoria didn't respond, he jerked his head toward the warehouse exit. "Well, come on."

"Can't it wait?" Victoria asked.

"No it can't. We've got a job to do."

Owen stepped between Ramsey and Victoria. "Isn't it a little late to be paying attention to your job? If the FDIC had been doing its job in Contrary all along, you wouldn't need to hold any auctions and my mother would be twenty thousand dollars richer."

Victoria touched Owen's arm and stepped around him. "That's all right. The work will have to be done sometime. Might as well do it now."

Owen watched Victoria follow Mitchell Ramsey through a double set of wooden doors and out of the warehouse. He was suddenly conscious that Jeb Stuart was staring at him. "What?" he asked.

"Nothing," the boy said. "But if I were you, I'd check that woman for tattoos."

Chapter Three:

Chiseled Crosses

The next morning, Owen was jarred from sleep by an insistent ringing. He punched the SNOOZE button on his alarm to stop the noise and give himself ten more minutes in bed, but the ringing didn't stop.

He opened one eye and stared at the alarm. It was six o'clock in the morning, too early for it to be ringing. By that

43

time, he was awake enough to realize the ringing wasn't coming from his alarm and he answered the phone.

"Owen? It's Thad Reader. Got time to come out and look at a crash scene?"

"Where are you?"

"Devil's Hairpin."

"How many dead?" He knew the location. It wasn't likely anyone could survive a crash there.

"Car went over the edge. We're still looking for bodies."

Owen sighed. It was going to be a messy scene. "Give me a half hour."

"Park at the turnout on Pigeon Point. Otherwise, your car will just be in the way. Give me a call and I'll send a deputy down for you."

"That's okay. I'll walk up."

"Still haven't gotten your cell phone to work hereabouts?"

The phone Owen had brought from California operated on the wrong frequency for West Virginia, and he hadn't bothered to replace it. At first, he didn't think he'd be around long enough to make it worth the bother. Then he found he enjoyed being free from incoming calls more than he missed being able to make outgoing calls.

"Even if I'd gotten a new phone, it probably wouldn't work around the hairpin. I don't mind walking. I can use the exercise."

"Then I'll see you when you get here."

Thad Reader was the sheriff of Raleigh County. He and Owen met when Owen's older brother George had a brush with county law enforcement. Since that time, Owen had worked with Reader on more than one occasion and he counted the sheriff as one of the few new friends he'd made since returning to West Virginia. Long-term consulting contracts were proving hard to come by in his native state, and the crash-scene investigations and expert witness work Reader steered Owen's way were more than welcome.

The Devil's Hairpin was a deadly switchback about halfway up Ragland's Ridge, fifteen miles south of Owen's mother's home in Barkley. The winding road leading up to the ridge was shrouded in early morning fog that cleared by the time Owen reached the turnout at Pigeon Point.

He parked his Saturn beside a patrol car from the sheriff's office, took his camera and a tape measure from the trunk, and began hiking up the narrow mountain road. Owen kept to the inside lane to avoid looking down over the sheer drop. The scarred face of the mountain was so close to the roadway in most spots he was forced to walk on the asphalt right-of-way. He didn't like the thought of sharing the narrow lane with wide mining trucks and was grateful to come upon an officer with a STOP sign controlling traffic at the head of a line of flares.

Owen followed the flares to the downhill leg of the Devil's Hairpin, where he found Thad Reader and another officer taking photographs.

Reader came down to meet Owen and walk him through the turn, stopping at the midpoint of the bend. "Car came downhill and went over the edge right here."

"No skid marks," Owen said. "Didn't try to stop."

"Looks that way."

"Fog, you think?"

The sheriff shrugged. "A little fog. Too much liquor. Not enough sleep. Who knows?"

Owen nodded toward the steep mountain wall that had been blasted away to form a ledge for the roadway. Two crude crosses had been chiseled into the limestone facing. "Not the first car to miss the curve."

"Six since I've been sheriff. A motorcycle, a coal truck,

two joyriding teenagers, a pillar of the community, and now this one. Half of them never touched their brakes."

"That's six in what? Twelve years?"

The sheriff rubbed his one good eye and nodded.

"County needs to put a guardrail on that curve."

"County needs a lot of things," Reader said. "More jobs and more revenue, mostly. Barely got enough money to fill the potholes on the busy roads."

"You'll have less money if somebody's survivor sues."

Owen started toward the edge of the curve. He had a bad case of vertigo, so he knelt and pretended to examine the roadway closely, then stretched out on his stomach and peered over the edge. The mountainside fell away sharply at first, then stepped down through a series of narrow ledges into a tree-covered slope that eased its way down to a winding creekbed.

There was some scarring on the tiered ledges, but no sign of the vehicle in the woods below. "Can't see the car," Owen said. "Who reported the crash?"

"Couple of campers along the creekbed heard the noise and called it in. Otherwise we might never have known about it."

A sheared sapling about ten feet down the vertical face of the mountain caught Owen's eye and he took out his camera and photographed it.

"See something?" the sheriff asked.

Owen pointed down the cliff face and the sheriff came to the edge and looked over. "That's a fresh break on that sapling," Owen said. "If the car had any speed at all going over the edge, seems like it should have cleared that twig easily. Could have cleared that first ledge too, but it didn't."

"Can you run some numbers, figure what speed would clear the first ledge?"

"I'll need some measurements, but that's easy enough to do."

Owen pulled back from the precipice and photographed a narrow groove gouged into the edge of the curve. "That gouge could have been caused by the undercarriage scraping the edge as it went over."

"Have to be going pretty slow to catch the undercarriage."

"Could be it was pushed."

Reader sighed. "That's why I called you. Thought it might not be an accident."

"Can I take a look at the car?"

"I've got some deputies down there, along with an EMS team. There's a fire road goes most of the way in. I'll drive you."

In the patrol car winding down the mountainside, Owen asked, "How's the reelection campaign going?"

Reader winced and grimaced. "Not so good. That nine-eleven stuff may have done me in."

As soon as the news of the attack on the World Trade Center aired, the sheriff had taken his deputies to guard both ends of the New River Bridge in neighboring Fayette County. His attempt to defend the highest bridge east of the Mississippi made the inside pages of several newspapers as human interest copy in the days following the attack and was almost forgotten until the late-night comedians picked up on it a few months later.

In the most popular variation, a monologing comic would hold his thumb next to his ear and extend his little finger to his lips, mimicking a terrorist making a phone call. "Okay, let's review the targets. There's the World Trade Center, the White House, the Pentagon, and (pause) oh, yeah, let's not forget that little bridge down in West Virginia."

The bit never failed to get a laugh, and the newspapers

picked up the story again, this time portraying Reader as a backwoods buffoon.

"You did what you thought was best at the time," Owen said. "Nobody knew what was going down. Not even the president."

Reader shook his head. "Doesn't matter. Folks used to say the only thing that could cost an incumbent his job was to get caught in bed with a live boy or a dead girl. Nowadays, I think a man could survive even that. What you can't survive is public ridicule."

The sheriff whipped the steering wheel around and turned off the narrow asphalt road onto a bumpy gravel trail through heavy woods. "Coldcock a suspect, shows you're tough on crime. Folks will still vote for you. Unless, of course, the poor stiff was a victim of profiling. Get caught copping a blow job from a teeny bopper and you're presidential material. Long as she doesn't disappear under mysterious circumstances." He thumped his palm on the steering wheel. "But get half the county laughing at you and you've got a tough row to hoe. As a candidate, you're dead meat."

The sheriff pulled halfway off the fire trail and parked behind another patrol car. A third patrol car and an ambulance were parked well ahead of them. None of the officers that came in the patrol cars were in sight, but an ambulance attendant in green scrubs sat at the base of a tree, smoking a cigarette.

"Car's about a hundred yards in, thataway," the attendant said, flicking ashes to indicate the direction. "No sign of any occupants yet."

"Maybe somebody shoved an empty car off the bluff just to junk it," Owen said.

"Car's no junker," the ambulance attendant said. "It's last year's Mustang. Cherry. Or at least it was until it hit the tree-tops."

"We ran the plates," Thad Reader said. "It's a rental. Renter's name is Mary Smith."

"Pretty common," Owen said. "Know anybody by that name?"

"Doesn't ring a bell. Woman's either got lots of relatives or damn little imagination."

Owen and Thad walked in the direction indicated by the EMS worker. The red Mustang lay on its top, its roof crushed to the level of the seatbacks. The driver's door was missing, and a large tree branch protruded from the grill.

Owen began snapping photos of the Mustang. The dense treetops obscured his view of the cliff face the car had bounced down.

He took a few close-ups of the undercarriage. "Looks like it scraped the edge of the roadway right here," he said, pointing to a long scar along the exposed edge of the underpanel. "Better have your boys scrape off a little of this coating and grit to compare with that notch up on the road's edge."

"So the car didn't go flying off the curve at full speed," Reader said.

"Doesn't look that way. But I'll run the numbers just to be sure."

A deputy burst into the clearing where the ambulance driver sat. "They've found a body. Stuck in the treetops."

The attendant stood and ground his cigarette underfoot. "They alive?"

"Don't know yet. Bring your kit."

The attendant went back to the ambulance and returned with a medical pack slung over his shoulder. Then Owen, the sheriff, and the attendant followed the deputy through the trees toward the cliff face. Along the way, they passed a dented hubcap, a red side-view mirror, and the missing driver's door.

The deputy led them to the base of a tall pine tree, where another deputy who looked to be barely out of his teens stood looking up through the thick branches.

"Gordo says it's a woman," the young deputy said.

"Is she alive?" the ambulance attendant asked.

"She alive?" the deputy called up.

There was no answer from the upper branches. Looking up, all Owen could see was the heel of the climbing deputy's boot. The branches rustled, and his left pant leg came into view.

"He's coming down," the young deputy said.

This was the part Owen dreaded. He hadn't been investigating crashes long enough to get used to the sight of mangled bodies. He probably never would.

A branch cracked, and "Son of a bitch" filtered down from the treetop. Then both legs of the descending deputy could be seen, along with two pale arms dangling from the body slung across his shoulder.

"Is she alive?" the ambulance attendant called up.

"What do you think?" the climbing deputy shouted down.

The ambulance attendant lowered his pack to the ground.

The branches bent and gave under the weight of the deputy and his load, revealing the top of the woman's head. Leaves and twigs clung to her short black hair. The woman's white blouse was torn, and an ugly wound ran the length of her left arm. Scratches crisscrossed her right arm, covering what looked like a raw open sore.

As the deputy descended through one more set of branches, Owen recognized the sore as the drop of blood at the tip of a dagger tattoo.

Chapter Four:

A Rolling Stone Gathers No Boss

"I don't exactly know the woman," Owen said to Thad Reader as they watched the sheriff's deputies help the EMS worker load the dagger lady's body into the waiting ambulance. "But I saw her take over the auction at one of Burt Campbell's warehouses yesterday."

Reader fixed Owen with his one good eye. "The FDIC auction? For the Contrary Bank?"

"That's the one. She took home damn near everything she bid on. Must have spent nearly fifty thousand dollars. Over

51

forty grand just for a single painting."

Reader looked back at the mangled Mustang. "Nothing like that in the car. No purse. No ID. Nothing."

"The trunk's sprung open." Owen nodded toward the body in the ambulance. "She didn't stay in the car after the first impact. It's no wonder nothing else did."

"I'll have my guys search the area. She must have had a purse, at least."

"I can help you lay out the search area," Owen said. "We know where the car left the road and where it ended up. Anything that fell out won't be far from a line between those two points."

"Be nice to find a purse and some ID. I'm betting her name wasn't really Mary Smith."

They watched the ambulance back up until the driver found enough space to turn around so that he could follow the fire trail out of the woods. Reader shoved his Mounties' hat back and scratched his receding hairline. "Woman comes out of nowhere, spends fifty grand at an auction, then winds up getting shoved over a cliff in a rented Mustang. What are the chances she really had a plain vanilla name like Mary Smith?"

"I agree. It looks less and less likely."

"Tell me again what she took away from the auction. So we know what we're searching for. Besides her purse and some ID."

"I don't remember everything. But I know she left the auction with a painting, a couple of movie posters, and a shoebox full of baseball cards."

"Baseball cards." Reader's face showed no expression, as if the woman's possessions were no more or less incongruous than the manner of her death. "And she'd paid forty grand for the painting?"

Owen nodded.

"What'd it look like?"

"Abstract, with a black frame and an orange arrow at its center. If it came loose from the car, it's likely to be as mangled as the Mustang, but you'll know it if you find it."

Reader tilted his Mounties' hat forward, shading his eyes. "Something tells me we aren't going to find it."

Ruth Allison tucked a wisp of gray hair back under the striped stocking cap she was wearing to cover the last traces of her chemotherapy. "So nobody knows anything about this woman?"

Owen waited for a gap in traffic so he could pull onto the main road from their cul-de-sac. He had plenty of time to make Ruth's appointment with her general practitioner, so he was in no hurry. "Not so far. Thad Reader's running her prints."

"What a horrible thing. Was she drunk, do you think?"

Owen pulled out into the stream of midday traffic. "Have to wait for the autopsy results."

"There's something you're not telling me. Sheriff Reader wouldn't roust you out of bed for an ordinary run-off-the-road accident."

There was a lot he wasn't telling his mother. He wasn't telling her the crash was no accident. He wouldn't tell her that until the investigation was complete. "It's the fifth death up there in six years, Mom. He's worried about lawsuits."

"Well, then, it's good he's hired you."

"God knows I need the work."

"What about that proposal you wrote for the state?"

"Still no word."

"But shouldn't you get that job? With all your experience, I mean."

Owen sighed. They'd had this conversation before. "That may not be all it takes, Mom."

"You mean they might want kickbacks?"

"I don't think they'll be that blatant. Kickbacks sent the last Attorney General to jail. That's why they decided to rebid the job. But the new Attorney General isn't exactly a friend of mine."

Ruth's face clouded over. "The new Attorney General?"

Owen glanced sideways at his mother. She blinked once and pursed her lips. They'd had several discussions about the new Attorney General, but it was obvious she couldn't recall them. "You know. Dusty Rhodes."

"Oh, yes. Dusty Rhodes."

Owen watched his mother's face soften as she processed the name and her memories of the man. "He may not be so bad as you think."

"Mom, he could not be as bad as I think and still deserve consecutive life sentences. He's a scumbag. He got where he is on shady deals and kickbacks, and he's left a trail of broken lives that probably include at least one murder."

"You don't know that for sure." Ruth continued to treat the conversation as if it were all new to her. Her spotty memory was the chief reason Owen had insisted she see a general practitioner in addition to her oncologist. "He'll have to give you the job. There's nobody in the state who's better qualified to do it."

"That may not be all it takes, Mom. He knows I worked against him last election."

Owen had an uneasy feeling about his bid for the state job, which entailed the inspection of several mine shafts in the vicinity of mining dams. The potential problem of dams built near underground shafts had been brought home forcibly just the past year when a mining dam burst through into a nearby shaft and flooded several hollows, blackening the Big Muddy and the Ohio Rivers with mine waste and killing three people.

The state was under a court order to assess the likelihood that the accident could be repeated at other dam sites and identify remedial measures. It was a job that Owen was well qualified to do, but it had been nearly two months since he had submitted his proposal and been interviewed. Something was delaying the Attorney General's decision. Since the job needed to be done quickly, the delay couldn't be a good sign.

"If you don't get the job, you ought to consider going back to California," Ruth said. "The worst of my chemo treatments is over. I'll be all right by myself."

"We don't know that you'll be all right. That's one of the reasons we're seeing a different doctor today."

"You belong back in California with Judith."

The mention of Owen's ex-wife added to his frustration. "We've had this conversation before, Mom. It's not clear that Judith wants me back or that I want to go back." He turned into the hospital parking lot. "But it's perfectly clear that she doesn't want to be here in West Virginia with me. And I'm going to stay here at least until we're sure you're all right and Jeb Stuart finishes his senior year."

"Well, then," Ruth said. "I want you to come with me to see this new doctor. I'll show you I'm all right."

The new doctor, Ann Rounkey, was a short, sturdy woman with a round, pleasant face and penetrating blue eyes. She greeted Ruth and Owen with a smiling, "Hey, y'all," that rolled out in a soft southern drawl rather than the harsher nasal twang of a native West Virginian.

Ruth grinned and returned the greeting. Then she

asked, "Is it all right if we do the mental test first and let my son watch? He's worried I'm a few marbles short of a full bag."

Owen reddened. "Mom, I never said . . ."

The doctor waved her stethoscope at Owen, cutting him off. "It's just fine if y'all stay." She pointed the earpieces of the instrument at him. "I just don't want you slipping answers to your mama behind my back, hear?"

Owen smiled, nodded, and retreated to a corner of the examination room.

The doctor took a clipboard from the long white shelf that ran the length of the room's back wall. "All right now," she said to Ruth. "Just y'all come sit over here next to me and I'll start by asking a few questions to see how well those marbles of yours are clicking together."

Ruth wheeled her chair over next to the doctor and rested one elbow on the edge of the white shelf. She didn't seem to be at all nervous. Judging by appearances, Owen thought, he was feeling more anxiety about the test than his mother.

The doctor led Ruth through a series of questions, asking her to name the year, the month, the day and date, the city and state, the hospital's patron saint, and the current president. Except for a slight grimace when she named the current president, Ruth answered all of the questions smoothly. She also had no problem with the next portion of the exam, in which she recalled and named objects called out by the doctor and spelled the word WORLD backwards.

The doctor then asked Ruth to complete a familiar saying and explain what it meant. The saying was, "A rolling stone gathers no (blank)."

Ruth smiled and, without hesitating, answered, "A

rolling stone gathers no boss." Then she paused. "No. That's wrong. Although it's not a bad answer, is it?" She tried again. "The real saying goes, 'A rolling stone gathers no moss.' "

Up to that point, the doctor had simply made check marks on her clipboard when Ruth answered correctly. Now she wrote what looked to be a full sentence on the answer sheet and asked, "And what does it mean?"

Ruth smiled at the doctor. "Why, it means if you keep moving, trying new things, you won't become hidebound."

The doctor made a short notation on the clipboard and said, "Now I'd like you to count backward from one hundred by sevens."

Ruth recoiled as if she'd been struck. "That's not . . ." She stopped in mid-sentence, held up her right hand, palm outward, and said, "One hundred." She stared at the doctor's clipboard. "Ninety-three."

The doctor made a small check mark on the answer sheet.

Ruth seemed stuck. She bit her lower lip and glanced back at Owen.

Owen tried the exercise himself, as if hoping that telepathy might unlock his mother's mind. It wasn't a natural progression, but he managed to count from one hundred down to two mentally before his mother spoke again.

Ruth locked her eyes on the clipboard. "Eighty-four. No that's not right. That's a multiple."

She lifted her gaze from the clipboard to meet the doctor's eyes. "Let me start over. One hundred. Ninety-three." Her voice trailed off. She shook her head and waved both hands in front of her face. "It's no use. I can't do it."

Ruth clenched her fists in her lap and hunched over them. "What's the next question?"

The doctor showed Ruth a sketch of a man missing his right ear and said, "Study this picture and tell me what's missing."

"His left ear," Ruth said, then quickly corrected herself. "No, that's wrong. It's his right ear that's missing."

Owen cringed inwardly, worried and embarrassed for his mother.

The doctor wrote another sentence on her clipboard, then asked Ruth if she remembered the three objects she'd identified earlier. When Ruth identified the three objects correctly, the doctor led her through a series of paper-folding tasks, then set aside her clipboard and said, "Well, that's all. You did quite well."

Ruth's shoulders slumped. "You don't have to humor me."

The doctor reached out and patted Ruth's clenched fists. "No. Really. You did well."

Ruth looked down at the fists in her lap and shook her head.

Owen started to move forward to help comfort his mother, but the doctor stopped him with a quick shake of her head. She stood and took her stethoscope from around her neck. "Maybe you'd best leave so we can get on with the physical exam."

"Of course." Owen backed toward the door of the examination room. "I'll wait outside, Mom."

Ruth still hadn't looked up. If she heard him, she gave no sign.

Owen paced the hospital hallway. He'd insisted on the exam because he'd been questioning his mother's memory. Now he found himself questioning the exam. How accurate could it be? What did it mean if a person couldn't count backwards by sevens? He'd be willing to bet that half the people in the hospital, doctors and patients alike, couldn't count backwards from one hundred by sevens on their first try.

"Why Owen, how nice to see you. What brings you to St. Vincent's?" The figure in the flowing white robes asking the question was Sister Regina Anne. She'd been in charge of the operating rooms where Owen worked as an orderly the summer after he graduated from high school. Now she ran the entire hospital.

"I'm waiting for my mother," Owen said.

The sharp angular planes of the nun's face were softened by her show of concern. "How is she?"

"I just watched her come apart because she couldn't count backwards from a hundred by sevens."

"The mini-mental exam." Sister Regina Anne frowned and nodded. "It's a difficult test to score. Patients taking it are so worried that their mental state might be deteriorating it affects their performance."

"That seemed to be happening with Mom. I've never seen her so flustered."

"Who's her doctor?"

"Ann Rounkey."

"Ann's a wonderful doctor. I'm sure she'll be readministering the test in the future. We'll be observing Ruth over time. You can't tell much from a single exam."

"It's just so frustrating. You know Mom. She's a strong woman. I remember watching her fix sandwiches for the divers searching for Dad's body. And she made it through chemotherapy without a single complaint, even though I never once heard her say the word cancer. Now she won't say the word Alzheimer's."

"Mental decline can be caused by many things besides

Alzheimer's. Those chemotherapy treatments had to be very stressful."

"But that exam . . ."

"That exam's only one indicator. I'll see that Ann keeps an eye on your Mom. We all will. Ruth's a wonderful woman. She's been a godsend to us here at the hospital with her volunteering." Sister Regina Anne took one hand from the folds of her robe and touched Owen's arm. "I'll remember her in my prayers. You could do the same thing."

"It's been a long time since I've prayed regularly, sister. I'm afraid God would say, 'Owen *who?*' "

The nun's clear blue eyes sparkled under her cowl. "Oh, there's no need to worry about God's memory."

In the car on the way home, Ruth slumped back against the passenger door as if trying to distance herself from her son behind the wheel. "It wasn't a fair test," she said. "That question took me by surprise."

"The counting backwards question?" Owen said.

"It wasn't on any of the sample tests."

"Sample tests?"

"They're on the Internet. The mini-mental test. You can take it yourself."

"You mean you practiced? In advance?"

"I got a hundred percent on all the practice tests."

Owen understood why Ruth had wanted him to sit in on the real exam. "That's bound to throw off the test's accuracy."

"It's no different from memorizing the eye chart for my driver's exam."

Owen felt his grip tighten on the steering wheel. "You memorize the eye chart?"

"I'm a good driver, Owen. You know that."

"Everybody thinks they're a good driver, Mom. But the accident rate for people your age is almost as high as the rate for teenagers like Jeb Stuart."

"Jeb Stuart's a good driver too. Besides, I don't drive after dark."

"That's a start. Next time, though, try taking your eye exam without cramming for it. Same thing goes for your next mental exam."

Ruth looked out the passenger window. The afternoon sun had disappeared behind a cloud and a few raindrops splattered off the car window. "Practicing didn't work anyhow. I missed two questions."

"I liked your doctor. What did she say?"

"She said I was within the norm. She didn't say what norm. The norm for loopy old ladies, I guess."

"Mom, it's no big deal. There'll be other tests."

"I missed two questions."

"The first was a tough question. The second you missed because you were frustrated over missing the first one."

Ruth traced the path of a raindrop down the windshield with her finger. "My mind is slipping, Owen. I can feel it."

The worry in her voice cut into him. He reached out and patted her hand. "You're getting older, Mom. A little slippage is natural. We're just trying to measure it. To make sure there's nothing to worry about."

"I can handle the slippage on the slope behind me. It's the cliff ahead of me I worry about."

He wanted to reassure her, but didn't know how. "It's no sin not to be able to count backward. Remember that green Triumph I had in college? By my senior year the transmission was so bunged up it wouldn't run in reverse. And I couldn't afford to get it fixed."

"So you drove it anyhow. I argued with you, but you wouldn't listen."

"I just had to be careful where I parked it. It had to be facing out with nothing blocking it. But I got by without a reverse gear."

"Is that supposed to make me feel better? You junked the car as soon as you graduated."

"Would it help if I ask the next ten people I meet to count backward from a hundred by sevens? I'll bet at least half of them won't be able to do it without a mistake."

"Why should I care what other people can or can't do?"

The fall shower was coming down in earnest now. Raindrops pooled on the windshield faster than the wipers could clear them away. Owen slowed to turn into his mother's cul-de-sac and parked at the foot of the sidewalk leading to the front porch.

He retrieved an umbrella from the Saturn's trunk and held it over the passenger door as he helped his mother out of the car. "We'll get Jeb Stuart and go out somewhere for dinner."

The front door of their house blew open.

Owen lowered the umbrella. "What the hell?"

A skinny, long-haired youth wearing a nose ring, a black T-shirt and ragged jeans burst out onto the porch.

Owen moved toward the house, blocking the sidewalk and pointing the umbrella at the boy. "Just hold it right there."

The boy stopped short, vaulted over the side railing, and started running toward the rear of the house.

Owen dropped the umbrella and ran after the intruder, chasing him through the narrow alley that ran between the neighbors' backyards and the foot of a steep hill.

When the alley ended, the boy crossed the street and

pounded down a cramped walkway beside a shallow creekbed. Owen plunged after him, not gaining ground, but not losing any either. He was close enough to make out the figure of a snorting dragon on the back of the boy's T-shirt, but not close enough to read the legend under the dragon. When he hit the creek walkway, he could feel his chest tighten. His breath came in short, sharp pants. He blinked and shook his head to clear the raindrops from his eyes.

The boy ahead of him splashed across the creekbed and started up a grassy hillside dotted with birch and poplar trees. Owen followed the boy across the creek, panting and losing ground. He could no longer make out the image of the dragon on the boy's back.

Owen started up the grassy slope when his feet slipped and he landed on his elbows, tracing two muddy tracks in the earth as he slid backwards. He got to his knees and swore at the boy's backside as it disappeared into the trees.

Owen stood unsteadily, gulping in air and rainwater. There was no chance of catching up now, or even seeing which way the boy turned when he left the cover of the trees.

Owen half walked, half slid down the slick grassy slope and ran back along the creek, through his neighbors' back-yards, and down the cul-de-sac leading to his mother's house. He pounded up the porch steps. The front door was ajar and he shoved it open, then stood stock still in the doorway, gasping to catch his breath and take in the scene in front of him.

At the top of the stairway, the banister had been knocked loose from its moorings and dangled white supports like broken teeth. Ruth Allison sat halfway down the stairs, cradling Jeb Stuart's head on her shoulder. The boy sprawled, trembling, holding his left wrist, which jutted at an awkward angle.

"I tried to stop him," Jeb Stuart said, hefting his wrist and grimacing. "But he caught me by surprise."

Ruth Allison ran her fingers lightly over the boy's sweating brow. "It's all right now. I've called nine-one-one."

"I'd just gotten home," Jeb Stuart said. "I was going upstairs when I heard a noise in the bathroom. I thought it was you, Ruth, but the door was half open. I knew something was wrong."

"Hush, child," Ruth said. "It's all right."

"I stood at the head of the stairs and called your name. Then this guy busts out of the bathroom and takes me right through the banister with a body block."

"Where was Buster when all this was going on?" Owen asked.

"Buster? Oh, my land, Buster," Ruth said. "Was he hurt too?"

Still winded from the chase, Owen took a deep breath and said, "I'll go hunt for him." He started for the rear of the house, calling the dog's name, when he heard a thumping noise punctuated by a faint yipping from behind the cellar door.

Owen opened the cellar door and a small black-and-white dog burst out, tail wagging. He looked up at Owen, danced on his two hind legs, then darted for the front of the house, stopped halfway into the living room, and scampered back to Owen.

Owen picked the dog up and examined him while walking back to the front stairwell. "Seems to be okay," he said to Ruth and Jeb Stuart. "Looks like the burglar shut him in the cellar. He started throwing himself against the closed door when he heard my voice."

Ruth reached out with her free hand and patted Buster's head. "Poor thing. You're just not big enough to defend yourself."

Owen sat the dog down on the floor. "He must have barked like mad. That's what got him shut away."

Buster scampered back and forth across the living-room floor, tail wagging.

"Doesn't look too traumatized by the experience," Owen said. The black-and-white poodle with the mutt cut was one of the few possessions he had claimed in the divorce proceedings. The dog was approaching ten years old, and still playful as a puppy. Well over fifty in human years, Owen thought, but you would have caught the guy.

Owen bent over and took a deep breath. As he straightened, he looked up at the shattered banister. "You're lucky you didn't break more than your wrist," he said to Jeb Stuart.

"You think it's broken?" The boy's forehead was producing more sweat than Ruth could wipe away.

Owen started for the kitchen. "I'll get some ice to keep the swelling down."

Buster followed when he heard the refrigerator door open.

"Some aspirin, too," Ruth called.

A siren sounded in the distance. Owen and Buster left the kitchen and went outside to meet the ambulance.

Chapter Five:

Hillbilly Heroin

Except for a young mother with a squalling infant, Owen and Ruth had the emergency room waiting area all to themselves. Thad Reader joined them while Jeb Stuart was in the operating room with the on-call orthopedic surgeon.

"What happened?" the sheriff asked. "I heard my dispatcher read off your address. By the time my deputies got to your place, though, the neighbors said you'd left in an ambulance."

"Jeb Stuart surprised a burglar in the upstairs bathroom," Owen said. "Boy knocked Jeb through the banister and ran. I drove up in time to see him clear the porch, but I couldn't catch him."

"What'd he look like?" the sheriff asked.

"Wore a nose ring and a T-shirt with a dragon and what looked like some band's tour dates on the back. Long stringy black hair. Looked to be in his twenties."

"How'd he get in?"

"We never lock our doors," Ruth said.

"Well, you better start," Reader said. "There's been a rash of break-ins in the last six months. Kids stoked on OxyContin, trying to get cash to feed their habit."

"OxyContin," Owen said. "Isn't that what hooked Rush Limbaugh?"

"Him and hundreds of others," Reader said. "It's a pain reliever. Doctors prescribe it for cancer, black lung, busted bones, and backaches. Comes in time-release tablets that give out little jolts over a twelve-hour period."

Across the room, the baby screeched and her mother stood and paced back and forth, smothering the child's cries against her neck.

"Trouble with OxyContin is, some drug-store cowboys played amateur pharmacist and figured out if you grind the pills up you can get the twelve-hour jolt all at once. It's a huge rush." Reader sighed. "But it's as addictive as cocaine. It's getting to be a real problem in the hollows. Folks call it hillbilly heroin."

The baby wrenched its face free from its mother's neck and screeched again. Ruth hurried across the room to offer help.

Reader shook his head. "West Virginia leads the nation in the consumption of OxyContin. Thirty-three states ahead of us in population, but none ahead of us in snarfing Oxys. Crime rate's tripled since it's caught on. I've seen maybe ten deaths in the past six months. Kids who just can't handle it."

The baby began squalling almost nonstop, pausing only long enough to catch a quick breath. Ruth was unable to comfort either the mother or the child. Finally, a nurse appeared to take the mother by the arm and lead her deeper into the heart of the hospital. The volume of the screeching grew lower and lower, and ultimately stopped after a door slammed shut somewhere inside.

"Street value of OxyContin's about a buck a milligram. Around a hundred times what a legitimate prescription costs. Comes in twenty-, forty-, and eighty-milligram tablets. Used to be one-hundred-sixty-milligram pills too, but they stopped making them when somebody figured out it was way too easy to OD on that much Oxy." Reader shrugged. "Kids who can barely count know the metric system now. Costs at least forty bucks for a starter hit of forty milligrams. You get hooked, though, and it takes more and more to get you high.

"Got a kid in my jail, swapped his pickup for two pills. High didn't last him a day. Caught him after he hotwired another pickup and wrapped it around a phone pole."

"That's awful," Ruth said.

"Moral is, keep your doors and windows locked. Town's not safe anymore. Was anything missing from your place?"

"We don't know," Ruth said. "We didn't have time to check."

"He wasn't carrying anything when I chased him," Owen said. "If he took something, it was small enough to fit into his pockets."

"Well, check to see if anything's missing when you get home," Reader said. "We'll talk to your neighbors, too. Could be he was working the whole block."

"What if he wasn't?" Owen said. "What if he targeted our house specifically."

"Why would he do that?" Reader asked.

"Strike you as strange that two people who came away from the FDIC auction with loot would be hit by robbers within two days?"

"You didn't tell me you came away with loot."

"Box of baseball cards."

"Same as Mary Smith?"

"Not quite. She was carrying about fifty grand more in art."

"Who's Mary Smith?" Ruth asked.

"We don't really know," Reader said. "She's the woman who went over the Devil's Hairpin. Found her purse in the woods. DC driver's license says Mary Smith, but it's a fake. We're running her prints."

"Anything else in the purse?" Owen asked.

"Ten dollars and a handful of change. Key to the local Motel Eight."

"Anything in the motel room?"

"Empty as a politician's promises. No cash. No clothes. No painting. No posters. No baseball cards." Reader removed his Mounties' hat and scratched his receding hairline. "Saturday, the woman pays out forty-eight grand in cash to an auctioneer. A day later, she doesn't have two tens to rub together."

"What are the chances she stashed her loot somewhere before the killer got to her?"

Reader shrugged. "Then why kill her? Why not keep her alive until she gives up the loot? And what makes her loot worth killing for, anyhow?"

"The woman showed a wad of cash at the auction. She probably had more with her. Maybe that's what attracted her killers."

Ruth grimaced. "You two are about as pleasant as my chemotherapy treatments."

"I met the woman who's curator of Caldwell's collection," Owen said. "Her name's Victoria Gallagher. I'll bet she'd give us a list of everybody who registered for the auction. Maybe somebody else had a break-in."

"Or broke in themselves," Reader said. "Seems like who-ever did in Mary Smith must have been at the auction. Other-wise, how would they know she got the loot?"

A young doctor in green scrubs wheeled Jeb Stuart into the waiting room. The boy's left arm was in a sling and his eyes were glazed. The doctor sported a sparse growth of black stubble on his chin and upper lip that looked to be either a failed beard or the product of a long duty shift.

"Your boy's going to be all right," the doctor said. "I put in a titanium bar and six bolts to make sure the wrist sets properly. I'll replace the soft cast with a hard one in two weeks. Another three to four weeks after that, and he should be good as new."

"Thank God," Ruth said.

The doctor smiled. "When you're young, you heal fast."

"Any lasting harm likely?" Owen asked.

"Shouldn't be," the doctor said. "He'll need a little phys-ical therapy when the cast comes off, to keep the wrist limber."

"But he'll be ready for the baseball season?"

"No doubt about it. Most likely part of the basketball season as well."

Jeb Stuart smiled. It was a vacant smile, aimed some-where beyond the concerned clump of adults surrounding him.

"I've given him a few pain killers," the doctor said. "Here's the prescription in case he needs more."

The doctor offered the prescription to Owen, but Thad Reader reached out and grabbed it. "OxyContin," the sheriff said. "Don't you guys ever get the word? There's an epidemic out there."

"There's no pain killer that can't be abused," the doctor said. "This one works better than most others when it's used legitimately."

Thad Reader handed the prescription to Owen. "My advice is to burn this and stock up on lots of aspirin."

"I'll be fine without any pills." Jeb Stuart started to rise unsteadily from the wheelchair. "Don't need this chair, either."

The doctor clamped his hand on Jeb Stuart's right shoulder and forced him back down into the wheelchair. "You need to stay in the chair until you reach your car. Doctor's orders."

The physician looked from Owen to Thad Reader. "I assume one of you has a car so he won't have to drive?"

"Oh, dear," Ruth said. "We came in the ambulance."

"I'll drive everybody home," Thad Reader said.

The doctor patted Jeb Stuart's right shoulder. "Then I leave you in good hands."

After taking Ruth and Jeb Stuart home, Owen and Thad Reader drove to the auction warehouse, where Victoria Gallagher and her FDIC overseer, Mitchell Ramsey, were taking inventory and packing items for shipping. Ramsey sat on a ladder, handing down modern first editions to a teenage girl who covered the books with bubble wrap and loaded them into a box. As he handed down each book, Ramsey called out the title, author, and condition for Victoria to record. He barely looked up when Owen and the sheriff entered.

"We called earlier about getting a list of your auction attendees," the sheriff said. "We'd like the names and addresses of everyone who registered to bid and a tabulation of what they spent."

Ramsey ignored the sheriff's request while he finished classifying the book in his hand. "*Men without Women*; Ernest Hemingway; condition, fine; dust jacket, near fine; signature, probably forged; minimum bid, five thousand dollars." He handed the book to the teenage girl, then glanced down at the sheriff. "I trust you have a warrant."

"We can get a warrant easy enough," Thad Reader said. "But there's been a murder and we're trying to minimize wasted motion. It's not as if we're asking for privileged information. The people were attending a public auction of government-owned artifacts."

"I've made a copy of the list of bidders," Victoria said, "along with a record of their purchases. You're welcome to take it."

"You didn't ask me for permission to copy that information," Ramsey said from his perch on the ladder.

Victoria ignored Ramsey, took several sheets of paper from her clipboard, and handed them to the sheriff. "Would you like me to make you a copy as well?" she asked Owen.

Owen smiled. "I wouldn't want to get you into any trouble."

"Oh, it's no trouble. You know, though, that many of the people attending the auction didn't register to bid."

"And many who did register didn't buy anything," Ramsey said. "We have work to do here, Victoria."

"I'm sure our little inventory can wait a few minutes," Victoria said. "After all, these gentlemen are conducting a murder investigation."

"Appreciate your help." Reader examined the list. "Looks like about half the folks were from around here, with another quarter from other parts of the state. The rest came from outside West Virginia. Four from Cincinnati, three from Columbus, three all the way from DC."

"There was a Cincinnati fan snapping up anything with a Reds Logo," Owen said.

Victoria pointed to a name on the list. "That was Mr. David Lewis. He paid us with a certified check."

"Mary Smith gave an address in the District of Columbia," Reader said. "Same as on her driver's license. But the license was fake."

"The money she paid was real," Victoria said. "Over forty thousand in cash for a single painting."

"What makes a phony painting worth that much money?" Reader asked.

"The real question," Ramsey said, "is why we didn't get more money for the other paintings. The bidders simply showed no appreciation for the works on display."

Victoria smiled at Owen. "Oh, several people appreciated the fake Klee."

"Not many could afford it, though," Owen said.

"Aside from Mary Smith, did anyone else pay with hefty amounts of cash?" Reader asked. "Or do anything else that struck you as out of the ordinary?"

Victoria took the list back and examined it. "About half the bidders paid in cash, but it was mostly small amounts. Aside from Mary Smith, the only bidder who paid more than a thousand dollars in cash was this man." She pointed to a name.

The sheriff read the name aloud. "Paul Cote. He's from DC, same as the woman calling herself Smith. What do you remember about him?"

"He was disabled," Victoria said. "He had only one arm and walked with a limp."

"He finished second on most of Mary Smith's big bids," Owen said.

"Think he was shilling?" the sheriff asked.

"Excuse me?" Victoria said.

"Running up the bid with no intention of buying," Reader said. "Increasing the house take."

Ramsey bristled on his perch. "I'll have you know we run an honest auction. We're the federal government, after all."

"When is your next honest auction?" Reader asked.

"We haven't set a date, just a location," Ramsey said. "The next auction will be held in the District of Columbia."

Reader nodded toward the boxes of first editions. "Is that where you're taking the books?"

"We're shipping them to our offices in the District," Ramsey said. "We expect the people in that venue to be much more appreciative of our wares."

"More appreciative of fakes and frauds, you mean?" Owen said. "I'd say you couldn't have picked a better place than DC. It's the home of the federal government, after all."

Chapter Six:

Fair and Unfair Trades

Riding home from the warehouse in the sheriff's car, Owen said, "So you're going to check the bidders' list to see if anyone else had a break-in?"

"Or looks to be a candidate for breaking in themselves," Reader said. "There's a good chance whoever did in Mary Smith was at the auction."

"The kid that hit our house and knocked Jeb Stuart through the banister wasn't at the auction. I would have noticed him."

"Killer didn't have to be at the auction. Could be Mary Smith was bidding for a third party who didn't want his identity known."

"And he killed her to cover his tracks?"

"Or maybe she tried to double-cross her employer by taking off with the loot."

Owen shook his head. "Doesn't make sense. If she was planning a double-cross, why go through with the auction? Why not just take the money and run?"

"Good point. Cash is a lot more liquid than a phony Paul Klee painting."

The sheriff pulled up in front of Ruth Allison's house, let Owen out, and followed him inside. Ruth was in the living room, watching a *M*A*S*H* rerun with the sound turned down to a whisper. When Owen and the sheriff entered, she switched off the TV and put her finger to her lips. "Shh. Jeb Stuart's asleep upstairs."

"Good," Owen said. "He needs the rest."

"I just stopped in to see if you've had a chance to check whether anything was missing from your house after the break-in," Reader said.

"There was some money in the telephone drawer," Ruth said in a stage whisper. "Bills. I don't know how much. The drawer's empty now. But I don't know how much was in it. I didn't forget. I just never keep track."

"It couldn't have been much more than twenty dollars," Owen said. "It's Mom's petty-cash drawer."

Reader looked up at the broken banister. "And Jeb Stuart surprised the burglar in the bathroom? Money and drugs. Could be it really was just a hophead looking to support his next fix."

"Or it could be he was looking for our baseball cards," Owen said. "I still think it's just too much of a coincidence that two people who were at the auction were attacked within two days."

"I keep forgetting about your baseball cards," Reader said. "Where are they kept?"

"Jeb Stuart has my old room," Owen said. "I put a false

top in the closet when I was in high school. That's where he keeps the card collection."

"My son used to hide his collection of *Playboy* magazines there." Ruth smiled at Owen. "Nothing wrong with my memory."

Owen returned her smile. "I only bought them for the cartoons."

"Then you won't mind that Miss March of nineteen-seventy is no longer on the other side of the Reds team photo hanging over the bed," Ruth said. "I took it down when we moved Jeb Stuart into the room."

"That's more than I need to know," Reader said. "Was there any sign the burglar found the cards?"

"No. That was the first thing Jeb Stuart checked when we got home."

"But they were pretty well hidden," Owen said.

"From anyone but your mother," Reader said. "Did you buy anything else at the auction?"

"No. Nothing but the cards."

"Which you got for two hundred and fifty dollars," Reader said.

"Owen. You paid two hundred and fifty dollars for a box of cards you hadn't even seen?" Ruth sighed. "You're as bad as your father."

Reader laughed and nodded. "You tell him, Ruth."

"They're worth at least what I paid for them, Mom. In fact after all that's happened, I think I'll get all our cards appraised. Jeb Stuart and I can drive to one of those card shops in Cincinnati this weekend. It'll help to take his mind off his wrist."

To prepare for the trip to Cincinnati, Owen and Jeb Stuart tried to estimate the value of the cards in their collection.

This task was far from straightforward. The catalog values were heavily dependent on the condition of the cards, rated from poor to mint, with six levels in between. There was even a super-category labeled "rated by experts" which seemed to multiply the value ten-fold.

Neither Owen nor Jeb Stuart had any idea how their two shoeboxes full of cards stacked up against the catalog categories. The cards from Owen's personal collection dated back to the mid-sixties, but showed a lot of wear. Had they been in mint condition, the catalog prices suggested his shoebox hoard could be worth as much as ten thousand dollars. The cards from the auction shoebox, on the other hand, looked as if they'd never been touched by human hands, but were mostly from the mid-eighties and, on the face of it, didn't appear to be worth much more than the two hundred and fifty dollars Owen had paid for them.

The trip to Cincinnati hugged the Ohio River for most of the distance. The roads had improved since Owen was a boy, but he could still remember the excitement of following the river to a Reds game. Now, with Jeb Stuart sharing the ride and the prospect of setting a value on their stash of cards, the damp river smell and the rush of the wind against the car made his skin prickle with the old thrill of anticipation.

The baseball card shop they'd found in the Cincinnati phone book, Brian's Books and Cards, didn't look like the kind of place that was likely to hand over ten thousand dollars for a shoebox full of baseball cards. Set in a strip mall, the tiny shop was flanked by a Laundromat and a bail bondsman. Inside, the front of the store featured glass cases packed with bobble-head dolls representing a range of teams and stars, autographed baseballs, and glossy eight-by-ten photos of current players. A glass counter along the side of the shop held a cash register and rows of baseball cards neatly displayed in plastic holders. The rear of the store was given over to bins of vintage comic books encased in glassine envelopes backed with stiff cardboard.

Two boys who couldn't have been older than twelve or thirteen huddled over the comic collection at the rear of the store, arguing the relative merits of Superman and Spiderman. Near the cash register, a slightly older boy wearing an orange Gore-Tex vest smiled at Owen and Jeb Stuart, each of whom was carrying a shoebox full of cards, and asked, "Can I help you?"

The boy staffing the cash register looked to be younger than Jeb Stuart, and Owen instinctively tucked his shoebox under his arm like a football, ready to do a quick reverse around the bobble-head dolls and out of the shop rather than entrust his treasure to someone so young.

Seeing Owen's hesitation, Jeb Stuart took the shoebox he was carrying under his good arm and edged it onto the counter beside the cash register. "We've got some cards we'd like you to look at."

Owen shrugged and followed Jeb Stuart to the counter. The boy in the Gore-Tex vest shoved aside two black loose-leaf binders to make room on the glass countertop. "Let's see them."

When Owen set his shoebox down on the counter, Jeb Stuart reached over and removed the lid. "Let's do the older cards first."

The boy behind the counter took out an inch-thick stack of cards held together by a rubber band. "Oh, wow. These are vintage Topps." He removed the band and slipped it over his wrist. "You shouldn't use rubber bands on cards like these. It notches them."

Jeb Stuart took the blame for Owen's teenage transgression. "Yeah, well. We didn't know."

The boy spread the cards out on the counter and held out his hand to Jeb Stuart. "I'm Richard, by the way."

"Jeb Stuart."

"What did you do to your hand?"

"Fell on it wrong."

"Tough." Richard looked at Owen, who stood back from the counter. "This your dad?"

Jeb Stuart smiled back at Owen. "Guardian, more like."

"Cool." Richard hunched over the cards on the counter. "Gee. You've got a Pete Rose rookie card. And look at all the Frank Robinsons."

Jeb Stuart had both elbows on the countertop so that his head was inches from Richard's as they both examined the cards. "Yeah, Owen's a real Cincinnati fan. He's got lots of dupes of the old Reds players."

Owen continued to hang back. Watching the two boys reminded him of how he'd felt about the cards when he was their age.

Richard raised his head from the two-person huddle. "These are great. But Brian really ought to look at them himself. I mostly know today's players. Mind if I call him?"

"Please do," Owen said. He felt all three of them could use a little adult supervision. On the one hand, he was happy to see Richard and Jeb Stuart wrapped up in his forty-year-old cards. On the other hand, they were smudging a potential ten-thousand-dollar treasure cache.

While they waited for Brian to arrive, Richard and Jeb Stuart sorted through the first shoebox and Owen poked around the rest of the shop, listening to Richard's occasional cries of "Awesome," or "Hey, look at this."

At the rear of the shop, Owen found that the *MAD* magazines he'd read when he was a boy were worth twenty to thirty dollars apiece. Too bad he hadn't saved them along with his baseball cards. The thought of swapping his memories for hard cash made him feel like a cartoon character with dollar signs for eyeballs. He looked around for a Scrooge McDuck comic to check the resemblance, but found that Brian was primarily into superheroes and early horror comics.

Richard looked up from Owen's shoebox long enough to sell two Action Comics to the boy who'd been a Superman advocate and answer a telephone query, but he returned to Jeb Stuart and the shoebox as if drawn by a magnet. Hunched over the collection, the two boys issued a series of appreciative murmurs, interspersed with exclamations as they passed the icons of Owen's youth back and forth.

"Hey, look. Vada Pinson."

"Here's another Frank Robinson." Jeb Stuart turned his head toward Owen. "Who'd the Reds get when they traded Robinson?"

"Milt Pappas."

"He never amounted to much, did he?"

"Had a couple of 30-30 years with the Reds before they traded him to Atlanta. Robinson, though, put up MVP numbers for the Orioles. Took them to four World Series."

"Hit five hundred eighty-six home runs, lifetime," Richard said.

"Fifth highest, all time," Jeb Stuart said.

Robinson's home-run total had been in the news a few years ago when Barry Bonds passed it. Owen felt a pang every time he saw the one-time Reds player's name. Even at age thirteen, he'd felt the Reds were making a lopsided trade. Why couldn't the Reds management have seen it?

Owen looked over some of the newer baseball cards in the display case. They'd come a long way since he'd peeled off bubble-gum wrappers to find out what cards were inside.

Now there were cards with embedded uniform swatches, autographed horsehides, and slivers from bats. One card had Ken Griffey Junior's picture and autograph next to a swatch from a "game-worn" jersey. Another had a slice shaved from Barry Bonds' bat. Like pieces of the True Cross, Owen thought. How many forests had died perpetuating the myth of that manufactured relic?

The bell over the shop door tinkled and a red-headed man with sideburns and a bushy moustache entered. A faded orange T-shirt advertising Brian's Books and Cards identified him as the proprietor, and he headed straight for the shoeboxes on the counter, asking, "What have we here?"

"Guys want to know what these cards are worth, Brian," Richard said.

Brian pulled a three-inch-thick catalog out from under the counter and plopped it next to the shoeboxes. "Well, let's take a look."

"We know what the catalogs say," Owen said. "But the prices go by condition, and we don't know how to grade the condition."

"Biggest things to look for are centering and edge wear." Brian took a magnifying glass from inside the display case and picked up one of the Frank Robinson cards. "Image has to be centered on the card and the corners can't be fuzzy or rounded. This card is well centered, but the corners show a lot of wear." He held the magnifying glass so Owen could look at the frayed corners. "Looks like it's had a lot of handling."

Owen smiled. "It did. Quite a while back."

Brian passed his hands over the cards as if he were a priest delivering a benediction. "Looks like you started collecting about the same time I did. What are you? About fifty?"

"Later this year," Owen said.

"Reds had it going back then." Brian tapped the Robinson card. "Till they let this guy go."

Owen commiserated by frowning and nodding. "For Milt Pappas."

Brian loosed something between a snort and a laugh at Pappas' name and returned the Robinson card to the shoebox. "Those rounded corners drop that card well below mint. I'd put it around twenty dollars."

Twenty dollars was less than one-third of the mint value quoted in the catalog. Owen imagined the sound of a cash register slamming shut. He told himself he didn't want to part with that card anyhow.

Brian began examining the cards more quickly, returning most to the first shoebox and splitting the remainder into two stacks. "Off-centering, blurry images, faded colors, rubber-band notches, frayed corners, any little blemish takes the card from mint to near-mint."

He held up a Hank Aaron card. "Corners are really important. Some sharpies shave the edges to get the corner points back." Brian grimaced. "Untrained eye, you can't tell unless you hold the shaved card up next to an unshaved card. I can always tell, though. Even when they press the cards first to enlarge them before cutting." He rubbed his thumb against his middle finger. "Just feels thinner."

"They press the cards before they shave the edges?" Owen said.

"Oh, yeah. This store was a lot more fun before cards got to be big business. Now you got to watch out for doctored cards, counterfeit cards, forged autographs . . ." Brian shrugged. "I'd guess eighty percent of the autographed stuff you see has forged signatures."

When Brian had finished sorting, most of the cards had been returned to the first shoebox, leaving two small stacks on the counter. Then he turned to the second shoebox. He withdrew a fistful of cards, fanned them like a bridge hand, examined them front and back, and then put them back in the box. He did the same thing with two more handfuls and said, "Whole different batch of booty here. These are mostly mid-eighties."

"Just got them at auction," Owen said. "Sight unseen."

"The whole box?"

Owen nodded.

"Mind if I ask how much you paid?"

"Two hundred and fifty dollars."

Brian cocked an eyebrow, not giving anything away. "Could be worth that, I guess." He checked his catalog, wrote three numbers on a piece of paper, and thumbed through the cards in the auction shoebox. Finally, he took four cards from the box and set them aside. Then he ran his tongue around his mouth as if he were savoring a rare wine vintage, cleared his throat, and said, "Okay, let's do the box with the older cards first. Some nice stuff there. The Pete Rose rookie card's worth around five hundred dollars by itself. Trouble is, no more than eight or nine of the other cards are mint or near-mint. You did what I did. You handled your cards. Sorted them, traded them, flipped them, played with them. Am I right?"

Owen nodded.

Brian shrugged again. "Who knew? You've got some cards I'd rate very good to excellent. They'd bring about a third of the mint value." He pointed at the shoebox holding the bulk of Owen's old card collection. "Most are just run of the mill."

Brian turned to the second shoebox. "Now, this newer box, the one you got at the auction. It's mostly cards from eighty-four and eighty-five. All in mint condition. Trouble is, somebody's skimmed it and taken out the valuable cards. Eighty-five was a good year for rookie cards. You've got Mark

McGwire, Kirby Puckett, Roger Clemens, a few others. The cards in this box are still in numerical order, and somebody's taken out those three rookie cards."

"Let the buyer beware," Owen said.

Brian held up the four cards he'd set aside. "On the other hand, mixed in with the rest, you've got four copies of Mark McGwire's rookie card. Be worth a hundred fifty dollars each if they weren't all fakes."

Brian handed Owen one of the cards. "Registration's just a little off. Somebody photographed the real card, then made copies from the negative."

"Looks good to me," Owen said.

Jeb Stuart and Richard picked up the other fake McGwires and examined them.

"They're doing great things with photographic images now," Brian said. "Makes it a lot easier to counterfeit cards and a lot tougher to detect fakes. Couple of days ago a friend of mine in DC had a guy walk in with three copies of a fifty-two Mantle card. Two were counterfeit, but one was a pure mint original. My friend paid twenty grand for it on the spot."

"You think the seller made copies from the original?" Owen said.

"Most likely. If he did, he probably made more than just two. No way to prove it, though. Shop owners just have to get the word out, keep an eye out."

Brian collected the fake McGwire cards and put them back in the shoebox. "Anyhow, this box would have been a real bargain if you'd gotten all the cards in the eighty-five set. As it is, it's worth about what you paid for it."

Brian spread his hands over the two shoeboxes. "If you want to sell, most card shops will give you around fifty percent of the catalog value after discounting for condition. Or you could leave a few with me on consignment, see how well they move. Best thing, though, if you want to sell, is to put them up on eBay."

"What do you say, partner?" Owen asked Jeb Stuart. "Shall we sell some or sit on them?"

"What do you want to do?" Jeb Stuart asked.

"Not my decision," Owen said. "I gave the cards to you. We're partners now, remember?"

"But you gave them to me before you knew what they were worth."

For Owen, the value of the cards had peaked as he watched Richard and Jeb Stuart oohing and aahing over them just before Brian arrived with his magnifying glass. "Now we both know what they're worth," he said. "I'll go with whatever you decide."

Jeb Stuart picked up the few cards Brian had left on the counter and put them back in the first shoebox. "Then let's head home." He paused, retrieved one of the Frank Robinson cards from the box and handed it to Richard. "Thanks for helping us."

"Oh, wow," Richard said. "I can't take this."

"Sure you can," Owen said, proud of Jeb Stuart for making the offer. "We want you to have it."

Richard took the card like a devout communicant receiving the host. "Well, thanks."

They were almost out the door when Richard said, "Hey, wait," and came out from behind the counter to hand Jeb Stuart a card. "It's one of the new Griffey Juniors. With a uniform swatch."

Jeb Stuart tried to hand it back. "But that's your . . ."

Richard waved him off. "It's okay. It's this year's card. I can replace it. Brian gives me a discount."

Back in the car, Jeb Stuart showed Owen the card Richard had given him. Owen rubbed his thumb over the embedded uniform flannel. "You did good. It's a lot better trade than the one the Reds made when they got Milt Pappas for Robinson."

Heading home, they stayed on the Kentucky side of the Ohio river, following a new freeway and crossing into West Virginia just below Ashland and its oil refineries. They stopped to eat at a Burger King outside of Huntington, and Owen took the opportunity to phone Thad Reader.

"Those cards we got at auction weren't worth much more than we paid for them," Owen said. "Doesn't seem likely they're what the burglar wanted."

"Unless he was a diehard baseball fan, then, he was probably just looking for cash so he could score some hillbilly heroin."

"Didn't look like a baseball fan to me."

"Here's something will interest you," Reader said. "We got a report back on Mary Smith's prints."

"And?"

"Real name is Lotus Mae Graham. Just got out of the Federal Prison Camp for Women at Alderson two months ago."

"What was she in for?"

"Passing bad checks. And get this. Her cellmate there was Mary Kay Jessup."

Owen realized from Reader's pause that some reaction was expected, but he couldn't muster one. "Name doesn't ring a bell."

"Mary Kay Jessup replaced Burt Caldwell as executive director of the Contrary Bank. She was one of Burt's first skirts. She's doing thirty years for fraud, conspiracy, and misplacing three quarters of a billion dollars."

Chapter Seven:

Fabricated Fakes

In the newspaper photos taken at the time of her trial, Mary Kay Jessup was a smartly dressed, attractive middle-aged blonde whose hands always seemed to be fluttering away from her body. Seated in the interview room of the Federal Prison Camp for Women at Alderson, West Virginia, her orange uniform looked to be a size too large, her lack of makeup and thinning gray hair pushed her well past middle age, and her hands were clasped sedately on her lap.

Thad Reader and Owen Allison sat down opposite Mary Kay at the gray institutional table and Reader said, "We'd like to talk to you about Lotus Mae Graham."

"I'm happy to talk about Lotus Mae," Mary Kay said, fixing her eyes on the sheriff's badge, "but I should tell you that except for our jail cell, she and I have very little in common."

"I understand," the sheriff pulled a sheaf of papers from

the folder on his lap and scanned the individual sheets. "According to her rap sheets, Lotus Mae was sent here for passing bad checks."

"I believe that to be true."

Reader continued to scan the sheets. "She never kited a check for more than two hundred fifty dollars, yet she showed up at an auction last weekend with at least forty-eight thousand dollars in cash. Any idea where she'd get that kind of money?"

"Could be she was thrifty. She certainly showed no tendencies toward extravagance when we roomed together." Mary Kay plucked at the oversized orange cuff on her prison uniform. "She always wore the simplest frocks and rarely, if ever, went out."

"We understand that your shopping opportunities and social life are somewhat limited here," Reader said. "That's why we were surprised at the amount of money your ex-roommate was carrying with her at the auction."

"Why are you asking me about it?"

"The auction was held to dispose of some of your old bank's holdings, and she roomed with you for nearly two years."

"You're auctioning off the bank's property?" Mary Kay lifted her hands from her lap and raised them shoulder-high in a gesture of surrender. "It's come to that, has it?"

"It's come to that because someone at the bank misappropriated seven hundred and fifty million dollars and left your depositors holding a lot of empty sacks," Owen said.

Mary Kay raised her right hand as if she were taking an oath. "At my trial I swore on the King James Bible I had no knowledge of the whereabouts of that money."

"The jury believed otherwise," Reader said.

"Justice is certainly blind. Did my roommate purchase anything at the auction?"

"A painting after the fashion of Paul Klee, some movie posters, and a box of baseball cards."

Mary Kay raised her eyebrows. "A Paul Klee painting?"

"It was fake," the sheriff said.

"Fake or not, I'm surprised at Masie. I'd have guessed her tastes would have run to black velvet paintings of dogs playing poker."

"We thought she might have been bidding on your behalf," Reader said.

"On my behalf?" Mary Kay's eyes widened and she made a show of looking around at the bare gray-green walls of the prison's interrogation room. "I'll admit this place could use a little brightening up, but I'm thinking the inmates' tastes would probably run more to posters of Paul Newman than to a forty-thousand-dollar painting by Paul Klee."

"So you have no idea how Lotus Mae came by forty-eight thousand dollars?" Reader asked.

Mary Kay shook out her oversized cuffs. "There's nothing up my sleeves. I don't have that kind of money. Why don't you ask Lotus Mae where she got it?"

"We could ask her," Reader said. "But we'd have to wait a while for the answer. She was killed the day after the auction."

Mary Kay's hands dropped to her lap and wrestled with one another. "Killed?"

"Murdered," Reader said. "Someone ran her car off a cliff and tried to make it look like an accident."

"And the painting?"

"Nowhere to be found."

"And the money? What about the fifty thousand dollars?"

"She spent most of it at the auction. All she had when we found her was ten dollars and change."

"My God."

"Did she mention any enemies on the outside when she was your cellmate?" Reader asked.

"None."

"So you've no idea who might have wanted to kill her?"

Mary Kay looked down at her clasped hands. "None."

The sheriff rose and dropped a business card on the interview table. "If you think of anything that might help us, please let me know."

Mary Kay made no move to pick up the card. "I'm not going anywhere. You know where to find me."

Owen and Thad Reader waited on a side road in the sheriff's patrol car while a large lumber truck negotiated the narrow space between the stone columns that anchored the main gate of the woman's prison.

"Building a new dorm," the sheriff said. "This prison is the county's only growth industry."

"Lots of the state's counties don't even have one growth industry," Owen said.

"What did you make of Mary Kay Jessup?"

"She seemed genuinely surprised when you told her Lotus Mae Graham was dead."

"Surprised and a little scared."

The lumber truck went by and Reader drove his patrol car out past the stone columns and guard house that marked the prison entrance. "She knew more than she let on about Lotus Mae's trip to the auction, though."

"She knew the Klee went for around forty grand by itself," Owen said. "We never told her that."

"That info had to come from someone at the auction."

"Most likely Lotus Mae herself."

"Most likely it was Jessup that bankrolled Graham."

"How could she do that from a prison cell?" Owen asked.

"She's in prison, but her husband Homer's a free man. He stuck with Mary Kay through a lot of years when she was rumored to be sleeping with Burt Caldwell."

"So his reward's custody of their four-million-dollar house and whatever she managed to shield from the bank examiner."

"And the size of that stash could come to tens of millions."

"Not a bad prize for turning a blind eye on a little adultery."

"Not bad at all." Reader tapped his glass eye. "Now me, I've been turning a blind eye on the world ever since Vietnam, with nothing to show for it but a few disability payments."

When Owen returned home that afternoon, Ruth pointed him toward a stack of mail on the dining-room table. "Something there from Charleston. Could be about that job you've been waiting for."

Owen picked up the letter on top of the stack. The return address told him it was from the Office of the West Virginia Attorney General. The lack of heft told him it was bad news. Announcements of winning bids didn't come on a single page in a number-ten envelope.

Owen's shoulders slumped. "Oh, Christ. It's bad news."

Ruth had followed him to the table and stood behind him. "How do you know?"

"Good news would have come in a bigger package. Or by phone."

"Aren't you going to open it? To be sure?"

Owen tore at the end of the envelope, ripping off the tip of the enclosed letter. He let the envelope drop to the table and unfolded the single sheet. It was a form letter that read

Dear Bidder:

Thank you for your interest in Request for Proposal

Number 02-1857, to Assess the Risk of Failure of Impoundment Dams Located Near Underground Shafts.

The Office of the Attorney General has decided not to award a contract pursuant to this procurement at this time. In the event that a new procurement is announced, you will automatically be placed on the bidders' list.

(Signed) Antonia Harris
Administrative Assistant

Dear Bidder, he thought. They hadn't even bothered to personalize their rejection. He'd given them a hundred pages that included closely reasoned logic, a detailed work plan, and impeccable qualifications, along with a supporting presentation, and all they could manage in return was a three-sentence form letter with two misspellings.

"I can see from your face I don't have to ask what it says," Ruth said.

Owen handed her the letter. "They decided not to award the contract."

" 'At this time.' The letter says, 'At this time.' What does that mean?"

Owen shrugged. "I don't know."

"But you said the job had to be done. There's a court order."

"It does. There is."

"Then they'll do it eventually."

Owen felt drained, empty. "Maybe. I just don't know."

"So you'll win it eventually. You're better qualified to do that job than anybody in the state."

"Mom, I'm better qualified than anybody in the country. I gave them a great proposal at a reasonable price. If they wanted me to do it, they could have awarded me the contract."

"So you think they want somebody else?"

"Either that or they just don't want me."

"Why would that be?"

"The Attorney General is Dusty Rhodes. We're not exactly bosom buddies."

"But would he ignore a court order? On a job this important? Just to get even?"

"He's done lots worse." Owen felt lost. Stupidly lost, like someone who'd ignored all the warning signs leading into a swamp. He should have known better, but he'd wanted the job too badly, counted on it too heavily, let too much ride on the award.

"You'll have to tell your entourage," Ruth said.

"My entourage?"

"Your young friend, Emily." The word "friend" had more spin than a politician's press release.

"Mom. She's a qualified mining engineer. And she's not the only person I took on to bid this job. I needed a team of experienced inspectors who wouldn't run for daylight the first time the mountains moaned."

"Well, there's no questioning her experience. She's got a ready-made family. Even though she is at least twenty years younger than you."

"So you keep reminding me. Where are your memory lapses when I need them?"

"That's neither funny nor fair. I'm sorry if I upset you, but you do need to call your friend Emily. And everyone else who was depending on the job."

"I think I'll call the Attorney General's office first. See what I can find out about their future intentions."

Owen started by calling the woman who had signed the "Dear Bidder" letter. She said she had issued the letter at the instruction of her supervisor and had no additional information on the procurement. Her supervisors were equally close-mouthed, saying only that they had decided against moving forward with the contracting process and refusing to speculate when or whether the job would be rebid.

After three calls, the only remaining link in the chain of supervisors was Dusty Rhodes himself. Owen stared at the phone, not wanting to give the Attorney General the satisfaction of knowing that the cancellation of the procurement had hit a nerve.

Actually, the cancellation had hit a whole bundle of nerves. Owen had been in West Virginia for almost a year and had run through his savings over six months ago. He needed a source of income that was steadier than the random accident investigations tossed his way by Thad Reader. His 401k plan had tanked when the Internet bubble burst, and there were penalties for early withdrawal, even if the plan had enough money left to make early withdrawal worthwhile.

Owen slammed the phone down on its cradle so hard that Ruth heard the noise and returned to the dining room. "Did you learn anything by calling Charleston?" she asked.

"Nothing they hadn't already told me in their three-sentence letter." Owen shook his head. "I've got to find more work."

"Your rent here's paid up in perpetuity. We've been doing all right so far."

"I'm a little old to be living at home with my mother."

"You came home to help me through my sickness. Let me help you through this bad patch."

"This bad patch is a hole deeper than the New River Gorge."

"Maybe you could get a job with George."

"My brother the highway commissioner." Owen sighed, expelling air as if he were experiencing a slow leak. "I wasn't cut out to be a bureaucrat, Mom. I tried it once and it didn't work. Besides, there's a hiring freeze in his department."

"Have you talked to Judith lately? Maybe there's work in California."

"That would mean leaving you here on your own."

"If it got the two of you back together, it would be worth it."

Owen waited until noon before calling his ex-wife Judith at her Palo Alto, California, law offices. After listening to the story of the procurement cancellation, she said, "I'm amazed you ever thought Dusty Rhodes would award you a contract after what you did to him during the last election."

"I worked against him, is all."

"That's a euphemism if I ever heard one. You worked against him the way Grant worked against Lee. You exposed the way he was using his environmental legislation to line his own pockets. You almost cost him the election."

"Too bad I didn't."

"The point is, you can't really have expected him to give you a job after you nearly cost him his."

"I thought I might be able to sneak in under his radar."

"Think he'd ever be able to sneak in under your radar?" Judith answered her own question before Owen could open his mouth. "Not bloody likely. And his radar's a lot better than yours. He's got the whole state at his disposal."

"Maybe so, but I expected him to run a fair competition."

"What makes you think he didn't?"

"If he had, I would have won. My proposal was great, my price was low, and I nailed the oral. There's nobody in the country better qualified than me to do this work."

"Owen, we've had this conversation before." He could

hear the exasperation in Judith's voice. "It's a city mouse, country mouse kind of thing. You think all you have to do to get work is to do a better job than anyone else. You concentrate on doing the work well. It's an attitude peculiar to people who grew up in small towns and Midwest cities, and it may still work in the private sector there. But it doesn't work in the public sector anywhere. Because people from the big cities have figured out how to win the jobs whether or not they do the work well."

"You see Rhodes as a city mouse."

"He's a carpet bagger from New York who saw a power vacuum and filled it."

"And I'm the country mouse."

"Think back. I've heard you complain over and over that public jobs don't always go to the best qualified firms. Sometimes the people awarding the jobs can't tell good work from bad, sometimes they don't care, sometimes they're on the take, and sometimes they have totally different criteria."

"This conversation is too depressing. I just called to see if you're still monitoring the mail to my PO box there in Palo Alto."

"I've been forwarding anything that looked interesting. There hasn't been much."

"But you've only been forwarding notices about jobs I can do from here."

"Per your instructions."

"Better start forwarding jobs that need a California presence as well."

"Is your mom well enough for you to leave her?"

"She's the one that suggested I broaden my job search."

"That wasn't what I asked. How is Ruth?"

Owen checked the dining-room doorway to see if Ruth

97

was still within earshot. "She has her ups and downs. Some-times her mind purrs along like a well-oiled engine. Other times it leaks like a cracked radiator."

"You were going to have her diagnosed. What did the doc-tors say? Is it Alzheimer's?"

"The doctors don't know what to say. She beat their tests by cramming on Internet info."

"I didn't know you could do that."

"Add it to your bag of tricks."

"Let's get back to my original question. Is Ruth well enough for you to leave her if there's work back here?"

"I'd have to make some kind of arrangements for home care. I can't go on much longer without steadier work."

"What about your hot young honey? Could you leave her?"

"Oh, for Christ's sake. My hot young honey is a figment of Mom's imagination. She's a mining engineer who signed on to work the state contract if I got it."

"Your mom tells me you've been seeing her outside of business hours."

"What business hours?" Owen heard himself shouting and lowered his voice. "The problem is I've got no business hours. Neither does she. We play tennis, see a movie now and then. It's nothing serious."

"Sorry. I had to ask." There was a short pause. Then Ju-dith said, "I still have hopes we'll get back together."

"We'll need to be in the same city for that to happen."

"That's why I asked if you were serious about coming back here to California to work."

"There are cities here. We could be together here."

"We've been through this before. My law practice isn't portable. I can't transplant it to West Virginia. Besides, it looks as if you can't find work there yourself."

"There's still the job with the Attorney General's office. They'll have to rebid it."

It was Judith's turn to raise her voice. "Have you been listening at all? Dusty Rhodes is under a court order to get the job done and he still hasn't hired you. If you depend on that job for your survival, you've got all the life expectancy of a fly caught in a Cuisinart."

"There's got to be a way."

"There's no way. I know Dusty Rhodes. He may forget a favor, but he'll never forget a slight. And what you did to him was far worse than a slight. You'll never be under his radar."

After he hung up, Owen sat at the dining-room table staring at the phone and the Attorney General's letter. His mother was right. He needed to call Emily Kruk. But he hated to be the bearer of bad news. Emily needed the job at least as badly as he did. And he still didn't know what the Attorney General's office would decide about a rebid.

A divorcée with a young daughter to support, Emily had moved back to West Virginia from Colorado in order to live with her mother and the convenience of a built-in babysitter. It was her hope that the child care provided by her mother would allow her to work full-time. But full-time work was slow in coming. Mechanization and environmental protests had lowered the number of mining jobs available, and an ingrained prejudice against women supervisors had kept her from getting any of the few available jobs.

Owen had met Emily when he was doing some limited mine inspections in the aftermath of a dam failure. She was solid technically, laughed easily and often, and was fun to be around. But he hadn't thought of her as anything but a coworker until he was forming a team to bid on the Attorney General's study and his mother commented on their age difference. Then he noticed Emily's auburn hair and blue eyes and they'd started playing tennis together two mornings a week and going out to an occasional movie.

Their relationship hadn't progressed beyond tennis and movies, and she seemed content to leave it at that. Whenever Owen thought about pushing further, something held him back. There was the age difference, for one thing. Shortly after they'd started playing tennis regularly, a middle-aged man rallying against his son on an adjoining court asked Owen if he and his daughter would like to join them in a game of doubles. Emily, who was twenty-eight but still looked young enough to be carded frequently in bars, laughed about the man's assumption and called Owen "pops" once or twice. Just twice, actually. Then she stopped when she saw he didn't take it well.

He told himself that the age difference was holding him back. That and the fact that he'd put himself in the position of Emily's boss for the purpose of the proposal, so that any overture might be construed as sexual harassment. That was silly, though. How could there be sexual harassment when they hadn't won the job, there was nothing sexual going on, and the only harassment of note had occurred the two times she'd called him "pops."

Owen picked up the portable phone and walked around the dining-room table. He didn't want to call Emily and be the cause of disappointment until he knew exactly what the Attorney General's office intended to do to fulfill the court order mandating special mine shaft inspections. Judith's admonition to the contrary, there was still some chance they'd get the job. He put the phone back in its cradle. He'd wait until he knew for sure the job was lost before calling Emily.

★ ★ ★ ★ ★

Owen returned to the phone several times over the remainder of the afternoon, but he kept thinking of excuses for not calling Emily. When he finally picked up the receiver, it was Victoria Gallagher's number he dialed.

He was convinced that Lotus Mae Graham's death was somehow related to the holdings of the Museum of Fakes and Frauds, and Victoria had promised him a personal tour. When he offered to trade dinner for the tour, she accepted immediately. He was careful not to say he was working with the sheriff, but she had seen the two of them together and he let her assume his visit was part of the official investigation.

Victoria met him at the door of the museum a little after the posted closing time of 5:30. She was wearing a tailored blue suit, and her gray-streaked hair was tied back in a severe bun that accented her oval face. Her smooth skin made it difficult to guess her age, but he imagined she must be at least forty, certainly no more than ten years younger than he was.

"I'm glad you called," she said, leading him into the museum foyer. "Where would you like to start?"

"I guess I'd like to understand what makes a painting that's a known fake worth forty thousand dollars."

"Then this is where we'll start." She stood aside and motioned for him to enter the main room of the museum, the one-time living room when the house had belonged to a coal baron. A small gold plaque beside the door read

GALLERY OF ARTISTIC ARTIFICE

Inside, the room itself was dark, an effect heightened by the rosewood paneling. The only illumination came from the lights attached to the frames of the paintings that lined the paneled walls.

Owen recognized a Picasso, or what he thought was a Picasso, a gray cubist painting entitled *Woman with Mandolin*. Beside it hung the head and shoulders of a male done in harsh jagged strokes and signed by Giacometti. Next to the Giacometti hung a clown face supposedly painted by Dubuffet. The room was lit with the colors of paintings done by artists imitating other artists.

"My God," Owen said. "I never realized all this was here. I've always headed straight for the Civil War and baseball rooms."

Victoria smiled. "Stonewall and the Babe. They're our most popular exhibits. But dollar for dollar, this room houses the greatest share of the museum's investment." She pointed at the Giacometti. "That was done by the same artist who painted the Klee you admired. He turned out so many Giacomettis, with such impeccable provenances, that art experts warn museum curators that sixty percent of the Giacomettis on the market are fakes."

Owen whistled silently. "He must have bought paint by the gallon instead of by the tube."

"Actually, he mixed his paint with K-Y Jelly. Said it added fluidity to his strokes."

Owen glanced sideways at Victoria. Her expression gave little away, but the edges of her almond eyes crinkled with amusement. "That's what it promises on the tube," he said.

"Eventually, the jelly was one of the things that gave him away. But he kept producing forgeries for a long time."

"Slippery devil. How did he manage it for so long?"

"The art world tries to hush up its forgeries. Gallery owners, dealers, auction houses, they all traffic in image and social consciousness. They can't afford to have a crisis in public confidence."

"How did the museum come by this copy?"

"When the collector who bought it found out it was fake, he came to us. He didn't want any publicity. We took it off his hands for twenty thousand dollars. About a tenth of what he paid for it."

Owen turned to the painting next to the fake Giacometti, *Woman with Mandolin*. "Who painted the Picasso?"

"We don't know. If a painting speaks to you, though, what does it matter who painted it?"

"How much did the museum pay for it?"

"I don't know that either. Burt kept a lot of those details to himself. And that painting was here when I came on board."

"When was that?"

"About fifteen years ago. Just as we were moving into this building."

"How did you find enough fakes to fill it?"

"It was hard at first. Burt had started the museum in a small room at the bank. Suddenly he had to fill all these rooms. He loved it though. He did a lot of research. And once we were established, anyone who'd been bilked knew they could bring him their fake paintings and forged documents and get a good price. Eventually we got enough fakes to fill this museum and two warehouses."

Victoria smiled, remembering. "It wasn't easy when we first moved in and had to fill all this space, though." She moved her index finger toward her lips. "Can you keep a secret?"

Owen watched the finger pause in front of her pursed lips. Her nail polish was fiery red, matching her lipstick. "I have at least twenty I'll carry to my grave."

Victoria raised her right eyebrow. "I'd love to hear at least one."

"Is that a test?"

"Of whether you can keep a secret? No, that was just a little mild teasing." She looked around the gallery, pretending to make sure they were alone. "Here's your twenty-first secret."

Victoria adopted a stage whisper. "When we first moved in and needed to fill the space, Burt Caldwell manufactured a few fakes himself."

"He faked fakes?"

"Not many. But a few." She led him toward an adjoining room. The gold plaque on the door read

LIBRARY OF LITERARY LEGERDEMAIN

The Library of Literary Legerdemain was lined with glass-doored bookcases. Four large display cases occupied the center of the room, one facing each wall. Victoria led Owen to the nearest display case, which held a complete set of signed first editions of the works of F. Scott Fitzgerald. All of the books but one lay on their backs, exposing their flawless covers. One book stood upright on its bottom edges, its pages fanned open to reveal the signed title page.

Still holding Owen's hand in her cool grasp, Victoria used her free hand to point at the upright book. "See that copy of *The Last Tycoon*?"

"The one with the posthumous signature?"

Victoria nodded. "Burt Caldwell hired a man to fake Fitzgerald's signature."

"What'd he do? Just look in the yellow pages under 'forgers'?"

"People were bringing him forged documents all the time. Fake letters, phony signatures, bogus autographs. He managed to trace a few of the more competent forgeries back to their source."

Victoria unlocked the display case and handed Owen the copy of *The Great Gatsby*. "A man in Pittsburgh did these Fitzgerald signatures. He was happy to work for Burt. He felt he couldn't be prosecuted if his signatures were clearly labeled forgeries."

Owen looked at the book in his hands. Two disembodied eyes stared up at him from the blue dust jacket, which showed no signs of wear. "So all the Fitzgerald signatures are forged?"

"Along with most of the Hemingways and Faulkners."

Owen handed *The Great Gatsby* back to Victoria. "I don't get it. A first edition of *Gatsby* or *The Last Tycoon* must be worth a fair hunk of money even without an autograph. Why mark the books up with forged signatures?"

"If this were a true first edition of *Gatsby*, it would be worth around thirty thousand dollars, even without the signature. A real signature would multiply the value five- or ten-fold. But Burt wasn't trying to sell the books. He just liked fooling people." Victoria returned the book to the display case. "Most of the works in these cases aren't true first editions. They're later editions or library copies that have been doctored to look like firsts."

"And signed by hired pens?"

Victoria nodded.

"Must have been tempting for a bank president to have a forger or two on the payroll."

"Oh, Burt never mixed the bank's business with the museum's."

"What makes you so sure?"

The question seemed to take Victoria by surprise. She ran a red thumbnail across her lips, examined it, and then said, "I guess I think I knew the man."

"But you said he enjoyed fooling people."

"Here, in this museum. Not down the street. Not in the bank."

"But all that money went missing."

"That was on Mary Kay Jessup's watch." Victoria closed both hands around her key ring. "We should have seen it coming, I guess. The woman lived like a queen. Burt lived more like a monk."

"From what I've heard, he was hardly celibate."

Victoria frowned. "I wouldn't know about that. I just meant he seemed other-worldly. Flashy possessions didn't interest him."

She locked the glass door on the display case and turned toward Owen. "Is there something else I can show you?"

Owen tried to read her face. The question seemed pointed, but her smile was non-committal, almost overly polite. "What did you have in mind?" he asked.

The amused wrinkles returned to the corners of her eyes. "Why, anything in the museum. Anything at all."

"The baseball exhibit, then. I never leave without looking at the baseball exhibit."

She took his hand and led him up the oak stairway. "That's right. You took one of our boxes of baseball cards home from the auction."

"I wanted to ask you about that. There was a nearly complete set of nineteen-eighty-five cards in the box. But someone had skimmed off the most valuable pieces."

She paused at the top of the stairs. "That's very strange. I don't think anyone had looked at those cards in over fifteen years."

"Why not?"

"Burt sort of lost interest in baseball cards after we moved into the new building. He'd already cornered the market on

106

the most valuable fakes, like the Wagner and the Mantle. All that was left was keeping up with the new rookie cards. But they were never going to be as valuable as the older cards. And the new copy machines made it much easier to turn out fakes."

They stopped in front of the pyramid of cards on the posterboard display that had attracted Jeb Stuart. The apex of the pyramid held a forgery of the 1910 Honus Wagner card that had commanded four hundred fifty-one thousand dollars at Sotheby's. The bottom row held more modern rookie cards.

Owen pointed at the bright and spotless 1985 Mark McGwire rookie card. "That's the newest card in the display, and it's over fifteen years old."

"That's about when we moved in and Burt lost interest in the cards. He started going after equipment. Bats, balls, gloves, helmets, uniform jerseys."

"There weren't any cards from the nineties in the box I bought. The eighty-five set and some eighty-six cards were about the newest."

"What cards were missing from the eighty-five set?"

"Tony Gwynn. Roger Clemens. Mark McGwire."

"That is strange. As far as I know, no one looked at those cards after Burt stopped keeping up with them. But he couldn't have taken out the valuable cards. Back then, he wouldn't have known which rookie cards would be valuable later."

"So somebody took them recently."

"I guess so."

"Who had access?"

"Me. My staff. And, since the failure, all the feds."

"The head fed, Mitchell Ramsey?"

"Oh, yes. Even those young girls who helped us take inventory had access. But we never tried to catalog the individual cards in those shoeboxes. We just checked randomly to make sure there weren't any really old items."

"Like how old?"

"Oh, before World War II. Those missing cards, what would they be worth?"

"Somewhere between forty and a hundred and fifty dollars apiece."

"That's one of the reasons Burt lost interest in the cards. You'd have to counterfeit whole batches of the newer rookie cards in order to make the forgeries worthwhile. Having just one in the museum wouldn't cause anyone's jaw to drop."

She swung their interlocked hands toward the display case. "We only added the McGwire card after he broke the Maris home-run record."

"He didn't hold the record long."

"Burt died before Bonds broke McGwire's record."

Even though they'd reached their destination, she still hadn't released his hand. Owen was acutely aware of the balls of her fingers touching his knuckles and the back of her hand resting against his thigh.

Victoria laughed. "Is that a cell phone in your pocket, or are you glad to see me?"

Owen blushed. "Oh, hell. I'd forgotten it. It's my mom's phone. It's on 'vibrate.' "

He fished the cell phone from his pocket and brought it to his ear. When he recognized Ruth's voice, he mouthed, "My mom" to Victoria.

Ruth's voice was hesitant. "Owen, I'm sorry to bother you, but could you possibly come home? Jeb Stuart's hurt his wrist again and seems to be in great pain."

"Did you give him aspirin?"

"Of course. It doesn't seem to help. Owen, he's all sweaty. I think he should see a doctor."

"I'll be right home."

Owen returned the phone to his pants pocket. "I'm sorry," he said to Victoria. "That was my mom. The boy that's staying with us is having some problems. He broke his wrist and it seems to be giving him trouble."

"Is there anything I can do?"

"Just give me a rain check on dinner. I've really enjoyed . . ."

Victoria silenced Owen by putting a finger to his lips. Then she looped her arm around his neck, rose up on her toes, and raised her lips. "One rain check, coming up."

Her lips were cool against his. Taken by surprise, Owen put one arm around Victoria and took a step backward, bracing himself against the baseball card display with his free arm.

The display case scraped against the wood floor. Strobe lights flashed and sirens sounded.

Victoria pulled back, disengaging their lips. Her face flushed red and redder as the strobe lights flashed. "Oh, God," she said. "I forgot to turn off the upstairs alarm."

Chapter Eight:

The Meebie Weebie Deevie Dance

It took five minutes for the first patrol car to arrive. It contained a short, stocky female officer whose name tag read DOWNEY and a lanky male deputy named Gillis.

While Downey went off to look around the museum, Victoria tried to explain to the skeptical Gillis that she had triggered the alarm by accident in the middle of an after-hours tour.

Gillis was copying the information from Victoria's ID into a pocket notebook when his partner returned. "Man, you should see the surveillance equipment they've got hooked up," Deputy Downey said. "It's all state-of-the-art stuff."

"The museum's founder ran a bank," Victoria said. "He was very security-conscious."

Downey shook her head. "Boy, most banks would kill for the setup you've got right here. Every room has surveillance cameras, trembler switches, strobe lights, sound-activated recorders, and some stuff I didn't recognize. It's like you're trying to protect the Crown Jewels. Or Dolly Parton's endowment, at least."

Owen's heart sank when he heard the words "surveillance cameras." Even with a starring role, he didn't want to stick around for the premier viewing. "Look, can we go?" he said. "I was responding to an emergency call when I bumped the baseball card display and set off the alarm."

"Emergency call," Gillis said. "You a doctor?"

"Not a medical doctor."

"So what's the emergency?" Downey asked.

"My son. He broke his wrist. It's giving him trouble. I need to get him to a doctor."

A half smile played across Downey's face. "What do you think, Gillis? Think we should let them go?"

"The sheriff knows us both," Owen said. "Check with him. He'll vouch for us."

As if on cue, Thad Reader strode through the main door of the museum.

"This guy says you'll vouch for him," Gillis said.

"You search him?" Reader asked.

"Not yet."

"Why not?"

"He said he knew you."

"Half the second-story men in the county know me," Reader said. "You run his ID, check his record?"

The tall deputy turned to Owen. "All right, mister. Up against the wall."

111

Owen looked from the deputy to the sheriff. "Hasn't this gone far enough?"

"He's okay," Reader said. "And she's the curator of the museum. Take their statements and let them go."

"I forgot to turn off the upstairs alarm system and we bumped the card case," Victoria said. "That's my statement. I've been making it over and over for the past fifteen minutes."

Deputy Downey backed off toward the doorway where she'd gone exploring earlier. "Before you let them go, sheriff, there's something you ought to see." She pointed toward the doorway. "The surveillance center's right through here."

Reader told Owen, "Wait here. I'll be right back," and followed his deputy through the door.

The sheriff returned in less than two minutes, wearing a smile that kept threatening to stretch into a smirk. "Well, Ms. Gallagher, it appears you were telling the truth about bumping the card case. The surveillance tapes confirm your story."

Something between a sigh and a soft moan slipped from Victoria's lips.

"So you're both free to go," the sheriff said. "Just in case we need to contact you again, though, maybe we could get a rain check."

At the words "rain check," Deputy Downey turned her head and covered her mouth with her hand to suppress a giggle.

"Rain checks are generally pretty good things," Reader said, rushing his words. "I hope Jeb Stuart's okay, Owen. There's just one thing, though, before you go."

Owen stopped at the museum exit. "What's that?"

"Either take your cell phone off 'vibrate' or carry it in your vest pocket. You don't want people getting the wrong impression."

Reader's smile stretched well past a smirk and erupted in a belly laugh.

"Thank God you're home," Ruth said, meeting Owen at the door. I almost called a cab, but there was no money in the telephone drawer."

Jeb Stuart lay trembling on the living-room couch. His right hand clutched his left wrist, still in its soft cast. Sweat beaded over his eyebrows and upper lip, and the white pillowcase propped against the arm of the couch bore the damp outline of his head. "I'm sorry, Owen," the boy said. "But it hurts pretty bad."

"No need to apologize," Owen said. "Did you take the aspirin?"

The boy nodded and emitted a soft grunt. "Still hurts."

"We'll go back to St. Vincent's emergency room," Owen said, starting up the stairs to his bedroom. "First, though, let me get that painkiller prescription."

Acting on the sheriff's advice, Owen had not bothered to fill the OxyContin prescription given them by the emergency-room doctor. In the face of Jeb Stuart's agony, that seemed like a really dumb decision, he thought as he rummaged through the drawer in his bedside stand where receipts, ticket stubs, business cards, and other small slips of paper nested and multiplied. The prescription should have been near the top of the loose piles, but he couldn't find it anywhere. When he'd dug deep enough to uncover receipts dated a month before the FDIC auction, he gave up and herded Jeb Stuart and Ruth into his car for the trip to the hospital.

As the Saturn's headlights blended with the twilight,

Owen asked Jeb Stuart, "What were you doing to stir up the pain?"

"Just horsing around with some guys. I fell on it."

Owen tried to keep his voice under control. "You fell on it?"

Jeb Stuart clutched the soft cast tightly to his chest. "It didn't hurt much at first. Now, though, I think I may have broken it again."

Owen swore under his breath, then said nothing more until they arrived at the emergency room. The room was empty of patients and a middle-aged Indian physician took Jeb Stuart in for diagnosis right away.

Left with Ruth in the waiting room, Owen paced between rows of multi-colored plastic chairs. "What the hell was he thinking? Horsing around?"

"Don't be too hard on him," Ruth said. "He's only a boy."

"He's a senior in high school."

"That's what I said. He's only a boy."

Owen stopped pacing and stood beside his mother's chair. "This parenting stuff isn't all bonding and baseball. Did you have this kind of trouble with George and me?"

"When you were just boys?"

"When we were seniors in high school."

Ruth cocked her head to look up at Owen. "With George, I had to get a DWI charge reduced to reckless driving. I was lucky the judge remembered your dad."

"I never knew that."

"And you had that pregnancy scare with Robin whatshername."

"You weren't supposed to know about that."

"I'm your mother, Owen. I know everything." Ruth shook her head. "Knew everything. Once, anyhow."

Owen squatted beside his mother's chair and took her hand. "You're still pretty sharp, Mom."

"About as sharp as a used hanky. We both know better. I'm forgetful." She stared over Owen's shoulder into the distance. "Your father used to say I had the memory of an elephant."

"I've never understood that saying. What's an elephant got to remember, anyway?"

Ruth smiled and pulled her gaze back to focus on Owen's face. "Don't try to humor me. I'm missing things. We both know it."

"What things?"

"Money. Have you raided my petty-cash drawer recently?"

"No. Why?"

"It always seems to me there ought to be more in it than I find there. And tonight, when I wanted to take a cab here, there was nothing in it at all."

Owen released his mother's hand and stood up. "Do you remember putting anything in?"

"No. That's the trouble. It seems like I remember, but I'm never sure. It could be I'm remembering something from months back."

Owen didn't like what he was hearing. Either his mother's memory was slipping further, or someone in the house was stealing her petty cash. "Maybe you should write down what you put in the drawer. And what you take out. Treat it like a checking account."

"If I can remember."

The doctor returned with Jeb Stuart. While the boy stood holding his cast and staring at the floor, the physician said, "X-rays show he's added a hairline fracture to his other troubles. I have rewrapped the cast. So long as he takes it easy, the wrist should heal quite well."

"What'll the new fracture do to the recovery time?" Owen asked.

"We'll leave the cast on a week or so longer. Just to be safe."

"And when the cast comes off, he'll have full flexibility?"

The doctor's brow furrowed. "We cannot guarantee that."

"The doctor who saw me before said there'd be no problems," Jeb Stuart said.

"He did not know you would add a fracture to the bones you had already broken."

"I need to have my wrist good as new. For baseball."

The doctor seemed to take Jeb Stuart's statement as a demand rather than a concern. "We will do the best we are able. But we do not give guarantees."

"What about something for the pain?" Owen asked.

"Doctor Cronin prescribed a two-week supply of OxyContin. Surely you must have some of that left."

"We never filled the prescription," Owen said.

"We were a little leery of OxyContin," Ruth said. "But aspirin didn't work tonight."

The doctor shrugged. "Then I suggest you fill your old prescription."

"That's the problem," Owen said. "I seem to have misplaced it."

The doctor lowered his glasses and stared at Owen over the rims.

"Once we started using aspirin, I didn't keep track of the prescription," Owen said. "I didn't think we needed it."

The doctor sighed. He seemed to be trying to decide whether Owen was a clever drug dealer, or just a naive parent. Finally he tilted his glasses up, took out his prescription pad, and began writing. "I'll give you enough to last for four days."

Then, turning to Jeb Stuart, he added, "But you should only use it if you're really in pain."

In the car on the way home, Owen said, "That doctor looked as if he wanted to prosecute me for misplacing the first prescription."

"He didn't seem sure I'd heal back proper," Jeb Stuart said.

"He was just reluctant to promise too much," Ruth said.

"It just seems like they ought to know more about what they're up to," Jeb Stuart said.

"The fresh break seemed to throw him," Owen said. "If it looks as if things aren't going well, we'll find a specialist."

"Will our insurance cover a specialist?" Ruth asked.

"If it doesn't, we'll find the money somewhere," Owen said, trying to put more conviction than he felt into his voice.

Owen gripped the steering wheel and stared at the winding road picked out by his headlights. He was afraid of what he was thinking, but he was afraid not to think it. Still, it wasn't fair to confront Jeb Stuart with his fears. Not until he'd had a chance to look harder for the missing prescription, and until Ruth kept better records on her stash of ready cash.

The next morning, Owen turned his room upside down, opening drawers, emptying wastebaskets, and looking at every loose scrap of paper. Could he have inadvertently thrown it out? He didn't see how.

Was it loose in a pocket somewhere? He opened his closet door. Most of his clothes were still back in California, so there weren't that many pockets to check, and all he found in them was a little loose change.

His worry grew into a gnawing fear. They'd filled the new prescription on the way home from the hospital, and Jeb Stuart had taken one of the four tablets. Owen had kept the remaining three. He'd hold them, dole them out one tablet a day, no more, and watch for signs of trouble. What signs? He had no idea.

Thad Reader would know what signs to watch for. Owen started downstairs to call the sheriff. He'd just hit the bottom step when Ruth called out to him. She was bringing in the morning mail and handed him a thick brown envelope. "Something from Charleston."

He opened the envelope and extracted an inch-thick sheaf of stapled sheets. It was a proposal request from the Attorney General's office. They were rebidding the inspection job he'd just proposed on. He thumbed through the pages, looking for changes in the original bid packet. They'd have to alter something to justify the rebid. He found a few cosmetic changes, but the kicker was at the end of twenty pages of proposal preparation instructions. A boxed-in notice read:

THIS PROPOSAL REQUEST IS ONE HUNDRED PERCENT (100%) SET ASIDE FOR CERTIFIED DISABLED VETERAN BUSINESS ENTERPRISES

That was it, then. They'd rigged it so he couldn't compete on his own. It wasn't unusual for states to set aside a percentage of proposed contracts for minority business enterprises (MBEs), woman-owned business enterprises (WBEs), or disabled veteran business enterprises (DVBEs). Contractors called it the Meebie Weebie Deevie requirement. But the Deevie portion rarely exceeded four percent. He'd never seen a proposal request with a hundred percent set aside for disabled veterans.

Owen sat down on the staircase. As a small businessman who much preferred to work alone, he'd started out hating the Meebie Weebie Deevie dance that usually ate up fifteen to twenty percent of government contracts. Eventually though, through painful trial and error, he'd found capable partners who had more to offer than just their ethnicity, gender, or war service. But those partners were all back in California. West Virginia was uncharted territory.

What he needed to do was find a local firm run by a disabled veteran and offer his services as a subcontractor willing to bid on the Attorney General's revised proposal request.

He'd started downstairs to call Thad Reader. Now he rose from the staircase and went to the phone. Reader was a vet, and, while Owen never thought of him as disabled, the eye he lost in Vietnam qualified him for disability payments. Maybe he'd know of a registered Deevie that would welcome help in bidding on the Attorney General's inspection contract.

"Try Rusty Oliver," Thad Reader said on the phone. "He's the local poster boy for disabled veterans. For years, you'd see him panhandling in downtown Barkley, working the rush-hour traffic, sitting at a busy corner on his scooter with a little cardboard sign saying 'HOMELESS VETERAN—GOD BLESS.' "

"Just like the big cities," Owen said.

"That must have been where he got the idea. Course, Barkley's idea of a rush hour is three cars at a traffic light. Rusty never could find a corner busy enough to support him."

"How'd he ever get a business together?"

"Got religion. Cleaned up his act. Checked into the Barkley Springs Retreat and dried out. When he left the Springs, he was a new man. Got certified as a Deevie, pulled down a couple of state contracts, kicked back a little to the right people, and now he's a shining example of individual entrepreneurship."

"Sounds like you don't much care for him."

"I didn't much care for the old Rusty, that's for sure. Cleaned up his puke in my jail cell once too often. He was bitter with soul rot, one of those permanent victims who blamed the war for everything from hangnails to hangovers. I can't help thinking the old Rusty's still there somewhere under the new improved version, like a cracked foundation or a metastasized tumor."

"Not exactly a ringing endorsement."

"Hey, what do I know? If it's a Deevie you're looking for, though, Rusty's your man. He's got the certification, more Charleston connections than a phone bank, and he must be making five times my salary."

Owen wondered if it was the salary difference that accounted for Reader's negative view of Oliver. He decided to change the subject. "Anything new on the Lotus Mae killing?"

"Nothing that breaks it. We came up with a funny coincidence on the auction, though."

"What's that?"

"You know, we were looking for people who had taken home winning bids to see if they'd been visited by robbers, like you and Lotus Mae. Turns out Lotus Mae wasn't the only bidder to make up a false background. The guy you said was bidding against her had a phony ID too."

"The one-armed man?"

"Think he might have been in cahoots with the dagger lady?"

"If they were in cahoots, they weren't entirely clear on the concept. They kept bidding each other up."

"Got a point there. So, chances are Lotus Mae and the one-armed man didn't know one another."

"I didn't say that. I just don't see how they could have been working together."

"Just seems like too much of a coincidence that they were both using phony IDs."

"May not mean anything," Owen said. "It's a little like having the same birthday. You get fourteen people in a room and the odds are good two of them will have the same birthday. You just don't know which two."

"I was never much good at math. But if the top two bidders at an auction are using phony IDs and one of them winds up dead, I'm thinking it's more than a statistical quirk."

"Any leads on the one-armed man?"

"Nothing. With Lotus Mae we had prints. This guy left nothing behind."

"You know," Owen said, "I was actually calling about another problem altogether. It's Jeb Stuart."

Reader's voice dropped an octave and Owen could hear the concern in it. "What about Jeb Stuart?"

Owen related the boy's story about horsing around, the hairline fracture, the missing prescription, and the possibility that Ruth's petty cash had been filched. As he listed each occurrence, he felt his conviction lessening. When he'd finished, he said, "Laid out like that, it all seems pretty circumstantial. I feel a little stupid even thinking he'd try Oxy."

"No need to feel stupid. Those are definite warning signals."

"What would you advise?"

"Last time I gave advice to teenage boys, the Vietnam war was on and they wound up in body bags."

"My teenage days are well behind me, and I'm the one who needs advice."

"Well, you should have burned that first prescription."

"It's too late for that. We never filled it."

"No, but you never burned it, either. Now that you've got the new prescription filled, you're doing the right thing in controlling the dosage. But watch Jeb Stuart when he takes it. Don't let him grind it up to get the full hit all at once."

"Anything else?"

"Talk to the boy."

"Confront him? With such skimpy evidence? It'll seem like I don't trust him."

"You don't. You shouldn't. There's too much at stake."

"You're right. It's just that my tolerance for confrontation has always been pretty low."

"I'll help if you want. I can talk to the boy, tell him some horror stories. Show him a few vegetables."

"No. I appreciate the offer. But it's my job. I'll get back to you if my confrontation doesn't work out."

"Good luck. He's a good kid. Lot of promise there."

Owen thanked the sheriff and hung up. Although he'd dreaded bringing up the subject of Jeb Stuart and drugs, he felt pretty good about the call. And about Reader. His stay in West Virginia had increased his store of good friends by at least one person. But he could take no joy in the tasks ahead of him.

Emily's voice on the phone always seemed to be coming from a smile, even when she said, "Haven't heard from you in a while."

"I was waiting until I had some good news to report," Owen said.

"And do you?"

"No. But I have a better handle on the shape of the bad news. And I just couldn't wait any longer."

The smile left her voice. "You mean we lost the job?"

"Not exactly. But we might as well have. They decided not to award it."

"Why would they do that?"

"If I were paranoid, I'd think it was because they didn't want to give me the job."

"But the job has to be done."

"They think so too. They're rebidding it."

"So? Why don't we just bid again?"

"Can't. It's a hundred percent set aside for disabled veterans."

"Can they do that?"

"They just did. It's pretty smart, really. Who's going to argue a disabled veteran doesn't deserve a government job?"

"But is there a disabled veteran that can do the work?"

"Most likely, a certified firm will front for somebody who can do it."

"Like us." The smile came back into Emily's voice. "Why shouldn't we hire ourselves out to a disabled firm?"

"That's a great idea for you. I'm not sure it works for me."

"Why on earth not?"

"The reason they abandoned the first procurement was to avoid giving the job to us—to me, actually. The Attorney General and I aren't exactly best buds." Uncertainty replaced the smile in her voice. "So what are you saying?"

"We should go separately to a Deevie and sign up. I've got the name of one with good connections. It's run by a guy named Rusty Oliver."

"Go separately?"

"You're a mining engineer. You've got perfect credentials for the job. This guy Oliver will have to take you on board. It'll give him real credibility."

"Your credentials are better than mine."

"Doesn't matter. I'm the kiss of death on this job. You're better off going alone to see Oliver."

"But you'll talk to him too?"

"Of course I'll talk to him. I need the work. I just don't think he'll listen."

"All right. I get it. It's just that I was looking forward to having us work together, is all."

"So was I."

After hanging up, Owen realized that they normally would have made a date for movies or tennis. Why hadn't he suggested it? He certainly expected to go on seeing her. Platonically. Now there was a qualifier he hadn't used before. Nobody but Ruth thought their relationship was anything but platonic. It didn't bear thinking about. He'd see Emily again. The fact was, though, that right now he had more important things to worry about than movies and tennis.

The screen door slammed, a sign that Jeb Stuart had just arrived home. Owen got to the living room in time to see him start up the stairs two steps at a time. "Hey," he said.

Jeb Stuart stopped halfway up the stairs. "Hey."

"How's the wrist?"

Jeb Stuart propped his cast on the banister. "Doesn't hurt much, but . . ."

"But what?"

"That new Indian doctor. The one in the emergency room. He said he didn't know if it would heal back proper."

"He was just being cautious."

Jeb Stuart raised the cast, palm outward, as if he were about to catch a baseball. The tips of his fingers peeked out over the tufted wrapping. "I mean, it's my glove hand, so it's okay if it's a little stiff for fielding. But I need to be able to handle a bat."

"We'll just have to wait and see." Owen took a small stoppered cylinder out of his pocket. "Think you'll be needing a pain pill?" Jeb Stuart rotated the cast back and forth. "Don't know. Feels okay right now."

Owen put the cylinder back in his pocket. "Well, let me know."

"Maybe I should take one, keep it in case I need it. Just to be sure."

Owen patted his pocket. "This stuff is too dangerous to take on spec and stockpile. If you need it now, I'll give it to you now. Otherwise, it'll stay put away."

"Hey, it was your idea. Don't come on like I'm some sort of druggie."

"Look, I'm sorry. It's just we've got to be careful with this stuff. I don't want you taking any chances. Understand?"

"You sound like my father."

"Somebody has to. This stuff scares me. I don't know what else to do. It's serious business. It could ruin your life."

"All right. All right. Keep your stash. If my wrist hurts I'll just gobble a few aspirin."

"That's the best thing. I'll be around if you need the stronger stuff." Owen sighed. He should have planned this talk better. He felt more like a pusher than a parent.

Jeb Stuart started back up the stairs.

"How are you fixed for money?" Owen asked.

The boy reached the top of the stairs and turned around. "Okay, I guess. Why do you ask?"

Owen hesitated. He couldn't say he'd asked because cash might be missing from the telephone drawer. Ruth wasn't even sure there had been any cash there to begin with. "No reason. Just feeling generous, I guess."

"Sheriff write you a check?"

Owen gave a noncommittal shrug and checked his wallet. A ten and a five. Thad Reader wouldn't be cutting checks for the accident investigation until the end of the month. What the hell. He met Jeb Stuart at the halfway point on the stairs and handed him the five. "Don't spend it all in one place."

"Excuse me?"

"That's what my mom used to say when she gave me money in high school. The joke was, it was never enough to spend in more than one place." Owen watched Jeb Stuart fold the bill into his wallet. "I guess nowadays it's hard to spend a five in more than one place. That will barely get you into a movie."

Jeb Stuart tapped his wallet and returned it to his hip pocket. "I'll do my best to spread it around. Thanks, Owen."

"I just want you to know, if you ever need money, for whatever reason, you should feel free to come to me."

Jeb Stuart looked puzzled, as if he expected Owen would have more to say. When he didn't, the boy backed up the stairs. "Okay. I'll let you know. Appreciate it."

Owen retreated down the stairs. He felt petty and ineffective, like a small-time gambler who'd just lost his rent money in a game he barely understood.

Rusty Oliver's office was on the tenth floor of the tallest building in Charleston. The waiting room was bigger than any office Owen had ever occupied and commanded a view of the gold dome of the state capitol.

It had taken Owen a week to get an appointment, and he had the distinct impression that it was given reluctantly. At the precise time set for the appointment, however, a hulking black man whose muscles were clearly outlined under his black T-shirt entered the waiting room and motioned for Owen to follow him.

Oliver's private office would have had the same view of the capitol dome as the waiting room if the picture windows hadn't been covered in heavy black floor-to-ceiling drapes.

The drapes darkened the back half of the room, which was cut in two by a conference table that was a few feet short of an airport runway. Track lighting over the table lit the runway and focused harsh spotlights on visitors, leaving the area behind the table in dim shadows.

When Owen entered, Rusty Oliver maneuvered his wheelchair around the conference table into the brightly lit half of the room to meet him. A thick scar snaked down Oliver's cheek from the patch that covered his left eye to the corner of his mouth. His black hair was slicked straight back and he wore a black silk necktie with a charcoal suit coat that seemed to be welded to his upper torso. A black lap robe that Owen guessed was cashmere covered Oliver's legs.

Oliver shook Owen's hand and wheeled himself back into the shadowy area behind the conference table, where he stopped his chair under a trapeze that hung from the lighting track. When Oliver saw Owen looking at the trapeze, he grabbed the bar, did a quick chin-up, and let himself back down into his wheelchair. "Helps me keep in shape," he said.

Oliver punched a button on the wheelchair's armrest and the trapeze moved from its position overhead to a point above a leather couch along the side of the room. "Also helps me get from one piece of furniture to another without bothering Billy Ray." He waved a hand and the black man backed out of the office.

"Good man, Billy Ray," Oliver said after the door had closed. "Served with me in 'Nam. You ever in 'Nam, Dr. Allison?"

"Call me Owen, please. No, I had a college deferment."

"All the way through the war?"

"It carried me through graduate school. By then the war was over." Owen recalled the draft board secretary in Raleigh County, who couldn't understand why he wanted to keep going to college once he'd gotten his bachelor's degree. After all, he was just an engineer, not a doctor or lawyer. "My draft board didn't see many requests for graduate school deferments."

"Wish I'd been smart enough to get me a deferment. I was just a poor hick from the hollers, marching off like John fucking Wayne." Oliver smoothed his lap robe. "Got carried back like Larry fucking Loser." Oliver raised his hand in a dismissing wave. "But, hell, I wasn't alone. West Virginia lost more boys per capita in that war than any other state. Crazy fools, all of us. Filled with red, white, and blue bullshit. Plum near killed me. Broke my body, broke my spirit. I was a wreck for damn close to twenty years."

"What pulled you out of it?"

"I found Jesus." Oliver smiled, daring Owen to respond. "I know, you're going to tell me you didn't know he was lost."

"I thought it, but I wasn't going to say it."

"Hell, that's what I would have said too, before I saw the light. Had me one of them near-death experiences." Oliver took a weathered cigar box from his desk and balanced it on his lap. "I was in my chair panhandling the rush-hour traffic at Main and Jefferson. You know that island that splits the four traffic lanes?"

Owen nodded.

"I'd take my chair out there with a cardboard sign and this here cigar box, work the traffic lanes when cars stopped for the red light. I was pretty wasted when I did that. Get one driver to roll down his window and fork over, though, and you'd get one or two more before the light changed. Herd instinct, I guess.

"Anyhow, this one night a big storm blows in around dusk. Thunder, lightning, whipping winds, the works. Kind of gully washers I used to see in 'Nam, when I'd promise God anything if he'd just let me get out in a minimum number of pieces.

"Rain's coming in horizontal sheets, so nobody's going to roll down their window to give me a handout. I should have given up, but I was wasted with no place to go anyhow, so I just sat there like it wasn't blowing up a storm."

Oliver hunched his shoulders and bent forward in his wheelchair, as if reliving the downpour. "It gets dark, and there's no more than one or two cars waiting through each red light, but still I sit."

He jerked his head upright. "Then I see it. Headlights fishtailing toward me. Some driver has lost control, and I hear that squishing sound of wheels skidding on wet pavement. The car jumps the curb and comes straight at me and I'm thinking, 'Good. This is it. Good.' "

Oliver pounded his fist into the palm of his hand with a loud splat. "But the car stops short. Well, almost stops short. Bumps me hard enough to send my chair shooting backward into the intersection. Now I'm hearing horns honking and brakes squishing while I'm trying to grab onto my own wet wheels."

Oliver crisscrossed his arms in front of his chest repeatedly as if he were fighting off an angry swarm of bees. "One set of headlights slews by me from the left, while another skids to a stop just before it reaches me. Time speeds up, like I'm in some silent film, and I hit the opposite curb before I can get my chair under control. By the time I get it stopped, though, I've gone from thinking, 'God, it's finally all over,' to 'God, I want to live.' "

"And I figure God wants me to live, too. I mean, I just sailed backward through that intersection, missed two cars, and wound up sitting on the opposite curb like I was just waiting for the light to change."

Oliver spread his hands, palms down, in an umpire's "safe" sign. "Then the light changes, and the backed-up traffic moves. Nobody stops to see if I'm hurt. I wheel myself across the street with the light and go back to the traffic island."

Oliver lifted the cigar box from his lap and shook it. Coins rattled and thunked against its sides. "This cigar box is still sitting there by the curb, not a penny spilled. I pick it up, but I'm not staying on that traffic island."

He put the box back on the polished tabletop. "Instead, I find me a sheltered doorway, wait out the storm, and nap through the night. Come dawn, I wheel myself to the sheriff's office and promote me a ride to Barkley Springs Retreat. They take me in, sober me up, and put me in touch with God and the Disabled Veteran folks. Got me a lease, got me a business, got me a Deevie certificate. Never looked back."

Oliver leaned forward, centering himself in the beam of one of the overhead spotlights as if he were expecting applause. Instead of clapping, Owen reached into his briefcase and pulled out the Attorney General's proposal request. "I've come about this job that's up for bid."

"I know. I'm going to bid it. And I've sort of been expecting you. You're persona non gratis in the Attorney General's office. Believe me, I know what that's like."

Owen held out the proposal request but Oliver made no move to take it. "I bid on this job the first time it was advertised."

"Wrote a great proposal, I hear," Oliver said.

"But they cancelled the procurement."

"So you've got no recourse."

"No recourse?"

"Even if you think the process was rigged and rotten, you

can't sue or protest, because the state's under no obligation to award a contract."

"I hadn't thought of suing," Owen said.

"Just as well you didn't. You'd have no case. It's not like they awarded the job to somebody unqualified. They just didn't award it at all."

Owen shoved the proposal request across the conference table toward Oliver. "I've still got the proposal I wrote. It will work for this rebid. I thought maybe we could strike a deal. You let me run the proposal through your Deevie firm. You get the profit, I get the work and a steady paycheck."

Oliver shook his head. " 'Fraid I can't do that."

"Why not?"

Oliver shoved the proposal request back toward Owen. "You can't win that job. You never heard me say this, but the Attorney General's not gonna give that contract to any firm that's got you on its payroll."

Owen slipped the proposal request back into his briefcase. "So I guess you're not worried that I'll find another disabled veteran firm and bid against you."

"Trying to win that job with you on the team would be like painting racing stripes on your sneakers and trying to win the Indianapolis Five Hundred on foot. Any firm that tried it would be a loser from the get-go."

Owen closed his briefcase and stood up. "Thanks for your time. And your candor."

"Well, hell. My time's easy enough to come by nowadays. And candor don't cost me nothing. Tell you what, though. I know what it's like to be out of work. I can't put your name in my proposal, but if we win, we're gonna have to hire a brace of inspectors. I could hire you then and nobody'd know the difference."

"That's a better offer than the Indianapolis Five Hundred. Let me think about it."

"We can't put it in writing, but I'll honor the deal." Oliver wheeled himself around his desk and held out his hand.

After Thad Reader's rundown, Owen had come prepared to dislike Rusty Oliver, but he found himself warming up to the man. He shook the offered hand.

"One thing, though," Oliver said. "You mind working for a woman?"

"Depends on the woman."

"This one's a mining engineer. Interviewed her yesterday. Think I'll use her to head up my proposal team. Name's Emily Kruk."

HITLER'S DIARIES

In April 1983, the West German magazine *Stern* announced that it had uncovered sixty-two volumes of a diary kept by Adolf Hitler from 1932 to 1943. The diaries, which were authenticated by a number of historians and handwriting experts, were allegedly pulled out of the wreckage of a plane that crashed near Dresden during the last days of World War II and smuggled across the Iron Curtain thirty years later by the brother of a West German memorabilia dealer named Konrad Kujau, who sold them to *Stern* for an estimated three million dollars. The diaries contained no mention of the Jewish pogrom and portrayed Hitler as "a kindly, gentle, and not very bright utterer of platitudes." When chemical tests showed the diaries' bindings and paper to be of post-war manufacture, the forged documents were traced to the memorabilia dealer Kujau, who, together with a *Stern* reporter, was sentenced to four years in prison.

From the Museum of Fakes
and Frauds' Hall of Historical Hoaxes

Chapter Nine:

Don't Look Back

So the job would probably come, Owen thought, but it would come slowly. The proposal wasn't due for another month. After that, there'd be at least a month of evaluation and another month of negotiation before a contract could be signed.

133

All measured in bureaucratic time, where a month's worth of work could easily consume sixty days.

He'd have to find something to occupy his time while he waited. There were still a lot of loose ends dangling from the museum auction and the Lotus Mae Graham murder. He wanted to see Victoria Gallagher again, so he called her with a proposition.

"Let me get this straight," she said over the phone, "you want to meet the forger Burt Campbell used?"

"It would help me to understand the museum's workings. And its holdings."

"He's in Pittsburgh, you know. That's a four- or five-hour drive."

"We could make it there and back in a day."

"It would have to be a Saturday or Sunday."

He could sense that she was warming up to the idea. "Could you set it up?"

"It's been years since I visited him with Burt. He may be out of business. And he may not remember me."

"He's a man. Trust me. He'll remember you." He imagined he could hear her smile.

"I'll need some excuse for visiting him."

"Why not get some more posthumous signatures for the museum?"

"We'd need to find a few first editions of books published after the authors' deaths."

"That could be expensive. Why don't we use baseball cards instead. I'll find some from old-time stars and stars who died young. Hall of Fame card sets aren't hard to come by. We can get him to autograph cards issued after the players died."

"And we're doing this because?"

Owen stifled the urge to be truthful, to say, "Because I'd like to spend more time with you." Instead, he said, "There's seven hundred and fifty million dollars missing from Burt Caldwell's bank, and at least one person has been killed after buying auctioned merchandise from Burt Caldwell's museum. I'd just like to get a better feel for your operation."

"A better feel." He could hear the smile in her voice again. "That's hard to turn down. I'll try to track down our forger."

"In the meantime, I'll try to track down some cards that can be signed posthumously."

Owen rummaged through his collection of cards with Jeb Stuart and called Brian's Card Shop in Cincinnati. With the help of Jeb Stuart, Brian, and UPS, he assembled a batch of cards suitable for posthumous signatures. Then he waited for Victoria to call.

When four days passed without a call, Owen began to worry. Had the forger gone out of business? Was Victoria having second thoughts? He was debating whether or not to call her when the phone rang.

"Sorry it's taken me so long," Victoria said, "but he's changed his phone number at least twice since we worked with him."

"But he's still in business?"

"Oh, yes."

"I've got cards for Ruth and Gehrig, Satchel Paige, and a Roberto Clemente commemorative for him to sign. I'm working on more."

"A Roberto Clemente commemorative signed by the player himself. That's good. We can use that in the museum."

"Do I need to bring anything besides the cards?"

"Bring signature samples. The more the better. He likes to see a range of signatures. I know he's already got Ruth and Gehrig. He's done them for us in the past."

"I'll bring as many as I can find. Can he see us this weekend?"

"I don't see why not. I got the impression he needs the business."

The trip to Pittsburgh followed Interstate 79 diagonally across West Virginia from Charleston to Morgantown before cutting north into Pennsylvania. The last time Owen had made the trip, the Interstate hadn't been built and the roads hugged the hollows and followed winding stream beds with the railroads. Now the Interstate skimmed across the midsection of the state's green mountains, following a gently curving path made, not by nature, but by occasional blasts that left exposed walls striped with limestone and coal rising next to the thoroughfare. For most of the distance, though, green, tree-covered slopes rose up on either side of the roadway and rolled ahead of them, unbroken by any sign of civilization beyond route markers, signs announcing they were traveling along the Jennings Randolph Highway, and an occasional black billboard with white lettering that read:

STOP DESTROYING MY MOUNTAINS
—GOD

Just south of Stonewall Jackson's birthplace in Clarksburg, a roadside sign announced that the next exit led to the Stonewall Jackson Lake and Lodge.

"I didn't know Jackson was born near a lake with the same name," Owen said. "What are the odds on that?"

Victoria smiled. "The lake came much later than the birth. It's a man-made recreation area. I'm guessing it's not more than twenty years old."

"Think that's really Jackson's elbow you've got on display in your museum?"

"I think the Confederate that carried it through the rest of the war believed it was Jackson's elbow. He credited it with his survival."

Owen shrugged and returned Victoria's smile. "Whatever gets you through the night."

"There's no doubt the museum's stacks of Jackson's personal Bibles are bogus, though. If Stonewall had carried every one of the Bibles bearing his signature into battle, his horse would have pulled up lame."

They passed another sign announcing they were on the Jennings Randolph Highway and a second one directing them to the Stonewall Jackson Lake.

"Nice to see a man-made project named for a real hero instead of some politician," Owen said.

"West Virginia politicians aren't all bad. I've watched the current batch in action a few times. They take their job seriously."

"The politicians that were around when the Interstate was planned took their jobs seriously too. They were seriously corrupt."

"Wasn't that before your time?"

"My dad was in the Highway Department then. The highway commissioner and two of his cronies went to jail for taking kickbacks and rigging bids. I believe the Attorney General did time too. The governor was indicted along with his buddies, but the jury let him off."

"See, our politicians aren't all bad."

"The governor went to jail two years later for bribing the jury that set him free."

"Guess I walked into that," Victoria said. "As far as I know, though, Jennings Randolph never went to jail."

"That makes him a rarity among West Virginia politicians," Owen said. "Maybe he deserves to have an Interstate named after him."

The address they were looking for was on the third floor of an office building in downtown Pittsburgh. The interior of the building's elevator was a dirty beige with waist-high scrapes and scratches marking years of furniture turnover. The frosted glass window on the door opposite the elevator on the third floor had been neatly lettered in gothic script to read:

LYLE C. UNDERDUNCK

HANDWRITING
ANALYSIS
and
CALLIGRAPHY

Inside, the office had all the charm and order of a homeless encampment. On the side facing the one windowed wall, every flat surface was littered with dust-covered piles of paper whose edges were yellowed. Rusting metal file cabinets lined the three windowless walls. Either the floor or the file cabinets needed leveling.

Above the file cabinets hung framed certificates, diplomas, signed portraits of presidents, and autographed photos of celebrities. Three desks formed a U under the grimy window. In the center of the U, nearly hidden by the mounds of clutter, sat a man with a straggly white moustache and kangaroo-sized pouches under his eyes.

As Owen and Victoria entered, the man placed his lit cigarette carefully on the one clear corner of desk space, unfolded his tall frame into a stooped posture, and shook their hands. "Surprised to hear from you. Been quite a while."

He waved Owen and Victoria toward a pair of folding chairs in front of the listing file cabinets and collapsed back into his own swivel chair. "Surprised to hear from anybody, actually. Goddamn computers have all but put me out of business."

Owen looked around the office. There was no sign of a computer, although two or three could easily have been hidden by the mounds of paper.

"You won't find one of those infernal machines in this office. They've damn near ruined me. Folks use them to turn out made-to-order certificates and diplomas. Nobody needs calligraphy anymore. Except for a few wedding invitations, I might as well shut up shop." Underdunck blew his nose into a wrinkled handkerchief. "Damn dust. Hell, computers are even doing handwriting analysis. FBI uses them to detect forged signatures."

He paused and examined his handkerchief. "Not that anybody really needs to forge signatures anymore. Computers have taken that over too. Just swipe a code, punch a button, and *zap*, somebody's funds get sent to somebody else's offshore account."

He wrapped the handkerchief around his little finger, worked it in and out of his left nostril, and returned it to his breast pocket. "Forgery's turned into a lower-class crime. Folks steal checkbooks, get groceries and a little cash back from local supermarkets. They don't even try to get the signatures right. Nobody checks their ID. Nobody raises an eyebrow. Nobody cares. Banks expect it. Hell, they even allow for it. It's cheaper to write off the bad paper than check every signature."

Underdunck retrieved his cigarette from the corner of the desk, took two deep drags, and flicked the ashes toward the floor. The drifting sparks disturbed a fat gray cat that had been dozing in a lower desk drawer. The cat uncurled, climbed across Underdunck's lap and curled back up on the windowsill.

Underdunck shook his head. "Forgery's a lost art. Only folks even trying to duplicate signatures are husbands signing for wives or business partners signing for each other."

Owen looked at the autographed pictures hanging on the wall. "What about celebrity autographs?"

"Oh, there's a market there, I guess. I've heard that something like eighty percent of the signatures on jock junk are bogus. It's like the supermarket forgeries, though. Strictly amateur night. Nobody tries very hard to get it right. The buyers want to believe they're getting the real thing."

Underdunck frowned and winced, causing the bags under his eyes to bulge even farther. "It's disgusting, the shoddy workmanship you see on sports signatures. Other day, a friend told me he saw an autographed Barry Bonds baseball with Bonds' name spelled B-a-r-r-*i-e*."

"What about autographed first editions, like the ones you signed for Burt Caldwell?" Owen asked.

"Those will fetch more money than most baseball cards and celebrity autographs. Trouble is, you've got to get your hands on a first edition. With big-name authors, that can get expensive."

"How did Caldwell manage it?"

"He could afford the cheaper editions. For the more expensive ones, Burt mostly bought up used library copies. Collectors turn up their noses at library copies, so you can get them pretty cheap. Then he'd spruce them up so you couldn't tell they'd come from libraries. Sand off any edge printing. Tip in fresh end papers. Takes an expert restorer to do that well. Easiest thing for me is to let somebody else do that work. Then I'd sign the copies they doctored."

"Show Owen the sample signatures you copied," Victoria said.

Underdunck went to one of the leaning file cabinets, came back with a manila folder, and spread the sheets from the folder across the mounds of paper on his desk. "I like to work from a range of signatures, so I had Burt bring me as many samples as he could find."

The sheets spread on the desktop had samples of the signatures of F. Scott Fitzgerald and Ernest Hemingway from a variety of sources. There were copies of signed title pages from *This Side of Paradise* and *The Sun Also Rises*, copies of both men's signatures from the pages of a magazine, and a copy of a letter signed by Fitzgerald that looked like a page from a biography.

"Where did Caldwell get copies of these signatures?" Owen asked.

Underdunck shrugged. "Collectors' magazines, mostly. Biographies, dealer catalogs, bibliographies. They're not too hard to come by."

"Ever forge any business signatures?" Owen asked.

Underdunck's face hardened. He lowered his thick glasses and stared over the top of the lenses. "For Burt Caldwell?"

"Lots of money went missing from his bank."

Underdunck waved his hand to take in his surroundings, trailing cigarette ashes from the desk to the windowsill. "Look around you, mister. I'm ass-deep in moldy papers. This office look to you like I had any share of a seven-hun-dred-and-fifty-million-dollar rip-off?"

The loud, angry question woke the cat, who vacated the windowsill and climbed onto Underdunck's lap.

Underdunck dumped the cat on the floor, swept up the signature samples from the desk and returned them to the file cabinet. The door of the cabinet screeched as he shut it and turned toward them. "You said on the phone you wanted some signatures from me."

Victoria opened her briefcase and took out the baseball cards and sample signatures Owen had collected. "We want you to sign these cards for the museum." She showed the cards to Underdunck. "It's the same principle as *The Last Tycoon*. They're all cards the subjects couldn't have seen in their lifetimes. This top one, for example, is a Roberto Clemente commemorative edition."

"Pretty slick." Underdunck laid the Clemente card on the one clear spot on his desk and surrounded it with the sample signatures. Then he sat in his swivel chair and flexed his long, knobby fingers. He reminded Owen of Victor Borge making elaborate preparations for a comedy riff at the piano.

Underdunck picked up a ballpoint pen and ran it over one of the sample signatures. "Thing that gives most forgers away is the shaky line," he said. "They slow down to match the shape, but they lose the flow. Work too fast, on the other hand, and you get the flow but lose the shape."

He ran the pen over the sample signature one more time, then signed the card itself with a flourish and handed it to Owen.

Owen compared the forged signature with the samples. "They might be carbon copies."

"What else you got?" Underdunck asked Victoria.

She handed him a card and two sample signatures.

"Satchel Paige," Underdunck said. "The old Satchelfoot. Now there was a character. Too bad there's no room on the card for his sayings."

" 'Don't look back,' " Owen quoted. " 'Someone might be gaining on you.' "

Underdunck nodded. "The one I always liked is, 'How old would you be if you didn't know how old you was?' "

"I've never heard that one," Owen said, thinking that he'd been feeling far older than fifty lately, even though his birthday was still a month away.

Underdunck duplicated his previous ritual and signed the Paige card.

Victoria handed him two more cards. "Sign these and we'll call it quits."

"My old buddies Ruth and Gehrig. I can sign them in my sleep." Underdunck rummaged through his desk drawer and came up with a fountain pen. "Ballpoints weren't around much before the Second World War, and Gehrig died in nineteen-forty-one."

He flexed the fingers of his left hand, took the pen in it, and dashed off both signatures.

"You signed the two lefties' cards with your left hand," Owen said. "Could anyone tell the difference if you'd signed them right-handed?"

"Nobody who's likely to visit your museum. A good hand-writing expert could tell the difference. I daresay I could fool the FBI's computers with either hand."

Underdunck handed the signed cards to Victoria, who counted out four fifty-dollar bills and laid them on the one clear corner of the desk.

Underdunck picked up the fifties and riffled them with his long fingers. "Museum doing well, is it?"

"Well enough," Victoria said. "The FDIC is forcing us to sell off some of our collection."

"I read a magazine piece on your collection. It mentioned you had the only signed copy of *The Last Tycoon*. I felt a little twinge of pride." He fanned the fifties like a poker hand. "Thinking of raising my rates. What with my computer competition and the economic downturn, I can barely make ends meet. Occurred to me it would be a shame if people found out you were fabricating your own fakes."

"I'd be careful where I spread that rumor if I were you," Victoria said. "Don't forget, you came to our attention because we've got samples of your work that weren't intended as museum pieces."

Underdunck shoved the fifties into the top drawer of his desk. "Naturally, I'd hold the price line stable for an old and valued customer like your museum."

Victoria slipped her briefcase strap over her shoulder and started to leave. "Don't think for a minute we don't appreciate it."

In the car on the way home, Owen said, "My God, the man's a whacked-out anachronism. I wouldn't have been surprised to see him pick up that cat and use it to blot his signatures."

Victoria smiled. "Like Peter Sellers in that movie about the tontine."

"*The Wrong Box.* I liked the way you handled his little extortion ploy."

"I learned quite a bit from Burt Caldwell."

"Underdunck seemed quite upset when I asked if he'd ever forged business signatures."

"He's probably done it, but I'd be willing to bet he never did it for Burt Caldwell. That wasn't the office of a big-time forger."

They drove in silence for a short time. Owen found he was comfortable with the silence, and with Victoria.

When they crossed the state line from Pennsylvania into West Virginia, Victoria said, "Can we stop for dinner? I know a great restaurant in Morgantown."

Owen took the Interstate exit marked for Morgantown, and they found themselves on Jerry West Boulevard. "Now that's the way to name a boulevard," Owen said. "Pick someone substantial. Forget those fly-by-night politicians."

"Who's Jerry West?"

"Who's Jerry West? You sure you're from West Virginia? He's the pride of East Bank High School, all-everything from WVU, Mister Clutch with the Los Angeles Lakers. That's his silhouette dribbling on the NBA logo."

"Must have been before my time. NBA. That's basketball, isn't it?"

Owen couldn't tell whether she was kidding or not. "That's basketball. It's the sport where you're most likely to find dribbling. Unless you're into drinking games."

"So they named a boulevard after him. Pretty impressive."

"When I was growing up, half the high-school kids in West Virginia thought they named the state after him."

Victoria pointed down a side street. "Turn here."

Owen turned onto a street pock-marked with potholes. The sidewalks were cracked, and parking meters tilted in different directions. "You sure about this?" he asked.

"I'm sure. Burt Caldwell and I stopped here a couple of times." After they'd driven four or five blocks, she nodded toward a tall, boxy building with a blue canopy over the entrance. "This is it. Park anywhere."

"The Hotel Morgan?"

"It was built in the twenties. But they renovated it just recently."

Victoria led Owen through the dark, wood-paneled lobby to a pair of elevators. A sign in front of one of the elevators announced that it was shut down until they could get parts from its year of manufacture to complete the renovation.

"Kind of makes you wonder whether the one working elevator has been repaired or not," Owen said.

"Stop thinking like a failure analyst." Victoria pushed the elevator button. "Relax and enjoy the trip."

A placard next to the working elevator invited hotel guests to dine at the Pinnacle Club on the eighth floor. "Pinnacle Club," Owen said. "Must be a throwback to the days when you had to be a private club in order to serve liquor."

"Careful, you're dating yourself."

"I must have read about it in the history books."

When they arrived at the eighth floor, a sign announced that the piano bar on the patio was open from six p.m. to eleven p.m. Owen checked his watch. It was a few minutes after six o'clock. "Things are looking up. I'm a sucker for a piano bar."

They were the first to be seated on the patio, which was dotted with fringed, ten-foot-square canopies that provided intermittent shelter for wrought-iron tables and chairs. A large canopy covered the patio's centerpiece, a polished baby grand where a suntanned man with a thick mane of wavy white hair was playing "My Funny Valentine."

The white stucco patio walls were high enough to shield them from the Morgantown street scene, but low enough to permit a view of the nearby mountains, which were rimmed with red by the setting sun.

"Fire on the Mountain," Owen said.

Victoria shielded her eyes. "It's breathtaking."

The piano player did a little riff and asked them for requests. Victoria requested "Someone to Watch Over Me," and Owen asked for "Send in the Clowns."

"Sondheim," Victoria said. "I would have figured you for Willie Nelson."

"They're not mutually excusive," Owen said. "I would have asked for 'Funny How Time Slips Away,' but I noticed the man at the piano had forgotten his guitar and I didn't want to embarrass him."

A young man wearing a tuxedo and a plastic name tag that announced his name was Johnnie appeared and asked if he could bring them drinks.

"I better not," Owen said. "I've got to drive the rest of the way to Barkley tonight."

"Go ahead and order," Victoria said. "I can drive from here on in."

"You sure?"

"Positive."

Owen ordered a glass of merlot, while Victoria asked for plain tonic water with a twist of lime.

When the drinks arrived, they clinked glasses and Owen asked again, "You're sure you don't mind being the designated driver?"

"Not at all." Victoria ran her hand along the silver chain around her neck. "Actually, I don't drink. I'm a recovering alcoholic."

"Oh. I didn't know."

"It's all right. It's been fifteen years since I've had a drink."

"That's quite a record. My brother George just passed his third year in AA."

"I have Burt Caldwell to thank for my recovery, actually. He paid for my stay at Barkley Springs. They dried me out and got me started in AA."

The patio began to fill with patrons. A college-age couple at the next table moved their chairs together so they could sit side by side holding hands and facing the pianist.

Owen found himself wondering how close J. Burton Caldwell had been to Victoria. Then he wondered why he was wondering, but only briefly. He waited until the pianist finished playing Victoria's request and said, "Caldwell sounds like an enlightened boss."

"Oh, yes." Victoria's tone and expression were non-committal, as if she were answering a telephone survey.

A group of twelve college students took over four tables along the patio wall. The six boys wore letter sweaters in the WVU colors, old gold and blue, and alternated holding up their index fingers and saying "Number one again," creating a mini-wave. The girls giggled and tried to shush them.

"First football game of the season today," Owen said.

"Did you play?"

"My high school was too small to field a football team. I never much enjoyed the game anyhow. I played baseball in high school, but didn't try out at Marquette. Studies took too much time."

"Do you regret not playing in college?"

Owen shrugged. "I guess. But it's pretty low on my list of regrets."

"I'd like to hear that list sometime."

The pianist finished "Send in the Clowns," and a thick-necked boy with a blonde crew cut from the student group shouted, "Hey, let's hear the Mountaineer Fight Song."

"God," Victoria said. "Remember being that young and clueless and exuberant?"

"Young and clueless, maybe. Never that exuberant."

"I suppose you were shy and retiring."

"Shy, certainly. But winning never gave me the high those kids are on. It's losses that are stored up in my memory banks. Our baseball team won the state championship my senior year, but what I remember most is losing in the final my junior year when I walked in the winning run."

"What was it Satchel Paige said? 'Don't look back?' "

The crew-cut boy in the letter sweater struggled to his feet. "What about that fight song? You know how it goes don't you?" He pumped a fist against the night sky and chanted, "Hail, West Virginia!"

About half the patrons ignored the boy. The other half either tried to stare him down or looked expectantly at the pianist.

The pianist nodded, smiled a fight song kind of smile, and bent over the keyboard. He had barely played the first line when lightning streaked across the sky, followed closely by a sharp thunderclap.

"Evidently God is not a Mountaineer fan," Owen said.

A few dollops of rain plopped on the canopies and splattered on the patio floor. Then water began sheeting down. The pianist stood and rolled his stool under the keyboard. "Sorry folks, there will be a short intermission."

Two waiters in tuxedos hurried out with a fitted canvas cover to protect the piano.

Johnnie appeared, waited out a thunderclap, and said, "I can serve your dinner inside." As the patio emptied, he led them to one of several small dining rooms with gold flocked wallpaper and built-in shelves bearing tiny figurines arranged to depict Currier and Ives scenes. Fresh flowers were centered on the white linen tablecloth and Owen was glad to see the Mountaineer rooters had been banished to a different room.

Their waiter disappeared and came back with a full wine glass for Owen and a fresh glass of tonic water for Victoria. "Rain watered down your drinks."

"Think the piano bar is likely to reopen?" Owen asked.

"We've been listening to the weather forecast. There's no telling how long these showers will last." He ran his hand through rain-slicked hair. "If you don't mind my mentioning it, though, you may want to rethink your trip to Barkley. There are tornado warnings from Ironton all the way across the Ohio Valley."

"They should have passed through by the time we get there," Owen said.

The waiter shrugged. "I were you, I wouldn't want to drive in that muck. It's a real toad strangler."

"Think the hotel might have a couple of rooms available?" Owen asked.

"It's Saturday. I'm sure we can find something. Would you like me to check with the front desk?"

Owen raised an eyebrow at Victoria.

She smiled and nodded. "Please do. There's no reason to be extravagant, though. We'll only need one room."

The hotel room was nearly large enough to be a suite, with a long couch facing a TV set, a double bed, and two easy chairs flanking a small table. "Our man Johnnie did well by us," Owen said. He picked up the phone to call his mother while Victoria explored the room.

"Owen, thank God you called," Ruth said. "There are tornado warnings all along the Ohio and Kanawha Rivers."

"I know, Mom. We've stopped in Morgantown. It's raining pretty hard here too. We're going to wait out the storm and drive in tomorrow morning."

There was a long pause as Ruth absorbed the plan to stay overnight. Then she said, "I don't think Barkley is in the path of the tornado."

"We'd have to cross the path to get home, though."

"Jeb Stuart is still out too. I'm worried about him."

Owen checked his watch. "It's only eight o'clock. He'll be all right."

"I don't know. He's been acting strange ever since he broke his wrist. And it's really storming out there."

"He's a good kid, Mom. He won't take any crazy chances."

"I wish you were here."

"We'll be home early tomorrow. Love you."

Owen hung up. He heard water running in the bathroom, so he settled onto the couch and flipped through the local TV channels. He was getting the baseball scores from ESPN when Victoria emerged wearing a terrycloth robe and drying her hair. "Wait'll you see the bathroom." Owen poked his head around the bathroom door. The bathtub had been outfitted with jet nozzles and squeezed under a marble ledge.

"It's a whirlpool bath," Victoria said. "Too bad there's only room for one. Why don't you try it?"

Owen undressed in the bathroom. His shirt was still damp from the sudden shower and he hung it from the towel rack next to Victoria's white blouse. He filled the tub with the hottest water he could stand, slipped into it, and punched the whirlpool button.

Hot jets pulsated against his back and legs. He held his breath and slid down so his head was under water and the rear jet was working against his neck muscles. When he surfaced and cleared his eyes, Victoria was standing next to the tub. "How is it?"

"Wonderful."

She slipped out of her robe and stepped across him to sit on the marble ledge.

"I thought you had gauged the maximum capacity of this tub to top out at one person," Owen said.

Victoria traced a circle on his inner thigh with her bare toe. "I think we can make it fit."

MISTER RAM-WHAT-AM

In the early 1900s, "Doctor" John R. Brinkley of Kansas made a fortune charging $750 to provide male patients with the transplanted glands or testicles of a billy goat.

This surgical procedure purportedly improved sexual prowess and was touted with advertising copy that read, "Just let me get your goat and you'll be Mr. Ram-What-Am with every lamb."

While some of the thousands of males receiving testicular transplants reportedly found that the operation improved their sexual performance, the American Medical Association labeled Brinkley a "giant in quackery." Their branding did not stop Brinkley from becoming a millionaire by 1920 or from running for governor of Kansas in 1932 as an independent. He had enough name recognition to receive 244,000 votes, finishing third behind Republican Alf Landon's 278,000 votes and the Democratic candidate's 272,000 votes.

From the Museum of Fakes
and Frauds' Hoaxers Hall of Fame

Chapter Ten:

The Other Side of Paradise

Owen was the first to wake the next morning. He propped himself up on one elbow and looked at Victoria. While he remembered falling asleep in her arms, sometime during the night she'd rolled away and turned her back to him. Freed of the bands that held her ponytail, streaked gray hair fanned out across the navy blue pillowcase. Two military dog tags attached to a silver chain had worked their way around her neck and dangled between her still shoulder blades.

Owen smiled at the memory of the tags bouncing between her breasts the night before and slipped two fingers under the silver chain. Trying not to wake Victoria, he took one of the metal tags between his thumb and forefinger and raised it enough to read the embossed name.

Victoria stirred and asked, "Whatcha doing?" in a sleepy voice.

Owen released the tag and kissed the nape of her neck. "Just checking your ID. Who's Jonathan Keller?"

The pillow muffled her voice. "Jealous?"

"Curious."

"What time is it?"

"Six-thirty."

"Too early to be jealous."

"Sorry, I didn't mean to wake you."

She rolled over to face him and tucked the blue sheet under her armpits. "Jonathan Keller was my grandfather. He was gassed in the first World War. My mother gave me his dog tags for luck when I went into Barkley Springs."

"And they helped you get through?"

"The man lived for ten years with lungs so damaged he could hardly climb a single flight of stairs. I kept thinking that what I was going through wasn't nearly so bad and wouldn't last nearly so long."

Owen recalled the cloth scapulars with pictures of saints the nuns had hung around his neck in grade school. When had he stopped believing in them? "But you're still wearing the tags, what? Fifteen years later?"

"I need to be reminded of the strength in his genes. I'm not out of the woods yet."

He gathered Victoria into his arms. "You're in a safe place now."

Victoria closed her eyes and smiled. "Ummm. Paradise."

Owen shivered. "*This Side of Paradise.*"

Victoria nuzzled his neck. "Close enough."

Owen sat bolt upright, pulling the sheet with him. "No. The Fitzgerald book. That's what been tugging at me."

Victoria recovered her half of the sheet. "Here I thought I was the one that had been tugging at you."

"I was speaking metaphorically."

"I love it when you talk dirty."

"No. Listen. Caldwell gave Underdunck a whole batch of Fitzgerald signatures."

Victoria shrugged. "The man liked to work from a range of samples."

"But most of the samples were copies of photographs from collectors' magazines. The signature from *This Side of Paradise* was a Xerox copy of the book's title page."

Victoria stifled a yawn. "So?"

"So Caldwell must have had his hands on a signed copy of *This Side of Paradise*. Like the one in the museum."

"But the one in the museum's a forgery."

"He wouldn't give Underdunck a forgery to copy. That wouldn't make sense."

"You think the museum copy might be real?"

"It would explain a few things."

"But we know that Underdunck forged the *Gatsby* signature. And *The Last Tycoon* is an obvious forgery. That was the whole point of the exhibit. A posthumous signature."

"I know. But there were four or five signed titles in the

154

Fitzgerald exhibit. What if one of them were genuine? A signed first edition of *This Side of Paradise* would be worth what? Thirty or forty grand?"

Victoria propped herself up on one elbow. "Why would Burt do a thing like that?"

"You said yourself he liked to fool people. There's seven hundred and fifty million missing from Caldwell's bank. Suppose some of it is sitting in your museum in plain view?"

Victoria smiled. "Wouldn't Mr. Know-It-All Ramsey from the FDIC be surprised. How can we find out if you're right?"

"Let's have the book appraised."

"Just take it out of the museum?"

"You're the curator. Can't you do that?"

"What if we're wrong? I don't want Mitchell Ramsey looking over my shoulder and laughing. And if we're right I don't want him confiscating our exhibits to pay the bank's debts."

"Then don't let him know. The exhibit's in a locked glass case. Copy the dust jacket and put it on another book. Then leave that book in the exhibit and take the Fitzgerald to an appraiser. Your man Underdunck is a handwriting expert. He ought to be able to verify the signature."

Victoria sat up beside him, gathering the sheet around her. "You think there are more, don't you? Exhibits where we've labeled the real thing a fake, I mean."

"I think there could be. It would explain why a woman might be murdered after buying a presumably phony Klee and a box of baseball cards."

"Those are gone. We can't have them appraised."

"But you've got a batch of baseball cards still on display that are labeled knockoffs. I know a man who can tell us what they're really worth."

"Let's just start with the Fitzgerald. I don't want to alert Mitchell Ramsey until we're sure." She traced a pattern on his bare back with her forefinger. "We've got about an hour before we have to start back. And I'm wide awake now."

"I don't know," Owen said. "The nuns in high school always told us to ask ourselves whether an hour of pleasure is worth a lifetime of shame."

"And what did you answer?"

Owen settled back on the bed and drew Victoria to him. "I could never decide. But I always wanted to ask the nuns, 'Please, sister, how do you make it last an hour?' "

Owen dropped Victoria at her apartment and made it to his home in Barkley by eleven o'clock Sunday morning. Ruth was sitting on the living-room couch waiting for him when he came through the door. It reminded him of the times in high school when he'd come home late after a date.

She looked up from the yellow scarf she was knitting. "Jeb Stuart didn't come home until three in the morning."

"How did he seem?"

"Distant. He didn't call. He's not the same boy. You should talk to him."

Owen didn't relish the prospect of a confrontation with Jeb Stuart. "You must have been up when he came in. Right on that couch, I imagine. Didn't you talk to him?"

"He said it was raining too hard to try the roads." Ruth pointed a knitting needle at him. "It was the same excuse you used."

"Mom, if you can recall the excuses I used when I was Jeb Stuart's age, you shouldn't have any worries about your memory."

"It was the same excuse you used last night."

"Last night? Last night there were tornado warnings."

"I know. At least you called. Owen, what do you know about that woman?"

"What kind of a question is that?"

Ruth stared down at the yellow scarf in her lap. "You registered as man and wife."

Owen stood stock still in the doorway, speechless.

"After you hung up, I called the hotel back. To see if that woman was registered separately."

"We didn't register as man and wife. I registered myself and said there'd be two in the room. Nobody asked if we were married. Nobody cared. And that woman has a name. Why don't we use it?"

"I'm sorry. It's just . . . Well, she's new to Barkley. She came out of nowhere and nobody knows anything about her."

"Mom, Victoria's been a museum curator here for fifteen years."

"That's what I mean. It's strange, is all."

"What's strange? That someone's still a newcomer after fifteen years? Or that your network hasn't been able to dig up any dirt on her?"

Ruth gave a half-hearted grin and returned to her knitting. "I said I was sorry. I just thought . . . Well, there's you and Judith."

"Mom, Judith is two thousand miles from here. We may get back together. We may not. I appreciate your concern. But it's really none of your business."

Ruth locked her eyes on Owen's. "You're my son, Owen. It will always be my business. I'm not trying to tell you how to live your life. I just worry about you, is all."

"Jesus, Mom. I'm almost fifty years old. Don't you think it's time you stopped worrying about me? Worry about Jeb Stuart."

"You will talk to him, then?"

157

"How'd we get back here?" Owen felt cornered. "I'll talk to him. That's what this whole conversation has been about, isn't it?"

Ruth looked up from her knitting. "Now's a good time. He's still in his room."

Owen stopped outside Jeb Stuart's bedroom door. He paused with his hand on the knob, thinking he ought to have a plan. When he had trouble formulating one, he asked himself, "What are you afraid of?" When he couldn't answer that question either, he knocked and entered.

Jeb Stuart was sitting up in bed, so that his gray Cincinnati reds sweatshirt peeked out over the rumpled sheet. "Hey," he said as Owen came through the door. "Hey," Owen said. The room smelled faintly of dried vomit and Lysol.

"What's up?"

"Mom says you didn't get home until three last night."

"I waited out the storm."

"You should have called. She worries about you. We both worry about you."

"It was raining too hard. You couldn't see ten feet in front of the windshield."

"That shouldn't stop you from calling."

Jeb Stuart shook his head. "Didn't think about it. You should have seen that storm."

"I've used that excuse myself. It never rains that hard that long."

"Yeah, well. I'd had a little too much . . ."

"To drink?" Owen finished the sentence, then wished he hadn't.

Jeb Stuart looked down at his rumpled sheet and shrugged.

"Look," Owen said. "If you had too much to drink, you

were right to wait it out. Sleep it off. I've done some work with the Highway Patrol and Students Against Drunk Drivers. I've seen what happens when kids your age drive after drinking. It isn't pretty."

When the boy didn't respond, Owen said, "Being drunk shouldn't stop you from calling. In fact, I'll make you a deal. Next time you've had a few drinks and think you're too drunk to drive, call me. Even if you're not sure, call me. I'll come get you. No questions asked."

"You weren't home last night."

You didn't know that at the time, Owen thought. Instead of pointing this out, he said, "I'm usually home. If I'm not, I'll let you know how to reach me." Jeb Stuart stared vacantly at the bedclothes.

"Listen, I've been there myself," Owen said. "Same place you were last night. Where do guys go to drink now? Is it still Gobbler's Knob?"

Jeb Stuart shrugged. "Sometimes."

"But not last night. It was raining too hard. Where'd you go last night?"

"Riley Stokes' place."

"He's still living with his uncle?"

"Uh-huh."

"How's that working out?"

"Okay, I guess."

"Riley's over eighteen, right? That how you get booze?"

"I thought you said, 'No Questions Asked.' "

"You're right. I'm sorry." He backed toward the door. "Look. I'm not going to be a hardass about drinking. But I will about drinking and driving."

Owen paused in the doorway. "If I catch you, your car's gone. And you better hope I catch you, because if the cops catch you, your car and your freedom are gone, along with a pile of cash. And if the odds catch up with you before I do or the cops do, it could be even more serious."

Jeb Stuart raised his hands in mock surrender. "All right. All right. I get it."

Owen backed through the door, closed it, and stood with his hand on the knob. He'd been accused of asking too many questions, but he couldn't shake the feeling that he hadn't asked enough. Or, at least, not the right ones.

"Lemme get this straight," Thad Reader said on the phone in a voice Owen imagined he reserved for speeding excuses and drunk-driving alibis, "you're telling me some of the fakes in Burt Caldwell's museum are actually real?"

"I'm telling you it's a real possibility," Owen said. "We're going to have appraised one of the books I think is genuine."

"Course, I hardly think there's anything illegal about labeling the real thing a fake. Unless you want me to arrest those folks for false advertising."

"It could help to explain why a woman who'd just bought a phony painting for forty grand and a shoebox full of baseball cards for almost four grand might wind up murdered."

"You'll have to explain that to me," the sheriff said, the skepticism back in his voice. "In this county, in this economy, forty grand is as good a reason for murder as four hundred."

"Suppose the painting was worth a lot more than forty grand. And suppose only one or two people know how much it's really worth. Then those people in the know have a vested interest in keeping quiet about the real value."

"At least until the auction's over."

"Even after the auction. There are more auctions coming

up. If the word gets out that some of the supposed fakes are genuine, there won't be any bargains left to bid on."

"So you're saying Lotus Mae Graham was bidding as an insider?"

"I'd be surprised if she'd ever been to an auction before. She'd roomed with Mary Kay Jessup. It's a safe bet Mary Kay sent her with inside information."

"Nobody more inside than Mary Kay."

"She may even have bankrolled Lotus Mae."

"Worth another trip to Alderson to talk to her about it. What about your friend the curator?"

"What about her?"

"Any chance she's on the inside too?"

"Not a chance."

"That was a pretty quick answer."

"I mean, I don't see how. She's going to sneak the Fitzgerald book out of the museum to have it appraised."

"So you've told her you think some of her fakes are real."

"She was with me when I got the idea."

"How'd she react?"

Owen tried to reconstruct Victoria's reaction with the bed sheet drawn around her and realized that his attention had been elsewhere. Not wanting to admit this, he said, "Seemed like the idea was brand new to her." Then he remembered that she had wanted to keep the possibility quiet. "I mean, even if everything in the museum was genuine, she couldn't profit from it."

"If all the pieces there were genuine, the feds would sell them off to pay back the bank's depositors. So long as the exhibits are worthless fakes, your friend's got a museum to run."

"So far it's all speculation anyhow. But I can't believe Victoria's keeping anything from me."

"That's what Sampson said about Delilah. When will you know about the Fitzgerald book?"

"I hope we can get it appraised this week."

"Let me know what you find out. In the meantime, don't let your lady friend give you any haircuts."

At two o'clock the next morning, Owen was working on the laptop in his bedroom to learn as much as he could about forgeries, art fraud, and the market for rare books. The Abebooks site put the value of a signed third edition of *This Side of Paradise* with no dust jacket at ten thousand dollars. He guessed that a pristine dust jacket on a signed first edition would triple that, at least, but no one on the Internet seemed to have a signed first for sale. He had a friend who could check recent auction records, but he'd have to wait until the late morning to contact him.

He was starting a Google search for Paul Klee forgeries when he heard a noise downstairs. The noise was faint, but he was sure he'd heard it. He lifted his fingers from the keyboard and listened.

The noise repeated itself. It seemed to have grown even fainter, but there was no doubt it was coming from inside the house. As far as he knew, both Ruth and Jeb Stuart were sound asleep. At least, they'd both gone to bed when the late evening news came on the TV.

Owen stood and slipped out of his shoes. Wearing only a T-shirt and blue jeans, he padded to his bedroom door and cracked it open. Nothing moved to disturb the shadows playing on the wall of the stairwell.

Had the burglar who'd injured Jeb Stuart returned? Was he looking for something in particular? Owen slipped out into the hallway. A floorboard creaked somewhere downstairs. For the first time in his life, he was sorry that he didn't own a gun. His father had owned several, but Owen had no idea where they were stored.

The last doorway before the stairwell opened into Ruth's sewing room. Owen peeked inside, hoping to find some kind of weapon. All he could see in the faded moonlight filtering through the windows was a cordless iron sitting on an ironing board.

Holding the iron in front of him like a shield, he tiptoed down the stairs, skipping the two steps he knew would creak. At the foot of the stairs, he stopped to listen and let his eyes adjust to the dark.

A scuffling noise came from the rear of the house. Too heavy for a rat, he thought. He crouched and moved along the wall of the dining room into the kitchen, where he stood facing two doors. The door leading to the basement was open, but the door to the breakfast room was uncharacteristically closed.

The sound of rustling cloth came from the other side of the breakfast room door. No light shone under the door, so whatever was making the noise certainly didn't belong there.

Owen's eyes made out two of Jeb Stuart's baseball bats propped in the corner of the basement stairwell. He shifted the iron to his right hand and carefully lifted a bat with his left. Another rustling noise came from behind the breakfast-room door.

He turned to face the door feeling faintly ridiculous, a stocking-footed gladiator with a flat-iron shield and a Hillerich and Bradsby broadsword. He reminded himself that there weren't likely to be any tigers on the other side of the door. If their burglar had returned, it was just a skinny teenager, probably strung out on drugs.

He bent his knees and took a few practice swings with his weapons. He'd hit low with the bat and high with the iron. He arced the bat under the iron, crossing his arms in midair. He'd always hated aluminum bats, but at least he wouldn't have to worry about keeping the trademark up.

He approached the closed door and drew a mental picture of the room on the other side. A round breakfast table sat in the center of the room, while a stacked washer/dryer combination occupied the far corner. A door in the near corner led to the backyard. That was probably how the burglar got in.

Owen decided to go through the breakfast-room door low and fast, hitting the light switch with the iron and moving to block the door to the backyard.

He flexed his knees, took a last one-handed practice swing with the bat, and burst through the door. The unmistakable stench of urine assaulted his nostrils.

He caught the light switch on the second try and crouched in front of the back door, clutching his weapons.

Jeb Stuart stood frozen in front of the washing machine, eyes wide and blinded by the overhead light. A stained sheet drooped from the mouth of the washer.

The boy's shoulders slumped. "I wet my bed."

Owen laid the bat and iron on the table and put his arm around Jeb Stuart. "It's all right."

"I didn't want to wake anybody." Jeb Stuart's eyes didn't seem to be adjusting to the light. The irises remained wide black circles.

Owen squeezed the boy's shoulder again and repeated, "It's all right." But he knew it wasn't.

Chapter Eleven:

Side Effects Include Death

"Why're we here?" Jeb Stuart asked. "You can't have me arrested. All I did was take pills that were prescribed for me."

Owen and Jeb Stuart were sitting in the narrow waiting area outside the sheriff's office. Across the counter, a female deputy ignored them to concentrate on a computer.

"I told you," Owen said. "We're not going to have you arrested. But I don't know how to help you, and the sheriff has lots of experience with OxyContin users."

"I don't need help."

"How can you say that after last night?"

Jeb Stuart shrugged. "I'm fine. I can quit anytime."

Thad Reader appeared behind the counter and lifted the gate flap to let them through. "Come on back."

The sheriff held the counter flap up as Owen passed through. When Jeb Stuart started through the gate, Reader stopped him and peered into his eyes. "Thought you had more sense."

"You going to read me my rights?" Jeb Stuart asked.

Reader lowered the counter flap behind Jeb Stuart. "What for? I'm not arresting you."

Jeb Stuart nodded toward the closed counter flap. "Sure doesn't feel like I'm free to go."

"You're not," Owen said. "Not until you hear what the sheriff has to say."

The sheriff led them down a corridor to his office. As Jeb Stuart slouched into a folding chair, he said, "All I did was fill my pain-pill prescription. There's no law against that."

"Where'd you get the prescription?" the sheriff asked.

Jeb Stuart was quiet. Then he said, "Dr. Holly."

"What'd he charge you? Two hundred dollars?" To Owen, Reader explained, "Holly's got a storefront out Route Ten. No receptionist. No exam table. Just a prescription pad and a cash box. You show up, tell him your symptoms, fork over the cash, and he gives you a prescription for OxyContin. Usually has a line a block long in front of his office."

"Can't you shut him down?" Owen asked.

"We're working on it." Reader turned to Jeb Stuart. "Today it's two hundred dollars. Tomorrow it'll be more. Thing about Oxy is, it takes more and more to get you off."

Jeb Stuart slumped down farther in his chair.

Reader reached into his desk drawer and brought out a manila folder. "Let me show you some pictures." He shoved an eight-by-ten photo across his desk. It showed the body of a young man on a morgue slab, covered with a sheet from the waist down. A small high-school yearbook shot was clipped to the upper left-hand corner of the larger photo.

"This boy OD'd on Oxy," Reader said. "He was about your age. His mother had terminal cancer. He stole her pills, sold some, popped some. Pretty soon, he needed to pop them all to get any kind of high. Then he took too many, washed them down with alcohol."

Owen winced, imagining what the boy's family must have felt. If Jeb Stuart was moved at all by the story, he gave no sign.

Reader took another photo from the folder. This one showed a pancaked auto with two sheet-covered bodies in the road next to it. Photos of a young, sideburned boy and a fresh-faced blonde girl were clipped to the corner of the accident picture.

"Here's a boy a little older than you," Reader said. "Got high on Oxy, went off the road. Took his girlfriend with him."

Jeb Stuart gave a sigh that seemed to convey more boredom than sympathy.

"Half the kids in this folder lost control of their cars," Reader said. "The others lost control of their bodily functions."

"I'm not out of control."

"Listen to the sheriff," Owen said. "Don't argue with him."

"What is this?" Jeb Stuart said, "Bad cop, bad cop?" Turning to the sheriff, he asked, "You got a men's room?"

"Down the hall to the right."

After Jeb Stuart had left, Reader shrugged and said, "I'm not getting through. At that age, kids think they'll live forever. The boy doesn't scare easy."

"You're scaring me," Owen said. "What can I do?"

"Cut off his supply. Get him into rehab."

"You're the one who needs to cut off his supply. How can you let those prescription mills operate?"

"Got to build a careful case against them. Need to be sure we're not jailing a legitimate doctor who's prescribing for patients with real pain." Reader shook his head. "Trouble is, when all this started, anybody with a bad back could get a prescription for OxyContin. This here's mining country. Bad backs are common as summer colds. Dave Jorgensen, he's running against me for sheriff, greets every voter by asking, 'Your back any better?' Makes them think he remembers them. Be surprised how often it works."

Reader picked up a pipe from the table and thumped it twice against the desk ashtray. "Anyhow, when folks with bad backs found out they could peddle their prescription pills for ten or twenty times what they paid for them, pretty soon we had an epidemic of bad backs."

"And a plague of doctors willing to prescribe OxyContin."

"Oh yeah. Eighty percent of the pills on the street come from legitimate prescriptions. There's no need for addicts to break into pharmacies."

"But you'd peg Jeb Stuart as an addict?" Owen felt helpless. "It's only been a couple of weeks."

Reader sighed. "Time's got nothing to do with it. Face it, Owen. He's on Oxy right now. Look at his pupils. And he's having trouble controlling his bladder."

"Tell me about rehab programs."

"Well, there's lots of possibilities. The state has a program, but it's not too pretty. I wouldn't want my boy in it. Private rehab clinics are probably your best bet. St. Vincent's has one. I've heard real good things about Barkley Springs. Trouble is, the private clinics charge big bucks."

"How big?"

"Last I heard, Barkley Springs was thirty grand."

Owen's heart sank. "Thirty grand? For a rehab program?"

Jeb Stuart stood in the doorway. "Don't need a rehab clinic. I can quit by myself. Anytime. Won't cost a cent."

"If you can quit anytime, quit now," Owen said. "Why do you need it?"

Jeb Stuart held up his cast. "Dulls the pain. Helps me pass the time till baseball season."

"Baseball season's five months off," Reader said. "You keep on taking Oxy, you won't last five months."

"Those people you showed me. In the pictures. They took Oxy along with other drugs. I'm smarter than that."

"Son," Reader said. "Oxy and smart don't belong in the same sentence. You take Oxy, you get so relaxed you can't control what else happens. Last night you were too relaxed to control your bladder. Get a little more relaxed, and you can't control your breathing. You want to know the clinical term for people who can't breathe?"

"I tell you, I can quit all by myself."

Owen looked at Reader. "Can it be done?"

"I've heard of it happening. But it's not easy. They don't call it 'hillbilly heroin' for nothing." Reader pointed his pipe stem at Jeb Stuart. "First week of withdrawing, you ache all over, your joints stiffen, and you feel like you're chasing a fart through a keg of nails. You'd sell your soul for one of those pills."

Jeb Stuart held up his hand as if to shield himself. "All right, I get the picture."

"It's not that you can't go it alone," the sheriff said. "It's just a lot easier if you've got a rehab center to support you. And you're less likely to backslide."

"I tell you, I can quit whenever I want."

"Well, son, I hope you're right," Reader said. "But from what I hear, it's like entering a kicking contest against a mule."

In the car on the way home, Owen said, "The sheriff thinks the only way to beat this is through a rehab program. Maybe we ought to consider it."

"What about school?"

"We'd have to check out the programs. I'm guessing most of them will help you keep up with your schoolwork."

"Then everybody would know."

"We could try to keep it quiet. Maybe claim you needed to go away to see a specialist for your wrist."

"Who'd believe that?"

Owen dug his fingers into the steering wheel. He felt as if he were losing ground, and the boy as well.

"Look," Jeb Stuart said. "I think I can quit on my own, without going away. Let me try that first. Soon as I get this cast off, I'll give it up."

"No. You need to quit right away."

"Why right away?"

"You heard the sheriff. The longer you use it, the more you need and the tougher it is to quit. And I don't want to lose you."

"So you bought those scare stories?"

"Didn't you?"

"That's what they always do. They show us pictures of fried brains to keep us from smoking pot. Red asphalt pictures to keep us from drinking and driving. But I don't know anybody with a fried brain or road rash. Those things never happen to people you know."

"They happen, though. You saw the pictures." Owen pulled up in front of his mother's house. "Look, I'll grant you some of the anti-drug ads are exaggerated. But the sheriff's stories were real. Whether or not you believe them, though, you've got two choices. Quit on your own or go to rehab. But you've got to do it now."

"Okay. I'll quit now. But I don't need rehab." Jeb Stuart left the car, took the porch steps two at a time, and went straight up to his room. Owen followed him upstairs and watched him throw himself on his bed as if he expected it to fight back.

When Jeb Stuart saw Owen in his bedroom doorway, he said, "I said I'd quit, okay? Don't you trust me?"

"I need to get a few baseball cards from your stash."

"How come?"

"Victoria needs some for the museum." Owen headed for Jeb Stuart's closet.

Jeb Stuart sat up on his bed. "Which ones does she need? I'll get them for you."

Owen reached up inside the closet and felt around the concealed shelf he'd put there when he was a teenager. "That's okay. I'll find them."

"Hey. This is my room."

"It used to be mine." Owen pulled down a shoebox full of baseball cards from the hidden shelf. "I'll just take the box, find the cards I need."

Jeb Stuart shrugged and sank back onto the bed.

Owen raised himself onto his toes and felt around the concealed shelf. "What's this?"

Jeb Stuart sat straight up.

Owen pulled down a plastic baggie holding two small

blue pills. "If you're going to quit now, you won't need these."

"You've got no right to search my room."

"Think of me as your support group." Owen held up the baggie. "Are there any more of these around?"

"No. That's it."

"I'll take your word for it. Don't forget, though. I know all the hiding places in this room. I used most of them myself."

"What did you have to hide?"

Owen thought about his stacks of dog-eared *Playboy* magazines, the Polaroid shot of Robin Hager flashing her breasts, and the crumpled pack of six cigarillos that had turned into a year's supply. "Nothing important. Nothing that would kill me, anyhow."

That evening, Owen logged onto the Internet to learn everything he could about OxyContin. He turned up government-sponsored sites that detailed the nature of the drug and documented related criminal activity; heartbreaking sites sponsored by the parents of teenagers dead of overdoses; sites sponsored by cancer patients praising the drug's pain-relieving potential; and sites promising addicts help ranging from hypnosis to religion.

Several sites sponsored by law firms were fishing for clients in class-action suits against the drug's manufacturer. One of the legal trawlers asked, "If you have taken OxyContin and suffered any serious side effects, such as addiction or death, please contact us for information regarding potential compensation."

The idea of soliciting the dead offended Owen. It was the kind of arrogant, blinkered nonsense he would normally forward to his ex-wife's legal office with an acerbic note. But he couldn't laugh at the image of overdosing teenagers lining up to sign onto a class-action suit just before they drifted off into Nirvana. The problem was too serious. Too immediate. Too close to home.

After three hours at the computer, Owen's eyes burned and his wrists ached. He'd always heard that the death of a child was the toughest situation a parent could face, but the loss of Jeb Stuart to OxyContin addiction seemed worse somehow. He couldn't help feeling it was his fault. If he'd paid more attention to the original prescription, listened more carefully to the doctor's warnings, been more suspicious of the missing money, or known how to interpret the boy's listlessness, all of this might have been averted.

Owen felt just as responsible for Jeb Stuart's predicament as the boy himself. In the lexicon of the Catholic Church, he'd been guilty of a sin of omission, and Jeb Stuart was suffering for it. He didn't know how to atone for his sin, but he knew he had to do something.

The Web site provided him with some information, a little more guilt, and the resolve to bear any cost to pull Jeb Stuart back from the brink of the abyss. While the sites offered no clear directions for the path back from the brink, they did provide contact information for several treatment centers, and he copied them all down.

Owen shut down his computer at two in the morning. For the second time that week, he heard a noise in another part of the house. This time the noise came from upstairs, in Jeb Stuart's room, and sounded like a whimper.

Owen knocked on Jeb Stuart's bedroom door and took the muffled response to be an invitation to enter. The boy was lying crosswise on his bed, curled into a fetal position around a crumpled blanket. The pillow next to his head bore a damp indentation from his sweat-soaked hair.

Jeb Stuart clutched his stomach. His face was flushed as red as the Cincinnati Reds emblem on his sweatshirt. "It hurts. It hurts like hell."

"Is there anything I can do?" Owen asked.

"You can get me those pills you took."

"No, I can't. I flushed them down the toilet."

"Shit. What am I going to do?"

"You're going to beat this thing. I'll get you some aspirin."

The four aspirin Owen took from the medicine cabinet looked small in his hand and he felt as if he were bringing a Band-Aid to staunch a spurting artery. But it was all he could think of to do.

Jeb Stuart eyed the pain killers and accompanying water glass with disdain. "Four aspirin. Woo hoo. Hello big spender." He downed the aspirin in one swallow, then gulped the rest of the water and returned the glass to Owen. Before Owen could set the glass aside, Jeb captured his wrist in a talon-like grip.

"We'll help you beat this thing," Owen said.

"Nobody can help. Don't want to beat it. Not if this is what it feels like." He tightened his grip on Owen's wrist. "I want those pills. Those pills you took."

"I told you. I flushed them."

Jeb Stuart released Owen's wrist, turned his back, and curled around his blanket. "Then you're no help at all."

Owen stood over the bed. The moonlight through the bare trees left a pattern of stripes on the boy and his bedclothes. He felt useless. As a support group, he was supplying about as much support as quicksand.

Jeb Stuart's back trembled in the shadows. Owen lay down on the bed and held him until the trembling subsided and the boy fell asleep.

★ ★ ★ ★ ★

"Everything I see now, I wonder if it's real or fake." Victoria was standing in the main hallway of the Museum of Fakes and Frauds, staring at a purportedly phony Picasso. "I mean, we've got provenance papers for most of these, but they're supposedly fake as well."

"I thought we agreed we'd start with the Fitzgerald book," Owen said.

"I know. It's just that everything looks a little different to me now. Did you come for the Fitzgerald?"

"No. Not exactly."

Victoria smiled, still looking at the Picasso. "Just couldn't stay away, huh?"

"There's that. Actually, I was hoping you could tell me about your experience with Barkley Springs."

Victoria frowned. "They saved my life. What more do you want to know?"

"That was fifteen years ago. What do you know about them today?"

"Why?"

"Jeb Stuart is hooked on OxyContin."

Victoria turned and gathered him into her arms. "Oh, Owen."

Owen hugged her tightly. A group of junior-high students entered the room and split up around the clinging couple as if they were an exhibit. A few girls giggled, and one boy whispered, "Whaddya think? Real or fake?" leading to more titters.

When the students had moved on, Victoria slid her hands down Owen's arms, clasped both his hands in hers, and pulled back from his embrace. "Oh, Owen. I'm so sorry. He seemed like such a button-downed boy."

"He was. I'm not sure he is anymore."

"Is he using now?"

175

"I took his stash. But he wants it. Badly."

"For Barkley Springs to do its job, the boy has to want to be there. Does he?"

"He thinks he can beat it on his own. To his own time-table."

"He can't. No one can."

Owen remembered Jeb Stuart's trembling the previous night. "I think you're right. But what are the chances Barkley Springs can help him?"

"Pretty good, I should think. If you can get him to go voluntarily. And if they'll take him. I understand there's a waiting list. Do you want me to call Russ Harden? He's the head doctor there."

"Would you?"

"Of course." She squeezed his hands and released them. "I thought you'd come for the Fitzgerald book. It's ready to go. Should we mail it to Underdunck?"

"I'd rather deliver it in person. And watch him evaluate it."

"You don't trust him?"

"There's that. If the book and the signature are genuine, he might be tempted to replace them with a forgery."

Victoria cocked her head and raised an eyebrow. "Maybe we could make another weekend trip. I know a few more interesting stops between here and Pittsburgh."

"I'd like that. But I need to get Jeb Stuart back on track first."

The main building of the Barkley Springs retreat was a brick house with a long colonnaded porch. Behind the main house, two long, low, stucco buildings met at right angles and formed a pie-shaped wedge against a curving creekbed. Dr. Russell Harden's office on the second floor of the main building overlooked the wedge-shaped expanse of grass between the stucco buildings and the creekbed. Patients in gray-green sweatsuits relaxed on the grass, sat on concrete benches, or walked along the creekbed. Each patient was accompanied by a white-coated attendant.

Dr. Harden, a slim fifty-ish man with thinning red hair whose face and hands were covered with pale freckles, asked Owen, "So far as you know, this is the boy's first drug experience?"

"I'm reasonably sure of it," Owen said.

"And you feel it was triggered by his broken wrist?"

"The wrist started him brooding. He was inactive for a while and worried about his future. And there was a prescription for OxyContin."

"Is there any history of drug abuse in his family?"

"The boy's father was an alcoholic."

Dr. Harden chewed on the earpiece of his rimless spectacles as he watched the patients on the lawn. "You understand, he would have to come here of his own volition?"

"I understand. Do you think you can help him?"

"We give no guarantees. But our approach has been successful with boys having a similar history."

"How successful?"

"We've managed to be successful over the years because we believe in the individual's ability to work their way free of the scourge of drugs. It's not easy, but the myths that recovery is impossible and that addicts always backslide are just that, myths."

"That's reassuring, but it doesn't answer my question. Just how successful is your program? What percentage of your patients kick their habits?"

Harden wiped his spectacles on the arm of his lab coat. "I'm not trying to dodge your question. I am uncomfortable trying to predict success without meeting the boy. So much will depend on his attitude and desire. It's really difficult to assign probabilities to such intangibles."

"But you must keep records of your successes and failures. All I'm after is some sense of your historical record."

"In order to get that kind of data, we'd have to track our patients for the rest of their lives. We don't have the resources to do that. I can tell you, though, that with similar cases we would expect to find three out of four of our patients drug-free after two years. That's a seventy-five-percent success rate."

"Or a twenty-five-percent failure rate."

"If you choose to look at the negative side, yes. But three out of four is still pretty good odds. Especially in the business of rehabilitating addicts. I'd invite you to check out our competition. They can't come close to our success rate." Dr. Harden counted off other programs by tapping the tips of his fingers with his spectacles. "The state programs can't match our facilities or our staff. There are at least four methadone programs within fifty miles, but they just substitute a less expensive addiction for an expensive one. And then there's the usual assortment of quacks and frauds hawking everything from hypnosis to faith healing. Try to get an honest success rate out of them."

"I have tried. I couldn't."

"Victoria Gallagher has talked to me about Jeb Stuart. I believe we could help him. And we're willing to reserve a place for him. But I understand he's not quite willing to come in on his own."

"No. Not quite yet."

Dr. Harden walked Owen to his office door. "I hope you'll be able to bring the boy around."

"Funny. I was going to say the same thing to you."

The doctor held out his hand. "Then good luck to the both of us."

Owen went down the stairs and out onto the wood porch of the main building. The sun was just beginning to set over the ridge and a faint breeze cooled his perspiring forehead. For the first time since he'd surprised Jeb Stuart beside the washing machine, Owen felt a twinge of hope.

Owen sat in the breakfast room with his laptop, assigning probabilities and dollar values to all the treatments and outcomes he could think of. No matter how many times he ran the numbers, or how much he played with the probabilities, the prospect of losing Jeb Stuart to drug addiction was so devastating that the mathematics said he should be willing to pay any price to avoid it. He didn't disagree with this analysis. He just wasn't sure where he could find the money for a month at Barkley Springs.

He heard his mother rummaging in the kitchen. She poked her head through the breakfast room door and asked, "Can I get you a cup of tea before I go to bed?"

"That would be nice. Thanks."

She nodded toward the computer. "What's got you so wrapped up?"

"Barkley Springs looks like the best treatment center for Jeb Stuart. But to get him in, I need to find thirty thousand dollars and convince him he needs to go."

"Thirty thousand dollars! Owen, this house didn't cost thirty thousand dollars."

"That's the going rate for treatment. A thousand dollars a day for a month."

"Maybe we should wait until February."

Owen's brow furrowed. "Why February?"

"Fewer days to pay for."

Owen didn't smile. It was the kind of offhand remark he might have made himself a short time ago. But that was before he had caught Jeb Stuart with his soiled bedclothes.

"I'm sorry," Ruth said. "I know it's not a joking matter. Look. This house didn't cost thirty thousand. But it's worth lots more than that now. And it's paid for. Why don't I take out a loan?"

"I can't let you do that, Mom. It's my problem. I brought the boy into your house."

"But you don't even have a regular job here in West Virginia. Where will you get that kind of money?"

"My retirement fund. My 401k plan has enough. I'll take it from that."

"Won't you need it when you retire?"

Owen shook his head. "When the stock market tanked, the fund took such a hit I don't think there'll ever be enough in it to let me retire. I might as well put the money that's left there to some good use."

"But isn't there a penalty for taking your money out early?"

"I feel like I deserve it."

Owen knocked on Jeb Stuart's bedroom door. He waited, then knocked again. When no answer came after the third knock, the Web site images of overdosed teenagers panicked him and he flung the door open.

Jeb Stuart lay on the bed with his eyes closed, snapping his fingers to music channeled through a large set of earphones. There was no indication he'd heard Owen enter.

Owen walked to the head of the bed and tapped the boy's shoulder. Jeb Stuart's eyes popped open and stared at Owen. His pupils had shrunk to the size of pinheads and his mouth had relaxed into a slack-jawed grin.

Goddamit, Owen thought. He reached out and tore the boy's earphones off. The thud of an unrecognizable rock lyric played through the discarded headset.

"Easy, man," Jeb Stuart said.

"You said you'd try to quit."

"I'll quit when I get ready to quit. No need to hurry."

"You'll quit now. I've reserved a place for you at Barkley Springs."

"You can't afford it and I can't afford to miss school."

"You can't afford not to. I want you packed and ready to go tomorrow morning."

Jeb Stuart scooted back against the headboard and propped himself up on his elbows. The effort seemed to leave him winded, and he sucked in a gulp of air before saying, "Tomorrow morning?" He shook his head. "No way. You can't make me. You're not my dad."

"That's right. I'm not your dad." A pair of dog tags that had belonged to Jeb Stuart's father hung over the bedpost. Owen lifted them off the bedpost and dangled them over Jeb Stuart's stomach. "Since you brought the subject up, let's talk about your dad."

The hand holding the dog tags shook, and the metal tags bounced and clanked at the end of their chain. "Your dad was an alcoholic, Jeb Stuart. If he'd had a chance to go to Barkley Springs, he might still be alive."

Jeb Stuart clasped the dog tags to keep them from clanking. "You don't know that."

"No, I don't. I do know he wasn't happy being hooked on alcohol. I know he wanted more from you. Expected more from you. So do I."

The boy released the tags and slumped back against the headboard. "It's too hard. Quitting is just too hard."

"It's a lot harder if you try to do it by yourself. That's what

Barkley Springs is for. They'll help you. They've helped to clean up lots of cases like yours."

"What about my teachers? What about coach?"

"I'll talk to the principal. She'll arrange to have your schoolwork sent to Barkley Springs. Your coach doesn't have to know anything about it. You'll be back long before the baseball season starts."

"Oh, man. It's just too much trouble."

"You've already shown me you can't quit by yourself. You want to be an addict all your life?"

"Tomorrow morning?"

"Tomorrow morning. Seven o'clock. They'll let you bring one bag." Owen started to tell him the bag would be searched, but decided to let him find out for himself. If he had more drugs, it would be an easy way to find them.

Jeb Stuart slid back down onto the bed and retrieved his headphones. "All right. You win. I'll be ready to go tomorrow morning."

It had been too easy, Owen thought. The boy had given in too easily. He wanted to believe Jeb Stuart would still be around, packed and ready to go in the morning, but he couldn't shake the fear that the boy might try to run away.

Owen took a blanket and an easy chair from his own room and sat the chair in front of Jeb Stuart's bedroom door. The padded armchair barely fit between the door and the banister the boy had broken through when he fell into the stairwell. He constructed a makeshift bed by setting a folding chair in the narrow hallway facing the easy chair. Then he settled into the cushions of the easy chair, propped his feet up on the folding chair, and draped the blanket over his legs.

He was pretty sure Jeb Stuart couldn't make it out of his second-floor window with his left arm in a cast. If the boy tried to leave, it would have to be through the door Owen was blocking with the easy chair. Blocking with his body, really. He hoped that would be enough.

Owen listened intently, but there was no sound from Jeb Stuart's room. He pictured the boy as he'd left him, lying on his bed, spaced out and communing with his earphones.

Owen had always been able to sleep anywhere, on floors, chairs, or airplane seats, in almost any position. At Cal Tech, he'd completed his PhD thesis by working days and evenings and sleeping on his desk at night, timing his catnaps so he was awake for the rounds of janitors and security personnel. Now, though, he found he couldn't get to sleep. He squirmed in the easy chair, worried that his presence in the hallway betrayed a lack of trust in Jeb Stuart. Well, so what? The stakes were just too high. If the boy didn't try to open the door, he'd never know Owen hadn't trusted him. And if he did try to run, lack of trust wouldn't be an issue. The only issue would be whether Owen could stop him. In a life strewn with failures, this was one job he didn't want to botch.

After two hours of squirming and fretting, Owen finally dropped off into a fitful sleep. He awoke to find Jeb Stuart looming over him. The boy stood in the doorway holding a duffle bag with his good arm and clasping a notebook filled with baseball cards between his cast and his chest.

The boy's pupils were still the size of pinheads, and he wore the puzzled expression of someone who has just been asked for a ticket on a ride he thought was free.

Owen tried to fight off his grogginess. "What time is it?"

"A little before four."

"It's too early. We don't have to leave until six-thirty. Why don't you go back to bed and get a couple more hours of sleep."

The boy dropped his duffle bag and stood with one hand

on the doorknob. There was no easy way around Owen and the armchair.

Owen made no move to get out of Jeb Stuart's way. Instead, he drew his blanket up around his neck and laid back in the armchair. "Go on. Get back to bed. You look like you could use some sleep."

The boy leaned on the doorknob for support. His expression went from frustrated to befuddled.

Owen nodded toward the card notebook. "And leave the baseball cards here. I've got something I need to do with them."

The boy blinked once, as if shutting out the hallway light might help him clear his head. Finally he tugged his duffle bag out of the doorway, said, "Okay, I guess I was a little early," retreated to his bedroom, and closed the door.

Owen breathed a sigh of relief as the door closed. He heard the sound of the duffle bag scooting along the floor, followed by the squeak of bedsprings.

Owen listed intently. After a half hour passed with no sound inside the bedroom, he decided there would be no more escape attempts. Some day, if everything worked out, he'd ask Jeb Stuart where he thought he was going with his duffle bag and the baseball cards. For now, though, he needed to get some sleep.

The sun had not yet cleared the ridge top when Owen, yawning, pulled up in front of the main entrance to Barkley Springs.

"It looks nice," Ruth said from the back seat.

In the passenger seat, Jeb Stuart, who had been quiet throughout the trip, emitted something that passed for a grunt.

Owen reached into his pocket and handed Jeb Stuart the

dog tags that had been hanging on the boy's bedpost. "I took these from your room. For luck."

Jeb Stuart barely looked at the tags and stuffed them into the pocket of his windbreaker.

"A friend told me that her grandfather's dog tags from World War I helped get her through her time here," Owen said.

"What friend was that, Owen?" Ruth asked.

"Just a friend, Mom." Owen took Jeb Stuart's stuffed duffel bag from the trunk and led the way up the steps of the colonnaded porch and into the main hallway of the retreat house.

Dr. Harden met them at the entryway with a burly male orderly who took Jeb Stuart's bag. "We'll take care of you from here on in," the doctor said. "You should say your goodbyes right here."

"Will we be able to visit?" Ruth asked.

"After he's been here a week," the doctor said.

Ruth hugged Jeb Stuart, whose hands hung loosely at his sides. "We'll see you in a week then, hon."

Owen shook Jeb Stuart's hand and put his free arm around the boy's shoulder. "Good luck." The boy's face had the same lost look Owen had seen when he surprised him feeding a soiled sheet into the washing machine.

When Jeb Stuart made no move either to return Owen's half hug or extricate himself, Dr. Harden took the boy's free arm and gently guided him toward the internal hallway. "Don't worry. We'll take good care of him."

Owen and Ruth watched Jeb Stuart follow Dr. Harden and the orderly down the long hallway toward the rear of the building. The boy didn't look back.

The sun had just cleared the ridge when Owen led his mother out of the main entrance onto the long wooden porch.

He blinked to clear his eyes. At the far end of the porch, a teenager with stringy black hair was watering the flowers in a clay planter.

The teenager wore torn blue jeans and a black T-shirt with a yellow dragon on the back next to what looked like a band's tour dates. It was the exact outfit worn by the stringy-haired burglar Owen had chased the day Jeb Stuart was injured.

Chapter Twelve:

Don't Mess with Dragons

Owen put his hand on his mother's arm and whispered instructions for her to wait on the front steps of the Barkley Springs Retreat. Then he started down the long wooden porch toward the thin figure watering the potted plants.

He moved slowly and carefully, both to avoid startling the waterer and to give himself time to consider a course of action. The last thing he wanted was to spook the boy into dropping his hose, vaulting the porch rail, and running away. If that happened, Owen knew from experience he could never catch up.

He'd try to seal off any escape path with his body, take the boy by the arm and turn him gently to check him out. If his quarry looked like the burglar, Owen would grab both his arms and lead him back to Dr. Harden's office.

Halfway along the porch, he was able to read the words on the back of the black T-shirt. The lines next to the golden dragon were not tour dates at all, but the admonition

DON'T MESS
WITH DRAGONS,
FOR YOU
ARE CRUNCHY
AND GOOD
WITH KETCHUP.

He closed in from behind. Water spritzed from the hose and a bee hovered above the spray, waiting its turn at the blossoms.

Owen took the free arm of the waterer and realized immediately that something was wrong. As he hesitated, the figure whirled and directed a quick spray of water at his face, saying, "Back off, perv," in a high-pitched voice.

Owen stepped backward and raised his hands against the spray. When he cleared his eyes, he was staring at the slim figure and pouting lips of a wary teenage girl.

"I'm sorry," he said. "I thought you were someone else."

"Well, I'm not."

Owen rubbed his eyes with his shirtsleeve. "I can see that."

The logo on the left breast of the young woman's T-shirt read "Barkley Springs," with the two mounds of the "B" displaced diagonally to form a mountainous background for an elongated white "S" representing a winding spring.

Owen stared at the logo. "Where did you get that T-shirt?"

"You didn't have to grab me to ask me that."

"I said I was sorry. What about the shirt?"

The girl gestured toward the front door of the spa with the hose. "Inside. There's a little shop. Employees get a discount."

Ruth appeared at Owen's elbow, asking, "What on earth is going on?"

Owen took his mother's arm. "I'll explain later. Right now, we're going back inside."

"We've been selling the shirts for three or four years," Dr. Harden said. "There are a couple of models. One has the AA prayer on the back. The dragon seems to be the most popular version, though."

Owen pulled his wet shirt front away from his clammy skin. "You only sell them to patients and employees?"

"Oh, my, no. We sell them to anyone. We even wholesale them through a few boutiques in Barkley. And Tamarack out Route Seventy-Seven carries them as well." Dr. Harden tapped the cash register in the tiny shop. "The sales help to subsidize our work."

"So anyone can buy them," Owen said. "Any idea how many you've sold?"

Harden shrugged. "We can get the exact number. But I'd guess we've sold at least five hundred by now."

"So it doesn't really narrow things down that the man who burgled our home and broke Jeb Stuart's wrist was wearing one of your T-shirts."

"I don't see how."

Owen mopped his damp brow with a handkerchief. "Whoever it was that burgled our house looked a lot like your Miss Varva from behind."

"Vonnie can be quite a handful. She's one of our successes. We took her off the streets, dried her out, cleaned her up, and she stayed on to help."

189

"We're probably not looking for one of your successes. You don't happen to recall any of your failures that might resemble Miss Varva?"

Dr. Harden scratched at his chin and examined the ceiling as if he might see a vision of the burglar there. "I can't think of any. But most of our T-shirt sales go through outside shops. There's a good chance your burglar was never a patient here."

"I think there's a good chance he was. I know you don't like to focus on your failures, but I'd appreciate it if you'd get me the names of any that might fit Miss Varva's description."

"Mr. Allison, one thing we promise both our successes and our failures is privacy. Our job right now is to cure Jeb Stuart. Finding your burglar doesn't get us any closer to that goal."

"Are you saying you won't help me find the burglar?"

"No. I'm saying I've already helped as much as I'm likely to be able to with your inquiries." Harden squeezed by Owen and Ruth and stood in the hallway outside the tiny shop. "Now, if you'll excuse me, I've got to get on with my own work."

Owen had promised Victoria he would find baseball cards to replace the ones in the museum display so that the display cards could be authenticated by an expert. Of the ten cards in the pyramid display, he felt he could duplicate five from his own collection and get the rest from Brian's Cards in Cincinnati. The only card that would be difficult to replace was the Honus Wagner at the apex of the pyramid.

After delivering Jeb Stuart to the rehab center, he went to the boy's room to retrieve the cards he needed as placeholders. As he took the shoebox and loose-leaf folders

down from the secret closet shelf, he recalled the guilty pleasure he'd always felt as a teenager retrieving treasures from
that hiding place. He also remembered Jeb Stuart's recent
upset over the invasion of privacy when Owen had pulled the
boy's stash of pills down from the hidden shelf.

Settling back on Jeb Stuart's bed with the shoebox and
loose-leaf folders filled with baseball cards, Owen understood another reason for the boy's agitation. The most valuable card in the collection, the Pete Rose rookie card, was
missing. His insides felt as empty as the plastic pocket that
had held the card as he stared at the hand-lettered notation

PETE ROSE—1963 (ROOKIE CARD)

that Jeb Stuart had taped to the page beneath the pocket.

Leafing through the notebook pages, Owen found four
other empty holders. In addition to the Pete Rose, four other
cards were missing. He guessed that the retail value of the
missing cards was close to six hundred dollars. He felt a certain sense of relief as he realized that Jeb Stuart had been
using the cards to finance his drug habit. At least the boy
hadn't been breaking into neighbors' houses or ripping off
electronics stores, two possibilities suggested by Thad
Reader.

Two of the missing cards, the Rose and a reverse-image of
Henry Aaron, were ones Owen needed as replacements for
the museum display. He'd just have to rely on Brian's Cards
for a few more replacements than he'd originally planned. He
didn't need substitutes for all the cards in the display. And he
didn't need authentic cards. Bogus cards would serve just as
well as placeholders while he had the display cards appraised.
He called Brian in Cincinnati and read him a list of the cards
he needed.

"You know I've got the Rose and the Aaron," Brian said. "Your boy just sold them to me."

When Owen was silent a little too long, Brian said, "Oh, Christ, you didn't know. I thought something was fishy, but your boy worked with Richard and they got along so well I didn't interfere."

"It's all right," Owen said.

"No, it's not all right. I gave him a fair price, and I'll sell them back to you for what I paid."

"Okay, but of the cards he sold you, I just need the Rose and the Aaron right now. And any of the others on the list I just read you. I'd especially like cheap knockoffs, if you've got some."

"You're not planning to pass them off as real, are you?"

Owen laughed. "Not really. But if you're worried about that, I'll sell them back to you in a couple of weeks at a discount."

"Sounds like you'd lose money on a deal like that."

"I'll make it up on volume. How many of the cards on the list have you got?"

"Well, there's the phony Mantle I told you about."

"The one your buddy in DC bought."

"Yeah. And I've got a real Ryan and a phony Gwynn I can let you have."

"That's great. Can you ship them right away?"

"I'll take them to the post office this afternoon. You should get them in a couple of days. What's the hurry?"

"It's kind of hard to explain. But I'll have a few more cards for you to appraise soon."

"Another shoebox?"

"Not that many. But I'm guessing you'll find them interesting."

"Bring 'em on."

★ ★ ★ ★ ★

The memory of their last trip to Pittsburgh, especially the stopover at the Hotel Morgan, caused Owen to push a little harder on the gas pedal as he sped along the Interstate with Victoria's head resting on his shoulder. They'd set up a return visit with Lyle Underdunck, and the quicker they finished their business with him, the more time they'd have to dawdle on their way home. As the green mountaintops flew by, Owen felt free and relaxed for the first time since he'd discovered Jeb Stuart's addiction.

He put one arm around Victoria and drew her closer. "I can't tell you how much I'm enjoying this."

"Ummm. The scenery is beautiful."

"It wasn't the scenery I had in mind. It's you I'm enjoying. We should do this more often."

She nuzzled his chest. Her hair smelled of lilacs. "Well, I've got a museum full of fakes. We could have them all checked out."

"Sounds like a great idea." Owen squeezed her shoulder. "How about doing them one at a time? Stretch it out. Make it last."

"Underdunck may catch on."

"So what? He'll be glad to get the business."

Underdunck's office seemed even more cluttered than it had on their first visit. There was barely room for them to stand between the stacks of cardboard boxes and shopping bags full of dust-covered books. Underdunck didn't bother to try to find chairs for the two of them. As soon as they handed over the museum copy of *This Side of Paradise*, he glanced at the cover, flipped to the title page, shut the book and handed it back to Victoria, saying, "You folks could have phoned this in. It's genuine."

"You hardly looked at it," Owen said. "How can you be so sure?"

"I appraised it for Burt Caldwell some years back, when he was deciding whether to buy it. I remember that tiny water stain on the corner of the dust jacket."

"So you're not surprised that it's authentic?" Owen said.

"Why should I be? Caldwell had quite a few valuable firsts. That Fitzgerald was part of a collection that included *The Great Gatsby*, a couple of Hemingways and Faulkners, and some Raymond Chandler mysteries. I appraised them and he bought them all. Never even haggled over the asking price."

"Do you remember the titles?" Victoria asked.

"There was the *Gatsby*, *A Farewell to Arms*, the Hemingway about the sun rising." Underdunck's brow furrowed. "Don't remember the Faulkner titles. Never could get into him. There were two or three Chandlers. I remember he had *The Big Sleep*."

"Don't suppose you kept records?" Owen said.

Underdunck shoved aside a stack of boxes that was blocking his access to a leaning file cabinet. "Got them somewhere. Trick is finding them."

"A list of the titles you authenticated would be really helpful," Victoria said.

The top file drawer screeched as Underdunck tugged it open. "Sounds like you're surprised Burt had a collection of first editions."

"He'd been displaying a lot of those books in his Museum of Fakes and Frauds," Victoria said, "as if they were just as phony as that copy of *The Last Tycoon* that you signed."

"Well, Burt was always quite a kidder." Underdunck pulled three dusty manila folders from the file drawer. "Maybe it was some kind of tax dodge."

"I don't see how it could have been," Owen said.

Underdunck moved a mound of paper to uncover a small copying machine. Then he copied a sheet from each of the manila folders. "These are lists of the three biggest collections Burt asked me to appraise. He bought all three." He handed the copied sheets to Victoria. "Could have done all this by phone and fax. Sorry you wasted the trip."

Victoria folded the sheets and tucked them into the pages of *This Side of Paradise*. Then she took Owen's arm and laid her head against his shoulder. "Oh, don't worry. We're not going to waste the trip."

The package from Brian's Cards arrived the next Monday. Owen added three cards from his own collection to the contents and took the whole batch to Victoria's museum. He waited with Victoria until the museum closed, when she deactivated the alarm system and the two of them replaced nine of the ten cards in the museum's pyramid display with the cards Owen had brought.

The only display card Owen had been unable to duplicate was the Honus Wagner card at the apex of the pyramid. As he slipped the museum's cards into plastic sleeves to take to Brian, he said, "Too bad I couldn't duplicate the Wagner card. Be nice to know whether it's real or fake. A real one brought four hundred and fifty grand at auction a short while back."

"If the other cards turn out to be real, I think we can assume the Wagner is genuine as well."

Owen put the plastic sheets holding the museum's cards into his briefcase. "Cincinnati's not much more than three hours away. If you take tomorrow afternoon off, we could be there before Brian closes."

Victoria shook her head. "You better make the trip alone

this time. Ramsey has us working overtime to get things ready for the next FDIC auction."

"I can wait until the weekend to go."

"No, don't. I'll still be working most of this weekend as well. You go ahead without me. I don't know anything about baseball cards, anyhow."

"It wasn't exactly your knowledge of baseball cards I was hoping to exploit."

Victoria batted her eyelashes. "Why, my goodness. What-ever do you mean?"

"You're better than my AAA Tour Book. You know all the best places to stop in route." Owen smiled. "And all the best rest-stop activities."

"You know, you don't have to travel to enjoy some of those activities. There's lots you can do right here in Contrary. Who was it that said, 'The best part of travel is coming home'?"

"I don't know. But I think it was Samuel Johnson who said, 'The man who is tired of Contrary is tired of life.' "

Brian smiled as Owen took the plastic card-holding sleeves from his briefcase and laid them on the counter. "See you've found a better home for your cards than a shoebox."

"I thought these might be worth a little extra care. Let me know what you think."

Brian carefully removed the Mantle card from its sleeve, held it by the edges to avoid smudges, and examined it with a magnifying glass. He slid it back into its case without com-ment and asked, "How's your boy?"

"I've got him in drug rehab."

"Christ, I'm sorry. If I'd known what was going on, I never would have bought those cards."

"It's not your fault. I appreciate your selling them back to me."

"Least I could do." He seemed to want to say more, but just shrugged. "Damn shame."

"What about the rest of these cards?"

Brian examined each of the cards in turn. By the time he got to the last one, the McGwire rookie card, he was no longer using the magnifying glass. As he put the McGwire card back in its sleeve, he said, "All genuine. All mint. Not a clunker in the lot."

"I thought so."

"The Mantle's the best I've ever seen. Probably bring you twenty grand if you work the card shows. I'll give you fifteen right now."

"Thanks, but it's not mine to sell."

Brian returned the magnifying glass to a drawer behind the counter. "I notice better than half those cards are like the ones I sent to you. But most of the ones I sent you were fake. Got something you want to tell me?"

"Not right now. Maybe in a week or so." Owen slipped the plastic-encased cards back into his briefcase. "Thanks for your help. What do I owe you?"

Brian held up his right hand, palm outward. "On the house. Worth it just to see the Mantle."

Owen held out his hand. "Well, thanks again. I'll fill you in on the card story as soon as I can."

Brian shook the offered hand. "Can't wait. Let me know how it goes with your boy, too. I sure hope he comes out clean. He seemed to be a real nice kid."

"He is."

Before he got back on the road to Contrary, Owen tried calling Victoria at work, but got no answer. He stopped for dinner in Ashland, Kentucky, just short of the West Virginia line, and tried calling her home, work, and cell phone numbers with no luck. He left messages on all three phones, saying, "It's what we thought. Every card was genuine. I'm just crossing the Big Sandy. Can't wait to see you."

Owen covered the roads between Ashland and Contrary in record time and pulled up in front of Victoria's apartment building just ninety minutes after stopping to eat. When no one answered his ring, he headed for the museum. Since she'd been too busy with work to join him on the Cincinnati trip, he expected to find her there or at the warehouse, cataloging items for the next auction.

Victoria's Dodge was parked in front of the museum and he pulled in beside it. Her car, and the fact that the front entrance was ajar after closing time, meant that she must be inside working. Owen took the museum steps two at a time, went through the entrance into the great hall, and stopped short. Something was badly wrong.

Where the fake Picasso had hung on the wall of the great hall, there was only a dim rectangular outline and two dangling electrical leads marking the painting's absence. Bare spots on opposite walls indicated that two other paintings were missing as well.

He called out for Victoria, and her name echoed off the newly bare walls.

His concern mounting, he ran to the curator's office. The door was unlocked, but the office was empty. Owen checked Victoria's answering machine and listened to his own voice saying he couldn't wait to see her. There was no sign anyone else had heard the message.

Victoria was missing. Paintings were missing. He tried to think logically, but worry about Victoria overrode reason. Victoria was missing. Paintings were missing. Was anything else missing?

He hurried to the literary room to check on those first editions he knew were genuine. The glass case containing the Fitzgerald first editions was open, and the only book left was the copy of *The Last Tycoon* with the bogus posthumous signature. The case that had held signed firsts by Hemingway and Faulkner was totally empty.

Owen called out again, not so much because he expected Victoria to hear him, but because he had the edgy feeling he wasn't alone in the museum.

He worked his way up the central staircase, pausing on each step to listen for some sound from another person. Hearing nothing but his own heartbeat and hesitant footsteps, he headed for the room holding sports memorabilia. A bat and several balls lay on the floor amid shards of glass from a shattered display case. The posterboard that had held the pyramid display of baseball cards was missing from the case, along with the cards he and Victoria had substituted for the museum's holdings.

The cards weren't the only items missing from the display case. Glass crunched underfoot as he paced back and forth, trying to remember what else the case had held. All that was left were two autographed pin-striped jerseys that had probably never belonged to Ruth and Gehrig, and a right-handed first baseman's mitt that had certainly never been worn by the left-handed Stan Musial. Owen was almost sure the display had once held a batting helmet, a catcher's mask, and many more autographed baseballs than he could see on the floor.

He needed to call the sheriff. It was one of the few times he missed his cell phone, but he knew he could use the phone in Victoria's office. He turned quickly to go back downstairs and his foot skidded on the shredded glass. The hand he threw out to steady himself glanced off the damaged display case and set off a piercing alarm. He felt a painful sense of déjà vu as the high-pitched squeal rose and fell and rose and fell.

From somewhere downstairs, he heard a door slam shut.

Chapter Thirteen:

Fruit of the Poisonous Tree

Owen ran down the oak staircase toward the main entrance with the alarm reverberating in his ears. The massive double doors at the foot of the stairs, which had been open when he arrived, were now shut tight. He couldn't budge the locked doors, and each time he touched the latch the alarm seemed to grow louder and more insistent.

Two narrow strips of red tinted glass framed the doorway.

Through the tinted glass, Owen could see that his Saturn was now alone in the driveway. Victoria's Dodge had disappeared.

He ran through the main hallway to the rear of the museum, only to find that the back door was also locked. He lowered his shoulder and butted the door like a blocking back, but it held tight. The windows on either side of the back door were bolted shut as well. Whatever mechanism had set off the screeching siren had evidently locked both the doors and the windows.

He had to get out, if only to escape the wail of the siren. He could feel his blood pressure rising with each beat of the pulsating alarm. Maybe the upstairs windows weren't connected to the security system. He ran up the back stairs and tried the window on the second-floor landing. It creaked and moaned as it slid upward, but it opened, letting in a gust of fresh air.

Owen straddled the window sill, then grabbed it and lowered his body until he dangled with his shoes about six feet above the ground. For some reason, the alarm sounded fainter outside. He let himself drop and broke the impact of the fall by tumbling backward onto his rump. As he stared up at the brick walls and open window, the alarm suddenly stopped wailing.

He scrambled to his knees just as a uniformed law officer rounded the corner of the museum. It was the same tall deputy who had answered the alarm when Owen and Victoria had set it off together. This time the deputy had his gun drawn and was saying, "Hold it right there, buddy."

The tall deputy, whose name tag read GILLIS, herded Owen around the side of the museum toward the front entrance where the deputy's squat female partner waited. "You again," his partner, whose tag read DOWNEY, said when she saw Owen. "I can't wait to see the videotape this time."

Downey stepped aside to let Owen and Gillis pass through the large oak doors into the main hall of the museum. "Holy shit," Gillis said when he saw the empty wall space that had held the missing paintings. "Looks like the alarm was for real this time."

Downey followed them in and asked Owen, "Got something you want to tell us?"

"The paintings were missing when I got here," Owen said. "The doors were open. I just walked in and found it this way."

"You picked a strange way to leave." Gillis turned toward his partner. "I caught him dropping from a second-floor window."

"I panicked when the alarm sounded," Owen said. "All the downstairs doors and windows were locked."

Downey twirled a batch of keys on a large ring. "It's the security system. It locks the museum down tight just as soon as the alarm goes off."

"So what brought you here?" Gillis asked Owen.

"I came to see my friend the curator."

"The one whose ass grabbing set off the alarm last time we were here," Downey said.

Owen kept silent, refusing to rise to the deputy's bait.

"So did you find your friend?" Gillis asked, twisting the word "friend," until it was off-center and off-color.

"No. She didn't appear to be here." He decided not to tell them about Victoria's car until he'd had a chance to contact her.

"But you found something that made you want to leave through a second-story window," Gillis said.

"I told you, the alarm panicked me."

"It's easy enough to find out what went on," Downey said. "I'll go have a look at the surveillance tapes."

As Downey disappeared down the hallway, Gillis asked, "That your Saturn out front?"

Owen nodded.

Gillis waved his hand at the empty walls. "Think if I looked in the trunk I might find some of the missing paintings?"

Owen dug into his pocket, came up with the car keys, and handed them to Gillis. "Be my guest."

"So I've got your permission to look, then?"

Owen nodded again.

"I'll be right back. Don't go leaving through any more windows."

Alone in the main hall, Owen looked at the bare walls and wondered about the missing paintings. Had Victoria taken them, along with the books and baseball cards? Was she the one who'd driven the Dodge away? He couldn't believe it. No, that wasn't quite right. The truth was, he didn't want to believe it.

Owen thought about trying to call Victoria again, but he was afraid of what he might find out if he contacted her, and afraid of what he'd think if he couldn't contact her. Why would she have taken the baseball cards from the exhibit, though? She knew they were fake. The real ones were in his briefcase.

His briefcase. His briefcase was still in the car. How could he have given his car keys to Gillis? He should have gone along with the deputy to make sure the search didn't go any farther than the trunk. Maybe it wasn't too late. He started toward the main entrance, then stopped short when Gillis came through the door. Owen's heart sank when he saw that the deputy was carrying the briefcase from the front seat of the car.

Owen had never understood the expression "shit-eating grin," but he was pretty sure if he looked it up the dictionary would have a picture of Deputy Gillis' face right at that moment. The grin never wavered as Gillis laid the briefcase on the side table under the space once occupied by the missing Picasso. It was still in place when Deputy Downey reentered the room from the side hallway. Downey's face bore no grin of any kind.

"Any luck?" Gillis asked.

Downey shook her head. "Not a lot. What about you?"

Gillis tapped the briefcase. "Some interesting stuff here. Why don't you go first?" he said with the air of a man who was confident he could overtrump any information uncovered by his partner.

Downey shrugged. "Can't figure it out. Looks like the surveillance system was turned off just after the museum closed. Didn't start up again until this guy here was poking around the baseball exhibit upstairs. Some of the downstairs cameras are still out."

"Baseball exhibit, huh? That fits with what I found in his car." Gillis snapped open the briefcase and pulled out the plastic holders containing the baseball cards Owen had just taken to Brian's Cards. "What I remember from our last trip here, these cards belong in that upstairs exhibit."

"I was bringing them back," Owen said.

"Of course you were," Gillis said. "Funny I didn't realize you were returning them. Maybe it's because the cards were locked in your car and you were crawling out of the back window."

"I took them to have them appraised."

"And the appraiser was?"

Owen gave them Brian's name and the phone number of his shop.

"And who gave you permission to take the cards out of the museum?" Gillis asked.

"The curator, Victoria Gallagher."

"Your friend from our last get-together," Downey said. "How can we reach her?"

Gillis wrote down the number Owen recited and tried calling both Brian and Victoria. "Funny, neither of those people seem to be answering their phones. Maybe you better come downtown with us."

"Downtown?"

Gillis read Owen his rights.

"This is ridiculous," Owen said. "You're holding me because you can't contact either of those numbers."

"We get to the office," Gillis said, "you can try calling them yourself. You're entitled to one call."

"Call your boss. I told him what I was doing. Give him a call."

"Our boss?"

"Sheriff Reader."

"I know who our boss is," Gillis said.

"Then you know how to reach him. Give him a call. He'll vouch for me. And he'll be pretty pissed if you run me in without contacting him."

Looking unsure of himself for the first time since he'd returned with Owen's briefcase, Gillis dialed the sheriff's number. He nibbled a thumbnail as he held the receiver to his ear. Then his face relaxed and he turned the earpiece so Owen could hear the busy signal.

Gillis hung up the receiver. "You going to come quietly, or do we have to cuff you?"

"I'll go quietly. But you'll keep trying the sheriff's number?"

"Don't worry," Gillis said. "Even if we can't reach him tonight, he'll be in first thing tomorrow morning."

The holding cell was tight and cramped, with a fold-down metal cot along one wall and a toilet next to it. Owen sat on the cot, listening to the indistinct buzz of voices in the outer office. From the booking officer's reaction, he would have guessed that the museum burglary was the biggest crime to hit Contrary since Prohibition moonshining.

Deputy Gillis came back to check on Owen every fifteen minutes, the way a collector keeps returning to the album page holding his prize specimen. Each time the deputy showed up, Owen asked him if he'd been able to contact the sheriff. Each time, the deputy shook his head, saying, "Sheriff's down county visiting his kinfolk. Cell phones don't work down-county."

"Will you please keep trying," Owen said. "The sheriff knows why I took those cards."

"You've got a phone call coming. You're welcome to try him your own self." Gillis hooked his thumbs under his gun belt. "Like I keep telling you, though, he'll be here in person come eight o'clock tomorrow morning. I was you, I'd use that phone call to get me a good lawyer. 'Pears to me you're going to need one."

The second time Gillis suggested that Owen call an attorney, the deputy used the phrase "lawyer up," and intimated that in his experience it was a sure sign of guilt.

Owen suspected that Gillis' only experience with "lawyering up" came from watching TV shows, but he also suspected that the deputy wasn't trying very hard to contact Thad Reader. It was after nine o'clock, close to bedtime for the only lawyer in West Virginia Owen knew well enough to trust. He took the deputy's advice and used his phone call to ring Guy Schamp.

Guy Schamp was at least thirty-five years older than Owen and roughly four inches taller than Owen's six feet. He was slim and slightly stooped, either from age or from bending to make eye contact with shorter companions. He'd flown fighter planes in World War II, and had gotten to know Owen when he'd defended Owen's great-aunt Lizzie against a murder charge.

The lawyer sat on one end of the fold-down cot, his long legs crossed in front of him. The sharply creased pants of his white-linen suit rode up to reveal yellow socks with clock faces on the ankles. From time to time he would interrupt Owen's story by raising a manicured finger and asking a question in a soft Virginia drawl that Owen knew he had cultivated to cover the nasal twang of a native West Virginian.

"So you gave the deputy permission to search the trunk of your car?"

"That's right. I gave him my keys."

"But your briefcase was in the front seat?"

Owen nodded.

"And was it open? Could he see the baseball cards through the window?"

"No. The briefcase was closed. Does it matter?"

"We could argue that you only gave permission for him to search the trunk, which would make the front seat off limits without a warrant and the briefcase made inadmissible as the fruit of the poisonous tree."

"Would that work?"

"Might. Depends on the judge. Trouble is, you gave the deputy the keys and you probably looked guilty as sin to him. After I got here, Gillis kept me waiting while he regaled two reporters with tales of your capture. The phrase 'red-handed' came up frequently."

"The sheriff will vouch for me."

"Better hope he does. I wouldn't want to have to defend you in court if he doesn't."

"Will it come to that?"

"You were caught dangling from the window of a burgled

museum with baseball cards from that museum in your possession. If nobody backs up your story about how you got those cards, I'd say you're looking at a tough trial."

"But Victoria Gallagher gave me the cards to have them appraised."

"And you didn't tell the police about Victoria's car?"

"No. I didn't want to involve her."

Schamp wrinkled his nose as if he'd inhaled a vile odor. "Owen, wake up and smell the disinfectant. Victoria Gallagher has left you holding the bag. She's the one who wanted to keep the appraisal secret. She's the one who stayed home while you went to Cincinnati. She's the one who's missing now. I'd say Amelia Earhart's a better bet to come back than your friend Victoria."

"I just can't believe she'd do it."

Schamp spoke slowly, as if he were instructing a dull student. "Suppose she didn't do it. Suppose someone else was driving her car. Then your lady friend's out of the way somewhere. Whether she's guilty or not, she's not likely to be available to testify on your behalf. And you're not helping yourself by keeping quiet about her car."

"All right, I'll tell them." Owen agreed with Schamp's analysis, but the decision still felt like a betrayal. Still, if Victoria had stolen the paintings, then he was the one who'd been betrayed. And if she hadn't, if someone else had taken her car, then she was in worse trouble than he was.

If Victoria was in trouble, he couldn't help her from inside a jail cell. Owen slammed his hand down on the metal cot so hard the bedding jumped. "You've got to get me out of here. Gillis can't hold me without charging me, can he?"

"Actually, he can. For twenty-four hours at least. But I don't think he will."

"Why not?"

"He knows you're a friend of the sheriff. He still has to answer to his boss."

"If that's the case, why am I still here?"

"The story plays better with the press if the deputy can say he has a suspect in custody. My guess is, he'll hold you just long enough to keep your release out of tomorrow morning's paper."

"So I'm stuck here just so Gillis can see his name in the *Barkley Democrat*."

"That's the bad news. The good news is he won't dare keep you overnight." Schamp checked his watch. "You should be out of here within half an hour." He stood and called for a guard. "I'll go make sure Deputy Gillis understands his options."

Instead of the jailer who had admitted Schamp, Deputy Gillis answered the lawyer's call. He turned a large iron key in the cell door, opened it, and stood aside.

"You're being charged with attempted burglary," Gillis said to Owen. "But I don't see you as a serious flight risk. You're free to go under your own recognizance. Just don't leave the county."

Schamp's face, which was cross-hatched with wrinkles, relaxed into a smile that deepened the horizontal wrinkles and obscured the vertical ones.

"What's so funny?" Gillis asked.

"Nothing," Schamp said. "You're about half an hour early, is all."

It started as one of those dreams that you want to hold onto, even though you know it must be a dream. Owen and Victoria were naked on a narrow cot, clinging and whispering to one another. They rolled over, and over, and over again and she was above him, her dog tags bouncing between her bare breasts. Then they rolled over again and left the cot, separating from each other as they dropped through space. Victoria reached out for him, but she began to fall faster and faster, disappearing into a black void. Owen kept falling, following her into the void, seeing nothing but darkness until he heard a loud thunk and awoke with a start.

He recognized the thunk. It was the sound of the morning newspaper hitting the porch. He'd been awake most of the night, unable to sleep. The one good thing about his insomnia, he'd thought as he'd tossed and turned, was that he'd be able to get to the morning paper before his mother had a chance to read it. But he'd fallen asleep at the last minute, with the sun creeping over the ridge line and crickets chirping in the backyard.

He threw off the sweat-drenched sheet and pulled on the same rumpled jeans he'd worn in the jail cell. There was still a chance he could get to the newspaper first.

He tore downstairs barefooted, only to meet his mother coming in from the porch. She was wearing a quilted robe and holding the folded newspaper under her arm.

"Owen, you're up early," she said. "I'll fix us some tea."

"I was hoping to check out the newspaper."

Ruth unfolded the paper and handed him the sports page. "Here's your part. Come on into the breakfast room. It'll be nice to have company this early."

As Ruth refolded the newspaper, Owen caught a glimpse of a picture of Deputy Gillis rousting him from a squad car in front of the jail, under the front page headline BOGUS BURGLARY. Unfortunately, his mother saw the picture too. She stopped halfway through the dining room and read the article with a deepening frown.

Ruth let the paper drop to her side and steadied herself

against the dining-room table. "Owen, what on earth is going on? This says you've been charged with burglary."

"Attempted burglary. But it's all a mix-up, Mom. The sheriff will straighten it out as soon as he gets in this morning."

"I don't understand."

Owen reached out for the paper. "It's pretty complicated."

Ruth kept the paper just out of his reach. "Don't tell me it's complicated. I'm not senile yet. Just tell me what happened."

"First, let me see what the paper says."

Ruth surrendered the newspaper. "All right. But I want to hear your side of the story as soon as you've finished reading."

Owen spread the newspaper out on the dining-room table and began reading.

THE BOGUS BURGLARY

Remember the joke about the Mingo County redneck who held up a poker game and made off with all the chips? Something like that happened at Contrary's Museum of Fakes and Frauds yesterday, when a gang of burglars broke in and made off with a bogus Picasso painting and several books with the forged signatures of authors like Hemingway and Fitzgerald.

Responding to the museum's alarm system, Deputy Lawrence Gillis interrupted the robbery in progress and apprehended one suspect, Barkley native Owen Allison, as he attempted to escape through a second-story window.

The article went on to sketch the history of the museum, describe Owen as a consultant sometimes employed by the county, and mention Deputy Gillis several more times before concluding, "Deputy Gillis remains confident that the remaining burglars will be apprehended soon. In the meantime, West Virginians would be well advised to postpone any Picasso purchases."

Owen handed the newspaper back to his mother. " 'Sometimes employed' implies I'm mostly unemployed."

"Never mind about that. Tell me what you were doing crawling out of a second-story window."

Owen sighed and told Ruth how he and Victoria suspected that several of the museum's "fake" holdings were actually authentic, taking her from their first meeting with Lyle Underdunck to his second-story escape into the arms of Deputy Gillis.

"And you saw that woman driving away in her car?" Ruth asked when he had finished.

"No, Mom. I saw Victoria's car leaving. I didn't see who was driving it."

"I warned you about her."

"Mom, you've warned me about every woman who wasn't Judith."

"And how often have I been right?"

"We don't even know that you're right this time." Owen felt his frustration building. "And maybe you should have warned me about Judith. She's the one who had the affair that killed our marriage."

Guy Schamp laid a sheaf of papers on the corner of Thad Reader's desk and handed him the top sheet. "This is a copy of an affidavit from Brian Forbes of Brian's Card Shop. My client, Owen Allison here, told Mr. Forbes that the cards he was having appraised did not belong to him and that he had no right to sell them."

Reader glanced at the statement, then handed it back to Schamp. "Doesn't matter. Forget about it. I knew Owen was having the cards appraised. We've dropped the charges against him." Turning to Owen, he said, "Sorry if my deputy gave you any trouble last night. Sometimes he's more interested in press clippings than police work."

"Is he after your job?" Schamp asked.

"No. But we've had enough run-ins so he wouldn't be too unhappy if Dave Jorgensen beats me in November."

"So you haven't been able to find Victoria?" Owen said.

The sheriff shook his head. "Not yet."

"I'm afraid something's happened to her."

"What's happened to her is she's taken off with the museum's most valuable items," the sheriff said.

"I can't believe she'd do a thing like that."

The sheriff waved his hand as if he were shooing away flies. "Why? Because she's good in bed? Owen, you're thinking with your dick."

Owen looked to his lawyer for support.

"Don't look at me," Schamp said. "I'm eighty-five years old. I can't remember the last time I thought with my dick. Enjoy it while you can."

"Wake up, Owen," the sheriff said. "You told me she was getting a line on the fake paintings. Now some paintings are missing, along with your friend Victoria. The other missing items are the books and cards you authenticated together."

"So why'd she take the cards?" Owen asked. "She knew I'd replaced the real ones with fakes to get Brian's appraisal."

"You didn't replace the Wagner. If it's real, it's worth more than all the rest combined."

Owen had run out of arguments. "You could be right. I may be thinking with other parts of my anatomy."

"Don't see it matters much whether you're thinking with

your heart or your dick. Or even your head," Reader said. "Whether Victoria is doing this or having it done to her, our job is still the same. We've got to find her."

Ruth got to the newspaper first the next morning. She was sitting at the breakfast table reading the front page when Owen joined her. She slid the front section across the table and poured him a cup of tea. "This paper is barely good for wrapping garbage. I only take it because they give me the day and date in big print right on the front page. And they usually get that right."

"Don't tell me it's worse than yesterday."

"No. But it's not as good as it could be. It just says a suspect was released. When you're arrested, they give your name and address. When they let you go, you're nameless, but still a suspect."

Owen sipped his tea and scanned the article. Sheriff Reader was quoted as being confident there would be a break in the case soon and praised his staff for their rapid response to the security alarm; Deputy Gillis was mentioned twice; there was no hint that the missing items were anything but fakes and forgeries.

Across the table, Ruth said, "Oh my God. It's outrageous." Her hands trembled as she folded the editorial page and passed it across to Owen.

The column below the fold was titled BLIND JUSTICE.

The strange case of the burglary at Contrary's Museum of Fakes and Frauds keeps getting curiouser and curiouser. The sheriff's office announced yesterday that it was dropping charges against the prime suspect for lack of evidence. Excuse us for asking, but how much evidence is necessary? The suspect was caught exiting a second-floor window of the museum with stolen goods in his possession. Of course, it helps that the suspect, Owen Allison of Barkley, is an old friend, associate, and sometime employee of incumbent sheriff Thad Reader. The suspect was also allegedly carrying on a clandestine relationship with the museum's curator, who is currently missing and, according to Sheriff Reader, a suspect in the robbery. It makes you think Reader's election opponent, local businessman David Jorgensen, has a point when he says, "A few people in this county may be getting the justice they pay for, but the voters aren't."

The tea burned in the back of Owen's throat as he stared at the newsprint. "I better call Thad Reader."

He dialed the sheriff's office and was patched through. Reader's voice was brusque, preoccupied. "Yeah, what is it?"

"Thad, it's Owen Allison. I just read this morning's *Barkley Democrat*. Looks as if turning me loose may have cost you a load of votes."

"Well, what the hell. I figure I balanced that by cinching yours."

"You'd have had mine anyhow. Except I'm still registered in California. You've got my mom's vote though."

Ruth was still frowning over the editorial, but she managed a curt nod.

"That's what I'm after," Reader said. "Quality votes. The hell with quantity."

"I'll tell her you said that."

"Hey, listen. What do you know about Victoria Gallagher's background?"

"Not much. She talked about a grandfather who served in World War I. I think his name was Keller. Why?"

"The real Victoria Gallagher was a ward of the state. She didn't know her parents, let alone her grandparents. We ran some prints from your friend's apartment. It looks like the woman using Gallagher's name is wanted on felony charges in North Carolina."

Ferdinand Waldo Demara Jr. (1921–1982) was one of the busiest imposters in American history. A high-school dropout, he was able to teach himself advanced skills, ingratiate himself with diverse employers, and inhabit a wide variety of roles. During the Korean War, he served as a lieutenant-surgeon in the Canadian Navy, where he took out tonsils, amputated limbs, and once successfully removed a bullet lodged within a fraction of an inch of a soldier's heart. At various times he taught English, French, and Latin to high-school students, psychology to college students, served as a Trappist monk, performed biomedical research into cancer cures, and passed himself off as an American soldier, a law student, a hospital orderly, a sailor, a deputy sheriff, and a guidance counselor in a maximum-security prison. His exploits inspired a best-selling book and a 1960 movie starring Tony Curtis.

From the Museum of Fakes
and Frauds' Hoaxers Hall of Fame

Chapter Fourteen:

Victoria's Secret

Thad Reader's desk was littered with several thick file folders. The sheriff shoved the thickest across the desk to Owen. A wallet-sized photo of a sullen, pockmarked woman was clipped to the upper edge of the file.

Reader nodded toward the photo. "That's the real Victoria

Gallagher. She was orphaned early and enlisted in the Army at the tail end of Vietnam. Mustered out after four years with a slew of drug and alcohol problems. She bounced between jails and rehab programs in the early eighties before she dropped off everybody's radar screens. Her prints are on file, but there's no sign of them in your Victoria's apartment."

Owen flinched inwardly at the phrase "your Victoria." "Whose prints did you find there?"

"Yours, for starters. Others we couldn't place. But most of them we traced to a woman named Claire Marie Weiler."

Reader tapped a second thick file. "Claire Marie ran a day-care center in North Carolina in the early eighties. Got swept up in the mass hysteria over child abuse. She and a teenage helper were accused of molesting their charges, holding satanic rituals, sacrificing animals, and a lot of other questionable acts."

"Let me guess. All the evidence was pried out of children's 'repressed memories' by a team of well-meaning witch-hunters."

Reader nodded. "Something like that."

"I thought all those charges had been pretty much discredited."

"For the most part. Turns out getting people out of jail can be a lot tougher than getting them in. Some states, everybody convicted of those trumped-up charges has been released. Other states, people are still serving time. North Carolina never caught Weiler, so there's still an active warrant out for her arrest."

Reader made a sour face and shook his head. "Not exactly law enforcement's finest hour. What I get from the official papers, Weiler and her husband tried to fight the charges, spent all their savings on lawyers, and the strain got to be too much. She started drinking, he filed for divorce, and she disappeared from sight."

"Disappeared before her trial?"

Reader flipped open the manila file folder and consulted the top sheet. "Last seen in 1987. Still a fugitive from justice."

"Fugitive from injustice, you mean. Those trials were a joke."

"Not to the parents. And not to the prosecutors."

"Come on. They ruined innocent lives on the strength of hoked-up testimony from impressionable kids."

"You'll get no argument from me."

"You can't blame Victoria for running from that mess."

"Claire Marie, you mean."

"She's still Victoria to me."

Reader extracted a photo from the manila folder. "Here's the last known picture of your Victoria before she disappeared."

The picture showed a thirtyish woman with long dark hair framing an attractive oval face. Unmistakably a younger version of the woman Owen had known as Victoria Gallagher. Somehow the phrase "your Victoria" didn't have the bite it carried when Reader had first used it.

"That's her, all right," Owen said. "The hair's darker and longer, but it's Victoria." The picture only deepened his sense of loss and frustration.

Owen pulled the sullen ID photo of the real Victoria Gallagher free from its paper clip and placed it next to the photo of the younger version of the woman he had known as Victoria. "Not even close."

"Wouldn't have to be. The real Victoria Gallagher didn't have many friends and Weiler wouldn't expect to run into anybody who knew her namesake in a little place as remote as Contrary." Owen felt a pang of betrayal. He'd told her everything, and she hadn't trusted him enough to share the central fact of her life. He realized he didn't have a photo of the woman he'd known as Victoria and asked, "Do you have a current picture?"

If Reader thought the question was strange, he gave no sign. Instead he opened a third file folder and slid a wallet-sized photo over to Owen. "Here's her employee ID."

It pained Owen to look at the current photo. He spread his hands over the three pictures: Victoria now, Victoria then, and the real Victoria. "Can I get copies of these?"

"What for?'

"I want to look for her."

"That's our job, not yours."

"I'm making it mine."

"God help us." Reader thumbed a buzzer on his desk. When Deputy Downey showed up in his doorway, he handed over the three photos and asked her to make copies.

"What happened to Victoria's husband?" Owen asked. He understood that he would go on calling her Victoria. It was Victoria he wanted to find. Not some stranger named Weiler.

"He's remarried. Living in South Carolina. Claims he knows nothing about his ex-wife's whereabouts. I'm sending a deputy down to interview him and take a look around."

"Can I go along?"

"Absolutely not. You're still a suspect in the burglary. You read the newspapers. The *Democrat* is already crucifying me for letting you go free. How will it look if I ask you to help find the likely perpetrator?"

"She didn't do it. She couldn't have done it."

"We've been through this before. That's your dick talking."

"No. No. I trust her. And I'll find her."

"You know something I don't?"

"I certainly hope so. But not about her disappearance." Owen moved both hands in front of him as if he were trying to mold an explanation out of thin air. "It just doesn't feel right. Her being guilty, I mean. On the way over here, I was expecting you to tell me she was an escaped axe murderer or something. And that sure didn't feel right either. Instead, you tell me she's the innocent victim of a hysterical witch-hunt. Suppose she came back to the museum and found the paintings missing. Her past alone explains why she'd want to drop out of sight."

Reader shook his head. "Owen, you're making this a lot more complicated than it is. Before we tracked down this identity thing, I would have bet the farm that your friend Victoria had run off with the paintings. Knowing what we know now, I'll bet the farm and my youngest daughter."

"You've only got sons."

"Then I'll bet my youngest daughter-in-law."

"She's the one you can't stand? The nagging vegetarian who landed your son with a hysterical pregnancy?"

Reader raised both hands in surrender. "All right. Have it your way. But think about this. If she's innocent, someone or something is keeping her under wraps. Or worse. If she's guilty, she doesn't want to be found. And she's good at hiding out. She's done it for over fifteen years."

"If she's in trouble, she needs my help. If she took the paintings, then she played me for a sucker. Either way, I want to find her. But I'll look a lot harder believing she needs me."

Deputy Downey returned with the photocopies. Reader handed them to Owen. "I can't give you much more help than these pictures. You're on your own. But for God's sake, be careful. The woman you're hunting has taken the identity of a missing person. The real Victoria Gallagher hasn't been seen for fifteen years. Think about that."

Owen put the current photo of the Victoria he knew on top of the stack of three pictures before pocketing them. "I am thinking about it."

★ ★ ★ ★ ★

The security procedures and bare walls reminded Owen of the Alderson Prison Camp where he and Thad Reader had interviewed Mary Kay Jessup. But the room wasn't part of a prison, and Thad Reader wasn't with him this time. Instead, he was in the visitors' quarters of the Barkley Springs Retreat with his mother, and the interview subject pacing on the other side of the spare green table was Jeb Stuart Hobbs, celebrating the completion of his first week at the rehabilitation center.

"I don't belong here," Jeb Stuart said for the third time. "You guys are wasting your money."

Jeb Stuart's statement had stung Owen each time he'd heard it. But he ignored it for the third time. "You're getting along okay? The school is sending your homework over?"

"Oh, yeah. Like nobody at the school was supposed to know I'm here." Jeb Stuart stopped pacing and pointed a shaking finger at Owen. "Little Dickie Ramella's been bringing my assignments. Surprised he can pull his nose out of the principal's behind long enough to make the trip. The way his tongue wags, we might as well buy prime-time TV ads telling everyone where I am." The boy resumed pacing. "I tell you, I'm ready to leave right now."

"You're system needs time to dry out," Owen said. "And you need more time to get used to drying out."

"That's all you know. Drying out's for alcoholics. That's not me. Druggies get clean. I'm no druggie, but I am clean. Clean as a whistle. Thing is, I could have done it just as easy at home. I tell you, I don't belong here. This place is for people with real drug problems. There are guys here who've been doping longer than I've been alive. One of them OD'd just two days ago."

Owen felt as if they were speaking two different languages,

and he desperately wanted to communicate with Jeb Stuart. "Has it been hard quitting?"

"Not too bad. Like a bad cold. The worst is over, though. I'm ready to go home."

Ruth had endured as much as she could. "Jeb Stuart Hobbs, I'm tired of listening to you talk like that. Owen here has cashed in his retirement money to send you to this place. You will finish this program without any more complaints or you won't have a home to come back to."

Stunned by Ruth's outburst, Jeb Stuart stopped pacing and sat down. "Yes ma'am."

"Now tell us a little something about your first week," Ruth said.

"Biggest news all week was Vonnie Varva turning her hose on Owen here. That must have been something to see."

"I thought she was the person who burgled our home and put your wrist in that cast," Owen said.

Jeb Stuart fingered the dog tags dangling from his neck. "Not a chance. Wasn't no girl did this to me. Besides, Vonnie's straight as they come. She's the poster girl for this place. Come here, dried out, and stayed on to help out."

"It was my mistake," Owen said. "I deserved to get splattered."

"Lucky you didn't try grabbing her brother," Jeb Stuart said. "I hear he's a real hardass."

"A brother?" Owen's eyebrows jumped to attention. "She has a brother? Have you seen this brother?"

"No. He busted out of here. Come here same time as Vonnie, but didn't last a week. Left his own legend behind, though. Know those two stone tigers on either side of the entrance gate? He left one of them in the fish pond. Nobody knows how he managed that."

"Must be a pretty big guy," Owen said.

Jeb Stuart shrugged. "Like I said, I never seen him."

"What's his name?" Owen asked.

"Vinnie."

"Vinnie and Vonnie? Sounds like twins."

"Can't prove it by me. Dr. Harden might know."

Owen rose from the table. "I think I'll pay the good doctor a little visit. I'll be right back."

Dr. Russell Harden looked up from his desk and smiled when Owen entered his small, book-lined office. "Mr. Allison. Come in."

"I hope I'm not interrupting anything."

"Not at all. My door is always open." He closed the file he'd been reading and laid a well-chewed pen on top of it. "So far, your boy is doing just fine. In fact, he's been a model patient."

Owen exhaled slowly, making a sound close to a sigh. "You wouldn't know it by talking to him."

Dr. Harden tilted his rimless spectacles forward and peered over them. "How so?"

"He's just spent most of our visit telling us we're wasting our money here."

"That's typical, I'm afraid. Most of our teenage patients think their parents have overreacted by sending them to us."

"But Jeb Stuart's treatment is going well from your standpoint?"

"Oh, yes. He's responded well to therapy, participates in group discussions, and the school tells me he's keeping up with his homework."

"Plays well with other children?"

Harden squinted over his spectacles, then smiled. "I guess I did sound rather like a bloodless report card. It's an occupational hazard. Please forgive me. I should warn you, though, that it's much too early to offer any sort of post-treatment prognosis. We've had model patients who, consciously or subconsciously, are just waiting to get out so they can go right back to drugs, and we've had patients who fought us tooth and nail but stayed clean afterward."

"Maybe they didn't want to come back."

"That's always a possibility. Still, you should be glad that Jeb Stuart is doing well so far." Dr. Harden adjusted his spectacles, turned his eyes to the file folder he'd been reading, and retrieved the pen from the top of the folder. When Owen made no move to leave, the doctor asked, "Is there something else?"

"As a matter of fact, there are a couple of things I wanted to ask you."

Harden returned the pen to the file folder. "Oh?"

Owen took the fifteen-year-old photo of the woman he still thought of as Victoria Gallagher out of his wallet and showed it to Harden. "Do you recognize this woman?"

Harden glanced at the photo, then scanned Owen's face as if he'd been asked a trick question. "Of course. That's Victoria Gallagher."

"Actually, it's not." Owen showed Harden a second photo. "Turns out this is Victoria Gallagher. Ever see her before?"

Harden shook his head, then pointed to the first photograph. "If that's not Victoria Gallagher, who is it?"

"Her name's Claire Marie Weiler. But she's the woman you treated as Victoria Gallagher?"

Harden frowned and nodded. "Oh, yes. One of our real success stories."

"And you've never seen the other woman?"

Harden examined the photo carefully. "Never."

Owen returned both photos to his wallet. "There's one

other thing. I understand from Jeb Stuart that Vonnie Varva has a brother."

Harden nodded. "Vinnie. Yes. Not one of our real success stories."

"A week ago, when Miss Varva sprayed me over a case of mistaken identity, I asked you if any of your failures might resemble her."

"Yes, I remember."

"You said no one came to mind."

"No one did."

"But you just told me Miss Varva's brother was one of your failures."

Harden's face reddened under his pale freckles. "In the first place, Miss Varva's brother bears scant resemblance to his sister. And in the second place, you continue to assume that your search for a petty burglar trumps our confidentiality agreement with our patients. Let me assure you, Mr. Allison, that it does not."

"Let me assure you, Dr. Harden, that the petty burglar you seem to be shielding could be linked to much more serious crimes."

Dr. Harden took two deep breaths and seemed to regain his composure. "Even so, Jeb Stuart is our chief concern here. Not your burglar. Let's try to remember that."

"I'm not likely to forget it. Do you have a picture of Vinnie Varva?"

Harden reacted as if Owen had requested a nude photo of his wife. "A picture?"

"A picture. It's not as if a picture will violate your confidentiality agreement. I already know Varva was a patient here. And I'm not exactly asking for sealed psychiatric records."

Harden hesitated. "I don't know."

"I can always come back with the sheriff." It occurred to Owen that Vonnie Varva might have a picture of her brother, but he didn't want to let Harden off the hook. Besides, given their history, Vonnie was even less likely to cooperate with him than Dr. Harden was.

Harden rose from behind his desk. "I'll see what I can find." He left the office to go directly across the hall. Owen heard the squeal of a file door opening and the whirr of a copy machine.

The doctor returned with a snapshot of a smiling, beefy young man with straggly hair. The snapshot was attached to an employment application that listed Varva's current address as the Barkley YMCA. The application was three years old.

"You're right, he doesn't look much like his sister from the front," Owen said. "I take it he didn't get the job."

"He gave us enough trouble as a patient. I wasn't about to ask for more. Does he look like the person you chased?"

"I'd need a rear view to answer that. I mostly saw the burglar from behind. But Jeb Stuart had a better look."

Thad Reader glanced at the picture of Vinnie Varva and flipped it back across his desk to Owen. "So Jeb Stuart thinks this is your burglar?"

Owen picked up the picture. "He said the burglar's hair was longer. And it all happened pretty fast. But he thought that could be the guy."

"Interesting. We've been looking for Varva for six months ourselves. He's wanted for a convenience-store holdup and is a suspect in a couple of burglaries."

Owen tapped the picture with his forefinger. "Got a more recent photo than this one?"

Reader retrieved an album filled with mug shots, leafed

through it, and showed Owen a picture of a pasty-faced young man with stringy black hair. "Shot's about a year old."

"It's the burglar I chased, all right," Owen said. "But you haven't been able to find him?"

"We'll look harder now that we know he's still around. I'd kind of assumed he'd left the county."

"I didn't expect him to be in hiding," Owen said. "That makes it a lot tougher."

"If my job were easy, everybody would want to do it. Think of the mess that would make on election day."

"Long as I'm here," Owen said. "Can I see your files on Victoria Gallagher and Claire Marie Weiler?"

Reader tilted his head forward and squinted over his spectacles. "What for?"

"I want to trace their whereabouts over time. At some point they must have crossed paths."

Reader took off his spectacles and rubbed his eyes with his thumb and forefinger. "I don't know. If it gets out that I've let you see files on a case where you're a suspect, the *Democrat* will crucify me."

"The news doesn't have to get out."

Reader shook his head. "It will, though. My office has been leaking like a rusty colander. I'm guessing half my staff will be voting for Jorgensen on election day."

"Can we wait until the opposition factor goes home?"

"Sad to say, I've got enemies on every shift." Reader pointed the earpiece of his spectacles at Owen. "Tell you what. We'll pretend you're still looking at mug shots. I'll set you up in the interview room and have Deputy Downey load you down with mug-shot albums. Meantime, I'll see that the case files for Weiler and Gallagher are in the same room. You act like you're reviewing mug shots and go through the case files when nobody's looking. When you're done, call Downey and tell her you've identified Vinnie Varva as the burglar who ransacked your home."

Reader gathered up the case files on Weiler and Gallagher and the album of mug shots and led Owen to a small, nearly bare room at the rear of the building. He put the two case files in the bottom drawer of the room's lone file cabinet, installed Owen at a pale green institutional table with the album of mug shots, and called Deputy Downey to order more mug shots.

The deputy showed up struggling under the weight of four heavy albums. She deposited them on the table next to the album Reader and Owen had opened.

Reader tapped the stack of albums, saying, "These should keep you busy for a while." Then he led Deputy Downey to the door, turned to tell Owen, "You're on your own. Holler if you see a familiar face," and closed the door.

Owen waited for a few minutes, leafing through the open album of mug shots to pass the time. Then he retrieved the case files of the real and fake Victorias from the file cabinet and began taking notes. In the case of the real Victoria, he listed every city named in her file, along with the dates she'd been there, as well as the names of every acquaintance or counselor mentioned. She'd been jailed twice, for narcotics possession in Lexington and for shoplifting in Charleston, and had been in and out of treatment centers through most of the eighties. Owen copied down the name, date, and location of each treatment center.

Owen felt vaguely guilty going through the police file of his Victoria, Claire Marie Weiler. Why hadn't she told him? Why hadn't he asked about her past? The woman's pre-trial record was sparse. She was born in 1958 in Raleigh, North Carolina, where she'd gone to high school. She'd graduated from the University of North Carolina with a Bachelor of Arts degree in 1980, married Johnny Earl Weiler in 1982, and settled in Asheville. None of the cities named matched any of the places on the real Victoria's list.

The bulk of the file on the fake Victoria was given over to the details of her arrest and the charges of molestation and rape. Owen found the charges sickening, both for their outrageous detail and for the pain they must have inflicted on his Victoria. Two five-year-old cousins, with their memories "restored" by child-guidance professionals, had testified to animal sacrifices in a dark basement, fondling by a red-headed clown, and penetration with broom handles and coke bottles.

The Weiler's day-care center had no basement, no animal carcasses were ever found, and there was no physical evidence of molestation on either child. A search of the center, however, uncovered a clown suit in a storage hamper with other costumes.

He felt saddened and outraged at the injustice that wrecked Claire Marie Weiler's life and turned her into a fugitive named Victoria Gallagher. He could trace his own setbacks, his divorce and business failures, to bad choices and poor decisions. But at least the choices and decisions were his own. What happened to his Victoria was like being hit in a crosswalk by a red-light-running drunk at high noon.

Thad Reader cracked open the door of the interrogation room to ask how things were going.

Owen riffled the pages of the thickest file. "Still about an hour to go. This stuff from Victoria's trial seems like a cruel joke."

"Lot of that going around at the time. Day-care owners are still in jail in Massachusetts."

"Makes the Salem witch trials look like models of jurisprudence."

Reader nodded. "I'm having pizza sent in. Pepperoni and mushrooms. Want to join me for dinner?"

"Aren't you afraid the papers might accuse you of coddling criminal suspects?"

"I'll leave off the mushrooms. Show I'm tough on crime."

F IS FOR FAKE

Hungarian-born Elmyr de Hory was one of the most prolific art forgers of all time. He bought and reused old canvasses, tore blank pages out of old books to get properly aged drawing paper, forged records of authentication, bribed experts, and inserted pictures of his fakes in genuine art books. De Hory was exposed in 1967 when 44 post-impressionist canvasses sold to a Texas millionaire were appraised as forgeries and fellow Ibiza resident Clifford Irving penned his biography, *Fake!*. De Hory subsequently painted Irving's picture for the cover of TIME when the author was himself convicted of fraud for faking Howard Hughes' autobiography.

Facing possible prison term, de Hory committed suicide in 1976. According to Orson Welles, who told the painter's story in his last full-length film, *F is for Fake*, de Hory left behind hundreds of masterworks still assumed to be genuine and a large number of exposed fakes which have become valued collector's items.

From the Museum of Fakes
and Frauds' Hoaxers Hall of Fame

Chapter Fifteen:

Going Once

Owen still had twenty pages of the Weiler file to finish when Reader appeared in the doorway carrying a two-liter container of Coke and a large pizza from Johnny Angelo's. He set aside the file to clear space on the table and followed a slice of pizza with a swallow of Coke from a paper cup before asking Reader, "How's the campaign going?"

"The *Democrat* won't let up on me. They claim I'm ignoring the obvious in the museum burglary."

Owen wiped his mouth before attacking a second slice of pizza. "With me being the obvious suspect?"

"Right. The rest of the state's newspapers have picked up on the theme. Did you see today's *Gazette*?"

Owen shook his head. "We only get the *Democrat*."

Reader left the room and returned with a copy of the *Charleston Gazette*. He folded the second section to an article entitled MUSEUM ROBBERY REMAINS A MYSTERY. The lead sentence of the article read, "Sheriff Thad Reader of Raleigh County, who brought the state notoriety by sending deputies to guard the New River Bridge in the aftermath of 9/11, has his hands full with the theft of bogus paintings from Contrary's Museum of Fakes and Frauds."

The article went on to list the items missing in the bold daylight robbery, quote FDIC representative Mitchell Ramsey's observation that even fraudulent artifacts could have significant value, and speculate on the whereabouts of the missing curator. There was no mention at all of Owen.

"Seems like a pretty straightforward article to me," Owen said. "I don't see that it helps you or hurts you."

"They bring up that nine-eleven stuff again. The newspapers just won't let it alone."

"What the hell. So you sent men to guard the New River Bridge. Who knew how many targets there were at the time? Or what they were likely to be. The feds sent troops to guard Disneyland, for Christ's sake."

"But it pleases the national press to make us look barefoot

and backward. As if nothing in West Virginia could be worth saving."

"But this isn't the national press. The reporter covers the state capitol. And he doesn't come down too hard on you." Owen pointed at the article. "The quote from Victoria's boss is interesting, though."

"Ramsey, the FDIC guy?"

Owen nodded. "He seems to be saying some of the museum's holdings are worth more than anyone thought."

"He's just using the burglary to hype their DC auction this weekend. There's a piece on it inside that section."

"Think he suspects some of the fakes are real?"

Reader examined the pizza slice he was holding, considering the question. "I interviewed him after the robbery. He seemed pretty surprised anyone would go to the trouble of stealing those paintings."

"Maybe his surprise was just as phony as the paintings the burglars left behind. Maybe he was in on the theft."

Reader swallowed half the slice and wiped his mouth. "I haven't ruled him out. I'm a trained investigator, after all."

"Even if he didn't have anything to do with the theft, it might have tipped him off that some of the museum's holdings aren't fakes."

"Be interesting to see what he puts up for sale this weekend."

"And who comes to bid on it." Owen eyed the last slice of pizza and decided to leave it. "This whole mess started at the FDIC's first auction. As a trained investigator, shouldn't you take in the second one this weekend?"

Reader smiled. "I was planning to do just that. As a public-spirited citizen, would you like to join me?"

The second FDIC auction of museum holdings took place at the Hyatt Regency in Arlington, Virginia, across the Potomac River from Washington, DC. Thad Reader and Owen Allison drove to Arlington in separate cars, then met in the hotel coffee shop before going to the ballroom where the auction was to take place. Reader had brought along a young deputy whose name tag read SINCLAIR, but whom the sheriff referred to as Zeke.

As the three men entered the hotel ballroom, it was obvious to Owen that the FDIC had added several refinements to the Arlington auction that weren't in evidence at the first auction in Contrary. Instead of signing in by hand at a long table, bidders registered by computer in a separate meeting room and received a four-color catalog displaying the items to be auctioned. The catalog was a distinct improvement over the Xeroxed lists supplied at the Contrary auction.

In the ballroom itself, bidders occupied plush leather seats instead of folding chairs, and nearly all the seats were filled when Owen arrived with Reader and his deputy. The auctioneer, who stood at the podium chatting with Mitchell Ramsey, wore a navy-blue ascot instead of the bolo tie favored by his Contrary counterpart. Next to the podium, two young women in black sheath dresses staffed phone lines to handle call-in bids.

For Owen, the biggest difference between the Contrary auction and the current affair was Victoria's absence. He kept scanning the Arlington crowd in the irrational hope that she might show up.

The omnipresence of armed guards marked another difference between the Arlington auction and its Contrary predecessor. Pairs of uniformed security personnel wearing Sam Browne belts and holstered revolvers stood guard at the doorways to the registration room, the ballroom, and the display room where the items to be auctioned were available for viewing. Inside the display room, more guards stood at either end of the four long rows of tables that held the items themselves.

Owen wandered up and down the display aisles, hoping to find some baseball memorabilia. He concluded that autographed bats and trading cards were too down-market for this up-market event. He was about to return to the auction ballroom when he saw a familiar face.

Lyle Underdunck stood in front of a glass case containing first editions by Faulkner, Hemingway, and O'Hara. A printed sign inside the case warned that the author's signatures on the title pages were suspected forgeries.

"Admiring your handiwork?" Owen asked Underdunck.

"It's not all my work," Underdunck said.

"Some of the signatures are real, you mean."

"That's why I'm here. I thought I might pick up a few bargains." Underdunck moved away from the glass case, as if afraid his gaze might give away the location of any first editions with legitimate signatures.

Owen followed Underdunck out of the display room and saw Thad Reader standing at the rear of the auction ballroom. He reached the sheriff at the same time as a bald man wearing a bright-orange shirt open so far at the throat that its collar points nearly hid the lapels of his blue blazer.

"Hey there, sheriff," the bald man said.

Reader held out his hand. "Almost didn't recognize you, Jesse. Last time I saw you, you had a lot more hair."

The man ran his hand over his bare, shiny dome. "Yep, no more trips to the barber for me." He opened his lips in a wide grimace and let his upper plate clack down onto his lower plate. After he'd worked the plate back into position with his tongue, he grinned and said, "Nor to the dentist neither."

Reader stretched his lips into a thin half-smile. "Owen,

this is Jesse Jessup. You've met his wife, Mary Kay. Jesse, this is Owen Allison."

Jessup shook Owen's hand. "Oh, yes. Believe I've seen your name in the papers. Here to case the joint, or are you figuring on bidding?"

"Just here as a spectator. Will you be bidding?"

"Got my eye on a few pieces. Hear this gal Joan Miro is a real comer." He pronounced the name Mah-Roe, so that it took Owen a few seconds to realize Jessup was talking about the Spanish painter.

"Not likely to come very much farther," Owen said when he'd translated Jessup's twang. "Been dead for a while now."

"So I hear," Reader said.

"That so?" Jessup clapped the sheriff on the shoulder. "Well, I got to find me a seat before they all fill up."

Owen watched as Jessup's cowboy boots clacked off across the inlaid parquet floor. "Think we should tell him Miro's not a gal?"

"He knows," Reader said. "Jesse's not as dumb as he acts."

"Thank God for that. His act gives hillbillies a bad name." Owen recalled their interview with Mary Kay Jessup in the Alderson prison. "Hard to imagine him and his wife as a pair. They been married long?"

"Long as I've known them. Mary Kay was quite a looker in her prime."

"Didn't you tell me she had something going with Burt Caldwell?"

"So folks said. Jesse stuck with Mary Kay through the rumors. Now Caldwell's dead, Jesse's wife's in jail, and he's sole proprietor of a fifty-room mansion in the hills above Barkley."

"Not nearly so dumb as he acts."

Mitchell Ramsey ascended the podium to announce that the auction was about to begin. As bidders filed in from the display room, a stocky, bearded man with one arm entered through the main door and struggled past several seated bidders to take a seat in the center of the second row.

Owen nudged Reader and nodded toward the one-armed man. "There's the big bidder from the first auction."

"The one who dropped out of sight." Reader gave a quick wave of his hand and pointed out the newcomer to Deputy Sinclair, who was standing beside the main exit. "Anybody else you recognize from that first affair?"

Owen shrugged. "The only other bidders I really remember are the dagger lady and a Cincinnati Reds fan." He looked around the ballroom, which was filled with dark-jacketed males and business-suited females. "Don't see any baseball caps in this crowd."

Owen scanned the backs of the bidders' heads once more. He knew that if Victoria were in the crowd, she'd be disguised, and he had the crazy hope he'd be able to recognize her erect posture from the rear. He realized how futile that hope was when he kept losing his focus and all the pearl necklaces, ear lobes, white collars, and women's necks started to look alike.

Owen nudged Thad Reader again. "There is one person I meant to point out earlier." He nodded toward Lyle Underdunck. "That blue suit on the aisle in the back row is the man who forged signatures for Caldwell."

"That makes at least three folks we need to keep an eye on," Reader said. "The forger, the one-armed man, and Jesse Jessup."

"All the unusual suspects."

The auctioneer stepped to the podium. Instead of relying

on the rapid-fire delivery of his Contrary counterpart, he spoke in mellow, sepulchral tones as if he were inviting each bidder to join him in a conspiracy.

The first items to be auctioned were the modern first editions Owen had seen Underdunck examining. The forger didn't bid on the first three novels offered, two Hemingway titles and O'Hara's *Appointment in Samara*. All three went for between three and four thousand dollars apiece to different bidders.

"Four grand for a book," Reader whispered to Owen. "Makes me think I ought to visit our library."

"The books seem to be genuine first editions, even if the signatures are suspect," Owen said. He noted that the winning bids were nearly double what comparable volumes had brought in Contrary. Either the change in venue or the publicity generated by the theft had pumped up the bidding considerably.

Underdunck made the opening bid on the next book, Faulkner's *The Sound and the Fury*. Other bidders raised the price to three thousand dollars when the one-armed man joined the competition. By the time the bid reached five thousand, Underdunck and the one-armed man were the only two bidders left.

"It's like those two know something the others don't," Reader said, as Underdunck and the one-armed man carried the bidding to seven thousand dollars.

"Underdunck certainly does," Owen said. "I'm guessing that's Faulkner's real signature on the title page."

"Still doesn't make me want to join in the bidding," Reader said.

The one-armed man had the same hesitant way of bidding Owen remembered from the previous auction. Each bid was preceded by a long pause, then delivered in a raspy voice that sounded as if it had been torn from his throat by a torture in-strument.

After the one-armed man's rasped bid of seventy-five hun-dred dollars, Underdunck mopped his brow, shook his head, and retired from the bidding.

Neither Underdunck nor the one-armed man bid on the next four offerings. When Faulkner's *Sanctuary* went on the block, however, both men joined in the bidding, driving the price past five thousand dollars and leaving competitors be-hind. This time Underdunck took home the prize with a bid of fifty-five hundred.

Owen checked the program. Two Chandler mysteries were scheduled to be auctioned off before a batch of indi-vidual paintings went up for bid. He leafed through the pages, which had obviously been printed before the museum robbery. The stolen Picasso appeared on the page following the first editions, and Owen recognized one other missing painting among the pieces promised for auction.

Neither Underdunck nor the one-armed man bid on the two Chandler mysteries, which went for three thousand dol-lars apiece, or on the two paintings which followed in the pro-gram. Owen thought the paintings looked undistinguished, and wasn't surprised when neither fetched more than the minimum bid of five hundred dollars.

The auctioneer announced that the fake Picasso listed in the program was not available and skipped to the next painting in the program, an imitation Joan Miro entitled *Bleu VI*. The painting featured a red slash of color that appeared to be striking a series of six black balls against a sky-blue back-ground.

The one-armed man opened the bidding for five hundred dollars and outbid all comers until there was no immediate answer to his bid of four thousand dollars.

241

The auctioneer raised his gavel and intoned, "Going once, going twice . . ." and was just about to slam the gavel down when Jesse Jessup shouted, "I bid five thousand." It was his first bid of the afternoon.

The one-armed man glared at Jessup, hesitated, and rasped out a bid of fifty-five hundred.

Jessup smiled into the glare and bid seven thousand.

When the one-armed man upped the bid to seventy-five hundred, Jessup gave his auction paddle a dismissive wave and said, "I'll raise to ten thousand."

The two men went on trading bids, with Jessup either countering the one-armed man's hesitant offerings immediately or waiting until the auctioneer announced, "Going once . . ." and inserting a last-minute bid with a broad smile.

When the bidding passed thirty thousand dollars, Reader said, "To hell with libraries, I'm going to get me a brush and some paints."

The back-and-forth bidding continued until Jessup raised the level from forty-five to fifty thousand with a quick bid that barely beat the auctioneer's gavel. The one-armed man slumped in his chair and shook his head, waving off any further bidding.

The auctioneer banged his gavel to award the painting to Jessup, who exhaled noisily, making a "Whooee!" sound that was part relief and part hog-call.

The crowd reacted with a smattering of laughter and applause, which the auctioneer silenced with a bang of his gavel.

Mitchell Ramsey announced that the next two paintings in the program were not available for bidding and the auctioneer skipped to a series of fox-hunting prints. The one-armed man slumped deeper and deeper into his chair with each bid on the hunting prints. Finally he rose and made his way to the main exit, where he had a short conversation with the secretary at the welcoming desk before leaving the ballroom.

Reader nodded to his deputy, who followed the man out the door.

When three more fox-hunting prints had been auctioned off and neither the deputy nor the one-armed man had returned, Reader and Owen followed their trail out of the auction ballroom.

Reader's deputy was standing at the end of a short hallway leading to two restrooms. The deputy nodded toward the door of the men's room. "He went to the setup room, picked up the book he won, and then stopped off in that restroom."

"How long's he been in there?" Reader asked.

The deputy shrugged. "Not too long."

"You go outside," Reader said. "Cut him off if there's an exit we can't see from here."

"What's he done?" the deputy asked.

"Maybe nothing. But we want to question him about the Lotus Mae Graham murder."

The deputy hurried toward the hotel exit while Owen and Reader pushed through the restroom door. An orange-suited janitor with black hair and a moustache to match was mopping the floor under the row of sinks.

A pair of feet was visible under the door of one of the four toilet stalls.

Reader slammed open the doors of the three unoccupied stalls. All empty.

The janitor straightened and rested both his hands on the top of his mop handle. "Can I help you guys?"

"Did a one-armed man come through here?" Reader asked.

The janitor tilted the end of his mop handle toward an

open window at the end of the row of urinals. "Somebody was going out that window when I was coming in. Happened so fast, I didn't count his arms."

Reader leaned out the window, which opened onto a parking lot. "It's a bit of a drop." The sheriff nodded toward the occupied stall. "Wait here," he said to Owen. "Check out the arms on that guy when he's done."

The sheriff straddled the window sill, let himself down until he dangled by both hands, and dropped about four feet to the ground just as Deputy Sinclair appeared in the parking lot.

The occupied stall opened and a short, stooped elderly man headed for the row of sinks and washed both his hands. The janitor resumed mopping.

Owen went to the window and leaned out. "No luck here. See anything out there?"

The deputy shrugged.

"He got by us somehow," Reader shouted to Owen. "Wait there. We'll backtrack and join you."

Owen shut the window, glad he didn't have to follow Reader through it into the parking lot. He turned and nearly slipped on the mop-slickened surface as the janitor wheeled his mop bucket out of the restroom door. The stooped man followed him out.

Owen looked in each of the toilet stalls for some sign of the one-armed man. He felt faintly foolish doing it, but something didn't seem right to him.

Deputy Sinclair came through the restroom door and held it open for Reader. "I don't understand how he got by me."

"Out the window, that's how," Reader said.

"But the doorman was taking a smoke break in the parking lot. He didn't see anybody come out of the window."

"He couldn't have been watching the window the whole time," Reader said.

"Should we call the Arlington cops, ask them to look for a one-armed, bearded man before he gets too far away?"

"I don't have a lot of faith in the local police," Reader said, "and it's not as if we've got any evidence he's connected with the Graham murder."

"His disappearance this time sure looks suspicious," Owen said.

"The guy might not be too hard to find," the deputy said. "How many bearded, one-armed men can there be in this city?"

Owen stood staring at the window. Something was wrong with the picture. "That window's a tough drop for a one-armed man." Then he saw them. Two plastic saw horses were stacked in the corner under the last sink. The saw horses read

CAUTION
WET FLOOR

Owen looked from the stacked saw horses to the still-wet mop tracks leading out of the restroom door. "Christ," he said. "It was the janitor."

Reader, Owen and the deputy charged out of the restroom and ran down the main hotel corridor, throwing meeting room doors open. The mop stood in its wheeled bucket behind the third door they opened.

Reader made a quick search of the room, then reached into the murky mop water and pulled out a soaked strip of gauze and a mane of wet hair that lay draped across his hand like a dead animal.

He shook the discarded beard at his deputy, spattering water on the floor. "You wanted to know how many bearded, one-armed men there were in this city? I'd say about one less than we counted on."

THE GREATLY EXAGGERATED DEATH OF TITAN LEEDS
Early in the eighteenth century, a man named Titan Leeds
published an astrological almanac full of questionable pre-
dictions. When Benjamin Franklin introduced a rival publication, *Poor Richard's Almanac*, in 1733, he predicted that
Leeds would die on October 17, 1733, at 3:29 p.m. Even
though Leeds failed to die at the appointed time and continued to publish his almanac, Franklin insisted that the
death had actually occurred and that Leeds' publication had
been taken over by associates misusing his name. Subsequent editions of *Poor Richard's Almanac* perpetuated this
hoax, memorializing Leeds on each anniversary of his
"death."

As the public came to believe that Leeds' publication was
in other hands, sales of his almanac declined while those of
"Poor Richard" climbed. When Leeds actually died in 1738,
Franklin praised the publisher's associates for finally admitting the fact of his death.

From the Museum of Fakes
and Frauds' Hall of Historical Hoaxes

Chapter Sixteen:

A Death a Day

Owen, Thad and Deputy Sinclair raced to the parking lot. No
cars were leaving. None were arriving. There was no sign of
the escaped janitor.

"He could be anywhere by now," Reader said.

"He could still be in the hotel," Owen said. "Maybe he's even got a room there. Maybe the Arlington cops would help us look."

Reader's mouth stretched into a look of disgust. "What would we tell them? That we're looking for a formerly one-armed man?"

"I'm sorry," Deputy Sinclair said. "I let him get away."

"We all let him get away." Reader patted his deputy's shoulder. "Forget it. He's not home free yet."

"He's got to be our man, though," Owen said. "He was the missing piece at the first auction. Then he shows up at the second one in the same disguise."

"Why the same disguise?" Deputy Sinclair asked.

"Why not?" Reader said. "It worked once. He had no reason to think we'd be watching for him. Besides, nobody looks too closely at the disabled. All you see is the handicap. When he shucked it, he fooled us all."

Reader and Owen turned to walk back to the hotel. "So you think he had something to do with the Graham murder?" Deputy Sinclair asked, catching up with them.

"He's the most likely suspect," Reader said. "Hell, he's the only suspect."

"So far." Owen said. "Maybe we ought to keep an eye on your friend Jessup, though."

"Why?" Reader asked. "He wasn't even at the first auction."

"Lotus Mae Graham outbid the one-armed man for an expensive painting and wound up dead. Jessup just did the same thing. Both of them were probably acting as agents for Jessup's wife."

"Good point." Reader stopped at the hotel's revolving door and turned to his deputy. "How about you head back to the auction. When it's over, bring Jessup to me. I'll want you to stick with him and his painting. Ride all the way home with him if that's where he's headed."

"Where'll you be?"

"I'm going to check with the hotel people. Look over their reservations. See if anybody remembers a one-armed man."

"If he registered here, he probably used both arms to do it," Owen said.

"Even if he did, he had to change sometime. Maybe some of the hotel staff saw him coming or going." Reader nodded toward the registration desk. "I'll hang out here for awhile. See what I can turn up."

"Want me to stick around too?" Owen asked.

"No. He's seen you twice at both auctions. If he's still around, you might spook him."

Owen tapped Reader's Sam Browne belt. "You think you won't spook him wearing that uniform?"

"I've got a change of clothes in the patrol car. And I've just come by a fake beard that could turn me into a master of disguise. I figure I'm all set for a little undercover surveillance."

Owen laughed. "That wet beard would make you about as inconspicuous as a nun in a nudist colony. Maybe you just better stay out of sight."

"I plan to do just that."

Owen got back to Barkley at two o'clock Sunday morning and went straight to bed. When he awoke, Ruth had hot tea and a newspaper waiting for him at the breakfast table.

She shoved the front section of the newspaper across the table. "You've been out of the news for three days now. I'm surprised the *Democrat* is able to stay in business."

Owen scanned the front page of the paper. Something was out of place, but he couldn't put his finger on it. Then it came to him. The football scores in the corner box were high-school scores. Sunday's paper should have the results of college games. "Mom, this is yesterday's paper."

"It's just like the *Democrat* to get the date wrong." Ruth's teeth worked on the back of her lower lip. "I guess I didn't notice." She left the table to hunt through a stack of newspapers beside the rear door. Finally she looked up, puzzled. "I can't seem to find today's."

Owen took a quick look through the newspapers near the top of the stack. Then he went through the kitchen and dining room to the front door. The morning newspaper was on the porch, still encased in its blue plastic wrapper. Owen felt a sharp pain in his stomach and flinched when he bent to pick up the paper.

He wiped the worried look off his face, tucked the paper under his arm, and returned to the breakfast table. "Mystery solved."

"Where was it?"

"Still on the front porch."

The worried look he'd tried to hide showed up on his mother's face. "It must have been delivered late."

Owen gave his mother the front section of the paper and kept the rest. He rifled through the pages, looking for anything about the burglary or the auction. "Nothing here. What about your section?"

Ruth raised her eyebrows. "Nothing about you. But there's a lot here about your friend."

"My friend?"

"The Gallagher woman. Except this article says that's not her real name. Ruth folded the paper and handed it across the table. The headline below the fold read

BURGLARY SUSPECT
FOUND TO BE ESCAPED FELON

Owen scanned the article. He couldn't bring himself to read the details. The sheriff must have wanted to show some public progress on the case. Either that, or one of his deputies leaked Victoria's real identity.

"Did you know about this?" Ruth asked.

"The sheriff told me. It's a trumped-up charge."

"If it's a trumped-up charge, why didn't she tell you herself?"

It was a question he didn't want to think about. He set the paper aside. "Can't we talk about something else?"

Ruth shrugged. "All right. What did the man say about your job?"

"What man? What job?"

"The man who wanted to hire you. The one from Charleston."

"Rusty Oliver? I haven't talked to him recently."

Ruth's face crumpled. "Oh, my. I thought I'd given you the message."

"It's all right, Mom. When did he call?"

"It's not all right. I was sure I'd told you."

"You're telling me now. When did he call?"

Ruth winced as if Owen were trying to beat the information out of her. "I don't know. A few days ago."

"What did he say?"

"He just asked that you call him. He said he had a job for you." She clenched and unclenched her hands and stared at her open palms. "I don't think it was too long ago. It was since we visited Jeb Stuart. I wrote it down somewhere. Maybe you can call him right now."

"It's Sunday morning, Mom. I'll call him tomorrow."

"I lose track of the days." Ruth sighed. "I'm sorry, Owen. My mind just isn't what it used to be."

"That's all right." Owen reached across the table and

patted his mother's hand. "Nobody's mind is what it used to be. We're all losing brain cells at a fantastic rate."

"It's not the cells I've lost that worry me. The ones that are left seem to be grouping for a mass escape."

It took a short time for Owen's eyes to adjust to the darkness of Rusty Oliver's office. In that time, Oliver guided his wheelchair out from behind his runway-length conference table, shook Owen's hand, and gestured him toward a leather couch along the side of the room.

A ceiling spotlight illuminated a stack of reports on the glass coffee table in front of the leather couch. Oliver's wheelchair was just outside the range of the spotlight, but reflections from the glass table caused shadows shaped by his eye patch and moustache to play across his face as he spoke.

"No need to ask what's new with you," Oliver said. "Your name was in the papers most of last week."

"Not one of my finest hours."

"Well, some good could still come of it. Seeing your name reminded me I had a job that might fit your qualifications."

"The mine-inspection job?"

Oliver shook his head. "Hasn't been awarded yet. Like I explained, though, that's a state job. Dusty Rhodes would never let me hire you direct for that one."

"So this isn't about mine hazards?"

"No. I just come by a federal grant to look at high-crash locations on state roads."

"Why is that a federal problem?"

"States can be a little reluctant to find fault with their own roadways. Could open them up for all sorts of liability." Oliver lifted a slim report and slid it across the glass table to

Owen. "So the feds have set up a pilot program. They want somebody to look at the crash sites, suggest fixes, and set repair priorities."

"That's what you want me to do?"

Oliver reached into his shirt pocket and pulled out a business card. "Your card reads 'failure analyst.' I had you checked out. Folks hereabouts still talk about the way you stuck it to Amalgamated Coal over their flooding."

"Half the folks doing the talking lost their jobs when Amalgamated pulled out of the state. They don't appreciate me much."

"Still, it was a helluva job you did."

Owen picked up the grant report. It had been issued by the Federal Highway Administration. He recognized the name of one of the authors. "I've worked with Norm Paulhus before. He's a good man."

"Because it's a federal job, nobody in the state administration is likely to give us grief for hiring you. Interested?"

"Hell yes."

"Good. Thought you might be." Oliver nudged a second report across the glass table. This here lists West Virginia's fatal crash locations for the past ten years. Got them ranked high to low."

"What about the police accident reports?"

"I can get them for you. Just tell me what you need." Oliver smiled broadly under his moustache. "Got to warn you, though, if you're working for the feds, there's no such thing as an accident." He put enough backspin on the word "accident" to bounce it off the wall behind them.

"Oh, yeah, that's right." Owen remembered that someone high up in the Department of Transportation had decided that the word "accident" was too forgiving. "They're called crashes now, aren't they?"

"Got to keep your buzz words up-to-date."

Owen leafed through the listing. "There are over five hundred crash sites here."

"Think how many more there'd be if they'd been calling them accidents instead of crashes."

"Boggles the mind."

"We just have to look at the top fifty sites."

"I see the Devil's Hairpin is number eleven on the list."

"It'd be higher, except not many cars use that road anymore."

Owen remembered the search for Lotus Mae Graham's Mustang. "I was just up there."

"Then you've got a head start." Oliver handed Owen a computer disc. "Here's the computer file of that report. The budget is fifty grand. Gives you a thousand bucks a site. Think you can do her for that?"

Owen would have done the job for a lot less just to have the work. But he hesitated a beat before saying, "I don't see why not."

"Why don't you write me up a little two-page proposal with a budget to keep things formal. List the sites you want to look at first. We'll get you clearances from the state."

"I can get the clearances myself."

Oliver shook his head. "Better let us do it. I don't want you on Charleston's radar screen. Dusty Rhodes can't stop me from hiring you, but there's not much point in rubbing his nose in the fact that I've done it."

"Fine by me. When can I start?"

"Soon as you get me your proposal."

"You sure all you need is two pages? For fifty grand?"

"I already got the grant. One of the perks of being a disabled vet." Oliver rapped his knuckles on the arm of his wheelchair. "Figure I've earned it."

★ ★ ★ ★ ★

The first thing Owen did when he got home was write the two-page proposal Oliver wanted. Then he transferred the fatal-crash data to his own computer and sorted the sites by county and frequency. He brewed a pot of tea and set it next to the laptop on the breakfast-room table. The ladder-back chairs grouped around the table were the same ones he'd sat in to do his high-school homework. He leaned back on his chair and heard the rickety creaking that had always brought his mother running with a warning that a backward fall could cause epilepsy. He tilted the creaking chair forward, lowering its front legs to the floor, and examined the data.

Over four thousand traffic deaths in ten years. A death a day. He scanned the names of the victims. He'd only visited West Virginia intermittently over the last ten years, but there were still some names he recognized.

Lotus Mae Graham led the list of the names he knew. Then there was Lucian Renuart, a neighbor's college-age son, who had slammed into a bridge abutment where a four-lane freeway had been shoehorned into a two-lane bridge; J. Burton Caldwell of the First National Bank of Contrary, who had gone off the road near the Devil's Hairpin; and Bob Bauer, a high-school classmate who'd been broadsided by a drunk driver.

Putting names to the statistics made the job seem more real to Owen, more personal. The victims whose names he recognized all had one thing in common: none of them were wearing seat belts. He looked at the ten-year totals. Less than a third of the four-thousand–plus fatalities had been wearing seat belts when they crashed. Owen shook his head. Getting drivers to buckle up would save a lot more lives than anything he could hope to do on his new job to make fifty sites a little safer.

He scanned the list of high-crash sites. As with the names of victims, he found he was already familiar with a few of the locations. There was the Devil's Hairpin; the intersection of Main and Jefferson in downtown Barkley; and a railroad crossing outside of Charleston that had always been a magnet for drag-racing teenagers.

One of the crash sites that didn't come close to making the top fifty caught Owen's eye. Rooster Run. Only one fatal accident had been reported on the road over the past ten years, but Owen knew about it. It had happened during his brother George's term as highway commissioner, and George had told Owen the story.

Rooster Run had been an unpaved dirt road for most of the twentieth century. Until the late nineteen-eighties, there was only one house on the road, and it belonged to a family of moonshiners named Crofter.

Hamp Crofter, the youngest son of the family, had lived on Rooster Run all of his life. He was a teenager at the tag end of Prohibition, and learned to drive outrunning revenue agents on back-country roads. As the century wore on, the demand for moonshine dwindled and all of the Crofters except Hamp and his wife Lucida either died or moved away. His wife told the police later that Hamp always backed out of the driveway without stopping, as if revenuers were still on his tail.

In the late eighties, the county covered the road with asphalt and developers put two new homes at the end of Rooster Run. By the early nineties, a full-scale subdivision had been built along the road. Most of the home owners learned to slow down around the Crofter house and listen for the sound of Hamp's pickup, but in 1995 a newcomer in an SUV broadsided the truck when Hamp came barreling out of his driveway.

"I told him and told him," Crofter's wife testified, "but he never paid me no mind."

Owen found himself thinking about Crofter's story a lot since he'd first heard it. It struck him that he was a lot like the ex-moonshiner, selling a service that fewer and fewer people wanted to buy, not keeping up with the times, not paying attention while the world around him grew more and more dangerous, just waiting to be broadsided. At least he still buckled his seat belt.

He reorganized the list of sites by county, got a map of the state, and used a red pen to mark the locations of the fifty sites he had to visit. Then he took a blue pen and plotted those locations where the real Victoria had spent time. He made up a schedule of site visits that left him with a little extra time at those locations, attached the schedule to the two-page proposal, and slipped the proposal into an overnight envelope.

He leaned back in his chair and smiled at the familiar creak. It felt good to be working again.

Three of the sites on Owen's list of fifty were within twenty miles of Ruth's home in Barkley: the Devil's Hairpin, the downtown intersection of Main and Jefferson, and a poorly banked curve on Interstate 64. He knew it would be easy for him to get encroachment permits for those sites close to home, so he decided to start with the location he knew best, the Devil's Hairpin.

He'd taken measurements and photographs of the Devil's Hairpin to document the death of Lotus Mae Graham, but those observations had focused on the marks left by her Mustang. Now he needed to take more general measurements of site distances, road curvatures, and pavement slopes for traffic moving in both directions.

He waited until mid-morning when the fog had lifted and work traffic had dissipated before driving up to the switchback with a load of orange cones, blinkers and warning signs. He parked his Saturn at the Pigeon Point turnout, took his camera from the glove compartment, and unloaded stacks of orange cones from the back seat. He'd started walking up the narrow mountain road with a load of cones when he heard gears grinding on the uphill climb behind him.

Something about the unsteady whine of the oncoming motor caused Owen to stop walking and use the parked Saturn for shelter. The whine grew louder and a battered blue pickup rounded an uphill curve, swerving from lane to lane. The pickup's horn blared when it came within range of Owen's car, and its rear fender scraped the edge of the Saturn's front bumper as it shot past.

Owen watched the pickup swerve across the center line toward the edge of the roadway before it disappeared around the Devil's Hairpin. He braced himself for the sound of a crash in case the truck couldn't hold the curve or met an oncoming car. No crash came, and the roar of the pickup's engine grew fainter as it continued up the hill.

Owen's shoulders shook. He sat the orange cones on the ground and took several deep breaths. Between the narrow, curving roadway and the wild drivers it attracted, it was a wonder the site wasn't number one on the state's list.

He kept as close as possible to the scarred face of the mountain as he laid out the traffic cones, both to keep out of harm's way and to avoid looking over the edge of the roadway at the steep drop to the hollow below. He hadn't expected that there would be much traffic on the mountain in the late morning hours. The careening pickup, though, made him wish that he'd brought a few more warning signs, and maybe even one or two extra workers to make the job go more quickly.

No other cars appeared as he laid out the cones and set up caution signs to narrow the traffic lanes and direct drivers away from the lip of the curve where he needed to work. With the cones positioned, he started by measuring the lines of sight approaching the switchback from each direction.

Falling rocks had pockmarked the asphalt on the inside of the curve, shrinking the paved roadway and forcing drivers toward the outer lip of the switchback. Owen dropped to his knees and crawled to the lip of the roadway to avoid aggravating his fear of heights as he measured the radius of the hairpin curve.

The edge of the roadway had eroded in spots, making the curve even more dangerous. They should have installed a guardrail when the road was built, Owen thought. They probably thought there wasn't enough room for one. Or enough money.

Owen stretched out on his stomach and peered over the edge of the curve when taking his final measurements. The mountainside fell away sharply, then stepped down through a series of narrow ledges onto a tree-covered slope. Trees dotted the ledges and even sprouted from the side of the mountain itself, their bare limbs stretching upward like clutching hands toward the sparse sunlight rationed by the surrounding ridges.

Owen drew back from the edge and rose to one knee to jot down measurements in his notebook.

He heard it before he saw it. A dull roar from above, mingled with a series of thunks that he thought at first must be a rockfall. As the roar grew louder and the thunks closer, he realized something big and nasty was headed down the hill toward the switchback.

Then he saw it. The battered blue pickup scattered orange cones like bowling pins as it came straight at him.

He tensed his shaky legs and launched himself over the edge.

Chapter Seventeen:

Out on a Limb

Owen bounced once off the sloping face of the cliff and clutched at the branches of a birch tree sprouting from a narrow ledge. The first branch he grabbed snapped under his weight, and he felt a panicky rush of fear when a second branch bent almost double before it broke his fall. He clung to the slender branch, dangling in midair, and watched the pickup's right front wheel leave the roadway.

Brakes screeched and a shower of sparks shot from the undercarriage as it scraped the edge of the pavement. The truck's bed swerved outward as the driver tried to regain the roadway, but the rear wheel followed the front over the edge and the pickup tilted, tottered, and rolled sideways off the cliff.

The truck tumbled as it dropped, shearing the limbs off a solitary birch, bouncing off a tapered shelf, and plunging into a tree-covered slope.

Owen turned away at the sound of the crash, wrapping his legs around the trunk of the tree and bracing himself against the shock of an explosion.

No explosion came, and the mountainside was eerily quiet.

Watching the truck drop through space into the hollow far below dizzied Owen, and he closed his eyes to clear the image from his mind. He felt the birch bending under his weight, and he shinnied farther down the trunk of the tree, which was rooted in a narrow shelf about a foot wide and fifteen feet below the edge of the roadway. While the trunk seemed strong enough to hold him, the face of the cliff was too steep to climb upward, and the tumbling truck had just shown him the only way down.

He kept his eyes closed and tried to imagine the scene on the roadway. The pickup had scattered the warning signs and traffic cones on the uphill side of the hairpin curve. Surely anyone driving by would see the upended cones, realize there had been an accident, and call the police.

If anyone drove by, that is. Fifteen minutes crept by with no sound of any cars on the roadway above.

Owen knew he couldn't climb back up to the roadway. And he didn't dare even look down into the valley below. In *Vertigo*, Alfred Hitchcock jolted the viewer's perspective by pulling his camera away from a target as his lens zoomed in on it to produce a dizzying effect that mimicked a fear of heights. But dizziness was only a part of Owen's phobia. A bigger part was the pull of the void, the fear of falling, the dread that he might relax his grip and let himself plunge through the expanse below.

He closed his eyes and clung to the trunk of the tree. If he looked down he knew he'd be tempted to loosen his hold and give in to the fear.

He heard a car bumping downhill toward the Devil's Hairpin, heard it stop, heard the car door open and slam shut.

"Down here," he shouted. "Over the edge."

Words floated down from the roadway. A man and a woman were moving around directly above him. He could make out snatches of their conversation.

"Think anybody'll mind?" the woman said.

"Hell, they're just laying there," the man replied.

"Down here. Hey, down here," Owen shouted.

"They'll look right smart in my garden," the woman said.

"Leave the damn cones alone," Owen shouted. "Look over the edge."

The car door slammed again and the engine thrummed on downhill. Owen's anxiety multiplied as he realized that the woman and her husband had just taken away the overturned cones that might signal other drivers that an accident had occurred.

How long had it taken before anyone discovered Lotus Mae Graham's car? At least half a day. Owen wondered if he could last that long, wedged between the tree trunk and the cliff. He had at least four hours till sunset. What would he do after dark?

What would Ruth do when he didn't show up for dinner? He had no way of knowing. He was often late for dinner. How long would she wait before trying to get help to track him down? Even if she got help, she didn't know he was headed up the Devil's Hairpin.

He looked up the sheer cliff face. At its highest point, the tree was still at least ten feet below the level of the roadway, and the upper branches were too slender to support him. He looped his right arm around the tree trunk and went through his left-hand pockets with his free hand. Car keys, comb, wallet, and his father's tape measure. Then he shifted hands and located a handkerchief, pocket knife, and pen in his right-hand pockets. He tried to pull the knife free from his jacket pocket, but it caught on the clasp of his pen and sent the pen falling through space. He swore and closed his eyes to keep from watching the pen drop. He never heard it hit, and swore again as he realized he wouldn't be able to write down what had happened or leave notes for Ruth and Jeb Stuart in case he didn't make it back up to the road.

For a brief moment, he was sorry he'd never bothered to replace his cell phone, but there would be no reception on the mountainside anyhow. Just as there was no satellite coverage in most of West Virginia for the global positioning system that would have made it easier for him to map his road measurements.

He felt in his pocket for his tape measure, the poor man's global positioning system. The size of a small saucer, it barely fit into his jacket pocket, but its curled metal tongue could extend for a length of thirty feet. He wouldn't need the whole thirty feet to reach the edge of the roadway. Fifteen feet should be enough, if the metal extension would just stay rigid as he unreeled it.

Owen tied his handkerchief to the end of the tape measure, making a small white flag that hung limply as he unreeled the metal rule, inching it upward along the side of the cliff. When the limp flag had risen about six feet, it snagged on an overhead branch. Owen reeled the tape in a few inches to shake it free of the branch and then started it back up the side of the cliff, playing out the tape a few inches at a time. The flag crept slowly upward, topping ten feet before it rippled slightly in a breeze and the tape bent backward under its own weight, drooping downward toward the valley.

Owen reeled the tape back in without looking down into the valley's depths. On the road above, a car rounded the hairpin turn without stopping.

Owen climbed as high as he could up the sloping tree, feeling the trunk bend under his weight, and used his pocket knife to cut off a few slim branches that could block the upward path of the tape measure. Then he inched the tape upward again, keeping the flag close to the cliff face and reversing the face of the rule so that if it bent again it would lodge against the mountainside instead of drooping downward.

This time the handkerchief rose twelve feet, clearing the edge of the roadway, and the concave face of the tape scraped against the side of the cliff without collapsing.

Owen twisted in his unsteady perch and looked up at the roadway's edge. With a little practice, he found that he could wiggle the reel just enough to cause the flag to bounce and flutter without dislodging the tape. He didn't know if the flag was high enough to catch the eye of a driver, but he feared the tape would collapse if he tried to inch it any higher.

The next time he heard a car approaching the curve, he jiggled the tape measure and watched the handkerchief bounce. The sound of the car's engine continued around the curve and down the hill. Then, just before it was out of earshot, he heard a car door slam. The driver must have stopped in the pull-out beside Owen's Saturn.

For a moment, there was no sound at all. Then he heard

footsteps approaching the curve. The hum of voices accompanied the footsteps. Young voices. He couldn't make out all the words, but one high-pitched voice seemed to be repeating variations of "It's a waste, man," over and over.

"Down here," Owen shouted. "It's not a waste."

A teenager wearing a backward baseball cap pushed aside Owen's handkerchief and looked down along the length of the tape measure. The boy's face barely changed expression when he spotted Owen. Either he was used to seeing fifty-year-old men dangling over sheer drops or he'd been hoping to find something more exotic.

"Hang on there, pops," the boy shouted down. "We'll go get help."

Owen sat in the passenger seat of Thad Reader's patrol car at the Pigeon Point turnout, sipping a Coke while three deputies and two volunteer firemen collected the remaining traffic cones and warning signs still on the roadway. After they'd finished packing away the signs, one of the firemen, a burly brick of a man with a full beard who had rappelled down the mountainside to cinch a safety belt around Owen's waist, knocked on the car's window.

When Reader lowered the window, the man leaned down to say, "Be going now. Don't try that again, hear?"

Owen reached across the sheriff to shake the fireman's hand. "Don't worry, I won't. Thanks again for pulling me up."

The fireman smiled and patted the rope coiled around his shoulder. "All in a day's work."

Reader watched the firemen leave the turnout and steer their rig back onto the narrow asphalt roadway. "Those boys don't get near enough credit." He turned to Owen. "So this guy clipped your car on the way up the hill, then came straight at you on the way down?"

The image of the onrushing pickup caused the Coke to shake in Owen's hand. "Straight at me."

"Doesn't sound like an accident. Sounds more like attempted murder."

"The guy went over the edge himself," Owen said. "Who'd plan that? Besides, why would anyone want to kill me?"

"You've been digging around some pretty nasty stuff."

"It's not like I've unearthed anything. I've kept you posted on what little I've found."

"You sure you haven't been holding out on me? Maybe trying to protect your museum mama?"

Owen shook his head. "You know everything I know."

"But nobody's running pickups at me."

Reader's walkie-talkie squawked. He held it up to his ear and said, "Reader here. Talk to me."

Owen strained to hear the voice on the other end, but he couldn't make out more than a few words.

Reader closed his glass eye and massaged the eyelid with his forefinger as the staticky voice rose and fell. Finally he nodded once, said, "Got it," and switched off the handset. "Well, we can stop hunting for Vinnie Varva."

Owen raised his eyebrows.

The sheriff replaced the handset under the dashboard. "He was driving the truck that forced you over the edge."

"So you were right. There's no chance it was an accident."

"Chances of that are longer than lottery odds." The sheriff tapped his fingers on the steering wheel. "It's not likely he was acting on his own, though. Vinnie Varva couldn't organize a circle jerk at a porn-star orgy. Somebody sicced him onto you."

"Who, though?"

"Who knew you were out here?"

"I filed an encroachment permit. It's public information."

"Somebody'd have to know where to look for that. Who were you working for?"

"Rusty Oliver."

Reader made a sour face. "Old repentant Rusty."

"I don't see how he could be connected to Varva."

"They both put in time at Barkley Springs."

"But Oliver graduated with honors a few years ago while Varva flunked out recently. Besides, Varva's first contact with me came back before I ever met Rusty."

"When he burgled your home and racked up Jeb Stuart, you mean."

Owen nodded. "Maybe Varva just followed me up the mountain and saw his chance. His first pass seemed a little haphazard."

"Like I said, Vinnie was never much on planning. Whoever was behind him, though, isn't likely to stop."

"But I don't know anything."

"Vinnie's bosses don't seem to think that."

"Maybe I should take out a full-page ad in the *Democrat* saying 'I don't know shit.' "

Reader fixed his good eye on Owen. "Maybe you should think harder about what you do know. Maybe you were getting too close to something."

"Too close to what? I was measuring an accident site I'd already visited with you."

"They weren't after you because you were up here. It must have been something that happened before. You sure you don't know where your curator is? You're not holding out on me?"

"If I knew where she was, I'd be with her. I'm not holding out on you."

Reader pressed a button on the side panel of his car and

the doors locked with an audible click. "Maybe I should clap you in jail."

"On what grounds?"

"On the grounds that you're withholding information on criminal activities."

"What information?"

Reader shrugged. "I don't know. If I knew, I couldn't charge you with withholding it."

"What's that? Some rural lawman's version of Catch-Twenty-Two? How many times do I have to tell you I don't know anything?"

"Maybe a little quiet jail time would help you sort out what you do know. Think of it as protective custody."

Owen felt his throat tighten. "You're kidding, aren't you? Or are you trying to make up for the bad press you got letting me go after the museum burglary?"

"Could be the best thing for you." Reader jerked his thumb toward the car window. "Somebody out there wants you dead."

"I've just started this new job. And I need to take care of my mom."

Reader nodded toward the Devil's Hairpin. "You couldn't do either of those things if you'd wound up riding Vinnie's bumper over that curve."

Owen tried to avoid looking at the curve and the drop beyond it. "But I didn't wind up on his bumper."

"You may not be so lucky next time." Reader nibbled his lower lip and stared off over the valley. "Tell you what. You don't fancy my county hospitality, maybe I'll send Zeke Sinclair around to keep an eye on you."

"I thought he was watching Mary Kay Jessup's husband."

"Jessup locked his painting away in a vault for safe keeping. I figure if the painting's safe, he must be too."

A deputy rapped on Reader's hood. When the sheriff lowered the window, the officer said, "We got pictures of everything and cleaned up all the cones. We're ready to go."

Reader gave the deputy a thumbs-up sign and turned to Owen. "You okay to drive?"

Owen started to balance the empty Coke can on the back of his hand, but had to grab it before it fell off. "Steady as a rock."

"Steady as a rock in a landslide, maybe. Why don't you let me drive you home? I can get a deputy to bring your car in."

Owen felt a strong desire to be alone. "That's okay. I can drive myself."

Reader hit a button on the side panel and reached across Owen to open the passenger door. "All right. But take it slow going back down the mountain. I'll be right behind you."

"I was expecting you a lot earlier," Ruth said as soon as Owen came through the front door. "Your dinner's in the oven."

"Sorry I'm late. There was an accident. Up on the Devil's Hairpin."

"Was anyone hurt?"

"A man drove his pickup over the edge. I was a witness."

"Oh, Owen. How awful."

Owen started for the kitchen, hoping his mother wouldn't ask any more questions about the accident. But Ruth stopped him, saying, "Owen, wait right there."

Owen stopped in the kitchen doorway, thinking of ways he could describe the accident without mentioning his dive off the cliff.

"You've got a phone message." Ruth pointed to a Post-It note affixed to the cabinet over the phone. "I wrote the message down and taped it up there at eye level. See, it's right there."

"I can see it, Mom."

"That way you won't miss any more phone messages. Don't you think that's a good idea?"

Owen realized he would rather have answered questions about the accident than watch his mother, once so quietly competent, make a major fuss over such a simple action. "It's a fine idea, Mom."

Ruth stood with her arms folded, waiting. "Well, aren't you going to read your message?"

Owen pulled the message free from the tape. It read, "CALL BRIAN," and listed a number for BRIAN'S CARDS as well as a home phone number for Brian himself.

Owen dialed the home number. "Brian? It's Owen Allison. What's up?" Brian's voice was rushed, as if he were afraid the connection might be cut off before he finished talking. "You know those cards I gave you? The phony ones you used as placeholders so you could run the museum's cards by me?"

"I hope you don't want them back. They went missing in a burglary."

"Well, they're not missing anymore. Some woman has been selling them on eBay. Trying to pass them off as real."

GHOST IN A JAR

In March 2003, an eBay seller put a "Ghost in a Jar" up for auction. His sale site described his discovery of two jars in a rotted wooden box found in an abandoned cemetery. When one of the jars broke, a black mist seeped out and a mysterious "black thing" had haunted the seller for over twenty years. He was finally advised that if he sold the jar, the ghost would accompany it to the home of its new owner. The auction site included the warning that the seller would NOT BE RESPONSIBLE FOR ANYTHING THAT HAPPENS ONCE THE TRANSACTION IS COMPLETE.

The auction, which started at $99.00, generated thousands of legitimate bids, including a winning bid of $50,922 from a questionable source. It also generated endless dialogues, copycat auctions of such items as "Ghost Poop in a Jar" and "A Vacation Home for the Ghost" (an empty jar), as well as a separate site operated by the International Association of Past Life Therapists, which offered individual ghosts in a jar (no two alike), guaranteed to bring good luck, for a flat price of $29.95.

From the Museum of Fakes
and Frauds' Cubicle of Computer Cons

Chapter Eighteen:

A Killing on eBay

Owen and Thad Reader were waiting outside the door of Brian's Card Shop in Cincinnati when he opened the next morning. Brian went straight to a small safe under the counter by the cash register, talking as he squatted down and rotated the combination dial.

"Got a buddy in DC who runs a shop like mine. He was skimming eBay when he came across a listing from a woman who claimed she had to sell her husband's collection of baseball cards because he'd walked out on her."

The door of the safe swung open. Brian reached in and extracted a baseball card encased in a small plastic baggie. "My buddy looked at what the woman was offering for sale and saw a chance to make a killing. Anyhow, he bid on a couple of cards.

"Bought this Mantle rookie card for four grand. Way below market value." The shop owner stood and handed the baggie to Owen. "Turns out it's the fake I gave to you."

"How do you know?" Reader asked.

"I mark my fakes so other dealers won't be fooled." Brian handed Reader a magnifying glass. "Take a look."

Reader took the card from Owen. "What am I looking for?"

"See the copyright symbol? There's a faint mark between the inner *c* and the outer circle."

Reader focused his good eye through the magnifier without squinting. "Oh, yeah. I see it."

"It's right there at ten o'clock on the circle," Brian said. "That's my sign. Other dealers use different positions on the copyright. Anyhow, my buddy got his bargain in the mail, saw that it was a fake, and contacted me."

Reader handed the card and magnifying glass to Owen. "Unhappy, was he?"

"He figured I'd put it on the market somehow. He's still a buddy, though. He didn't want to prosecute or alert eBay so long as I'd make good on his loss."

"So the card you gave me was the only Mantle fake you've ever marked?" Owen said.

"Only Mantle rookie card I've ever had in my shop, real or fake. And it was a pretty good fake."

"You and Victoria know this card was marked?" Reader asked Owen.

"No. But Victoria knew it was a fake. She wouldn't try to sell it as real. It wouldn't make sense. It would just bring the police."

"Only if the buyer could spot the fake," Reader said.

Owen handed the card back to Brian. "For that kind of money, wouldn't the buyer have it appraised? Get it authenticated?"

"Usually the seller does that before he puts it up for auction. My buddy was so eager to get a bargain he didn't worry about authentication."

"But he worried afterward," Owen said.

Brian nodded. "Afterward, he saw my mark and knew he'd been taken."

"See, it doesn't make sense," Owen said. "Victoria wouldn't try to pass a fake off as real."

"She knew it was a fake," Reader said. "She didn't know it was marked."

"It's not Victoria," Owen said. "How can we find this eBay woman and prove it?"

Brian booted up the computer next to the cash register. "Check out her site. She's still got some cards up for bid." He scrolled down eBay's baseball card offerings until he came to an auction headed by bold letters reading

HUSBAND LEFT ME
MUST SELL COLLECTION.

"There were only ten cards in the museum display," Owen said. "She's offering lots more than ten cards."

"She's offering random packs of five cards. That's pretty standard. But she's also listing individual cards. Some of them match the ones I gave you." Brian pointed at the screen. "See, there's the McGwire rookie card."

"I'll bid on one of those cards," Owen said.

Reader shook his head. "No. If it's Victoria, your name will alert her. I'll have somebody on my staff bid."

"I'll bid on one of those five-card batches right now," Brian said.

"The auction doesn't end for a week," Reader said. "How can we find out where she is without tipping her off?"

"eBay must have records," Owen said.

"I'll get the Attorney General's office to take a run at them," Reader said.

"Is that necessary?" Owen said. "Calling Dusty Rhodes into a case like this is like inviting a shark into your hot tub."

"A little legal muscle can't hurt," Reader said. "Most outfits are more likely to pay attention to a state's Attorney General than a lowly county sheriff."

"So long as I'm bidding, I can try asking the seller a question through email," Brian said.

"We'll try it both ways," Reader said. "You go in through the bottom with a bid and I'll go in through the top with the Attorney General."

Owen stared at the block lettering reading HUSBAND LEFT ME. "I can't believe Victoria's on the other end of that ad."

"She may not be," Reader said. "But whoever is knows who looted her museum."

Buster scooted into the kitchen, tail wagging, when he heard Owen open the oven door. The oven was cold, and the roast inside looked as if it could have been there for a week.

The poodle stood on his hind legs, savoring the possibilities.

Owen moved between Buster and the oven door. He started to call his mother to ask about the roast, then decided just to dispose of it.

Ruth came into the kitchen as Owen was following Buster out the back door. The roast peeked out over the top of the garbage bag. "What's that?" she asked.

"Just the garbage, Mom."

"I can see that, but what's that sticking out of the top of the bag?"

"Left-over pot roast."

"Left over from when?"

"Must have been the night I missed dinner. The night there was an accident on the Devil's Hairpin."

"That was some time ago." Ruth paused, and her face clouded over. "Wasn't it?"

"Five, maybe six days."

Ruth sighed. "I just don't remember."

"It's all right, Mom. I'll take care of it." He followed Buster out the back door.

The morning drizzle had left a shallow pool in the upside-down lid of the empty garbage can. Owen poured out the pool, dumped the garbage, and stared at the discarded roast as Buster pawed the can and whimpered.

The doctor had tried to help him sort out the warning signals. It was no big deal to forget to serve a vegetable course that was part of a dinner. But to forget the whole dinner? Or the main course?

Still, there had been a lot going on that day. And she had told him his dinner was in the oven, hadn't she? He put the lid on the garbage can, closed his eyes, and turned his face upward toward the drizzle. If he couldn't remember, how could he expect Ruth to?

When he got back inside the house, Ruth was standing in the doorway between the kitchen and the dining room holding a yellow Post-It note. "Your friend the sheriff just called. I was making a note so we didn't forget it."

Thad Reader's voice on the phone was measured, but there was as much excitement behind it as Owen had ever heard him express. "I think we're finally getting somewhere. I just finished up with the eBay people. They were really helpful."

"Was it the Attorney General's juice?"

"Hell, I never should have bothered bringing him into it. They have a policy, the eBay people. They won't let anyone sell who doesn't give them a real street address."

"So you can't just rent a post-office box for a quick scam."

"Right. Except these mailbox stores will give you a street address. Turns out that's what our seller's done. She gave eBay an address at the Mail Boxes, Etc. store in downtown Barkley."

"So the burglar's from Barkley?" Owen was sifting the evidence for links to Victoria.

"Can't tell. Barkley's the only town around here big enough to support one of those mailbox stores. I'm on my way there now. Want me to swing by and pick you up?"

"I'll be ready."

The manager of Barkley's Mail Boxes, Etc. was a rail-thin, older man with a prominent adam's apple framed by chin stubble, a maroon sweater-vest, and a polka-dot tie.

"I don't remember all of my customers," the manager said. "Some I barely see."

"What about number four-sixty?" the sheriff asked.

The man's adam's apple bounced once as he swallowed hard. "Four-sixty? That would be Miss Lajoie. Has she done something wrong?"

"We just need to contact her. Do you have an address where she can be reached?"

The manager's eyes darted toward the wall of mailboxes and returned. The adam's apple bounced twice. "I don't believe so."

"Could you check, please?" Reader said. "It's important."

The manager looked through a Rolodex file. "No. Nothing here."

Reader reached out and inspected the file to see for himself.

The manager seemed pleased to have his veracity verified. "Many of our customers prefer to remain private and anonymous."

"I understand," Reader said. "How does Ms. Lajoie pay you?"

"Cash in advance. Many of our customers prefer to deal in cash."

"To preserve their anonymity."

"Exactly."

"Can you describe Ms. Lajoie?"

"Mid-thirties, I'd say. Kind of attractive, in a flashy sort of way."

Owen showed the manager the picture he carried from Victoria's ID. "Is this the woman?"

The manager squinted to study the photo. "Hair's different. Real different. More subdued like. It could be her, but I really don't think so."

"How often does she come in?" Reader asked.

"Once a week or so. Fridays, usually."

Reader gave the man a card. "I'd like you to call me the next time she comes in."

The manager taped Reader's card to Lajoie's Rolodex file. "I can do that. What's she done, anyway?"

"We'll let you know as soon as we've had a chance to talk to her."

Outside the store, Owen said, "Man seems a tad taken with this Ms. Lajoie."

"He does at that."

"Wouldn't surprise me if he tries to warn her before he calls you."

"That would be my guess too. I believe I better put a deputy into plain clothes and have him watch this place."

The corner of Main and Jefferson in downtown Barkley was one of the locations on Owen's list of high-accident sites. Since it was also only one block away from the Mail Boxes, Etc. store where the payments for the stolen baseball cards had been sent, he decided to make it the next site he reviewed for Rusty Oliver. It would give him an excuse to keep an eye on the mail drop, on the off chance Ms. Lajoie was really Victoria.

Owen spent the next day videotaping traffic at the intersection. In the late evening, when the traffic had died down, he measured slopes, sight distances, curb heights, and signal timing. Then, because he thought there must be some mistake, he remeasured everything.

He was standing in the tree-lined traffic island that divided Jefferson videotaping the site again the next morning when Thad Reader stopped at the light in his patrol car.

"The fuck you think you're doing?" the sheriff shouted out of the driver's window.

"Trying to figure out why there are so many accidents at this corner."

"So you just happened to pick this site when I've got a man up the street watching the mail drop?"

"It helped me decide."

"You got some crazy idea you're going to warn her?"

"Who?"

"Don't play dumb with me. Victoria. Your museum mouse. I couldn't believe it when Conine told me you were out here poking around."

"Conine the deputy you've got watching the mailbox? Or the one you've got watching me?"

"He's watching the mailbox. Off and on."

"Thought so. He's been about as unobtrusive as a black ant in a bowl of sugar."

The light changed and the car behind Reader honked. He turned on his flasher and waved the traffic around his car. Then he turned his attention back to Owen in the median strip.

"Conine's new, he's out of uniform, and nobody here in Barkley is likely to know him. Now with you, it's a different story. If he's an ant in a sugar bowl, you stand out like a tarantula in one. Do me a favor. Take your pictures some other day. After we've caught whoever rented that mailbox."

"It's not Victoria," Owen said it loudly, as much to make himself believe it as to be heard over the traffic.

"You don't know that."

"The store manager didn't recognize her picture. And she never would have tried to pass those phony cards off as real."

Brakes squealed at the end of the line of stopped cars.

"That's the trouble with this intersection," Owen said. "Cars come barreling off the freeway without slowing down, round that curve, and are surprised by the back-up at the stoplight."

"Needs a warning sign ahead of the curve."

"I'll be recommending that."

"Good. Then you can pack up that camera and get away from here."

"There's something else screwy about this intersection."

"Get in. If I stay here any longer, we're going to stack up enough traffic to cause an accident ourselves."

Owen hurried around the patrol car and climbed into the passenger seat just as the light turned green.

Reader pulled away from the traffic island and through the light. "What else is screwy about that intersection?"

"That's the corner where Rusty Oliver got religion."

"You mean where he got knocked backward in the rain, dodged four lanes of traffic in his wheelchair, and wound up headed for Barkley Springs and rehab?"

"That's his story. I just don't see how it could have happened."

Reader let loose a short, sharp laugh. "No shit, Sherlock."

"For his story to work, a car would have had to jump the median curb, hit him head on, and knock him backward off the median."

Reader grunted.

"But the way the trees are spaced on the median, no car could have jumped the curb and hit him head on. And even if it had, the curb cut would have stopped his chair before it hit the cross traffic."

"Don't tell me you believed his story."

"You hear him tell it, it's pretty convincing."

"Man wakes up in his own puke one morning too many and decides to change his ways and take the cure. But that's not near as good a story as the out-of-control wheelchair." Reader looked over at Owen. "Lemme ask you. You think Saint Paul actually got knocked off his horse by lightning on the road to Damascus?"

"You mean when he promised God he'd renounce his libertine past and sin no more?"

"That's his story. More likely, he woke up in a whore-house one morning with pimples on his pecker and decided he'd better mend his ways."

"I must have missed that gospel."

"It's one of the ones they didn't print. The lightning-spooked horse makes a better story. Same for Rusty Oliver. He just didn't have Matthew, Mark, Luke, and John doing his public relations."

Reader's two-way radio squawked. He pulled the receiver from its holder and held it to his ear. After listening to a staticky voice, he said, "We'll be right there."

He returned the radio to its holder under the dash and made a U-turn. "That was Conine. He's just nabbed a woman picking up mail from box four-sixty."

When they arrived at the mail drop, Deputy Conine was holding onto the arm of a woman in her late twenties. Nearly six feet tall, she was wearing tight black Spandex pants and a red-leather jacket that was fighting a losing battle with her bosom. She kept maneuvering to keep the batch of envelopes under her free arm as far from the deputy as possible.

"You can't hold me," she told Reader as soon as she saw his uniform. "I haven't done anything wrong."

"We'll decide that," Reader said. Then he asked his deputy, "She been read her rights?"

Conine nodded.

"What's your name?" Reader asked the woman.

"Lucille Lajoie."

Reader nodded toward the open door in the wall of mail-boxes. "Four-sixty your box?"

"I use it, yes. In my business."

"Which is?"

"Photography. I sell pictures."

Reader's face remained impassive as he fixed his good eye on the straining top button of the woman's jacket. "Pictures, huh? Portraits? Landscapes, maybe?"

"I sell pictures of me. On the Internet. Nothing illegal in that."

"Depends on the pictures."

"I'm over twenty-one. I've got rights."

Reader asked Conine, "You see our letter in that batch under her arm?"

Conine nodded. "It's the blue envelope. With the Roy Acuff stamp."

Reader took the envelope from the woman. "Pictures all you sell?"

"I have some friends. Investors. They share the box with me."

"It's the investor that's getting this blue envelope that interests us."

"My investors like to remain private."

Reader tapped the blue envelope. "The investor who gets this is trafficking in stolen goods. That makes you an accomplice."

"He's just selling pictures too."

Owen glanced at Reader. The card seller was a man. He felt a sense of relief that it wasn't Victoria, followed by a pang of regret that he was no closer to finding her.

"The pictures he's selling don't belong to him," Reader said.

"Son of a bitch." The woman's crimson lips tightened. "All's I do is forward his mail."

"Does he have a name?" Reader asked.

"Smith." Seeing the skeptical looks on the faces of the three men, she added, "That's what he told me."

"Is his address any more credible than his name?" Reader asked.

"What do I get out of this?"

"You get to be left alone," Reader said. "If you're lucky. If we nab Mr. Smith. And if you really have nothing to do with his business."

"I told you I don't."

"Then tell us his address."

The woman handed over a large brown envelope. "I was going to forward his stuff in this."

The envelope bore a Contrary address. "Blackberry Ridge," Conine said. "Pretty nice neighborhood."

"Can I go now?" the woman asked.

"Not until we've talked to your Mr. Smith," Reader said.

"He's not my Mr. Smith. Just an acquaintance."

"How'd you get acquainted?" Reader asked.

"Through my Web site. He bought some pictures. We got together. He wanted to invest."

"I'll just bet he did." Reader held out his hand. "Why don't you give us all his mail. We'll deliver it and save you the postage."

While Lucille Lajoie sorted through her envelopes, Reader turned to Conine. "Take her into headquarters and wait for my call."

"Shall I book her?"

The woman held up a handful of envelopes. Reader reached out his hand, palm up. The woman hesitated, then turned over the envelopes.

"Don't book her just yet," Reader said, pocketing the envelopes. "Wait until we've had a chance to talk with Mr. Smith."

The Contrary address was about twenty minutes away over winding mountain roads. Reader whipped his patrol car around the hairpin turns with an abandon that left Owen bracing his feet against the floorboards and his hands against the dash. On a rare straight stretch of roadway, the sheriff took one hand off the wheel and radioed his office to order backup and find out who lived at the address Lucille Lajoie had given them.

After a short pause, the office dispatcher said, "It's one of Doctor Younker's rental units. No telling who's got it this year."

"See if you can raise Doc Younker and find out."

Blackberry Ridge Road ran halfway up one of the hills overlooking Contrary. It was dotted with two-story brick homes spaced out of sight of each other. The homes weren't as opulent as the colonnaded houses of physicians on neighboring Pill Hill, but they were several cuts above the mobile homes and shanties lining the creekbed below.

A silver Cadillac sat in the driveway of the Blackberry Ridge address on the confiscated envelope. While he waited for backup, Reader parked at the foot of a small rise and asked his dispatcher to run the Cadillac's license plates.

When the dispatcher got back to him, Reader slapped his leg, turned to Owen and said, "Should have seen this coming. The Caddy belongs to Mitchell Ramsey."

"The FDIC guy? The one who's running the bank now?"

"That's the one," Reader said.

"Makes sense. He had the run of the museum and the warehouses as well."

Backup arrived in the form of the Mutt and Jeff team of Deputies Downey and Gillis. Reader sent Downey to the back door of the house while he rang the front doorbell with Owen and Gillis.

No one answered the rings.

Reader knocked loudly. Still no answer. "That's funny," he said. "Ramsey's car is in the driveway."

Reader tried the doorknob. The door was unlocked. He opened it a crack and called, "Mr. Ramsey."

There was no answer. Just silence.

Reader turned to Gillis and whispered, "You hear that?"

"What?"

Still no sound.

"That." When Gillis shook his head, the sheriff turned to Owen. "You hear it, don't you?"

"Sure sounds like foul play to me," Owen said. "Good reason to go on in."

"That's what I thought." The sheriff drew his revolver. "Gillis and I are going in. You wait here at the door."

Guns drawn and leveled, Reader and the deputy went through the front door. The sheriff motioned for Gillis to go upstairs while he covered the ground floor.

From the front doorway, Owen saw Reader's shoulders stiffen and hear him mutter "Shit" as he stopped suddenly at the entrance to the room opposite the stairwell.

Reader waved Owen into the house and called Gillis down from the stairs.

Mitchell Ramsey sat in a heavy armchair at the head of a long ebony dining table. His body listed to the left, as if over-balanced by the half of his head that was still intact. His right arm dangled over the arm of the chair, and a revolver lay on the floor under his lifeless fingers.

Unrolled on the table in front of him was the forged Modigliani painting that had hung next to the phony Picasso in the anteroom of the Museum of Fakes and Frauds.

Chapter Nineteen:

Burgling the Burglars

A photographer's flash bulbs popped at intervals, lighting up the white-coated coroner bending over Mitchell Ramsey's body with a strobe-like effect. Two plastic-gloved deputies wearing see-through booties over their shoes were

286

systematically working over opposite walls of the dining room.

The room felt tight and confining to Owen. He went out onto the porch, where he found himself staring into the faces of neighbors milling around between the coroner's ambulance and a patrol car with a blinking light bar.

One of the onlookers called out, "Something happen to old man Ramsey?"

Owen nodded, decided that the confining crush inside was preferable to the curious stares outside and went back into the house. He took a seat halfway up the stairs, out of the way of the crime scene investigators.

Thad Reader joined him there. "After a while, you get used to it."

"Jesus, I hope not."

"Coroner says Ramsey hasn't been dead more than a couple of hours."

"Think it really was a suicide?"

Reader shrugged. "Doesn't feel right somehow. There's no suicide note. Like he expected the painting to be all the explanation anyone needed."

"Funny how the Modigliani is facing away from him. As if he were showing it to somebody."

"There's that. Reader handed Owen a pair of plastic gloves and see-through booties. Want to poke around upstairs?"

Owen stared at the gloves and booties. "Might as well."

"It's not compulsory. Sounds like your heart's not in it."

Owen shook his head. "I was hoping the eBay auction might lead us to Victoria."

"May yet."

Owen pulled on the booties. "I don't know. I don't like the way people associated with the auction seem to be dying."

Mitchell Ramsey's bedroom was dominated by a black

lacquered armoire that took up most of one wall and was overrun with tiny Japanese figures. A smaller lacquered cabinet held a forty-two-inch Sony TV that faced a queen-sized bed. Black satin sheets had been stretched tightly over the bed, and a bookcase beside it held VHS tapes that ranged from a Picasso documentary to S & M titles.

"Early Hugh Hefner," Owen said from the doorway.

"Try to rein in your imagination." Reader opened the armoire and started going through the pockets of a checkered sports coat. "Let's look at what's here now. Not at what might have happened here."

Owen knelt and looked at the bottom shelf of the bookcase, which held a number of loose-leaf notebooks. The first notebook he opened was packed with clear plastic sleeves holding eight-by-ten glossy photos of Lucille Lajoie in a variety of tight-fitting leather outfits.

He held the notebook up so that Reader could see a photo of Lucille wearing a half-open kimono and knee-high red boots, posed against the armoire Reader was looking through.

"Must be a prospectus for her investors," Reader said.

The next notebook held about fifty plastic sheets, each with pockets for nine baseball cards. Most of the sheets had one or two cards missing from the three-by-three displays. Owen leafed through the notebook until he came to a page of cards he recognized: rookie cards from Roberto Clemente, Mark McGwire, Nolan Ryan, and Tony Gwynn, as well as reverse-image shots of Hank Aaron and Dale Murphy.

He took the Clemente card out of its pocket and examined the printing on the back. His eyes weren't good enough to see what he was looking for without help, so he took the card over to the window, where the light was stronger. Squinting hard to focus, he could barely make out Brian's faint mark in the copyright symbol.

He held the card up for Reader to see. "Bingo."

Reader left the armoire and crossed in front of the bed to look at the card. "One of Brian's?"

"Looks like six of Brian's. Everything that was in the museum except the Mantle card Ramsey sold to Brian's buddy, the Rose and Robinson rookie cards, and the Honus Wagner card we couldn't replace with a fake."

"But the Wagner's the most valuable card?"

"Over four hundred grand if it's real."

"And it's not in the notebook?"

"Not on the page with the other cards."

"Take a look at every page. Make sure it's not there."

Owen looked through each page of the notebook, checking the front and back of each card to make sure the Wagner hadn't been hidden behind a cheaper card. "Not here." He closed the notebook and leafed through the other two on the bookcase shelf. One held more pictures of Lucille Lajoie, while the other contained photos of a woman he didn't recognize who evidently owned an extensive wardrobe of leather and spandex outfits cut out to expose her breasts and crotch.

Owen held up one of the photos for Reader to see. "Think she got a discount for the manufacturing irregularities?"

"Doesn't look like baseball cards to me." Reader shut the armoire door and sat down on the bed. The black sheets bunched under his weight. "So what we've got is an apparent suicide with enough loot to link him to the museum theft. But the looted pieces likely to be the most valuable, the Wagner card and the phony Picasso, are nowhere to be found."

"Not yet, anyway."

Reader tilted his Mounties' hat back and scratched his forehead. "I tell you, it's looking more and more like somebody burgled the burglar."

The morning paper had a front-page picture of Attorney General Dusty Rhodes standing in front of a microphone on the steps of the state capitol announcing, according to the headlines, CONTRARY MUSEUM THEFT SOLVED.

Owen saw the picture as he sat down at the breakfast table. "Son of a bitch."

"I knew it would upset you," Ruth said. "I almost hid the paper, but I knew you'd see it sooner or later."

"The man made one unnecessary phone call and he's taking credit for cracking the case."

"Election day's less than a month away."

"It's less than a month away for Thad Reader, too. And he needs a boost."

"They mention him later on."

Owen spread his mother's home-made strawberry preserves on a slice of toast and began reading the article.

Ruth was opening and closing cabinet doors in the kitchen. "It's not a sign of anything to misplace a teapot, is it?"

"Not unless you find it in the linen closet."

"Thank God. I already looked there."

Owen heard the metal-on-metal sound of the oven door opening. "Here it is," Ruth said.

Owen munched his toast and read the article. "They don't mention Thad until the last paragraph, where it says, 'Sheriff Reader announced that the missing artifacts will be returned to the Museum of Fakes and Frauds.' "

"At least they mentioned him. I don't recall reading any retraction of their accusations about you."

Owen was reading a separate article on Mitchell Ramsey's

suicide that featured expressions of surprise from museum and bank employees and no comments at all from his FDIC superiors when Ruth appeared with tea. She poured a large mug for Owen. "Jeb Stuart comes home next week. Be nice to have him back."

"His cast comes off tomorrow."

"Will they do that at the retreat?"

"Sister Regina Anne is arranging to send a resident out there. Evidently St. Vincent's and Barkley Springs have reciprocal privileges."

Ruth seemed distracted. "That's nice."

"We've got one visiting day left. On Thursday. I thought I'd take some gloves and a ball. Want to come?"

"No. That place saddens me. Take Buster. He's the ball hawk in the family."

At the sound of his name, the black-and-white poodle wagged his tail and stirred from his position beside Owen's chair. Owen tore off a crust of toast and fed it to the dog.

"When does Stuart's cast come off?" Ruth asked.

"Tomorrow. We get to see him Thursday."

"I don't think I'll go. That place saddens me."

Owen sighed. "There's a lot of that going around." Ruth's repetition saddened him. He thought, though, that it might be a blessing to be able to forget a few things you've said or done. If he'd been able to forget Judith's infidelity, he might still be married.

He carried his empty tea mug and plate into the kitchen and called Thad Reader. "I see in the paper the Attorney General wrapped up the museum burglary."

Reader's voice was dry and humorless. "Christ. The guy made one phone call. Turns out we didn't even need that. Your buddy Brian could have gotten the address with an 'Ask the Seller' email. I should have listened to him."

"The newspaper made it sound like the case is all wrapped up."

"That what Rhodes wants the electorate to think."

"I guess he wouldn't want his picture on the front page saying the case is only half solved."

Reader made a sound between a grunt and a half laugh. "Well, it probably doesn't hurt to have Ramsey's killer, if there is one, think we buy the suicide."

"What does the coroner say about suicide?"

"No lab results yet. Turns out Ramsey knew we were coming, though."

"How'd that happen?"

"My deputy let Ms. Lajoie make a phone call when he booked her. She called her lawyer and her lawyer called Ramsey."

"So it really could have been a suicide."

"Can't rule it out. Not yet, anyhow."

"But the big-ticket items from the burglary are still missing."

"Ramsey could have hidden them away."

"And we still don't know what's become of Victoria."

"Claire Marie, you mean."

"Actually, we don't know what's become of either of them."

Reader responded with a full-fledged grunt.

"I'm on my way to Huntington to check out some accident sites. Thought I might cross the river into Kentucky and talk to one of the rest homes that treated the real Victoria."

"That was some time ago."

"Can't hurt to try."

"Well, be careful. Stop by my office and I'll make you a part-time deputy. Fix you up with a badge, a gun, and a letter of introduction."

"A letter of introduction will help. I really don't think I'll need a badge and gun to get information from a rest home."

"The badge will help too. You already work for me part-time anyhow, reconstructing accidents. Now that the Attorney General has pronounced the burglary case solved, you're no longer a suspect. It won't hurt to make your relationship with my office official."

"I've never carried a gun in my life."

"It's for your own protection. The accident rate seems to go up whenever you're out in the streets measuring."

"It's the Heisenberg principle."

"The hell it is. It's somebody out there who wants your ass on a platter. And his name's not Heisenberg."

On either side of Route 60 between Huntington, West Virginia, and Ashland, Kentucky, two concrete abutments formed a gate in the flood wall that protected the West Virginia city from the Ohio River. The abutments were just as high as the fifteen foot wall, but twice as wide, and notched to accept the log-like extenders that closed the gate and stretched the wall across the roadway when the river approached flood stage.

So long as the river remained within its banks, traffic flowed freely between the abutments, which stood about five feet back from the edge of the roadway. According to Owen's records, though, the five-foot clearance hadn't been enough to prevent six cars from crashing head-on into the northern abutment in the past ten years, killing their drivers and passengers instantly.

The abutment still bore the scars of past crashes. The corner nearest the roadway had a bumper-high gouge deep enough to expose the rebar, and one of the U-shaped iron rungs that formed a ladder to the top of the wall had been mashed into a W by the force of a collision.

Owen was photographing the misshapen rung when a black pickup truck squealed into a U-turn, climbed the curb, and skidded to a stop between Owen's Saturn and the flood wall. The truck blocked Owen's path to his car, where he'd left his surveying equipment and the revolver that Thad Reader had given him.

He started to walk around the pickup to get to his car when the truck's door swung open, blocking his way. A middle-aged man wearing jeans, a battered leather jacket, and a straw cowboy hat that shaded his dark sunglasses swung down from the driver's seat. His mouth was drawn into a worried line, and it barely opened when he said, "Hi there."

Owen edged around the man and the open pickup door, working his way toward the Saturn. "Hi."

"Saw you taking pictures of the flood wall. Has there been another accident?"

"No. Not recently. I'm here trying to make sense out of the past accidents."

The man frowned but said nothing. His right hand reached into the inside pocket of his leather jacket.

Owen tensed his legs, ready to charge the man if anything resembling a weapon came out of the pocket. "I'm working for the feds. Trying to patch high-accident locations."

The man pulled a pack of chewing gum out of his jacket pocket and offered Owen a stick. "Well, this wall here sure qualifies."

Owen declined the gum and relaxed a little. He doubted whether many hit men gave out chewing gum to their victims. "Frankly, I'm not sure what the problem is. The sight lines are good in both directions, and the roadway's straight as a draftsman's ruler."

The man folded a stick of gum into his mouth. "Not from around here, are you?"

"No. Barkley."

"Well, if you lived around here, you wouldn't be wondering about those gouges in the cement. To folks around here, that wall is as much of a landmark as Hawk's Nest or the New River Gorge. For all the wrong reasons."

"Why's that?"

"About eight years ago, the Spring Hill High homecoming queen broke up with her boyfriend, a kid named Richard Jackson. They'd been going steady for three years, and Richard decided he didn't want to live without her. So he took his dad's Chevy, had a few beers, and drove full speed into that abutment. Gouged out that hunk of concrete and killed Richard instantly." The man pointed at the abutment. "That jut-out stove the car's front end in so far the headlights wound up facing each other."

Owen sucked in his breath. "Sweet Jesus."

"For a couple of years, the State Police carted that cross-eyed car from high school to high school as an object lesson on the evils of drunk driving. Then another Spring Hill Senior, a boy named Benny Fetty, took the wrong lesson from the car. He'd gotten a Dear John letter from his sweetheart and decided to follow in Jackson's tire tracks."

The man took off his straw hat and wiped the back of his hand against his forehead. "Great God Almighty. They were just kids. Their whole lives ahead of them, and they couldn't see past that damn wall. Folks around here started calling it the wrecking wall.

"The name caught on. Not more than a year later, a young woman, another high-school student, got pregnant

and decided the wall could be an equal-opportunity ob-
stacle."

The man seemed to shrink as he told the story. He took a
handkerchief from the hip pocket of his jeans and blew his
nose.

"All the crashes here weren't suicides," Owen said. "One
claimed four lives."

"Prom-night drinking. Just kids again. You got kids?"

"One. A boy."

"Well, then, you understand." The man folded his handkerchief, dabbed at something under his eye, and returned it
to his hip pocket. "The last death was another suicide. Just
last year. Another lovesick senior decided to add his own
notch to this infernal wall."

Owen was at a loss to know what to say. "I'm sorry."

"When I saw you taking pictures, I thought there must be
a new casualty."

Owen shook his head. "No. I was just trying to figure out
how to make the site safer. From what you've been telling
me, though, the trouble here isn't exactly a design
problem."

"No. It's not."

"Still, a guard rail could keep drivers from having a
straight shot at oblivion."

"Could you do that?"

"I can certainly recommend it." Owen held out his hand.
"My name's Owen Allison."

The man smiled and shook Owen's hand. "Gordon
Simmons."

"Forgive me for asking, but you seemed to be pretty
wrapped up in the victims' stories. Were you related to one of
those kids?"

"I'm principal of Spring Hill High School. They're all my

kids." Simmons climbed back into the cab of his truck. "Nice meeting you. I'll be looking for that guard rail."

Owen watched the pickup make a U-turn back into traffic. He recalled his apprehension when the truck pulled in, and he laughed out loud. A guard rail should be an easy sell, he thought. Some good could come out of all this after all.

Chapter Twenty:

A Lesson in Pigs and Pokes

The Queensbrook Lifecare Center was just outside a hilly resi-
dential section of Ashland, Kentucky, about ten miles from the
West Virginia border and five miles from the Country Music
Highway. The sprawling white frame facility looked brand new,

with stone pillars marking the entrance and white columns supporting a canopy over the receiving area. Owen wondered whether he'd been given the right information that Victoria Gallagher had been in rehab there over fifteen years ago.

The woman charged with guarding patient's records was reluctant to surrender any information to Owen. She even dodged his questions about the age of the facility as she scrutinized his letter of introduction through rimless glasses that she held up to her eyes like a pair of binoculars.

When she finished with the letter, she let her glasses dangle from their neck chain against her starched white blouse and squinted at Owen through slate-gray eyes. "How do I know you are who this letter says you are?"

Owen showed the woman his driver's license.

She tapped the sheriff's letter. "But how do I know this letter really came from the sheriff's office?"

"Call him."

She looked as if she believed Owen was trying to put something over on her. "Barkley's a long-distance call."

"Call him collect. Or ask the operator for time and charges and I'll pay them."

"Even if you are who you say you are and the sheriff is who he says he is, I'm not authorized to release any medical records to you."

"I don't need to see any medical records. I'd just like to talk to someone who was here when Victoria Gallagher was treated."

"The rest of the staff is not allowed to give you any information either."

"Look. I know the Boyd County Court remanded her here in July nineteen-eighty-eight."

"Then you know as much as anyone here is likely to tell you."

"It's a matter of identification. Someone took over Victoria's identity about that time. We need to know exactly when that happened."

"Identity theft is a serious business. I'm not at all sure. . . ."

"Oh, for heaven's sake, Maude. Let the man talk to Margot Durbin." The interrupting voice came from a cubicle behind the records clerk. A blonde pageboy bob framing a pair of horn-rimmed glasses peeked over the top of the cubicle. "Margot's been with us from the start. If anybody can help you, she can."

Owen shifted his attention to the pair of horn-rimmed glasses. "How can I find this Miss Durbin?"

"I've already paged her."

"Can I help?" The voice came from behind Owen, and he turned to see a petite nurse with an open, attractive face and gray hair tied in a single braid that dangled well below her waist. Her name tag read MARGOT.

Before Owen could answer, the records guardian broke in. "This gentleman is asking for information on a former patient, Victoria Gallagher."

"Victoria? Is she still around?"

"That's the trouble," Owen said. "We don't believe so. I'm representing the sheriff's office in Raleigh County, West Virginia. Someone has been posing as Victoria Gallagher for quite some time. I'm trying to find out when that impersonation started."

From behind the records desk, Maude said, "I've already explained that we cannot release any information from the patient's files."

Margot smiled sweetly at Maude. "Suppose you let me have Victoria's files so I'll know what information I'm not supposed to release."

The blonde with the horn-rimmed glasses emerged from behind her cubicle wall. "They'll be in storage. I'll get them for you."

Maude balanced her glasses on her nose and scrunched her eyes in what she intended to be a withering stare, which she aimed first at Owen, then at the gray-haired nurse, and finally at the blonde file clerk. When she found no one was paying enough attention to return her stare, it withered and died.

"Why don't we wait for the records in the cafeteria? We can talk there." Margot led the way down a cream-colored corridor. "This is our new wing."

The cafeteria was pentagon-shaped, with four walls containing glass doors that opened onto corridors of different colors and a fifth wall that featured a picture window overlooking a rippling creek. Two elderly patients in wheelchairs sat staring out the picture window.

Owen got an iced coffee for Margot and a Coke for himself. As he sat down at the tan Formica table, the nurse nodded toward one of the corridors leading from the cafeteria. "That green wing was all we had when Victoria was here. Twenty units. Now we've got a hundred and twenty. Handle all kinds of rehab: drug, alcohol, post-op, elderly care."

"You seemed surprised at the idea that Victoria might still be around today."

"At the rate she was using when she was here, she wasn't going to last long. She was here at least twice. Don't believe she lasted the full month either time."

Owen took the fake Victoria's—his Victoria's—museum ID photo from his wallet and showed it to Margot. "Is this the Victoria you knew?"

The nurse studied the photo, then studied Owen and shook her head. "Not a chance. The woman never smiled like that the whole time she was here."

Owen shoved the real Victoria's booking photo across the Formica tabletop. "How about this?"

"That's our girl. About three breaths away from interment."

The blonde clerk returned with a file folder that she handed to Margot while smiling at Owen.

"Thanks, Eunice," Margot said. "You'd best get back to Maude, or you might see some confidential information compromised."

The blonde smiled again, winked at Owen through her horn-rimmed glasses, and left the cafeteria.

Margot leafed through the file folder. "Looks like she was with us twice. August eighty-seven and July eighty-eight. Lasted two weeks the first time, twelve days the second. Both times she just disappeared without a word to anyone."

The nurse studied the last page of the folder. "We'd discussed sending her to Barkley Springs. Started the paperwork, but she wasn't around long enough for the referral to go through."

"Barkley Springs is where she wound up. By that time she'd morphed into the woman in the smiling photo."

The nurse examined the museum ID. "Curious."

"Would a Barkley Springs referral have been a usual procedure?"

"Back then it wasn't unusual. Especially for our toughest cases. The Springs had been around longer, had more staff, more beds, and some astonishing success stories. We were brand new at the game."

"But the referral didn't take."

"No. Barkley Springs was willing, but the patient didn't stay around long enough for us to effect a transfer."

"So the last time you saw Victoria was July nineteen-eighty-eight?" Owen jotted the date down in his pocket notebook. "You said Barkley Springs had some astonishing success stories. Was there anyone in particular you had in mind?"

"No one I can remember to talk about."

"But I imagine Queensbrook has had some success stories too."

Margot smiled and nodded. "Oh, yes."

"But none you'd care to talk about?"

"Are you investigating Victoria or doing comparison shopping?"

Owen's face flushed. "A little of both, I guess. I've got a boy who's hooked on OxyContin."

"I'm sorry. Of course we've had some successes here. At least, we've had a lot of graduates who are still clean and sober. You're never sure how long that will last."

"But none who'll give testimonials."

"No. The identity of our patients is something we keep private. I'd be happy to give Queensbrook a ringing endorsement though."

"As an employee, aren't you a tad biased?"

"Oh, I was a patient before I was an employee. One of the first. Sober sixteen years, eight months, and still counting."

"I'm sorry. I didn't mean to pry."

"That's all right. I'm happy to recommend the place."

"Do you have a card? In case I think of more questions when I'm back home."

Margot took a business card from the pocket of her white blouse and wrote a number on its back. "I'll give you my home number too. Call anytime."

Owen gripped the edges of the card and placed it between the pages of his pocket notebook. "Appreciate it."

Margot closed Victoria's file folder. "You said you were affiliated with the Raleigh County Sheriff's Office. What exactly does that mean?"

"I'm a private consultant. I help them out from time to time. Mostly with accident reconstruction."

"But this time you're helping them find a missing person?"

"Sort of. They deputized me for the duration of the search."

Margot shoved the two photos back across the table to Owen. She tapped the museum ID with a clear fingernail. "Would I be right in assuming there's something personal for you in this search?"

"The woman calling herself Victoria Gallagher was the curator of a museum in Contrary. Some of the museum's most valuable holdings were stolen and she went missing at the same time."

"I saw your Attorney General on Tri-State TV the other night. Claimed he'd just solved some big burglary. Was that the one?"

"Our Attorney General wouldn't know a solved case from a suitcase. There are still a lot of loose ends." Owen held up Victoria's museum ID. "Including this woman's whereabouts."

"You didn't answer my question about whether you took a personal interest in her whereabouts."

Owen returned both pictures to his wallet. "You could say I have a personal interest. I guess it must show?"

"Only to someone who's looking for it. She take something of yours?"

"Not exactly."

"Not an ex-wife, is she? I notice you're not wearing a wedding ring."

"No. There is an ex-wife, but she's not missing. You're not wearing a ring either."

Margot held up her left hand and stared at it longer than

necessary to verify the absence of a ring. Finally she said, "Widow."

"I'm sorry. Any children?"

"Two girls."

"Got pictures?" When Owen was young, Ruth had cautioned him to look at the mothers of the girls he dated if he wanted to know how they'd hold up over the years. Now he found himself looking at the daughters of interesting women to imagine how they must have looked when younger. He guessed that Margot's daughters would be beautiful.

Margot passed over a picture of herself between two laughing young women leaning over a birthday cake with two large candles in the shape of the number twenty-one. "Knockouts," he said.

"Why, thank you." Margot pocketed the picture, leaned forward, and propped her chin in a cup formed by the palms of both hands. "You have wonderful brown eyes. Anybody ever tell you that you look like Sean Connery?"

Owen gave an exaggerated finger snap. "Damn. I was trying for the Ernest Hemingway look." Thinking as he said it, how old is Sean Connery, anyhow?

As if she read his mind, Margot said, "After James Bond, but before Indiana Jones."

"Indiana Jones. That was what? Ten, fifteen years ago?" How old was Connery when he'd played Indiana Jones' father?

"Something like that. I didn't expect you to parse my compliment." She held a hand out in front of her eyes to bisect Owen's face. "The beard helps, but I think it's mostly the eyes."

Owen got up to leave. His chair scuffed the floor and he stared down at the table. "I didn't mean to be ungracious. I've just been a little sensitive about my age recently."

"Aren't we all?"

Owen met her eyes. "And thank you for your help."

"My pleasure. If you don't find what you're looking for in West Virginia, you might try over here in Kentucky. The light's a little better in our state. Easier on aging eyes."

Owen showed up at Barkley Springs with Jeb Stuart's catcher's gear under one arm and Buster under the other.

The receptionist smiled and patted Buster's head. "Cute dog. What kind is it?"

"Poodle."

"Doesn't look like a poodle."

"We cut him like an ordinary mutt. Don't want him putting on airs."

Buster wagged his tail.

"No matter how cute he is, I can't let you take him back to the patient's room."

"I thought we'd just play a little catch on the back grounds. Would you tell Jeb Stuart Hobbs that's where we'll be?"

"You go on out back. I'll bring him to you."

"I'd like to see Dr. Harden too. Would you let me know when he's free?"

The receptionist nodded. "Of course."

Owen carried Buster through the main auditorium and out onto the sloping grounds behind the residential wings. Two patients strolled with a white-coated attendant around the flagstone walkway that circled the grounds. A third patient sat with another attendant on one of the iron benches that faced the creek at the foot of the manicured grass. Vonnie Varva was sweeping leaves off the flagstone walkway, wearing the same black T-shirt that had caused Owen to mistake her for her brother. When she saw Owen, she took her broom back inside the retreat, leaving half the walkway unswept.

Owen laid the catcher's equipment down on the ground and took a tennis ball from his pocket. At the sight of the ball, Buster's tail began wagging like an over-wound metronome.

Owen underhanded the ball in a shallow arc that Buster scurried to intercept. The dog snatched the ball on the first bounce and brought it back, dropping it between his two front paws and using his nose to nudge it toward Owen's feet.

One of the patients on the walkway applauded, and Owen arced the ball a little farther out. Buster ran it down and returned with it clamped between his teeth. Instead of nudging his prize toward Owen, the dog passed him by and laid it at the foot of Jeb Stuart as he approached Owen from behind.

Jeb Stuart picked the ball up and heaved it back toward the far wing of the recovery building.

"Buster's such a kick," Jeb Stuart said as they watched the dog bound off after the ball.

"Good field, no hit," Owen said. "How does your arm feel?"

Jeb Stuart rubbed his left wrist with his right hand. "A little stiff."

Owen pointed toward the pile of catching gear. "Thought we'd test it out."

Jeb Stuart slipped the catcher's mitt onto his left hand and bent it double with his right.

"We'll start with some soft tosses," Owen said. "Give me a chance to warm up."

"Then I won't need the rest of the gear."

"Not just yet."

They stood about thirty feet apart and lobbed a baseball back and forth. Buster scampered between them, hoping one of the two would drop the ball.

"I miss Buster," Jeb Stuart said.

"You'll be home in another week."

"I'm ready now. I'm clean. I can stay clean."

"Stick with the program. It won't be much longer."

"Wouldn't it save a lot of money if I just left now?"

"We've already paid for the whole month. End of story."

They threw and caught in silence for a while. Then Owen said, "Want to try some harder tosses?"

"Sure." Jeb Stuart slipped into his chest protector and shin guards while Owen paced off the sixty feet and six inches between the pitcher's mound and home plate.

"This look about right?" he asked.

"Close enough for government work." Jeb Stuart put his catcher's mask on the ground to simulate home plate and crouched behind it.

Owen toed an imaginary pitcher's rubber and looked in at Jeb Stuart's target. His imagination produced the same announcement he always heard before his first wind-up: "Now pitching for the Cincinnati Reds, Owen Allison." It was delivered in the flat Midwest twang of Waite Hoyt, the radio voice of the Reds when Owen first followed baseball.

Owen wound up and launched his fast ball toward Jeb Stuart's glove. The ball bounced in the grass ten feet short of home plate.

"Need a little more mustard," Jeb Stuart called out.

Owen shook his head and tried again. This time the pitch caromed off the catcher's mask they were using as home plate.

Buster retrieved the ball as Owen ran his right hand over his pitching arm. He felt a twinge in his left shoulder and winced.

"Getting old," Jeb Stuart said.

Owen wound up and unleashed a pitch that sailed high over Jeb Stuart's head and carried all the way to the creekbed with Buster panting after it.

"I'd say that made up for the two short tosses," Jeb Stuart said. "Average the three together and you're right on the money."

Owen wound up again. Waite Hoyt's voice had disappeared. His next pitch hit Jeb Stuart's glove squarely in the middle, but it seemed to require much more effort than it should have.

Much to Buster's dismay, Owen's subsequent pitches all hit Jeb Stuart's target without mishap. To give both the dog and the boy more of a workout, they started a drill in which Owen deliberately threw pitches short of the plate and wide, forcing Jeb Stuart to slide over and block the errant throws. The boy moved expertly, but enough balls got through to keep Buster happy.

Owen's left arm was beginning to twinge with every pitch when the receptionist came across the lawn to say Dr. Harden was available to see him.

Dr. Harden sat behind the desk in his tiny book-lined office. "The boy's been a model patient for the last week or so."

"Does that mean he'll have a good chance of staying clean?" Owen asked.

"Usually. Sometimes people game the system, just waiting to bust loose the minute they get out." Harden stood and came around to lean against a corner of his desk. "But I don't think that's going on here. A couple of things have happened recently to put our boy's experience in a new light."

"Oh yeah?"

"One of his high school classmates was killed when he flipped his car off a plank bridge into Nameless Creek. Drowned in four feet of water because he was too doped up to unbuckle his seat belt and his buddies, who were thrown clear, were too doped up to help."

"I saw the TV report before they released the names. That wasn't the first fatal accident on that bridge."

"Another of our boy's friends nearly OD'd on OxyContin. Kid named Riley Stokes."

"I know Riley."

"Well, he pulled through. But it was touch and go there for a while."

Harden paused as if he'd lost his train of thought. "Anyhow, the upshot is, instead of looking like a wuss who couldn't keep up with his buddies, our boy is looking like the only smart one in his group."

"That news filters back here?"

"You bet it does. He has visitors from the school every day, bringing him homework."

"That reminds me." Owen took a typed form from his pocket and unfolded it. "The school asked me to get your signature on this form explaining Jeb Stuart's absence."

Harden glanced at the form. "They've never needed this before."

"Something to do with ADA funds, I think."

Harden signed the form and gave it back to Owen. Owen returned the form to his pocket. "So everything looks positive for Jeb Stuart?"

Harden nodded. "For now everything looks positive. Of course, he'll never be completely out of the woods."

"One other thing. You told me the Victoria Gallagher you treated fifteen years ago was the same woman who was curator of the Museum of Fakes and Frauds."

"Yes. That's right. Another of our real successes."

"Could you tell me exactly what dates she was here at Barkley Springs?"

Harden's features clouded over. "I hope you don't expect me to breach doctor/patient confidentiality."

Owen shook his head. "No. We know she was here. We just need to know when. And whether anyone referred her."

Harden hesitated. He seemed rooted to the corner of his desk.

"It's important to a robbery and murder investigation. If you like, I can have Sheriff Reader request the information officially."

"That won't be necessary, if all you need are the dates. With a boy here yourself, I'm sure you understand we have to be careful with our records."

Harden left his office and returned five minutes later with a thick file folder. "Victoria was here from August fifteenth through September fourteenth, nineteen-eighty-eight. There's no record of anyone referring her. She simply showed up on her own and committed herself."

Owen jotted down the dates. "Thank you. And thank you for your work with Jeb Stuart."

"It's good to see it paying off."

Thad Reader stood over his office copier, running off READER FOR SHERIFF flyers, as Owen reported on his visits to Queensbrook and Barkley Springs. When Owen finished, the sheriff said, "So you figure there's about a three-week window between the time the real Victoria Gallagher disappeared from Queensbrook and the time the new, improved Victoria Gallagher was getting the Barkley Springs treatment."

"So they must have crossed each other's paths during that time."

"Unless they were together at Queensbrook. You say the real Victoria disappeared from there?"

"Yes, but that wasn't unusual. She'd bailed out on the treatment there once before."

"Still, if they met there, it could explain her final disappearance."

Owen recalled his interview with Margot Durbin and smiled. "I showed them Victoria's, . . . I mean Claire Marie's, museum ID. They didn't recognize her. I didn't mention her name, though."

"She wouldn't have been using her real name anyhow. She was on the run, don't forget."

Owen didn't like thinking that his Victoria might have met the real Victoria before the real Victoria vanished. It led to the fear that his Victoria might have caused her namesake to disappear. He took a manila folder out of his briefcase and handed it to Reader. "Got some prints I'd like you to check."

Reader opened the folder and used the tip of a letter opener to leaf through its contents. "A school form, an accident report, and a business card. Lady wrote a phone number on the back of the card. We're not in the business of vetting your love life."

"Don't worry. It's strictly business."

"Her business or yours? Mind telling me what we're looking for?"

"Just running a hunch. I'm betting at least one of the prints is linked to a shady past."

"Counting your own? I'm assuming we'll find your prints here too."

"I tried to be careful with the card. But my prints are on the rest."

"And you're keeping your suspicions to yourself."

"For the time being." Owen pointed to a stack of pamphlets bearing a photo of the arch of the New River Bridge. "What are those?"

"Bridge Day's coming up. Third Saturday in October. All the surrounding counties got together to talk about traffic control. Don't want loonies jumping without parachutes or bungee cords."

"So you reserve the bridge for loonies with parachutes and bungee cords. Except I'm sure you didn't mean to use the word 'loonies.' You must have meant to say 'Vertically inclined thrill seekers.' "

"Don't want loonies blowing the bridge, either." Reader grabbed a pamphlet. "Look here. They crucified me for sending deputies up to watch the bridge on nine-eleven, but check out this pamphlet. They're not only closing the bridge to traffic, they're closing all the access roads under it. They're asking people to take shuttle buses in. And there'll be big signs prohibiting backpacks, coolers, and large handbags."

"You were just ahead of your time."

"A little too far ahead, I guess." He opened the pamphlet and pointed to a warning outlined in red. "Read this."

For security purposes, law enforcement reserves the right to stop, question, and screen any person attending Bridge Day.

The copy machine churned to a stop. Reader took down a clipboard hanging over the machine, filled in a line on a printed form, and initialed it. "Got to sign for these personal copies or my opponent will have my nuts on a platter."

"How's the campaign going?"

"Dusty Rhodes looks like a shoo-in for governor now that he's solved the museum caper. I look more like a shoo-out."

Owen held up the Bridge Day pamphlet. "Maybe you should use this."

"Use it how?"

Owen took the pamphlet and one of Reader's flyers and

sat down at a computer in the corner of the work room. "Ever hear of Rafe Caughlan?"

"Good ole country boy. Mingo County sheriff for quite a spell a while back."

"Guy Schamp told me a story about him."

"About the pig?"

"So you know the story?"

"Just heard rumors. Like I said, it was a while back. Before my time."

"Well, Guy goes back quite a ways. Way he told it, Caughlan's opponent in the sheriff's race accused him of having intercourse with a pig. Had photos to prove it."

"I hadn't heard about the photos. Hard to believe. Even in Mingo County."

Owen typed a few sentences into the computer and fiddled with the font size. "Anyhow, the way Guy tells it, Caughlan didn't have the chance of a snowball in hell of being re-elected. Half the county had seen the photos, and the other half had heard about them."

"Makes it tough to deny."

"According to Guy, this was back when election day was big business."

"Always has been in Mingo County."

"Big holiday, bursting with flags, bunting, and parades. They had marching bands, Kiwanis, Elks, Boy and Girl Scouts, convertibles carrying the coal queen and her attendants."

Owen pushed the PRINT button on the computer. "Anyhow, when the last tuba player had passed the band-stand and everybody thought the parade was over, someone pointed back down the street. There, walking along about a block from the end of the parade, was Rafe Caughlan."

Owen paused for effect. "And he wasn't alone. He was leading the pig on a rope. Had a red ribbon tied around her neck. According to Guy, the pig cleaned up real nice. Caughlan marched her right past the bandstand."

"I hadn't heard that part of the story."

"It's the most important part. According to Guy, Caughlan won by four votes. And the pig wasn't even registered."

"And your point is?"

"Well, it seems true that half the population will brag about what the other half's ashamed of." Owen took a scissors to the bridge pamphlet and Thad's election flyer. "But Guy claims there were at least three other points."

Owen took his sheet from the printer and moved the cut-out images around on it. "First, like Yogi Berra says, 'It ain't over till it's over.' "

He taped the images onto the printout. "Second, West Virginians will almost always vote for a rapscallion. Especially if he's running against a Republican."

"That's good for Dusty Rhodes, I guess. But I don't see how it helps me."

Owen smoothed out the sheet of paper and eyed it critically. "And third, there's a lot more pig fuckers out there than anyone realizes."

Reader laughed. "And damn near all of them vote. But I still don't see what that's got to do with me."

"Well, you've been taking heat for guarding the New River Bridge on nine-eleven. I figure it's about time you put that pig in a parade."

Owen showed the sheriff the flyer he'd just created. A photo of Thad Reader's face was in the foreground, under the arch of the New River Bridge. The caption read

VOTE FOR THAD READER.
HE GUARDED OUR BRIDGES.
WHAT DID YOU DO?

315

The accident site was just south of Mount Hope, where the two lanes of Route 61 narrowed and twisted suddenly, losing their urban bearings and turning rural without any warning. The site was easy to find. Three short wooden crosses had been erected to commemorate the most recent deaths. Freshly picked dandelions sprouted from a green vase sunk into the earth in front of the middle cross.

Owen parked his Saturn in a gravel turnout just ahead of the three crosses. He didn't need to read the details of the accident report to imagine what had happened to the crash victims. Five single-vehicle accidents in ten years. All fatal. Two motorcyclists, an independent miner, a dozing driver, and three drinking teenagers in a built-up Chevy. Probably lulled by the straight stretch of road and surprised by the sudden turn, all five drivers had run off the roadway and lost control on the weedy incline that fell away into a shallow creekbed.

He'd just opened his trunk when a blue pickup pulled off the road in front of his Saturn. The driver, a thin, freckle-faced man wearing jeans, a weathered bombadier's jacket and a New York Yankees cap, climbed down from the truck's cab and approached Owen. "Having car trouble?"

"No. I'm okay." Owen rested both hands on the lip of the trunk. The revolver Thad Reader had given him was buried under surveying equipment at the bottom of his father's black tackle box. The box sat in the rear of the trunk, barely within reach.

"Sure you don't need help?" The man reached into the pocket of his bombadier's jacket.

Owen leaned well into the car's trunk, pulled the tackle box toward him and fumbled with the latch.

The man's hand came out of his jacket pocket holding a cell phone. "I've got a phone here in case you want to call someone."

Owen quit fumbling with the tackle box and straightened up. "No, I'm okay. I'm just looking over this accident site."

"Accident site?" The man came around to the rear of Owen's Saturn, which had blocked his view of the three roadside crosses. "Oh, I see." He put his cell phone back into his pocket and held up his left hand, palm outward. "Well, I'll be hitting the road then."

"Thanks for stopping, anyhow."

"That's okay." The man turned back and stared at the crosses. "Are those fresh flowers in that vase?"

Owen swiveled his head to look at the dandelions. The instant he did it, he knew it was a mistake.

A tire iron slipped from the man's jacket sleeve into his right hand. The iron flashed upward, catching Owen just behind his left ear, and everything went black.

Chapter Twenty-One:

Harvesting Souls

Owen woke up in total blackness, with a sharp pain in his side and the thrum of a car's engine intensifying his headache. His knees were folded nearly to his stomach, and the cramped quarters and smells of rubber and engine oil told him he was in the trunk of a moving automobile.

His hands were free, and he felt around to find that the hard edge poking into his side was the corner of his father's tackle box. So he was in his own trunk. There must have been too much traffic on Route 61 for the Yankee fan to do anything but dump him into the Saturn and drive off.

Drive off to where? Where were they headed? Probably someplace secluded. He doubted that he'd been kidnapped to be delivered to a surprise fiftieth birthday party. More likely, the Yankee fan wanted to keep him from reaching that milestone.

He shifted his body enough so that he could grab the tackle box and pull it from his side to the hollow between his knees and stomach where he could open it. His left hand dug through the tools and tape measures and found the revolver Thad Reader had given him. A spanner wrench rattled against the side of the metal box as he pulled the gun free from the other tools. The weapon felt cold and awkward in his hand and did nothing to lower the level of his anxiety.

Could he use it? He knew he'd have to. He squirmed around so that he was facing the front of the car. He held the gun in his left hand and felt the forward wall of the trunk with his right. His fingers traced the outline of the panel that allowed access to the rear seat of the car. The salesman had called it a ski panel, and proudly demonstrated the way it could be opened from the rear seat by lowering the center arm rest, or from the trunk itself. Owen had never been a skier, but he'd found the panel useful for transporting surveyor's transits, tripods, and tomato stakes for Ruth's garden. Now he was especially thankful that the car's designers had anticipated the need to open the panel from the rear of the car.

He eased the panel open and a bright shaft of light illuminated the center of the trunk. He waited while his eyes adjusted to the light and peeked through the open partition. The back of the driver's neck was framed by the adjustable headrest bars, and Owen could hear him talking on his cell phone.

"Nameless Creek," the driver said. "Yeah, I know where that is. Just off the old Coal Hollow Road."

Nameless Creek, Owen thought. If that was where they were headed, the site was far enough off the beaten path so that there'd be no witnesses. He pictured a map of the local roads in his mind's eye. Nameless Creek was about a half-hour drive from the three crosses where he'd been knocked out. The trouble was, he had no idea how long he'd been unconscious. They could be twenty minutes from their destination, or just about to reach it.

He weighed his options. He could shoot out one of the rear tires through the trunk wall. That would stop the car. But it might cause a crash. Even if it didn't, the driver might hear the shot and know it wasn't a normal blowout. Then the driver would be alerted and Owen would be trapped inside the trunk. In any case, he'd still be faced with the problem of shooting the driver when the trunk was opened.

If he waited until they reached their destination, there might be more people to contend with. He had no clear idea who wanted him dead, so he had no idea how many might be there when the trunk opened. Then too, there was always the chance the driver might never open the trunk. More than one car occupant had drowned in the headwaters of Nameless Creek. The Yankee fan might just drive the car into the creek, let Owen drown in the trunk, and then stuff his body behind the wheel to make it look like an accident.

The revolver gave Owen the advantage of surprise, but if he waited for the driver to open the trunk, he might never have the chance to use that advantage. He peeked through the opening in the trunk. His best chance was to wait until the car stopped and shoot the driver.

He knew he was right, but he didn't want to admit it. Wild Bill Elliot and Owen's early cowboy heroes from Saturday matinees at the State Theater would never backshoot a man. But they'd never been trapped in a trunk on their way to Nameless Creek.

The Saturn's trunk was as confining as a coffin, but not nearly as comfortable. Owen imagined he could stretch his legs in a coffin, but he didn't want to find out. He wanted to live, even if he had to backshoot someone. Living was a day at the ballpark, a Sondheim song. Living was watching Jeb Stuart graduate. Living was a Marx Brothers movie, a Carl Hiaasen novel. Living was the chance to find Victoria.

The car slowed, then stopped. Owen could see the tip of a traffic light through the windshield. He tried to level the pistol at the base of the driver's neck, between the two headrest supports, but his hand wouldn't stop shaking. He blinked to clear the sweat from his eyes and tried to steady the gun with his free hand.

Before he could steady the gun, the car began moving. He'd have to wait until the next time the car stopped. He had to do it then. He had no choice.

He imagined a map of their route. Where would they hit a stoplight? Oak Hill, probably. If they were in Oak Hill now, though, they weren't more than five minutes away from Nameless Creek. Please God, he whispered. Let there be another light. Or at least a stop sign.

What was he thinking? God wasn't likely to answer a prayer that would lead to a killing. Look, God. Just let him stop and I'll try not to kill him. But you know and I know that if I don't shoot him, he'll kill me for sure.

As the car bumped along, he wondered how God would weigh the sure death of Owen Allison against the possible death of a Yankee rooter. He imagined the God of the Old Testament stroking his beard and saying, "Owen *who?*" He'd always suspected God was a Yankee fan. How else could you explain all those World Series wins?

How many stoplights would there be in Oak Hill? More than one, surely. But what were the chances that the next one would be red?

Owen recalled that Hank Williams had died in Oak Hill. He'd been on tour, and someone had stolen his cowboy hat when they took him from his car and tried to revive him. Owen doubted that anyone would steal the Yankee fan's hat. He wanted to give them a chance, though.

He heard the clang of a railroad crossing warning. They must still be in Oak Hill, Owen thought. He felt the car slow, then stop.

The train whistled, and he heard it enter the crossing as he steadied the gun against the side of the panel opening and aimed at the back of the driver's neck. He squeezed off a shot that reverberated inside the trunk. The gun slipped slightly along the side of the panel and he fired twice more into the back of the driver's seat. The driver slumped forward and the car's horn sounded.

The train rumbled past and the crossing arms lifted, but the car horn went on blaring. It was answered by the sweet cacophony of horns from the cars behind them.

Owen sat trembling on a bus-stop bench while Thad Reader's men photographed the Saturn and measured the angles of the bullet holes in the windshield and driver's seat. Reader brought an army-issue blanket, draped it over Owen's shoulders, and sat down beside him.

Owen gathered the blanket around his neck. "Did I kill him?"

"Not outright. Report from the emergency room says he's still breathing."

"Who was he?"

"Name's Tony Zimmerman. Two-time loser for narcotics possession. Did some state time and got referred to Barkley Springs. Name mean anything to you?"

Owen shook his head. "I couldn't think of anything else to do."

Reader put his arm around Owen's shoulder. "You did what you had to do."

"They were going to kill me."

"They?"

"I heard him on the cell phone. Talking with somebody. They were taking me to Nameless Creek. I think they were going to stage an accident."

"Good place for it."

"It's on my list of high-accident sites."

"The list you gave me? The one you wanted to check for prints with the business card and school form?"

"What'd you find out?"

"Prints on the card belonged to the nurse whose name was on it. Prints on the school form came from the guy who signed it, Doctor Harden. Your accident list, though, that was another matter."

"I thought it might be."

"Lots of prints. Most of them smudged. Most of the ones we could read were yours. One set, though, matched with a paper hanger named John Baker Collins. Wanted on a thirty-year-old warrant from Logan County. Man left a trail of bad checks from Memphis to Bluefield, then just disappeared."

"My guess is he reappeared as Rusty Oliver."

"Oliver handled your list?"

Owen nodded in sync with his trembling. "He's the one who gave it to me."

"So you think he was the one directing your driver to Nameless Creek?"

"It was on his list, so he'd know I'd have a reason to be there."

"Who else knew?"

"Far as I know, just Oliver and his assistant. His assistant helped me get encroachment permits for the accident sites, but he's not old enough to have been writing bad checks thirty years ago."

"Why would Oliver want to kill you?"

"He must have thought I was close to discovering his real identity."

"Didn't know you were trying to corner the market on forgers."

"I wasn't. But I'm guessing Oliver got his new identity from the same place as Victoria. And I was nosing around there."

"There being?"

"Barkley Springs. I think Doctor Harden's been supplying felons with fake IDs."

Reader jerked backward on the bench as if he were dodging a blow. "Whoa. Where'd that come from?"

Owen threw off Reader's blanket. He'd stopped trembling. "You'll want to pick up Oliver. I'll explain on the way."

Owen had to shout to make himself heard over Reader's siren. "I was pretty sure Victoria—my Victoria—wouldn't have harmed her namesake to get a false ID. Somebody had to get it for her."

Reader grunted. He'd been trying to raise Charleston on his two-way radio, but the reception kept cutting in and out as he wound around the mountain curves. A stream of static stopped, and he shouted, "Try his home, then his office," into the radio.

After another long stream of static, a voice identifying its owner as Chief Blatt of the Charleston Police Department said, "You sure you know what you're doing, sheriff? Oliver's got a lot of juice in this town."

"We're bringing a blender. Hold him till we get there."

"Anyhow," Owen said, still shouting over the siren. "The real Victoria was last seen at Queensbrook and the new Victoria first surfaced at Barkley Springs within three weeks."

Reader wheeled onto Interstate 64 going toward Charleston, turned off his siren, and replaced it with his flashing light bar.

Owen lowered his voice. "Queensbrook said they'd sent the real Victoria's paperwork to Barkley Springs, but Doctor Harden denied ever getting it."

"So one of them is lying."

"Or just forgetful. It was over fifteen years ago. But places like Queensbrook and Barkley Springs get a steady stream of alcoholics and drug addicts. Some will be on their last legs, and others will be looking for a fresh start."

The car radio squawked. Oliver wasn't at his home.

"Try his office," Reader said. "We'll meet you there."

"The nurse at Queensbrook told me Barkley Springs had a history of remarkable rehab successes. But I knew at least one of those successes was a retread rather than a rehab. And I suspected Oliver was too."

"Just because he embellished that story about his curbside conversion?"

"The prints on the accident list confirm he's not who he claims to be."

Reader frowned. "Not necessarily. You don't know who else might have handled that list."

"No one who might have been forging checks thirty years ago. Anyhow, Oliver will still have his prints when we catch up with him. We'll find out for sure."

"Why'd you give me the card with the nurse's fingerprints?"

"She was a graduate of Queensbrook. I wasn't sure whether Queensbrook or Barkley Springs was recycling IDs. It could have been either place."

"Or neither place."

"I guess I didn't want to believe Doc Harden was turning out phony IDs. He's been a lifesaver with Jeb Stuart."

"If you're right, he's been a lifesaver with the people who got recycled IDs, too."

Owen shrugged. "Maybe not with the people who gave up their IDs, though."

"Have to talk to him about that."

The radio squawked again. Rusty Oliver wasn't at his office either.

Reader's patrol car was just passing the golden dome of the state capitol. "Hang on a minute," the sheriff said. "We'll meet you there."

On Owen's past visits, Rusty Oliver had always kept his office dimly lit. Now, with the shades open and daylight streaming in, the office looked drab and shopworn. Oliver's wheelchair sat empty in the middle of the room.

"How far do you think he'll get without that chair?"

"A lot farther than he'd get with it," Owen said. "I doubt that he ever needed it."

"Glory be to God, a miracle."

The police chief they'd radioed, Denny Blatt, stood in the doorway. He had the open, blank look of a redneck, but instead of a beer belly, his spotless uniform covered a workout-flattened stomach. "Looks like whatever you had on Rusty sent him packing."

Reader smiled. "It was a thirty-year-old check-kiting warrant."

"You've got to be shitting me. Statute of limitations has run out at least twice on a dinky charge like that. Hardly worth getting my men out of the donut shops for that action."

Reader nodded toward the empty wheelchair. "Oliver didn't think so."

"It's likely we can upgrade the charge to counts of assault, kidnapping, and attempted murder," Owen said.

"Who'd he try to kill?" the police chief asked.

"Me."

"Then I'd say you're one lucky fellow. Rusty was used to getting what he wanted. He wanted you dead, I'm surprised you're not dead."

"Think you can stem your admiration for the man long enough to get out an APB?" Reader said.

"He's anywhere within the city limits, we'll get him for you," Chief Blatt said.

"His real name's John Baker Collins." Reader shoved the wheelchair with his foot, and it came to rest under the picture-window view of the state capitol. "He can't have much of a head start."

"He's good at avoiding the law, though," Owen said. "He's been doing it for at least thirty years."

"We need to talk to Doc Harden about that," Reader said.

* * * * *

Dr. Harden's small, book-lined office seemed to shrink as Owen and Thad Reader closed in on the doctor's desk.

"I don't see what you expect me to tell you," Harden said. "I can't discuss my patients. You have a boy here, Owen. You must know that."

"Let me tell you what we do know," Owen said. "We know two of your star graduates, Victoria Gallagher and Rusty Oliver, left here with false IDs."

Harden picked at a fingernail. "They left here with the IDs they came in with."

"We know two of your flunk-outs, Vinnie Varva and Tony Zimmerman, tried to kill Owen Allison here," Reader said.

"I'm sorry, but this is ridiculous. We can't succeed with every patient. And we're certainly not responsible for what addicts might do after they leave our care."

Reader sat on the edge of Harden's desk. "We know at least two of your patients, Claire Marie Weiler and John Baker Collins, both known felons, lost their identities in your system."

Harden's brow furrowed. He looked genuinely puzzled. "Who?"

Reader repeated the names.

"We have no records of those patients."

Reader leaned over Harden. "We think you destroyed their records so they could become Victoria Gallagher and Rusty Oliver."

"I told you, I'm not at liberty to discuss our patients."

"You won't be at liberty much longer if you don't start discussing them," Reader said. "You've been aiding and abetting felons."

"We've done no such thing. We've helped numerous patients escape the shackles of drug dependency. And I refuse to divulge their names to you."

"You don't need to divulge names we already know," Owen said. "We know Victoria Gallagher and Rusty Oliver graduated from your program. Oliver bragged about it openly, and Victoria admitted it to me. She's the reason I sent Jeb Stuart to you."

"And the persons now calling themselves Victoria Gallagher and Rusty Oliver were wanted felons when they came to you and have been accused of more serious crimes since they left," Reader said. "Forging their IDs makes you an accessory to their crimes."

"I don't know about Victoria, but I refuse to believe Rusty Oliver is guilty of any serious crime," Harden said.

"Believe it," Reader said. "Tony Zimmerman was working for Rusty Oliver when he tried to kill Owen here."

"Rusty Oliver has hired many of our patients, both those who completed the program successfully and those who didn't. He believes everyone deserves a second chance."

"But you won't help us find him," Reader said.

"I won't impair the doctor/patient relationship."

Reader slapped his hand down hard on the doctor's desk. "Bullshit. You leave me no choice, Doctor Harden. I'm taking what I know to the press."

Dabs of sweat appeared under the armpits of Harden's white lab coat. "That would be slanderous."

Reader shook his head. "No. If what they print isn't true, it could be libelous, not slanderous. But I won't be telling them anything that isn't true and verifiable."

Harden slumped in his chair.

"I'll just go over the way that Victoria Gallagher and Rusty Oliver emerged from Barkley Springs with brand-new IDs and went on to commit felonies. Victoria is suspected of robbing the Contrary Museum, while Rusty conspired to kill Owen Allison."

"Should make quite a story," Owen said.

The sweat stains under Harden's arms widened. "This is blackmail."

"No," Reader said. "This is sharing our findings with the fourth estate. Honoring the public's right to know."

Harden brought his hands together, fingers spread apart, closed his eyes, and tilted his head back as if he were praying. He opened his eyes and leaned forward. "I'll help you with these two cases if you promise me one thing."

"You're not in a position to bargain," Reader said.

"It's all right, Thad," Owen said. "Let's hear what he wants."

Harden sighed. "It stops with these two individuals. And you don't go to the press. We've helped a good many patients over the years. Most are leading useful lives. I don't want to see them compromised."

"We may be able to avoid that. But we can't promise anything," Reader said.

Harden gripped the edge of his desk as if it were a podium. "You've got to understand what we're doing here. Put it in perspective. We're harvesting souls. It's just like waiting for a heart transplant. You get on a list and when a suitable donor expires, you get an identity transplant."

"Who's on the list?" Reader asked.

"Well, you know about Victoria Gallagher and Rusty Oliver."

"The real Victoria Gallagher and Rusty Oliver were donors," Reader said. "I'm more interested in Claire Marie Weiler and John Baker Collins."

"Right. Well. We've saved draft resisters . . . ," Harden began ticking points on the fingers of his right hand, "witch-hunt victims like Claire Marie, the falsely accused, producers of medical marijuana, and people who just wanted out of dead-end lives."

"And at least one out-and-out felon," Reader said. "This Collins was wanted for check kiting."

"I didn't know about that," Harden said. "Look. We're not hurting anyone here. We're just in the business of giving deserving people second chances."

"What about the donors?" Reader asked.

"They're people with no hold on life. People with no living relatives. Dopers. Hopeless alcoholics."

"People who have come to you for help," Owen said.

"And we do our best to help them." Harden reddened. "My God. You don't think we . . . do anything to hasten the death of our donors? I've told you. It's just like waiting for a heart transplant. We don't interfere in the life process."

"But you probably don't give prospective donors all the care they might otherwise get," Reader said.

Harden's face tightened. "I resent that. We try our best to salvage every patient who comes through our doors. Some are just beyond saving."

"Even assuming that's true, you're still guilty of aiding and abetting felons," Reader said.

"In our view, the draft resisters, medical marijuana providers, and persecuted daycare operators never deserved to be felons in the first place."

"That's not your call," Reader said.

"Look," Owen said. "Even if we grant you the moral high ground here, you can't exactly advertise your services. How does someone get on your list for an identity transplant?"

"Burton Caldwell was a co-founder of Barkley Springs and a substantial contributor. He traveled in some shadowy places to stock his museum with fakes. And met some shadowy people."

"So this identity transplant business was Caldwell's idea?" Reader said.

"He enjoyed it, I think," Harden said. "He seemed to get a kick out of fooling people. He kept us supplied with subjects. I never knew exactly where he found them."

"I imagine he charged a hefty fee," Reader said.

"I wouldn't know about that. I told you, he supplied the subjects. We treated them as ordinary patients."

"But he supplied you with sizable contributions as well as subjects," Reader said. "And you supplied the donors."

Harden pursed his lips and nodded.

"Burt Caldwell's been dead now for what? Two or three years," Owen said.

"Yes, and our list of recipients has dwindled. A few of Burt's business associates still send us subjects. But it's been almost a year since our last transplant."

"Okay," Reader said. "You say you don't hurry the donors along. What becomes of their bodies?"

"We bury them. Here on the grounds. We have a licensed cemetery."

"But you don't bother to report the deaths." Reader pounded a fist into his palm. "Jesus Christ, do you have any idea how many laws you've been violating? Identity theft. Aiding and abetting. . . ."

"It's all in a good cause," Harden said. "Believe me. If you knew the lives we've turned around."

"How can I believe you when one of your ID transplants is out there trying to kill people?"

"That's an aberration. I had no idea this man Collins had a criminal record."

"What can you tell us about Collins?" Reader asked.

"And Claire Marie Weiler," Owen added.

"Very little, I'm afraid," Harden said. "We destroy all our records on the recipient once the transplant takes place. The records in our files are those of the real Rusty Oliver and Victoria Gallagher."

"And the man who sent Weiler and Collins to you is dead," Reader said.

"Burton Caldwell. That's right."

"So you really can't help us find these people," Owen said.

"I'm afraid not. Is it really so surprising? If I were doing heart transplants, would you expect me to keep tabs on my patients for the rest of their lives?"

"All right," Reader said. "At least we know what's been going on. We'll go after this man Collins ourselves. But we'll be getting back to you."

Dr. Harden slumped in his chair. "I expect so."

Outside Harden's office, Reader fumed for about four steps and then exploded. "Jesus Christ, do you believe that guy? He really thinks he's on a humanitarian mission. Like he's running an underground railroad for slaves instead of shielding common criminals."

"I think he believes what he's doing is right," Owen said. "He's holding out on us, though."

"You think he knows where Collins is?"

"I don't know about that. He may not even know *who* Collins really is. But I'm damn sure he knows Rusty Oliver is really J. Burton Caldwell."

Chapter Twenty-Two:

Third Thoughts

Thad Reader stopped short on the porch of the Barkley Springs Resort and grabbed Owen's arm. "You better run that by me again. Real slow."

"Think about it. Collins was last seen some thirty years ago. Before J. Burton Caldwell ever appeared in Contrary with his hazy background."

"All right. I'll give you that."

"Rusty Oliver's recovery coincides with Caldwell's reported death. Almost to the day. I've read the accident reports on Caldwell. DUI. Missed a curve. Car flamed out and gutted."

"So the ashes on display in the Contrary Museum?"

"They're the real Rusty Oliver."

Reader let out a short, sharp laugh. "Just another fake."

"Caldwell must have seen the bank collapse coming. He'd helped others get new identities. Stands to reason he'd want one for himself."

"When did you figure all this out?"

"While we were talking to Harden. It was pretty clear he'd never heard of Collins. But Collins' initials are the same as Caldwell's. It started me thinking. Collins morphed himself into Caldwell before he came to Contrary."

Reader squinted into the sun, which was setting over a nearby ridge. "So our murders all go back to Caldwell?" It was half a statement, half a question.

"I think he must have been behind Lotus Mae Graham's death. A car over the Devil's Hairpin. Sound familiar?"

"Worked that one to death, didn't he?"

"So to speak."

"But why take out Graham?"

"Because she outbid him. He hadn't counted on the FDIC auctioning off his museum holdings."

"You're saying Caldwell was the one-armed bidder?" This time Reader made it more a statement than a question.

"He liked pretending to be disabled. Probably figured people would remember the gimp and not the guy. He showed up at the auction to bid on the most valuable pieces."

"To keep people from finding out they were real and not fake?"

"Maybe. Could be he just wanted to reclaim his best pieces. Or to buy low and sell high."

"But he hadn't counted on anybody bidding too high against him."

"Not for self-proclaimed fakes. But Mary Kay Jessup must have figured out that the bank's money was going into some valuable museum artifacts."

"So she sent her freshly released cellmate to bid on them."

"But she didn't expect competition either. Neither Caldwell nor Graham came prepared to outbid someone who knew what the cards and paintings were really worth."

Reader smiled. "Would have raised a few eyebrows if they had."

"They didn't want to draw attention to themselves. So Caldwell let Graham win the Klee, then took it back and had her killed. Shoved her over the Devil's Hairpin."

"Can we prove any of this?"

"Not right now. But I'm betting if we find Caldwell, we'll find the missing paintings and baseball cards." Owen shook his head. "Shit."

"What's the matter?"

"All these deaths over faked fakes. Makes it seem less and less likely we'll find Victoria alive."

Reader was quiet for a moment. Then he said, "If anyone can tell us what happened to her it'll be Caldwell." The sheriff turned and put his hand on the door leading back into the retreat. "Let's go back and take in Harden. Get him to lead us to Caldwell."

Owen put his hand on Reader's arm. "Let's think this through. You're probably better off just watching Harden."

"Why's that?"

"Caldwell just disappeared today. Probably right after Zimmerman failed to kill me. I'm guessing he wasn't prepared to skip out."

"If he needs a new identity, he'll have to call Harden."

"Right now, Harden may not know where Caldwell's gone. If we pick up Harden, though, it's likely to spook Caldwell so that we never see him again."

"It's in Harden's interest to keep Caldwell out of jail.

Catching J. Burton Caldwell would shine a public light on his entire operation."

Owen moved his hand up to Reader's shoulder. "Hell, capturing J. Burton Caldwell would ensure your reelection. You wouldn't even have to distribute those flyers we printed. Just burn them in a victory pyre."

"So you're saying we should leave Harden wriggling free as bait for Caldwell."

"Right now, Harden thinks we're chasing a check kiter named Collins on a thirty-year-old warrant. He probably doesn't know Collins is really Caldwell. I don't think he's a flight risk."

"Even if he is, I can have my guys keep an eye on him." Reader nodded, then turned and started down the porch steps. "I like it. I think it'll work."

Owen stayed on the porch. "Wait a minute."

Reader stopped at the foot of the steps. "Don't tell me you're having second thoughts. I've already had enough for both of us. If you're uncertain now, we're well into third thoughts."

Owen shook his head. "No. Something just occurred to me. I think I'd like to see Jeb Stuart before we leave."

Owen remembered the nurse at the reception desk from previous visits. Middle-aged, caring, helpful in the past. He smiled and said, "I'd like to see Jeb Stuart Hobbs."

The once-helpful nurse frowned. "I'm sorry. That's the rehab wing. It's closed to visitors every day except Thursday."

Reader pushed forward and showed his badge. "We'd like to talk to Mr. Hobbs now. Outside of visiting hours."

The nurse glanced at Reader's badge and asked, "Is there some problem?"

"Only if you don't let us talk to Mr. Hobbs."

"I'm sorry. No visitors are allowed in the rehab ward today."

"This is Mr. Hobbs' guardian," Reader said. "And I'm sheriff of this county. We've just come from talking with Dr. Harden. You can check with him if you'd like."

"Okay, then I guess that won't be necessary." She smiled at Owen. "I know who you are. You were here a few days ago. With that cute dog. Another rule-bender."

"I'm sorry," Owen said. "It's important that I talk to Jeb Stuart."

The nurse turned to Thad Reader. "And I know who you are too."

Reader grinned. "You've seen my flyers?"

"No. But I've seen my brother-in-law's TV ads."

Owen and Thad looked at the nurse's name tag for the first time. It read ANNETTE JORGENSEN.

Reader sighed. "My opponent is your brother-in-law?"
The nurse nodded.

Reader narrowed his eyes. "I suppose you've experienced all that in-law friction they make jokes about?"

"No. We get along just fine."

"Maybe you better show us to Jeb Stuart's room," Owen said.

The nurse nodded toward a long white corridor. "Down there. Room twenty-thirty-two."

As they entered the corridor, Reader said, "I'm guessing she's not a vote I can count on."

"Didn't sound undecided to me. You weren't exactly straightforward with her, though."

"I said we'd just talked to Dr. Harden. I didn't say what we'd talked about."

Owen knocked on the door of room 2032. They heard a

hurried shuffling of papers, and Jeb Stuart's voice said, "Come in."

Jeb Stuart sat bolt upright at a desk that ran the length of one wall. A calculus textbook and loose-leaf notebook were open in front of him. Something had been shoved under a page of the loose-leaf notebook.

The boy was wearing black sweat pants and a maroon T-shirt with a Cincinnati Reds logo. His father's dog tags dangled from his neck. He looked from Owen to the sheriff and back to Owen. "Is something wrong?"

"No," Owen said. "We've just been visiting Dr. Harden. I had a question I wanted to ask you."

"You're not supposed to be here."

"Don't worry," Owen said. "We cleared it with the nurse at the front desk. It won't affect your release date."

"God, I hope not. I've only got two days left."

The sheriff moved around Jeb Stuart and leafed through the pages of his calculus text.

"So what brings you here?" Jeb Stuart asked.

"Remember my first visit after you started here?" Owen said.

"Yeah. I said I didn't belong. I was ready to go home then."

"You said one of the other patients had died of an overdose."

Jeb Stuart furrowed his brow. "Yeah. So?"

"Do you remember his name?"

"It was a weird name. Troublefield. Lou Troublefield. Is something wrong?"

"We've been trying to trace his suppliers." Reader lifted the top loose-leaf sheet. "What course it this?"

The sheet had been covering a heart-shaped locket. Jeb Stuart stared at the locket as he answered, "Calculus." A picture of an attractive blonde girl stared up from the locket.

Reader put the sheet of paper back on top of the locket. "Never had it. Never even offered it when I was in school."

"Owen helps me with it."

"That's good." Reader moved toward the door. "They treat you okay here?"

"Pretty good for a prison. Not so good for a resort. I'm ready to go home."

"We're looking forward to getting you back," Owen said.

"You should be okay." Reader put his hand on the door-knob. "They have a pretty good success rate here."

"We should go," Owen said. "Be back in a couple of days to take you home."

Jeb Stuart smiled. "See you then."

In the corridor outside Jeb Stuart's room, Reader said, "Cute kid."

"Jeb Stuart?"

"No. The cheerleader in the locket. Heard the boy hiding something just before we walked in."

"And you couldn't let it go."

"Occupational hazard. Could have been something a lot less innocent."

"Drugs, you mean. Sure glad it wasn't."

Reader shrugged. "Everybody's got something to hide."

"And it's your job to ferret it out. Think you'll go on lifting loose-leaf sheets until you know everybody's secrets?"

"Think I'll start with Doc Harden. I'm wondering if he remembered to report the death of Mr. Troublefield."

"Funny. I was wondering the very same thing."

The next day, Owen came in from walking Buster to find his mother holding a yellow Post-It note. "It's your friend, the sheriff. He wants to talk with you."

Owen could hear the excitement in Reader's voice. "Asking Jeb Stuart about that overdose victim was a stroke of genius. Turns out Troublefield's death was never reported."

"Just another seed for Harden's soul harvest."

"Troublefield had no relatives, not much history. A walking coke habit with a maxed-out credit card. Guess what, though?"

Without waiting for a guess from Owen, Reader answered his own question. "Somebody paid the card off. Five grand. A week after Jeb Stuart said the man died."

"So they're getting ready to recycle Troublefield's ID."

"Who for, though? Harden or Caldwell?"

"Could be a third party we don't know about. Troublefield died before Harden and Caldwell knew they'd been found out."

"They know now. They're not likely to give away a ready-made ID if they need it themselves."

Owen scratched his forehead with his free hand. "I don't think Harden's likely to run. Most likely, he'll try to get the ID papers to Caldwell."

"That would be my guess too."

"So if you keep watching Harden, eventually they'll make contact."

"Let's hope you're right." Owen heard voices in the background in the sheriff's office. Then Reader said, "What?" into a half-muffled speaker.

After a long silence, the sheriff came back on the line. "Know where Hopkins' Chevrolet is on Main? Meet me there as soon as you can."

The pennants over the used-car lot at Hopkins' Chevrolet hung limply in a light drizzle as Owen parked behind Reader's patrol car. He could see Reader through the large display window, talking to a man in a yellow-and-black checked sport coat.

As Owen approached, he heard the man saying, "Guy came in a cab. I figured that's good two ways. One, he had money. Two, he needed wheels right away. So I wasn't surprised when he didn't bargain too hard."

Reader turned to Owen. "Preston here's just sold a used Chevy Nova to a man who paid with Lucien Troublefield's credit card. That rang our alarm."

"Man seemed like a good guy," Preston said. "And the card checked out okay. Was it stolen or something?"

"Something like that," Reader said. "What did the guy look like?"

"Baseball cap, sunglasses, lots of freckles. Had his arm in a sling."

"Sling sounds like Caldwell's MO," Reader said.

"Freckles sound like Harden," Owen said. "Was the man left- or right-handed?"

Preston drew his left forearm across his stomach as if it were in a cast. "Right. It was his left arm in the sling. And he signed the papers right-handed."

"Caldwell is left-handed," Owen said. "Must have been Harden."

Reader made a sour face. "Couldn't have been. My guys are watching Harden."

"Better check on them," Owen said.

Preston watched Reader retreat to his patrol car. "The sheriff seems upset. What'd this guy do?"

"Helped to knock over a bank."

"No shit? How much did he get away with?"

"Millions."

"Christ. I knew I shouldn't have given him any break on the Nova's price."

Reader returned, grimacing and grinding a fist into his palm. "Harden went into the spa at eight this morning. My guy's been watching his car."

"Better send him inside," Owen said.

"I just did. But we both know what he'll find. Harden is a step ahead of us."

"Not quite a full step," Owen said. "He doesn't know we've tracked his new car."

"I put out an APB as soon as I got here." Reader's cell phone buzzed. He put it to his ear, said, "Talk to me," and glowered through the one-sided conversation. Finally, he said, "Wait there," and turned to Owen. "Big surprise. No sign of Harden."

He slammed his cell phone shut. "Son of a bitch. I should have put two men on Harden. But every spare body I've got is on loan-out for Bridge Day duty."

"Today's Bridge Day?"

"Third Saturday in October." Reader lifted his cell phone. "I'll pull Browning off the spa and send him up to the gorge."

"Maybe you should leave him where he is," Owen said. "I'm guessing Harden will be back."

"But he's already skipped."

"More likely he's taking the car and ID to Caldwell."

"Then we're missing them both."

Owen put his hand on Reader's shoulder. "We've got their car's plates and their credit card number. They won't get far."

Reader stared glumly at his cell phone. "They've already gotten farther than they should have."

The cell phone buzzed again and Reader put it to his ear. This time a smile played over his face as he said, "Watch it. But don't get too close. We're on our way."

He snapped the cell phone shut and hurried to his patrol car with Owen following close behind. When he reached the car, the sheriff shouted over the hood, "One of my guys working traffic on the New River Bridge spotted the Chevy. It's parked with all the other tourist cars."

Owen slipped into the passenger seat of the sheriff's car. "Anybody in it?"

Reader turned on his ignition and light bar. "No. But it won't be going anywhere for a while. The place is packed solid with cars and spectators watching the festivities."

"So you told your man to keep an eye on the car?"

Reader pulled out of the used-car lot with his light bar flashing. "From a distance. I don't want him getting too close and spooking Harden or Caldwell. If there's one thing my guys are good at, though, it's watching empty cars."

Chapter Twenty-Three:

A Bridge Too Far

The drizzle had stopped by the time Thad Reader and Owen
joined the line of cars inching their way onto the New River
Gorge Bridge. The sun shone on rainbow-hued parachutes
that blossomed over the gorge as jumpers hurled themselves
off the bridge and glided under the colorful canopies to the
shores of the rapid-streaked river eight hundred feet below.
Parachutists followed one another in close succession or
jumped in groups of two or three as spectators cheered from
the bridge and the rocky riverbank.

On the south end of the bridge away from the jumpers, two dozen nylon lines danced in the breeze and supported rappellers who took a slower route down than the parachutists and stopped at intervals to enjoy the scarlet and yellow patches of fall color that rose on either side of the gorge.

The two northbound lanes of the bridge had been closed to through traffic and were packed solid with parked cars, concessionaires, and milling spectators.

"Ever been to Bridge Day?" Reader asked Owen as they inched along the approach road.

"No. The bridge went up after I left for California. At the rate traffic is moving, I may miss this one too."

A few cars moved onto the berm in response to Reader's light bar. Reader waved as he passed the pulled-over drivers. "Longest single span bridge in the world."

"Feels like it."

"Not to worry. We're almost there."

A tall deputy waved Reader's patrol car through the cones that marked off parking for emergency vehicles. Reader pulled in and parked.

"If Harden brought a car into this mess, he's not trying too hard to get away," Owen said.

"Two hundred thousand people," Reader said. "Easy to lose somebody in the crowd."

"He must be counting on that. I'm guessing he probably left his car for Caldwell to pick up. Where is it?"

Reader got out of his car and waved the tall deputy over. "Where's the Chevy you guys spotted?"

"About a half mile back, parked with other cars on the bridge approach. We've got two officers watching it."

"Hope they're unobtrusive," Reader said.

"Porras is in plain clothes hawking peanuts. Downey's slumped down in an unmarked car pretending to sleep."

Reader smiled. "Got Downey on sleep duty, huh? Good choice."

"Thought you'd like it."

"Can we go take a look?" Owen asked.

"I don't want you anywhere near that car," Reader said. "Both Harden and Caldwell know you. I don't want you spooking them by hanging around their car."

"How can I help, then?"

"Circulate in the crowd. You know what they look like." Reader handed Owen a cell phone. "Take this phone. If you spot Harden or Caldwell, call me. Don't try to do anything on your own."

"If Caldwell's here, he's likely to be disguised."

"Why should today be any different?" Reader said. "Let's split up and work the crowd. Owen, you take the north end of the bridge. That's as far from their car as you can get. Try to blend in with the crowd. I'll work the middle of the bridge south. Gillis, you hang here and be ready to respond to calls from Porras and Downey at the car. That's where our guys are most likely to show up."

Owen took the cell phone and wandered off among the vendors. He bought a slouch hat that had West Virginia stitched on it in yellow script, dark glasses, and an orange T-shirt announcing that he'd survived Bridge Day. He hoped it would prove prophetic.

He moved among the vendors, passing booths that sold polish sausage, cotton candy, T-shirts, and roadkill recipes. Most of the crowd was pressed two and three deep against the bridge rail, watching the parachutists and rappellers.

Owen got close enough to the edge to see that the parachutists seemed to be aiming at a target formed by a circle of small stones laid out along the riverbank. Not wanting to elbow his way through the crowd or risk activating his vertigo, he backed far enough away from the edge so that he could see the rafters and rescue boats farther up the river, but not the parachutists and rappellers.

He didn't want to be distracted by the dare Devils anyhow. He was after bigger game. Caldwell had been responsible for the deaths of at least two people, and had tried twice to have Owen killed. Moreover, there was a good chance he would know what had happened to Victoria.

Owen turned his attention from the gorge and watched the people in the crowds. Blue jeans and T-shirts were the costume of the day. Parachutists traveled in groups with their packs slung over their shoulders. Rappellers wore thick gloves, with their brake clamps looped over their shoulders or hanging from their belts.

Most of the crowd was made up of non-combatants, spectators who didn't care to launch themselves into the void for the eight-hundred-foot drop to the riverbank below, but who crammed themselves together at the bridge edge to watch others do it.

What made the spectators watch? Was adrenalin transferable, like secondhand smoke? Or were they secretly hoping that a chute wouldn't open or a rappeller's grip would slip?

Owen's attention was drawn from the crowd at the bridge edge to a man purchasing a polish sausage at a booth set well back from the edge. The man was on crutches, and his right leg was imprisoned in a cast. From the rear, the man appeared to be the right height for J. Burton Caldwell, but Owen had only seen Caldwell seated in his Rusty Oliver role, and seated again as the one-armed bidder at the FDIC auctions.

He watched the man shift both crutches under his right arm so he could reach the wallet in his left hip pocket with his left hand. Owen felt a rush of recognition. As a lefty, he kept his own wallet in his left hip pocket.

The man turned and, still keeping both crutches under his right arm, put the wrapped sausage into a blue backpack.

Owen hung back, pretending to examine a purse made from roadkill pelts.

The man turned, his profile became visible, and Owen could see a fault line running vertically down the left side of his face. It wasn't a scar, more like a tan line. But it was in the exact spot where Rusty Oliver's scar had been.

The scar line clinched it. Owen could feel his heart pumping as he backed away, found a space between two vending booths where he couldn't be seen by his quarry, and called Reader. "I think I've found Caldwell. He's at a sausage booth near the north end of the bridge, starting back toward the south end. He won't be hard for you to spot. He's on crutches."

"We're on our way," Reader said. "Leave this line open. We'll find you."

Owen stayed hidden between the two booths until the man passed, and then fell in behind him.

The man took his time meandering through the crowd. Was he not used to the crutches, scanning the crowd for signs of police, or just enjoying Bridge Day?

Owen saw Reader approaching through the crowd. From the way the man's back stiffened, he must have seen the sheriff as well. He stopped in his tracks, but there was no place to run, even if he'd been able to. He started forward, then stopped again when he saw Gillis, the tall deputy, following Reader. The man turned and tried to get out of the stream of traffic by heading for a booth selling music boxes.

But Reader was on him. "Excuse me, sir," the sheriff said. "Could I see some ID?"

"It's in my car," the man said. "I was worried about pick-pockets. Is there some problem?"

"No problem. We'll just accompany you back to your car. Would you mind telling us your name?"

"Troublefield. Lucien Troublefield."

"Any relation to the Troublefield who disappeared from Barkley Springs a couple of weeks ago?"

The man, who had turned sideways to the flow of people when he saw Reader approaching, now tried to turn away from the sheriff. He turned halfway and saw Owen. The look of recognition on the man's face was a dead giveaway. The man slumped over his crutches as Reader clamped a hand on his arm.

"Maybe I just better read you your rights," Reader said. "Then we'll walk you back to the Visitors' Center. Nice and easy now."

They took Caldwell to the Visitors' Center above the bridge overlook. The center was overrun with tourists, but the ranger on duty let the sheriff use the administrative office. The office was small and spare, with a couch, a desk, and an easy chair. Reader placed Caldwell in the chair and sat on the edge of the desk. Owen sat on the couch with Deputy Gillis and the ranger found folding chairs for the two deputies who'd been watching the car intended for Caldwell.

"First off, let's cut out the shit about Lucien Troublefield," Reader said. "We know who he is and what happened to him. We know you did business in Contrary as J. Burton Caldwell, although that's not the first name we've got on you. We'd just like to clear up a few loose ends."

Reader leaned forward from his perch on the edge of the desk. "It could go a lot easier on you if you help us out a little. Fill us in on your death and rebirth."

"You talked to Doctor Harden," Caldwell said. "You already know what happened."

"Why don't you give us your version?" Reader said.

"I saw the bubble bursting. I knew the bank couldn't survive a downturn. Doctor Harden and I had helped many others get started with new identities. It was easy enough to manage."

"Easy for everyone but the real Rusty Oliver," Owen said.

Caldwell brushed at the shoulder of his suede jacket. "Doctor Harden told you we didn't harm our donors. Oliver didn't suffer in our hands."

"You sent him over the edge of a cliff in your pickup," Reader said. "He was burned beyond recognition."

"He was already dead when we put him behind the wheel," Caldwell said. "He felt nothing."

"His blood showed three times the legal limit for alcohol," Owen said. "That might have nudged him along the road to his death."

"I took his identity, not his life."

"That's one of the things a jury will have to decide," Reader said.

"So you started Oliver's consulting business," Owen said.

Caldwell grimaced. "It was a profoundly stupid business. Nothing to sell but my time and no way to leverage that. Still, if you started with enough money, it was easy to make it look successful." Caldwell shrugged. "And the government kept shoveling money at disabled veterans. Half my job was telling them how to do that."

"But you couldn't stay clear of your past life," Owen said. "You showed up in disguise at the FDIC auctions."

"I built that museum. There are some wonderful pieces in it. The government had no right to auction them off."

"The government didn't know how valuable some of the

351

pieces were," Reader said. "And you didn't want them to find out."

"I only wanted a few of the rarer pieces. I'd already tracked them down and paid for them once."

"So you showed up and bid on them."

"Nothing illegal in that," Caldwell said.

"But somebody else had figured out some of the museum displays were real and valuable," Reader said. "And Lotus Mae Graham showed up at the auction with a list of those displays."

"You couldn't outbid her without raising eyebrows," Owen said. "And running the risk that other people would figure out that some of your museum fakes were real."

"I could have outbid the Graham woman easily. I chose not to. The most valuable pieces were still in the museum."

"Lotus Mae left the auction with at least one of your favorite pieces," Owen said. "So you followed her and had her killed."

"Or had one of your lackeys do it," Reader said. "Who was it that ran Lotus Mae off the Devil's Hairpin? Was it Vinnie Varva? Or maybe it was Tony Zimmerman?"

Caldwell exaggerated a smug, bored look. "I don't know what you're talking about."

"You might as well help us out here," Reader said. "We've got enough on the bank scandal alone to put you away for at least as long as Mary Kay Jessup."

"That will depend on my lawyer and the jury, now, won't it? Why should I tell you anything incriminating?"

"How about incriminating others?" Owen said. "Mitchell Ramsey must have figured out that the museum holdings were worth a good deal more than their face value."

"Ramsey had been filching baseball cards from the warehouse shoeboxes for some time," Caldwell said. "I never got around to inventorying them properly. When he tried to sell them, he found we had many more genuine cards than fakes. It dawned on him that the cards in the museum's pyramid display were likely to be real, and valuable, so he stole them."

"And you know this because?" Reader said.

"Ramsey tried to sell the Honus Wagner card on the black market. I'd reestablished ties with a number of my sources after my untimely death. They thought they were dealing with Rusty Oliver, of course."

"So when the Wagner card came on the market, you tracked it to its source," Owen said.

"Same as we did with the other cards that showed up on eBay," Reader said. "But you got to him before we did."

"He tried to sell the Wagner card first," Caldwell said. "But it was too unique and too valuable to sell through eBay without triggering alarms."

"So you tracked him down," Owen said.

Caldwell screwed his face into an exaggerated expression of solicitude. "Man was filled with remorse. We pointed out the error of his ways and threatened to expose him publicly."

"We?" Reader said.

"Tony Zimmerman and myself. Tony could be quite persuasive. And Ramsey had quite a bit to hide."

"Including the fact that he had burgled the museum he was in charge of liquidating," Reader said.

"Including that fact, yes."

Owen could contain himself no longer. "What about Victoria Gallagher?"

"I honestly don't know," Caldwell said. "I assume Victoria caught Ramsey pillaging the museum and he found it necessary to kill her."

"You assume?" Reader said.

"We tested the hypothesis on Ramsey when we threatened

to expose him. It was just one of a long list of his transgressions," Caldwell said. "He denied any knowledge of Ms. Gallagher's disappearance. But then he denied everything, including the museum robbery and his affairs with Lucille the latex lady."

"Just one of a long list of transgressions?" Owen said. "You're equating murder with filching a Mark McGwire rookie card?"

"We only suggested that he'd murdered Ms. Gallagher," Caldwell said. "We had positive proof he'd stolen the cards."

"How do we know you didn't commit the burglary yourself and frame Ramsey?" Owen said.

"Ramsey was the one auctioning off the stolen goods. Ramsey was the one who committed suicide. I'm sure your autopsy showed that the wound was self-inflicted."

"Our findings were, shall we say, consistent with suicide," Reader said. "But there were a few facts that left us wondering. There was evidence that his legs had been taped to the chair earlier. And there was only one bullet in the suicide weapon."

"One should be sufficient from a close range," Caldwell said.

"It's your statement, though, that Ramsey was alive when you left him." Reader enunciated each word carefully, emphasizing "statement" and "alive."

"But clearly overcome with remorse," Caldwell said. "In my opinion, the thing that pushed him over the edge was the call from his latex lady's lawyer saying that you were on your way there to arrest him."

"So you took that call," Reader said.

"Oh, we passed its contents on right away," Caldwell said. "Ramsey just couldn't live with the prospect of public exposure."

"And you couldn't risk sticking around until we got to Ramsey's house," Reader said.

"I'm sure you'll appreciate that I had a good deal to hide myself," Caldwell said.

"It's curious that the most valuable pieces taken in the burglary, the Wagner card and the Picasso painting, are still missing," Owen said.

"I'm sure they'll turn up," Caldwell said. "Without admitting anything, I imagine restitution could be arranged."

"In return for?" Reader said.

Caldwell sighed. "Leniency, understanding. Lawyers would have to work it out." He frowned and scratched at the top of his cast. "The trouble with these elaborate disguises is that they always leave you with an itch you can't scratch." He tried to squeeze his fingers under the cast. Still frowning, he shook his head and held out his hand to Deputy Gillis, "I wonder if I could trouble you for that pen in your breast pocket?"

Gillis rose from the couch and handed Caldwell his ball-point pen.

Caldwell slipped the pen under the top of his cast, moved it back and forth, and smiled with relief. "Thank you."

He held the pen up to return it to Gillis. As Gillis bent to take it, Caldwell's cast fell away in two halves and a thin knife flashed in his hand.

He looped his right arm around the deputy's head and pressed the knife against Gillis' throat with his left hand.

"I'd advise all of you not to move," Caldwell said. "Especially you, deputy."

Caldwell released his grip on Gillis' head and rose from his chair, keeping the point of his knife lodged against the deputy's neck. His chin pointed skyward, Gillis straightened slowly as Caldwell rose.

Caldwell unsnapped the flap on Gillis' holster, retrieved the deputy's revolver, and cocked it with his right hand. "Now here's what's going to happen. The deputy and I are going to back out of this room and out of the Visitors' Center. If any of you move across the threshold of that doorway, I shall kill the deputy."

He took a step backward, guiding Gillis with the point of the knife. "I remind all of you that I have very little to lose here."

Caldwell and Gillis backed down the steps of the Visitors' Center and onto the walkway leading to the bridge overlook. The crowd on the walkway parted to let the knife wielder and his captive pass.

Reader, Owen and the two remaining deputies bunched around the doorway of the Center. "No farther, sheriff," Caldwell shouted. "Tell these folks to clear the pathway."

"Let them pass," the sheriff told the crowd.

The crowd jabbered and spilled off the walkway and onto the grass.

Caldwell backed along the curving walkway with Gillis in tow. About halfway to the overlook, he left the walkway and backed down a grassy slope toward a low wire fence that separated the Center's grounds from a dense woods.

When Caldwell reached the fence, he backed up against it and forced Gillis to his knees in front of him.

The crowd suddenly became silent.

With Owen and the sheriff watching from the Center doorway, Caldwell shifted his grip on the revolver and hammered the deputy behind his right ear. As Gillis pitched forward onto the grass, Caldwell leapt over the low fence and disappeared into the woods.

Owen, Thad and the two deputies ran to the fence, scattering the crowd of onlookers. The plainclothes deputy,

Porras, knelt to help Gillis, while Owen, Thad, and Deputy Downey scaled the wire fence. Owen started straight into the trees while Reader and his deputy moved along the fence toward the bridge.

"Not that way," Reader shouted to Owen. "There's nothing there."

Owen stopped short at a clearing that ended in a sheer drop into the gorge below. Shaken by the view over the precipice, he backed away from the edge and tried to follow the sounds of Reader and the deputy.

Owen picked his way through the dark evergreen forest until he broke out into sunlight and the sight of the bridge and Deputy Downey shedding her Sam Browne belt and shouting, "I'll go after him."

Reader clutched her arm, restraining her. "Don't bother. He's got no place to go."

They'd come out at the underside of the bridge. Owen followed Downey's gaze to see that Caldwell had climbed out onto the latticework of steel supports and was working his way, hand over hand, out across the span.

Reader shouted into his walkie-talkie, and Owen could see amber light bars of patrol cars flashing and moving toward either end of the bridge.

"He'll have to stay under the roadway," Reader said. "There's no way he can get back on top from where he is."

Owen watched Caldwell pick his way along the bridge supports. "He doesn't seem to know that."

About a quarter of the way across, Caldwell tried climbing the latticework to gain a hold on the concrete wall of the bridge itself, but there was nothing for him to grab onto.

"He knows now," Reader said. "He's stuck underneath."

Caldwell returned to the substructure and made his way toward the top of the steel arch supporting the center of the

357

bridge. He was far enough over the gorge now so that the crowd on the riverbank below could see him. A few onlookers pointed upward.

Caldwell passed the rappellers' nylon ropes and grabbed one for support. The rappeller below spun crazily and dropped thirty feet before he regained control.

The other rappellers stopped at various stages of descent to watch Caldwell pick his way along the steel substructure.

Oblivious to the drama under the bridge, parachutists continued to leap from the bridgeway and float to earth under colorful canopies.

Caldwell moved more slowly now, pausing to test the superstructure for a way up onto the bridge. He was far enough away so that he reminded Owen of a fly trying to find its way out of a closed car window.

Caldwell's foot slipped on a steel girder that was still slick from the morning's rain, and he grabbed another rappeller's line for support. The rappeller, who had stopped to watch Caldwell's progress, raised his fist toward the fugitive.

Sounds of applause drifted up from the crowd on the riverbank. "They think they're watching Harold Lloyd clinging to a clockface," Owen said.

Reader pursed his lips. "It's all part of the show to them. They think it's staged."

A jumper leapt from the bridge, did two forward somersaults, spread-eagled himself in mid-air, and waited until the last possible minute to release his chute. The crowd on the riverbank loosed a drawn-out "oooh" that turned into a high-pitched "aahhh" when the chute opened.

The jumper controlled his descent so that he landed in the center of the circular target of riverbank stones, eliciting strong rounds of applause from the crowds above and below.

Caldwell had reached the exact center of the bridge, where the parabolic support arch met the latticework substructure of the bridge roadway. From the other side of the bridge, a uniformed deputy began crawling across the substructure toward him.

"Who the fuck is that?" Reader shouted into the walkie-talkie. "Get that deputy off the girders."

A female voice came over the squawk box. "It's Deputy Ruddle, sir. He's going out to apprehend the fugitive."

"Get him the hell off the bridge support," Reader said into his speaker. "The fugitive has no place to go. He'll have to come back to earth eventually. We don't want to lose personnel going out there after him."

Reader switched off the walkie-talkie. "Goddamn Ruddle. I might have known."

In the center of the bridge, Caldwell saw the deputy starting toward him along the horizontal substructure. The fugitive tried to shift from the horizontal latticework to the parabolic steelwork of the supporting arch.

"He's trying to come down the far side of the arch to avoid your deputy," Owen said.

"Not a problem." Reader turned on his walkie-talkie. "We'll beat him to the foot of the arch."

Under the bridge, Caldwell climbed down a vertical I-beam to the curving steelwork of the support arch. He lost his footing, slid about ten feet down the arch, reached out to grab a vertical beam, missed, and tumbled off the steelwork.

Seeing him start to fall, the crowd below began its "oooh" roar. The roar built, then broke into scattered screams when no chute opened.

Reader switched off his intercom.

Down below, a rescue boat circled and headed to the spot

where Caldwell had ended his eight-hundred foot plunge by splatting into the New River rapids.

Reader pocketed his intercom. "Show's over. Damn fool never even came close to the target."

Chapter Twenty-Four:

A Slippery Slope

It rained off and on for two days following Bridge Day, the
kind of bleak, intermittent drizzle that never quite turns to
snow but reminds everyone that winter is coming.

Election day was only two weeks away. Placards supporting county candidates fronted every house and sprouted
like kudzu on vacant lots, fighting each other for sunlight and
viewing space. Thad Reader's placards just showed his name,
supported by the arch of the New River Bridge. They'd been
designed to reflect his 9/11 guard duty, but took on new
meaning after the Bridge Day plunge of J. Burton Caldwell.

The newspapers had been filled with stories of Caldwell's
real and faked deaths and his practice of concealing bank
funds in the Museum of Fakes and Frauds' collection. Nearly
every story mentioned Reader and included a photo or an interview with the sheriff who had routed out Caldwell and
chased him out onto the bridge span.

The rain finally stopped on Tuesday morning, and Owen
drove out of Barkley to the accident site where he'd been ab-

ducted by Tony Zimmerman. The site had changed appreciably since Owen's last visit. One of the three commemorative crosses had been sheared off at the base by someone who had lost control on the sharp curve of the off-ramp. Beyond the curve, a trail of broken cattails and muddy tire tracks led from the ramp all the way down to the shallow creekbed at the base of the ravine.

From the creekbed, two deeply gouged tire tracks slanted upward along a slight incline that led back to the main roadway about five hundred feet from the turnoff. Owen guessed that the tire tracks belonged to a pickup with four-wheel drive. The driver had turned into the spin and regained enough control to guide the truck down the steep slope to the creekbed. From there, he'd either made it out under his own power or called a tow truck.

The driver had been lucky. React quickly, point the front wheels downhill, and the worst you got was a bumpy roller-coaster ride to the bottom of the ravine. React slowly, though, or turn your wheels the wrong way, and you were in for a deadly roll.

A thin line between living and dying. The crisis comes when you least expect it, when you're reconnoitering after a battle, considering a job offer, or returning home after a hard day at the office. And there's no way to prepare, no practice course. Guess wrong, and you can lose the Confederacy, your wife, or your life. He retrieved the broken cross and reattached it to its base with duct tape.

He'd pulled out his camera and was photographing the site when the cell phone clipped to his belt played "Take Me Out to the Ball Game." Thad Reader's voice was on the other end of the line. "Finally got a cell phone that works here, huh?"

"Seemed like it was about time. So far though, Mom's the only one with my number. How'd you get it?"

"I'm out at your house."

Owen stared at the roadside crosses. He felt a stab of panic. "Is everything all right?"

"Your mom's fine. Neighbors saw her wandering about three blocks away and I happened to be driving by."

"I'll come right home."

"No need. I was on my way to see you anyhow. Where are you right now?"

"Route Sixty-One turnoff. Outside Mount Hope."

"Isn't that where Zimmerman clipped you? What are you doing there?"

"Thought I'd finish the job I started. Put in a few billable hours before the bureaucrats shut down the contracts Caldwell won as Rusty Oliver."

"Wait there for me."

Owen's apprehension returned. "It's a little out of your jurisdiction. Shouldn't you be campaigning closer to home?"

"Polls say I've got the election locked up."

"Polls?"

"My wife talked to all the in-laws. Half of them are either for me or undecided. Means I can't miss with the voting public."

"Didn't I tell you?" Owen said. "Bag Caldwell and you bag the election as well."

"Still not over till it's over, though. See you in a bit."

Owen had finished with his measurements and was packing his instruments in the Saturn's trunk when Reader pulled up behind him. Ruth was in the passenger seat beside the sheriff.

"What brings you out here?" Owen asked, addressing his mother as much as the sheriff.

"Neighbors called . . ." Reader began to answer.

Ruth interrupted. "I was looking for Buster. On Elm Street."

"The dog was at home," Reader said.

"That's why I couldn't find him on Elm Street," Ruth said.

"When I told your mom I was coming out to see you, she asked to ride along," Reader said.

"Thought I'd see what you were up to." Ruth looked at the three crosses. "This curve doesn't look so bad."

"It's not bad when it's dry," Owen said. "When it's wet, though, people have trouble holding it."

Reader got out of his car and pointed to the muddy tire tracks leading from the creekbed back up to the main road. "Looks like somebody lost it recent."

"Lost it on the curve," Owen said. "Managed not to roll, though."

"Lucky guy." Reader looked back up the roadway. "Guess what you need is a warning sign upstream."

"Wouldn't hurt," Owen said. "Half the drivers who lost it here weren't in shape to read signs, though."

"DWI?"

Owen nodded. "You haven't told me what brings you out here."

"Couple of leaf peepers came across Victoria's Dodge. In a gully off Camp Creek Road."

"Was she . . . ?" Owen couldn't form the words to complete the sentence.

Reader shook his head. "No sign of her."

Owen wanted to feel relief, or hope, but he sensed Reader was holding something back.

The sheriff reached into his pocket and pulled out a plastic bag. "My boys found these in the trunk." He held the bag out to Owen.

Owen reached out to take the bag, then stopped with his fingers extended as he recognized the silver necklace inside it.

"What is it?" Ruth asked.

"Dog tags." Owen forced his hand to close on the plastic bag.

"Whose dog tags?" Ruth asked.

Owen's senses suddenly became more acute. Sounds from the freeway pounded in his ear. He knew the answer without reading the tags. "They belonged to Victoria's grandfather."

"Did he die?"

Owen felt he had to shout to make himself heard over the noise. "He died. Gassed in the First World War."

"I'm sorry, Owen," Reader said. "I know you said she always wore them."

The traffic noise pulsed in Owen's temples. He had to get a grip. Respond. "I felt it. I knew if she were alive she'd contact me."

"Nothing's certain," Reader said. "It's not like we've found a body. Could be she ditched those tags and took on another new identity."

Owen shook his head. "She kept those tags through her first identity switch. She wouldn't part with them." He opened the fist he'd closed around the plastic bag. The edges of the dog tags had left red lines on his palm. "You need these back?"

Reader took back the tags. "Just for a short while. They're evidence. I'll see they get back to you."

"Caldwell had it right," Owen said. "Victoria must have interrupted Ramsey when he was looting the museum."

"Makes sense. My boys found the missing baseball cards in a hidey hole at Ramsey's place." Reader stared at the dog tags, then pocketed them. "Caldwell might not have been guessing about Victoria, though. Ramsey could have told him and Zimmerman what really happened. They had Ramsey strapped in that chair."

"I'm thinking they could be pretty persuasive," Owen said.

"It's a wonder they didn't beat us to the baseball cards. I'd have thought that would be the first thing they'd ask Ramsey."

"We must have interrupted them with our phone call," Owen said. "They couldn't very well stay and interrogate Ramsey knowing we were on our way over."

"Stayed long enough to make sure Ramsey shot himself."

"Could be they helped him along."

Reader nodded toward the gear clipped to Owen's belt. "That new cell phone mean you'll be sticking around?"

"For a while at least. Mom needs somebody to stay with her. And Jeb Stuart needs to finish this year of high school."

"Your stint as a part-time deputy worked out pretty good. Want to make it permanent?"

"You really in a position to make that offer? Ducks don't come much lamer than you. Elections are only two weeks away."

"I told you, my polls look promising."

Owen picked up a twig and scraped gobs of mud off his high-topped boots. "I don't know. This consulting gig is pretty glamorous work."

"I can see that."

Owen straightened and threw the muddy twig into the ravine. "Thing is, I'm pretty good at it. And it could save a few lives."

"We can keep you on part-time. Give you something stable you can count on when the consulting jobs are slow in coming."

"Let me think about it." Owen slammed the Saturn's trunk shut. "Talk to you after the election."

He walked back to Reader's patrol car and opened the passenger door. "Come on, Mom. We're going home."

Epilogue:

Diamond Necklaces

The April sun warmed the wooden seats and cast shadows of the bleachers along the first-base line. Owen sat in the stands behind home plate watching Barkley High School's baseball team warm up for the season's first home game. The stands only held a smattering of fans, but there was no place Owen would rather be than a baseball diamond in the afternoon sun. The rest of the world just didn't know what it was missing.

The crowds hadn't been any bigger when he'd played on this same diamond. Students would fill a gym to root for their basketball team or pack a stadium for Friday night football, but the players often outnumbered the fans in the stands at high school baseball games.

On the field, Barkley was taking infield practice. Jeb Stuart stood at home plate in his catcher's gear while a potbellied coach hit ground balls that the infielders scooped up and fired from base to base.

Thad Reader appeared alongside the grandstand and Owen waved from his seat just below the top row behind the backstop. Reader nodded and picked his way up the bleacher seats, waving to a few adult spectators and pausing to chat with an elderly woman holding a cowbell on her lap.

When he finally reached the next-to-last row of the bleachers, the sheriff sat down beside Owen and said, "Some tough life you've got, sunning yourself here in the middle of the afternoon."

Owen laughed. "That's what's so great about part-time work. It comes paired with part-time leisure."

Reader removed his Mounties' hat, closed his eyes, and turned his face toward the sun. "Sure beats sitting in a crowded courtroom."

"How's the hearing going?"

"Best guess is Harden will get off with a wrist slap. The statute of limitations had run out on all the ID swaps we could document except the one between Troublefield and Caldwell."

"And that one didn't take."

"Nobody wants to shut down Barkley Springs," Reader said. "The spa does a lot more good than harm. Case in point is standing right down there behind home plate."

The coach knocking out grounders had started double-play drills. He hit a sharp one-hopper to the right of the short-stop, who backhanded it cleanly and flipped it to the second baseman for the pivot and the throw to first. The first baseman threw home to Jeb Stuart, who rifled the ball back to the shortstop, making a seemingly effortless throw in his catcher's gear.

"Boy's got quite an arm," Reader said. "Got quite a future, too, thanks to you."

"Boy's always had a future." Owen nodded toward a heavyset man with a clipboard sitting in the front row and chewing on an unlit cigar. "That Cleveland scout was hanging around last year too."

"Boy came close to blowing it, though. You bailed him out."

"Jeb Stuart bailed himself out. Quitting OxyContin isn't something anybody does for you."

"You're the one that got him into Barkley Springs." Reader watched the Cleveland scout write something in his notebook. "Think the Indians will make him an offer?"

"Could be. But he's already got a better one. A full ride at Arizona State."

Reader whistled silently. "Good baseball program there, I hear."

"One of the best. Offer a degree in mining engineering too."

"Nice package. You put that together too?"

"I just pointed Jeb Stuart in the right direction."

Infield practice ended with each fielder charging toward home plate to scoop up a bunted ball and flip it to the catcher. After Jeb Stuart took the last throw, he turned his back on the infield, waved at Owen, and headed for the Barkley bench behind first base. On his way to the bench, he let his open palm trail against the wire backstop in a silent signal to three girls sitting in the front row.

The gesture was so slight anyone not watching the boy closely would have missed it, but both Owen and Thad Reader picked up on it.

"That blonde girl in the middle looks familiar," Reader said.

"It was her picture you saw in the locket in Jeb Stuart's room at Barkley Springs."

Reader raised his eyebrows in a "Tell me more" look.

"Her name's Elizabeth Jackson. She's a junior at Barkley Catholic. In my day they would have been called an item."

On the bench, Jeb Stuart leaned forward to unstrap his shin guards. Several thin chains dangled from his neck.

"Boy's got more neckwear than a Cuban pimp," Reader said.

"One chain holds the locket you saw. Another one's got his dad's dog tags. He wore them both through Barkley Springs."

Reader shrugged. "Whatever gets you through the night."

"Can't play this game without a few superstitions."

"You believe they work?"

"He believes they do. That's all that matters."

"But do you believe they work?"

Owen loosened the top button of his shirt and pulled out a thin silver chain holding two dog tags.

"Victoria's grandfather?" Reader said.

Owen nodded. "I understand they work whether you believe in them or not."

"Jesus. I couldn't tell you where my 'Nam tags are."

"You've got your glass eye as a keepsake."

"Never thought of it as a good-luck piece."

"What I hear, you were luckier than the guys on either side of you when the grenade exploded."

Reader tapped his thumbnail against his glass eye. "You got that right."

The home plate umpire, who to Owen didn't look much older than the players, called "Play Ball" in a squeaky voice, and Owen leaned back against the top row of the bleachers to take in the game.

The Barkley pitcher loaded the bases on a single and two

walks in the top of the first, but still managed to keep the visiting Logan team from scoring.

The Logan pitcher had more command in the bottom of the first, striking out two batters, but a shortstop error put a runner on second when Jeb Stuart came to bat.

Owen leaned forward and cupped his hands around his mouth. "Let's go, Barkley."

Jeb Stuart paused before entering the batter's box, scooped up a handful of dirt, sifted it through his fingers, and wiped his right hand across the front of his uniform jersey, touching his neck chains.

"You gotta believe," Owen said.

Jeb Stuart swung at the first pitch, a slider low and away. There was a thin plinking noise as the ball ticked off the bat and thudded against the backstop.

"Aluminum bats just don't have the right sound," Owen said as he watched the Cleveland scout make a notation on his clipboard.

The Logan pitcher came back with another slider.

This time the bat met the ball with a solid "plunk" and drove it deep into the gap between the center and right fielders.

The runner on second scored easily, and Owen and Reader leapt to their feet as Jeb Stuart rounded second base without slowing down. "He's going for three," Reader said.

Owen's head told him it wasn't a smart play with two out, but he felt his heart pumping at least as fast as Jeb Stuart's.

The second baseman took the throw from the right fielder, whirled, and pegged it on a low line to the third baseman. The ball arrived at third just as Jeb Stuart started his slide.

Dust plumed, and all eyes turned to the umpire, who seemed caught in a moment of indecision. His right hand formed a fist with the thumb extended in the OUT sign, then opened as he saw the ball trickle out of the third baseman's glove and spread, palm downward, in a SAFE signal.

The crowd cheered, the cowbell clanged, and Owen clapped wildly as Thad Reader slapped him on the back.

Jeb Stuart bounced up from the dust cloud at third base, laughing and waving at the stands.

Owen waved back, then fingered the chain around his neck as he watched the boy's dog tags dance and glitter in the afternoon sun.

About the Author

John Billheimer, a native West Virginian, lives in Portola Valley, California. He holds an engineering PhD from Stanford University and for the past thirty years has been Vice President of SYSTAN, Inc., a small consulting firm that specializes in transportation research. Over the years, he has investigated such diverse topics as commuter lane performance, mobile phone safety, drunk driving countermeasures, DMV service, video surveillance, and motorcycle safety. An early research project with the Norfolk and Western railroad took him back to the coalfields of his native state, where he observed the poverty, independence, and resourcefulness that mark the characters of his first novel, *The Contrary Blues*.

The Contrary Blues was the first book in the "funny, sometimes touching," mystery series featuring failure analyst Owen Allison. It was named one of the ten best mysteries of 1998 by the *Drood Review* and has been followed by four other mysteries set in Appalachia's coalfields. The second, *Highway Robbery*, explores West Virginia roadbuilding scandals, while the third, *Dismal Mountain*, covers the controversial topic of strip mining. The fourth, *Drybone Hollow*, deals with the false claims and scams that follow in the wake of a devastating flood, and the most recent, *Stonewall Jackson's Elbow*, tracks the aftermath of a seven-hundred-and-fifty-million-dollar bank fraud.

Billheimer is married with two children, and is an avid

tennis player and movie buff. He chaired the Transportation Research Board Committee on Motorcycles and Mopeds, and co-founded the California Motorcyclist Safety Program, a statewide program of mandatory training which saw motorcycle fatalities drop over seventy percent during its first fifteen years.

More information on John Billheimer and his books may be found at his Web site, www.johnbillheimer.com.